Charlotte

A compelling novel set in Victorian Suffolk and London: a case of unsolved crime within an outwardly respectable household. Charlotte, left by her father to bear the burden of the blame, broke away from her family to teach at a sort of Dothegirls Hall where Mrs Armitage knew her story but was prepared to keep quiet —up to a point. Was Charlotte responsible for the death of the little pupil? Was it a repetition of the first crime? In darker moments even she herself could not be sure.

By the same author

BLESS THIS HOUSE
THE BRITTLE GLASS
OUT OF THE NETTLE
SILVER NUTMEG
TO SEE A FINE LADY
A CALF FOR VENUS
THE DEVIL IN CLEVELY
  (AFTERNOON OF AN AUTOCRAT)
JASSY
QUEEN IN WAITING
THE ROAD TO REVELATION
HEAVEN IN YOUR HAND
THE TOWN HOUSE
THE HOUSE AT OLD VINE
THE HOUSE AT SUNSET
SCENT OF CLOVES
THE LUTE PLAYER
THE CONCUBINE
HOW FAR TO BETHLEHEM?
HESTER ROON
DEAD MARCH IN THREE KEYS
THE KING'S PLEASURE
THE LITTLE WAX DOLL
LOVERS ALL UNTRUE
A ROSE FOR VIRTUE

NORAH LOFTS

Charlotte

HODDER AND STOUGHTON
LONDON SYDNEY AUCKLAND TORONTO

Author's Note

THIS IS A WORK OF FICTION, BUT READERS OF REAL-LIFE CRIME stories will recognise in Part One some of the facts that came to light in what has been termed the Case of Constance Kent. Certain details—the unhappy family background, the nature of the crime, the mystery of the missing nightdress and the almost unbelievably fatuous behaviour of the police—tally more or less exactly.

The characters, however, are my own; and whereas those who write factually about a crime—especially one never satisfactorily solved—can only speculate about the motives and, indeed, the identity of the murderer, the writer of fiction, dealing in a more plastic medium, is able to say: This is how it happened.

Part Two owes nothing to the Case of Constance Kent. Incredible as it may seem, it is based on a first-hand account of a school in which my sister once tried to teach, a mere forty years ago. Here again the characters are my own; but I did not invent the oil-stove that was carried up and down . . .

PART
ONE

I

'FINISH YOUR MEAT, CHARLOTTE,' MRS CORNWALL SAID. 'I'VE told you before. It sets such a bad example.'

From under half-lowered lids Charlotte looked about the table. Five emptied plates. To whom do I set this bad example, she thought with wry humour. To ask the question aloud would be simply asking for trouble. She said, meekly, 'It is rather fat.'

The so-called fat and lean had been more than usually fat this week and very coarse as well: people who owed butcher's bills were not served with the best in any grade. Thinking of that and aware that she was feeling slightly queasy herself, Mrs Cornwall spoke more sharply.

'Eat it at once. I will not have good food wasted.'

Thomas, fourteen, growing rapidly and perpetually hungry, said, 'It need not be wasted, Mamma. I'll eat it for you, Charlie.'

Sticking together! They always did!

'That is another thing I have spoken about. Charlotte is far too old to be called by that ridiculous name.'

Vincent said, 'Charlie! Charlie! I shall call her Charlie!'

One could not suspect a child of four, one's own beloved son, of deliberate defiance; and yet there was a mischievous look on the handsome little face. With something less than her usual affection Mrs Cornwall said, 'That is because you are still a baby.'

'I am not. I am big for my age and very forward. Everybody

8

says so.' Then with a shift from indignation to what in anyone else Mrs Cornwall would have recognised as malice, he began to chant,

'Charlie is my darling, my darling, my darling,
Charlie is my darling, the young . . .'

The next word eluded him, so he leaned forward and rubbed his curly head against Charlotte's arm with an affectionate, puppyish gesture.

'Sit up, Vincent. Or you will get no pudding.'

Vincent sat up and regarded his mother with anger and astonishment. Mamma spoke like that to other people, never to him.

Charlotte rose and collected the plates. Nellie, the maid, brought in six plates and a bread-and-butter pudding which she placed before her mistress.

'We shall need only five plates,' Mrs Cornwall said, and rather ostentatiously returned one. 'Miss Charlotte was unable to finish her first course. She will not need pudding.'

Nellie threw Charlotte a look of surreptitious commiseration.

Mrs Cornwall served the pudding, helping Vincent first and then Adelaide who was always regarded as the elder of the twins. Perhaps their own mother had known which of them had first entered the world, but she had been dead for five years and Adelaide, as the one with the slightly larger share of their very limited wits, and the definitely more dominant personality, was always regarded as the elder.

A portion for Adelaide, one for Victoria, Thomas. The spoon hovered. The pork had been extremely fat, enough to take the edge off anybody's appetite. Then Mrs Cornwall remembered that a pregnant woman should eat for two. She helped herself.

The meal proceeded in silence. The twins never had anything to say to other people, and even between themselves had a way of communicating that demanded the minimum of words. Charlotte and Thomas had long ago learned that their stepmother, who had been their governess, had a way of twisting almost any remark into something meriting either correction or rebuke. Silence was best.

The pudding was eaten quickly. The twins were anxious to

9

get back to the sanctuary of their room at the top of the house, and to the fascinating work upon which they were engaged. Thomas was still hungry. Mrs Cornwall thought with longing of the moment when she could loosen her corsets and lie on her bed in a shaded room. Vincent had something in mind. Charlotte, with nothing to eat was putting up that infuriating front of not caring, sitting bolt upright, her hands folded in her lap, so that even her stepmother could not criticise her posture. Vincent carefully scraped up the last spoonful of his pudding, and then, cunningly addressing nobody in particular, said what had so often been said to him—

'Open your mouth and shut your eyes and see what the fairies will send you.'

Significantly—a tribute to his charm and his power—they all obeyed, knowing that he would put the spoonful into his own mouth and then laugh merrily. He had tried that trick before. But today he guided the spoon to Charlotte's mouth and while she half choked, he laughed, and looking at his mother said, 'Charlie did have some pudding!'

For the first time Agnes Cornwall understood why, outside the family, Vincent for all his beauty and charm and youth, was not much liked. Even Cook had said, 'I'm sorry, ma'am, I can't have Master Vincent in the kitchen. He's too mischief ul.' Nellie didn't care for him, nor had any of her predecessors: the man who helped in the yard and the gardener, said he was a young imp, a nuisance, a tittle-tattle who invented tales. Even Mrs Greenfield, the rector's wife had once said, not completely admiringly, 'Surely, he is very *precocious*.' Agnes had then thought—And why not? The child of love. His father is clever and I'm pretty smart. Apart from her ordinary mother love, Agnes Cornwall felt, on the fringe of her mind, a certain indebtedness to her son; he had timed his arrival so well; one year after her marriage ...

But she was annoyed with him now; the gesture, that merry mocking look. She said, 'Go upstairs, Vincent, and take your rest.'

'I don't want a rest. Babies have rests. I want to play. Charlie will play with me, won't you, Charlie?'

Charlotte said, 'If that is agreeable to your Mamma, Vincent.'

Your Mamma. Not mine. Charlotte had, five years ago, at the age of eleven, said, 'I shall never call her Mamma. You can

10

only have one mother and mine is dead.'

An offensive thing to say. But Charlotte had stuck to it, defying the small spiteful persecutions, and Papa's disapproval, and the recurring, day by day awkwardness of the matter of address. You couldn't very well say, 'Yes, Mrs Cornwall,' or 'No, Mrs Cornwall.' It sounded so stilted. So for five years Charlotte had said, 'Yes' and 'No' or 'I'm sorry' or 'Just as you say', with no other word tagged on and had thereby gained herself nothing except a name for being surly and without manners.

So now she agreed to play with Vincent if that was agreeable to his Mamma. And there was the problem. Charlotte was always willing to take charge of Vincent; she could amuse him for hours on end and she had nothing else to do. Rose Ellis, the nurse, up in the nursery, had the baby, Amelia, to see to and had shown, in the last few weeks, a streak of something that could only be called disobliging. 'When he is restless and noisy, he wakes the baby. I've only got one pair of hands, Madam.' More and more Charlotte had taken charge of Vincent during his waking hours. And the result of that had just been made manifest at the table.

'Thomas,' Mrs Cornwall said, 'can take you for a good long walk, darling.'

Thomas said—and for some reason every time he used the word which Charlotte would not, he felt like a traitor, 'Mamma, I am sorry. I have to go down to the school. Papa arranged it. Mr Macferson said three o'clock on Friday would be the best time for him. I am sorry, Mamma.'

'Oh, very well then,' Agnes Cornwall said, thinking of the bed in the room with the blinds lowered. 'Charlotte may play with you. A quiet game, in the shade. It is a very hot day.'

Adelaide and Victoria went across the black-and-white tiled hall, mounted the first flight of stairs, laid with crimson carpet, and went diagonally across the landing to the second flight, narrower, steeper, linoleum-covered. Their own room was spacious and, though shabby, comfortably furnished. Their current piece of work lay on a round table near one of the windows; a grey bodice belonging to Victoria which was being refurbished by the application of jet beads taken from an old cape. In this, to the wonder and admiration of all, Victoria would appear in church on Sunday morning. They would then

11

spend the next week in improving Adelaide's buff bodice by applying strips of brown braid. Although they were so almost identical that they often acted and were regarded as one person they never dressed alike. Long ago their own mother, thinking that their oddity had something to do with their twinship, had done her best to stress their individuality rather than their likeness. But as Mrs Greenfield once remarked, 'I can never tell which is which until I see them together.' Adelaide was taller, a little less rounded of figure. Victoria had the better complexion.

There was no obvious need for them to spend a sunny June day on making an old garment look new. They were fortunate young women. At a time when a man regarded himself as well-paid at twelve shillings a week, they had between them an income of six hundred pounds a year. They had come into their heritage when they were twenty-one, rather more than a year earlier. In five years' time, when Charlotte was twenty-one, she would be equally rich. Their maternal grandfather, a tough Scot who had come south and built up a successful business as a merchant in Bristol, had believed that lassies were delicate creatures, to be provided for. Males could fend for themselves, as he had fended. He had never liked his son-in-law and had gone to considerable pains to make sure that John Vincent Cornwall should not benefit directly from his marriage with Emily Burns. On the other hand, Emily must never lack. While she lived, the first Mrs Cornwall had enjoyed an income of nine hundred pounds a year, by her father's decree, her own; put into her own hand in quarterly sums. It was difficult for the hearty, successful man to visualise his own death, leave alone his daughter's, but he had faced that possibility. Should Emily die, her income reverted to the trust accumulating for her female issue.

The twins contributed a pound each towards the expenses of the household. Some six months ago Mrs Cornwall had made a suggestion that this sum should be increased to thirty shillings. Adelaide, always the spokesman, and always regarded as half-witted, said, 'We should have to consult Mr Watkins. He's the man who came to see us. All the way from Bristol. He told me ... He said it over and over again. We mustn't do anything about money without asking him first.' Such a cautionary word had seemed to Mr Watkins to be a necessity. Two half-wits with six hundred a year between them!

'I told him,' Adelaide said, 'that we intended to pay for our room and our food. That was just, I said. And he agreed. He thought a pound a week was enough, since we do not take tea.'

Mrs Cornwall's common sense told her that it was enough. Quite apart from the fact that they were under their father's roof. Bed and board, with the bed made, the room cleaned, and washing done was obtainable for ten shillings a week, in a stranger's house.

She said, 'Very well, I shall speak to your papa.'

Adelaide said, 'Yes, perhaps that would be best. Then Papa can write to Mr Watkins. That would be best.'

Mrs Cornwall spoke to her husband and he, always shifty and evasive and bad-tempered when money was mentioned, said, 'Oh, let it go. What difference would it make?'

'It beats me,' Mrs Cornwall said, 'what they do with the rest of it.'

That was a secret which the twins had confided to nobody. They were saving up to buy a house of their own. Their very own. A quiet house. In this one, remote as their room was, there were always disturbances. Vincent was noisy, chattered, played tricks; the baby cried; March, the gardener, and Catchpole the odd-job man, shouted at one another, just below their window; Thomas and Charlotte called to one another across the upper landing. Cook and whatever maid was employed were either quarrelling or chatting, quite late at night. And always, always, there was this troublesome question of time, meals arranged to suit other people. Their real grievance was that in this house they were not properly considered, were often called merely, 'the girls'. Where are the girls? The girls are late. We can't start without the girls. Their wishes, their timetable, was never once regarded. Even now, when they were paying their way.

Threading a bead on her needle, Adelaide said, 'That meat *was* nasty. In our house we will have chicken. Or cutlets.'

'And fish,' Victoria said. She also took a bead which stuck half-way along the needle. 'Too small,' she said, wrenching it off.

'Don't put it back with the others. We might get it again,' Adelaide said, sensibly. 'Not on the floor, Vikky! We shall only have to sweep it up.'

'No. Not on the floor,' Victoria said, retrieving the tiny

13

glistening speck. After that they worked in a companionable silence.

'What are we going to do, Charlie?' Vincent asked as Charlotte led the way into the front garden, into the deep shade of the massive copper beech.

'You'll see. And darling, your mamma does *not* like me to be called Charlie.'

'I know. Because you are so old.'

Because it is a pet name; used only by those who are fond of me. Even Nellie sometimes says 'Miss Charlie'.

'Yes. I am so old that I must be called Charlotte.'

'Charlotte. Charlotte. I can say it. I can say anything.'

He hopped, dragging on her hand.

'You're so clever, Vincent, that this afternoon I am going to teach you your letters.'

'I know my letters. A b c d . . .' He went right through, finishing up triumphantly, 'x y z'. He had a parrot's memory.

'But you don't know what they look like,' Charlotte said.

Between the entrance gate and the front door of the house the gravel drive made a swoop, so that most of the house looked out upon the lawn and the beech tree. Under the spreading, bronze-coloured branches nothing grew and the bare soil was dusty. She found a little stick and taught Vincent as she herself had been taught. Big A, little a. A is for apple; she drew the letters and the apple in the dust.

'Now you try.' Vincent took enthusiastically to this game. Charlotte felt that in a way she was fobbing him off, but she was disinclined for any more demanding pastime. The scene— not that it could really be called that; she could remember many worse—the *unpleasantness* at the table had upset her. Not to answer back, not to show any feeling had taken an effort. That because one had been unable to eat the grossly fat meat one should be denied pudding, seemed highly illogical. It was equally illogical to be upset by anything that Mrs Cornwall might say or do. Mrs Cornwall disliked her for a number of reasons; the refusal to address her as 'Mamma'; the occasional remark from someone who remembered the first Mrs Cornwall, that Charlotte was growing very much like her in appearance. Any reference to the dead woman annoyed the second wife; the fact that of the four children of his first marriage

14

Papa liked Charlotte best, far too mild a preference to be called favouritism, but noticeable from time to time: and lately, of course, Vincent's childish attachment. Trivial things in themselves, but cumulative in effect.

But, out of this dislike, the cause of much misery in the last five years, good might yet come. Fingering the letter in the pocket of her faded print dress, Charlotte foresaw that this evening, or some time over the coming weekend, she might count upon Mrs Cornwall as an ally.

Breathing hard from concentration, Vincent advanced to H for hat and then put down the stick.

'I know enough now,' he announced.

'You have been very good. What would you like to do now?'

'Go for a walk.'

'Darling, it is so hot.'

'I was going for a walk with Thomas,' Vincent reasoned, relentlessly.

'All right. We'll walk up to the farm and see the little pigs.'

'I want to go the other way.' A look of cunning and mischief sparkled on his face. The other way led to the village green, where the general shop sold sweets. But Charlotte was now completely penniless. When she left school at Easter she had had four shillings; she had spent one and elevenpence on a pair of stockings. Of the remainder Vincent had consumed almost all, in the form of cream-filled chocolate bars.

She said, 'Darling, I spent my last penny on Monday.' His face assumed such a doleful expression that she added hastily, 'I'll see what I can do. You stay here.'

She went swiftly and quietly upstairs to the girls' room.

Please, could you, between you, led me a penny?'

'What for?' Adelaide asked, shocked by this extortionate demand.

'To buy Vincent a chocolate bar.'

It was not sufficient reason. But, looking down at the round table Adelaide saw that the wood was visible through what remained of the black cotton on the reel.

'We want some more black cotton,' she said.

'Yes, we do. We want some more black cotton,' Victoria confirmed.

Adelaide rose, went to a desk and fussed about with keys

and a battered old cash-box, from which she took three pennies.

'That will be twopence and you can have a penny for going,' she said, generosity triumphing over parsimony.

'Oh, thank you, Addie. That is very kind.'

Generosity must be justified.

'It will save our time,' Adelaide conceded.

'Yes. It will save our time,' Victoria agreed.

In her own small room Charlotte donned an ancient straw hat and a pair of darned white cotton gloves. Nobody past childhood and with any pretensions to gentility would appear in the village lacking these accessories. From the pegs in the back hall she then took Vincent's white linen hat; remembered something and went to the kitchen door. Cook was stuffing a fowl, Nellie shelling peas.

'I'm going into the village. Is there anything you want?'

They both meditated deeply.

'I don't think so,' Cook finally said. 'Thank you.'

'It was nice of you to ask, Miss Charlie.'

They had agreed, time and again, that Miss Charlie was the best of the bunch—with the possible exception of Mr Cornwall who, when in a good temper, was a proper charmer: unfortunately his temper was not to be relied upon.

Vincent's hat, much washed, had shrunk considerably. Forcing it on over the thick golden curls, Charlotte said, 'Learning some letters has made your head swell.'

'Did you get it? The penny, Charlie?'

'Yes, I managed it.'

Taking her hand, hopping with joy, he said, 'I like you best in all the world, Charlie.'

'Charlotte. And that is not a proper thing to say. You must like your Mamma best.'

'What about Papa?'

'Yes, of course. You must like them both best.'

At the imposing gateway, stone pineapples topping the posts, they turned right into Bridge Lane. On one side there were some cottages, four comparatively new, built by Mr Brook the farmer and occupied by men who worked for him. March, their own gardener, lived in one of the old ones. His wife was gathering gooseberries. Next door was Mrs Whinney's, the yard, as usual, all aflutter with washing—Mrs Whinney, aided by her daughter, Carrie, washed for anyone who

16

could afford her modest charges. The remaining cottage was Catchpole's and its extremely dilapidated state proved that handyman though Catchpole might be across the lane at Stonebridge House, he did not expend much handiness on his own dwelling. From behind a window with one broken and two cracked panes an ancient, seamed, brown face peered and Vincent tightened his hold on Charlotte's hand.

'I don't like *her*,' he said. 'Is she looking at us? Nellie told Cook that old Mrs Catchpole could look at you and make something nasty happen.'

'That's just silly talk. Mrs Catchpole is just a very old woman. They say she is nearly ninety.'

She spoke with confidence; but at the same time she was bound to admit to herself that the old woman had a malevolent look. And it was undeniable that not so far from here something rather more than nasty had happened, when Thomas was six, and Charlotte was eight. Had Mrs Catchpole looked out that day? Nonsense!

'Anyway, I shouldn't like to kiss her,' Vincent said. 'She has a cracked face. You won't ever have a cracked face, will you, Charlie?'

'Charlotte. No, darling, I promise.'

'If you did I shouldn't kiss you.'

They crossed the humped stone bridge that gave the lane, and their own home, the names they bore, and walked on, Charlotte carefully averting her eyes from the woods where she and Thomas and Mamma had walked on what was to prove their last outing together. Presently they emerged on to the village green. It was dominated by a large and magnificent church, standing on a slight rise. Biddlesford had once been a small, but very prosperous wool town. It still had its ancient Guildhall, now used for various purposes. Set around the irregular oval of the Green were the Rectory, and Doctor Fletcher's house, both substantial, several smaller houses, most of them pretty in this month of roses, the forge, always busy, Potter's butcher shop, Wright's bakery, the inn—Catchpole's sister Sally had married the landlord there and Catchpole spent every evening with her—and the general shop, Fiske's, where almost everything was obtainable.

Charlotte bought the reel of cotton and put it into her pocket, feeling the letter again. A good hot dinner, roast chicken, fresh peas, new potatoes, should put Papa in a good mood. Her whole future might be decided this evening. She took the chocolate bar and held it delicately.

'We'll find somewhere cool for you to eat it,' she said.

'I want it now, Charlotte.'

The thought of a possible, imminent parting from him made her indulgent; and the church porch, the cool place which she had in mind, was not far away. She stripped the bar and put it into his eager little paw. But it was a very hot afternoon, and by the time they had climbed the sloping path, between the yews that were said to be even older than the church, the chocolate and the pink cream filling had begun to melt and he had changed the bar from one hand to another, wiping the fingers of the hand thus freed upon the white sailor suit, the everyday dress of thousands of little boys—not all of them English. He pushed back his hat, soiling that, too, and streaking his smooth brow.

'I shall have to wash you as soon as we get home,' Charlotte said.

But there was no time. No time at all. As Charlotte and Vincent gained the landing, Mrs Cornwall emerged from her bedroom.

'Where have you been?'

'To Fiske's, to buy a reel of cotton. And Vincent had a chocolate bar. I was just...'

'No need to tell me,' Mrs Cornwall said in her roughest voice. 'Look at him, just look at him. Eating in the public street,' she said, upgrading the village and the lane. 'Disgraceful. He's filthy, worse than a gypsy child. Suppose anybody had met you.'

'Nobody did.'

'Don't argue with me!'

Vincent's sensitive antennae had already conveyed to his very active mind enough information to enable it to place people in categories.

Mamma was nice to him, but often cross to Charlotte.

Papa was often nice to him, but had been known to be impatient and to say, 'Run away, Vincent. Go to Nurse.'

Nurse was horrid. She said, 'No' and 'Sit still' and 'Be quiet'. She held over him a vague threat, all the worse for being vague. She said, 'You go to sleep, or the bogey'll get you.' What the bogey was Vincent did not know, nor did he dare enquire. He thought of it as something rather like Tiger, the big shaggy dog, chained in the yard outside the back door. This animal, kept as a guard, regularly fed and watered but deprived of, and craving, human affection had once reared up, put his front paws on Vincent's shoulders and licked his face. A terrible experience which still haunted his dreams, and which gave the vague word, 'bogey' substance and reality.

Vincent did not like Nurse. He knew that Addie and Vikky disliked him; so did Cook and Nellie. Thomas was all right, neither friend nor enemy, but dull ... walking, playing with Thomas, dull.

In fact the only one to be completely relied upon was Charlotte and now, Mamma, with a cross face and a loud angry voice was frightening. He turned, clutched Charlotte about the knees and buried his face in her skirt.

'Go to Nurse,' Mrs Cornwall said, raising her voice even more. 'Nurse! Nurse!'

Another door on the landing opened. Mrs Cornwall said, 'Will you please take Master Vincent and give him a wash and some clean clothes.'

Then even Charlotte failed him. She reached down, loosened his clutching hands and said, 'Go along, dear. Papa will soon be home and you must be all smartened up to welcome him.'

Vincent went, unbefriended. Mrs Cornwall said to Charlotte, 'And I'll thank you ...' As the rector's wife had once said—'She does use some very unfortunate expressions ...'

'I'll thank you,' Mrs Cornwall said, 'not to take Vincent out of the house without my permission and not to go stuffing him with a lot of cheap rubbish.'

Charlotte employed her old tactics; silence, a blank expression; the gaze directed not at the angry face but at some point just over the speaker's shoulder and at some far distance.

Mrs Cornwall turned and went back into her bedroom. Charlotte's remark that Papa would soon be home had made its impact. He would soon be home.

The conjugal bedroom, like that of the twins, immediately above it, had two windows, one facing south, the other west. Agnes Cornwall went to them both and wound up the cream linen blinds. No direct sun streamed in for at this moment, four o'clock on a late June afternoon, the sun struck the corner of the house. But a benevolent, diffused light poured in, and in this light she sat down before the glass on her dressing-table and studied with distaste what she saw.

Pretty once. Thick, glossy hair, black as coal and eyes as blue as a cornflower—entrancing combination, an inheritance from her Irish-born mother. She'd had a skin the colour of cream. The first Mrs Cornwall had remarked it, kindly—'Miss Gooch, country air will soon put some colour into your cheeks.' That was—how long ago? Ten, eleven years. Eleven years should not have done such damage. It was the worry, the scheming, the uncertainty and the disappointment. Nothing had worked out as it should.

She had come to Stonebridge House when she was twenty-one, a healthy, well-set-up young woman, not exactly pretty, but comely, and lively, very different from Mrs Cornwall who was delicate and vague, who had borne the half-witted twins, then two babies who had died in infancy, then Charlotte, normal enough, and finally Thomas with his peculiar hands. After that she had been advised not to have any more children.

It had not been difficult to assume responsibility for the household; even less difficult to embark upon a violent love affair with Mr Cornwall; what was difficult was to conduct this love affair, and have full charge of the servants and of the children while Mrs Cornwall was around, vague, forgetful, but not unobservant and not uncritical.

Agnes Gooch had gone to work stealthily. 'But Mrs Cornwall, I am positive that you told me guests were expected tomorrow, not today. Cook would bear me out on that. If you remember you said tomorrow, because the pheasants would then have hung for a week.'

'Miss Gooch, I think you are mistaken. I said almost a week. I should never dream of inviting the rector for Friday. He always looks in on the choir practice on Fridays.'

'Yes, I thought of that. I actually mentioned it, but you assured me that this week was an exception.'

'Miss Gooch, of that I have no memory at all. And they are coming this evening? Oh dear. Mr Cornwall will be so displeased with me ...'

It was a game that could be played with infinite variations.

One move had been crucial, and like many such, virtually extempore.

'It is a lovely day,' Emily Cornwall said. 'The wild daffodils should be out in Tutt Wood. I used always to make a point of walking to see them. That was before Thomas was born.'

20

'They are out. And a sight to see,' Agnes Gooch said. 'Somebody in the village mentioned them to me yesterday and I went to look.'

'I think I shall venture,' said Mrs Cornwall who had hardly set foot off her own premises since Thomas's birth with all its disabling consequences. 'I'll take the children.'

Adelaide and Victoria had then reached the age where they resented being called 'the children' as much as they were later to resent being called 'the girls'. They made some excuse. Before leaving, with Charlotte and Thomas, Mrs Cornwall said, 'Miss Gooch, I seem to have forgotten. I remember the stile ... In order to find the daffodils does one turn left or right where the path forks?'

Miss Gooch said, 'Left.' Almost without thinking.

This was the outing which Charlotte remembered, waking, sleeping. Happily along the lane, past the cottages, over the stile. She carried a flat basket in which to bring some wild daffodils home; Mamma loved flowers, and those in the garden were not yet in bloom. Left, and left again; faint flecks of sunlight falling on dead bracken. 'Just the colour of your hair, Charlie,' Mamma said. A place in the path where one could only turn right; back into the heart of the wood, darkening now. Mamma said, 'I think we must have taken a wrong turning, my dears. We must try to retrace our steps.'

The air turned chilly, the wind moaned in the branches. They were hopelessly lost. And presently a sleety rain began to fall. Mamma said, 'I think we should sit down and rest for a little while. Come along, cuddle close.' She sat down, her back to the trunk of a stout tree and opened her cloak, like a bird's wings ...

Agnes Gooch, back at the house, had not fully understood John Vincent Cornwall's extreme agitation; she did not know that nine hundred pounds a year was involved ...

They were found, wet and chilled to the bone, and Thomas had something called pleurisy and almost died. His cough lasted for months.

After that Mrs Cornwall was deemed obviously unfit to do so much as take her children for a walk; lachrymose, confused and ineffective now, she relapsed into the invalidism, the incapacity that had finished her off.

But it had taken a full three years. For Agnes Gooch a hard

21

three years; fending off visitors, fending off enquirers. In and around Biddlesford the forgetful, delicate, gentle woman had been astonishingly popular.

Then there had been a little space. Agonising. Will he? Won't he? Like blowing on a dandelion head. In the end he had. Agnes Gooch had become Mrs Cornwall.

And nothing had been the same since.

Naturally nobody could expect open, respectable marriage, to hold the raptures and excitements of a clandestine love affair. But there should have been compensations, ranging from silk dresses to social acceptance. Neither was forthcoming. She had not even obtained possession of the dead woman's jewellery. Mr Cornwall said it belonged to the three girls and must be put away; stored in the bank, until they were old enough to wear it. She strongly suspected that he had disposed of it, for when the twins were legally of age and entered into their other inheritance the jewels did not reappear.

The stark truth was that Agnes Gooch, ruthlessly edging Emily Cornwall into seclusion, into melancholia, near madness and death, had not understood the financial situation at all. Nine hundred pounds a year had vanished overnight. Too late, John Vincent Cornwall explained, adding, 'And that means that I must look about for a job of some sort, blast it.'

He had found one—or one had been found for him—and he seemed not to find it too onerous, but Agnes realised that in marrying her he had made a sacrifice. He was still young enough, and handsome enough to have married another woman with money, a woman that his friends might have approved. Her shrewd hard mind concluded that although he had married her—as was only right—he had resented doing so and that this fact had led to the deterioration of their relationship. The knowledge, because it angered and soured her, furthered the process. She became a scold, always seeking to attain by stinging words the power over him that she had once exercised by means of charm. In this she was not entirely unsuccessful. John Cornwall liked any unpleasantness in his vicinity to be of his own making.

In the kitchen Cook hulled the strawberries which March had brought in, warm from the sun and summer-scented. Nellie washed the tea things and a few oddments. Suddenly she said, 'Well, pay-day tomorrow and I'm going to speak

22

about the nursery trays. Carry them up I must, but down I will not. If he say I am to, he'll get my notice.'

'She do get lazier and lazier,' Cook agreed. The prospect of losing Nellie did not profoundly disturb her. Maids seldom stayed long at Stonebridge House. Nellie was the third within a year, and better than most. The house was isolated, not enough young men about; nothing to do in Biddlesford in your free time, and Bereham very difficult to get to. Carrier's wagonette once a week, but it set out at ten in the morning and left Bereham at half past four sharp. Beattie Adams fully realised that a way of life which suited her very well wasn't attractive to the young.

'When he interviewed me—Norwich that was—he said he *knew* it sounded a big family, but the young ladies did their own rooms—which they do—and there wasn't much entertainment—which there ain't. But he never said the nurse'd got to be waited on hand and foot. And come to that nor she did, till lately. About Easter she started putting on airs and graces.'

'Thass true,' Cook said. 'When she first come I thought she seemed a decent, hardworking little thing. Mim as a mouse, too. I can't think whass got into her.'

'I know whass got *on* to her,' Nellie said, turning from the sink to impart this piece of information, 'and thass some rare good scent. Not stuff you or me would buy. Expensive.'

'I never spent a penny on scent in my life and never shall. Got something better to do with my money.'

'Count it,' Nellie said with a grin. Cook was a miser; saving up for her old age. 'I know about the scent,' she said, facing the sink again. 'Sometimes of a morning the nursery fair reeks. First I thought it was some new sort of baby powder, but it ain't. It's her ladyship. All scented up and nowhere to go, eh?'

Drying the cups Nellie considered her grievance and her threat and retracted a little. It might be silly to leave at the end of July. Young March was showing a definite interest; was horseman up at the farm and made better money than the ordinary labourer. Bob March and one of the new cottages in the lane would be just the ticket.

'I tell you what I'll do. I shall say I'm willing to do the extra for another five bob a month. Why don't you do the same? *You* have to haul down the trays my afternoon and evening off.'

' 'Twouldn't be a bit of use,' Beattie said, rising and going to the stove where a large saucepan simmered. 'There just ain't the money, old girl. They owe the butcher and I bet he ain't the only one.'

'How do you know?'

'By the muck we've been getting lately. Take that fat and lean we had today. All fat. And take this,' she prodded with a fork. 'Best silverside was ordered. If this is silverside I'm the Queen of England. I know brisket when I see it. Potter'd never dare send this if they wasn't in debt. And pretty deep, too. It'll be eatable,' she said, giving herself a pat on the back, 'I'm doing it so gently. Cold tomorrow with a bit of salad, it'll make a nice lunch. But that ain't the point.'

She stooped to the oven, withdrew a fowl and basted it tenderly. As she did so there was the sound of hooves and wheels on the gravel of the yard. The master was home. His voice, deep and resonant, said, 'Evening, Catchpole. Lovely day!' He had arrived home in a good mood.

He came into the kitchen, a tall, handsome man, carrying his fifty-two years very lightly. No grey yet in the thick wavy hair that had once been the dead-bracken colour of Charlotte's, but had darkened a little without losing its glow: no surplus flesh anywhere, and singularly few lines about the grey eyes or the mobile, sensual mouth. He was capable of looking bad-tempered, or merely glum, but such expressions were too fleeting to leave any permanent mark. He was selfish enough never to have given a thought to anybody else's troubles, and though he had had troubles of his own, bad patches, he called them, a multitude of varying experiences had bred in him the assurance that nothing *finally* ever went wrong for him. He'd been going through a bad patch lately; money short and Agnes nagging more than usual. She resented this, her third pregnancy, but she had brought it on herself. (There in the bed beside him, saying, 'I know you don't love me any more.' 'I'll show you...' It would be another mouth to feed, but it had put Agnes out of action for a bit, thank God.)

He came in, smiling.

'Well, have you been good girls in my absence?'

Beattie was in her fifties, but she responded, 'We done our best, sir.'

'And you've done me a good turn ... A horse,' he said, 'called Cookstown. Quite irresistible. But...' he lowered his voice and looked around with the cunning, the mischief that

24

was so like Vincent's. 'Well, you know how your mistress feels about horse-racing. So pouch it and say nothing.' He gave Cook two gleaming golden sovereigns and Nellie one.

'Thank you very much, sir,' Cook said. She had been at Stonebridge House for five years and had received similar bonuses three or four times. Nellie never had. Slightly more than a month's wages deposited in her hand like that. She was too much overcome to say more than, 'Thank you, sir.'

Mr Cornwall, sniffing the air upon which the scent of roast chicken and Cook's special stuffing lingered, said, 'Something smells very good. And I am starving...'

Catchpole leaned in and placed, just inside the door, the small valise which Mr Cornwall took when his work involved a night or two away from home, and the other, flatter bag which contained the papers which were to do with his work.

'I'll take this,' Mr Cornwall said, taking the flat one by its handle.

'I'll take that one up to your dressing room, sir,' Nellie said. She had done it often enough before, but never so willingly.

'And you can trust *us*. Not a word, sir,' Beattie said.

Carrying his bag of paper work John Cornwall left the kitchen by the door which opened into the back hall which, at a clearly divided line, where the linoleum ended and the black and white tiles began, became the front hall. He moved rather quietly; rather quietly he opened the door of the library and put his bag on the wide, leather-topped table. Agnes might be resting, either in the drawing room or the bedroom, both in the front of the house. If the day's luck held—he had won two hundred pounds at Newmarket that afternoon—she would go on resting, unaware that he was home. He needed, he deserved, a bit more time in which to savour his luck and he knew that the moment she saw him she would begin to nag and moan—about the bills, which he could now, thank God, pay, though he could not tell her how, about the heat of the day, which he could not help, and which he had, on Newmarket's wide open heath positively enjoyed, or about how she felt, or how one of the children had behaved. An hour's peace, a quiet drink...

In the kitchen Beattie said, 'Well, there you are. Four months of the rise you wanted and not even having to *ask* for it.'

25

And for herself two golden steps forward towards her secret goal. Beattie Adams had a sister, a few years older, named Fanny. Fanny's last employer had left her enough to enable her to buy a little cottage at Brancaster, up on the Norfolk coast and to assure her an income of two and sixpence a week for life. This, just enough to keep alive on, but not enough for comfort, Fanny supplemented by collecting and selling cockles, the free gift of the sea, available for all. Beattie had once, between jobs, taken a short holiday at Brancaster and enjoyed herself very much. And Fanny had said, 'You're welcome, any time.' But Beattie had thought—not as a dependant; when I come I must pay my way. She wanted to be sure that she could match Fanny's two and sixpence a week and help with the gathering of cockles.

'That was nice,' Nellie said. 'But...' She had a variable mind; it had swung from the determination to give notice because of Miss Rose Ellis's demands, to caution, because of the possibility of Bob March's being serious, to gratitude for the unexpected gift. Out of her confusion of mind she said, almost angrily, 'All the same, I don't like it here. I never did. Nothing to do, really with the trays ... or ... or ... Nothing I could put a name to. Tell you the truth, the moment I set foot inside that door I just didn't like the house.'

'Well,' Beattie said, 'it ain't the most convenient. But I've been in worse. Between here and the dining room is a fair walk, I admit. But on the level. Last place I was there was twenty-four steps between where the food was cooked and where it was eat. *And* five courses every blessed night.'

'It ain't that,' Nellie said. She was not a markedly articulate girl and she was attempting to describe the inexplicable. 'I never was nervous before, and here I am. I dunno whether you've noticed, but even my night off I'm always back before you go up. Sort of creepy, as though it could be haunted.'

'Well, I been here over four years and never seen anything worse than myself. I had a rare old fright once though.'

'Don't tell me. I don't want to hear.'

'Well you should, because it just shows you how daft them tales are. I woke in the pitch black and I heard a sort of thud, like a door and then footsteps, ever so slow on the landing. And then there was fumbling outside my door and the knob rattled ...'

'You're just trying to frighten me,' Nellie said. People were

26

all the same. She shouldn't have mentioned feeling creepy, just as you should never mention not liking things like spiders. Cook was plainly gloating over this tale.

'I'm trying to *show* you. It was just Miss Charlie, walking in her sleep. She used to when she was younger.'

'I think I should've died. What did you do, Beattie?'

'I lit my candle and got hold of my old flat-iron. I reckoned it was a thief, see? You never know. When you're earning, and you don't spend, some rogue might think ... But I was ready. And it was just Miss Charlie. I put her back to bed. Mrs C had been pretty nasty to her that day, I recall. Boxed her ears and put Thomas in the cellar. There's one good thing, she can't do that sort of thing nowadays.'

'There's other ways of being nasty,' Nellie said.

'Yes. Like March,' Beattie said, tipping peas into a saucepan. 'Just because I once told him not to come in here without wiping his feet, he'll do me down if he can. He know as well as I do that peas need mint. But will he bring it? Nip out, Nellie, and get a few sprigs.'

In the nursery, one room of which overlooked the yard, Vincent heard his father arrive. Nurse had been cross and horrid; she had washed him very roughly, not let him have jam on his bread and butter at teatime and afterwards made him do that most difficult of all things—sit still and be quiet. Even when he had asked a crafty question in a suitably muted voice, 'What are you sewing, Nurse?' she had not relented. 'Nothing to do with you. I told you to keep quiet.'

Papa's arrival meant release. Even if he should also be cross and say, 'Go away,' Vincent could go and find Charlie.

'Papa is here!' Vincent shouted. He threw himself across the room, out of the door, over the landing and down the stairs.

'Papa!'

Papa was not in a bad temper. He smiled, standing just inside the library door, and put his finger to his lips and said, 'Ssh! We mustn't disturb Mamma.'

'No. She's cross. So is Nurse.'

'Oh? What about?' Vincent was too young to wonder at the alert look, the sharpness of the question. He said, not without complacency, 'Me. Charlie gave me a chocolate bar and it melted. So Mamma was cross to Charlie and Nurse was cross to me.'

'Well, never mind. They'll get over it.' Papa rumpled Vincent's curls.

'Can I stay with you?'

'Yes, of course. Go in the library. I shan't be a minute. And be quiet.'

He went to the cellar door which was on the same side of the rear hall as the kitchen. The door opened on to a steep flight of steps, and ever since the twins could toddle, the door had always been kept locked, the key hung on a hook well out of reach. He wouldn't be a minute because he would not have to go far beyond the bottom of the steps, or brood, and ponder, choosing his evening's beverages. He knew exactly what was left in what had once been a pretty well-stocked cellar. One bottle of sherry; one of brandy. But sufficient for the day is the evil, or the good, thereof. Tomorrow morning he would drive into Bereham, go to Sadler and Palfrey's, pay his bill, get a fresh supply.

He carried up both bottles, took them into the library, opened the sherry, poured himself a glass, took Vincent on his knee, sipped and said genially, 'Well, and what have you been doing today, beside getting into a mess with a chocolate bar?'

'I learned to read,' Vincent said grandiloquently.

'Really!' He said the word too lightly, not sufficiently impressed. Vincent was slightly offended.

'Up to H for hat,' he said sternly. 'Big and little letters. Charlie showed me. Shall I show you?'

'Pray do.'

Vincent reached out, took up a pencil, and using it as he had used the stick, scrawled on the nearest piece of paper, admonishing himself, 'Big A, little a. A is for apple. Big B, little b, B is for ball...'

His father watched, not without interest; after all he was concerned with education, for the post that had fallen into his hands in the middle of the worst patch he had ever known, was that of inspector of the fairly recently established Board Schools. It was a gentleman's job; the poet, Matthew Arnold, was a school inspector.

Watching his son's plump hand, holding the pencil in a firm, if unorthodox way, John Vincent Cornwall thought—Of course he is as strong as some of the little wretches are at seven or eight: and how would this method apply to those who seldom saw an egg?

28

Vincent said, 'Big H, little h, H is for hat. And we stopped there because Charlie had to go and buy a reel of cotton for Addie.'

In the right, the suitably impressed voice, Mr Cornwall said, 'Well, for one afternoon's work you've done wonderfully well, Vincent. You really are a very clever little boy.'

He loved Vincent, completely satisfactory child. He had some feeling for Charlotte; every now and then she'd twist a word, turn a phrase in a way that amused him. It was a great pity that she and Agnes should have been at loggerheads from the first.

'Charlie said I was very good. She gave me a chocolate bar.' It was not just a simple statement; it said—come on, what reward do you propose to offer me?

'And I'll give you a sip from my glass. Just a sip.' It was a dark, sweet, brown sherry, not much to his own taste, and that was why it had been left to the last. It couldn't hurt a child. In France and in Italy, countries which John Cornwall had visited in his day, children drank wine and took no harm.

'I like that,' Vincent said. 'It tastes like toffee.'

A perceptive remark.

'You may have one sip more...'

The door opened and Agnes came in.

He slipped Vincent from his knee, stood up, went towards her, gave the meaningless, dutiful kiss that the occasion demanded. The sight of her lowered, though only slightly, the ebullience of his mood. This time her condition was making itself shown very early; she looked thick and heavy; there were patches of dark pigmentation under her eyes and the lilac-coloured dress did not suit her now-sallow complexion.

However, he said, 'Well, my dear. Here I am, back safe and sound. And how have things been with you?'

'I've had a very trying day,' she said, looking at him with disfavour. 'Vincent, go to Nurse.'

'No,' Vincent said positively. 'Not Nurse.' That glance, with its precocious spark of malice in it, took in the faces of both his parents. He offered a compromise. 'I'll go to Charlie.'

'That's a good boy. Run and find Charlie.'

'What are you drinking?' Agnes Cornwall asked as soon as they were alone. It was an accusation rather than a question.

'Some innocuous beverage called sweet brown sherry. The adjectives are indisputable. The noun is open to question.' It was a manner of speech which she found irritating. 'May I pour you a glass?'

'I feel quite poorly enough as it is. And I do not approve of children drinking.'

'A sip and a half,' he said, placatingly. And then, because she did not look placated, he added mischievously, 'I'll make a drunkard of him yet.'

She then made one of the speeches which he loathed, and in a way dreaded. What about the butcher's bill? Potter was now sending inedible meat; her lunch had been so indigestible that her rest had done her no good ... She moved on to Charlotte's misdemeanours, the bad influence she exercised over Vincent.

It was the kind of talk to which he had trained himself to turn a deaf ear. He poured and drank another glass of the despised but quite potent sherry.

When the tirade ended he was able to say, still lightly, 'Well, Potter shall have his pound of flesh first thing in the morning.' The allusion eluded her; the term 'governess' was, in her case a piece of self-promotion. The first Mrs Cornwall had advertised for a *mother's help, preferably one capable of giving first lessons to younger children.* The poor muddled woman had still at that time hoped that, relieved of some household responsibilities and with someone to help with Charlotte and Thomas, she still might fan the feeble sparks of intelligence in Adelaide and Victoria. She had soon seen through Miss Gooch's pretensions, but by that time the young woman had made herself so invaluable in other ways ...

'In fact, all bills shall be paid tomorrow,' Mr Cornwall said.

'How?' Suspicion now added itself to the other disagreeable ingredients of her expression.

'In the usual way. Coin of the realm.'

'Where did you get it?'

'I fell in with a gentleman who makes it by the sackful.'

He had always kept her in the dark about his financial transactions. Too late she had learned why the first Mrs Cornwall's death had ushered in a period of stringent economy.

'Have you been gambling?'

'My dear! How could I? Schools offer small opportunity. And that reminds me. I must change before dinner. The odour of well-matured corduroys is very pervasive.'

'The bills will be paid?'

30

'In full.'

He went upstairs, his good mood almost intact. Complaints about bills when one had money were very different from complaints about them when one did not know which way to turn.

As he reached the top of the stairs, the nursery door, to the left, opened and Nurse Ellis stood in the opening.

'Good evening, Nurse.'

'Good evening, sir. Is Master Vincent with you?'

'No. He went up to Miss Charlotte.'

'It's his bedtime. I expect you are glad to be home, sir.'

'I am indeed.'

He went to the door of his dressing room and Nurse called from the bottom of the second stairway. 'Master Vincent! Bedtime!'

Any meal with Papa at the table was better than one without him, and tonight his mood was especially good. He joked with Addie and Vikky about being the two best-dressed young ladies in East Anglia. He praised Charlotte for teaching Vincent so many letters so quickly. Even to Thomas, who all too often had the same effect upon Papa as Charlotte had upon Mrs Cornwall, he was friendly tonight.

'Well, my boy, you appear to have made a favourable impression upon Mr Macferson this afternoon. I had a word with him as I came home and he thinks you'll make a splendid pupil-teacher. You start after the Harvest holiday.'

Thomas blushed and wriggled in his chair, torn between relief at having satisfied Papa and a profound distaste for the future thus opening before him. He was an intensely shy boy, really only at ease with one person in the world—Charlie, and to be a pupil-teacher, and presently a teacher, was a painful prospect indeed. The idea of facing a class appalled him; but Papa had decided, and he had sense enough to see that his choice of occupation was very limited. The thing he really wanted to do would not provide him with a living for years, if it ever did.

Charlotte thought—now! Not only was the moment as opportune as any likely to present itself in the near future, but what she had to say would divert Papa's attention from Thomas. Papa's next remark might be, 'Well, have you nothing to say?'

31

So from her pocket she took the letter and said brightly, 'Papa, now that Thomas's future is settled, would you consider mine?'

He joked, taking the paper. 'What is it, Charlie? A proposal of marriage?'

But he read the letter gravely.

'Are you sure you want to do this?'

'Absolutely sure, Papa.'

'What is it?' Mrs Cornwall demanded.

'Charlotte wishes to become some kind of apprentice nurse. In London.'

'I think that is a most sensible idea.'

'Up to a point,' Papa agreed. 'Thanks to Miss Nightingale, nursing is now a most respectable profession.' Almost the only one which a middle-class girl could adopt without losing caste. And with Charlie gone Agnes would have one less thing to complain about. But ... He looked along the table and studied Charlotte. He had never loved his first wife; he had married her for her money, resented the restrictions imposed, been impatient with her ill-health, extreme sensitivity, impracticality. It slightly annoyed him when people like Mrs Greenfield said how closely Charlotte was growing to resemble her mother; it was superficial. Her colouring was his, and so was her spirit. Look how she'd managed this, without a word to anyone. In one way, however, Charlotte did resemble her mother; a kind of frail look.

'It's gruelling work,' he said. 'Heaving and hauling.'

'Children, Papa.'

'You have a point there. But you're only what? Sixteen. And you have never lived in London. I think you're too young.'

'But Papa, this is a scheme specially devised for the young. Like Thomas's pupil-teachership. I have all the particulars upstairs, in my room. It sounds a bit like school—except that the uniform is provided and two of us may venture forth into the streets—instead of the baker's dozen in a crocodile. The uniform may be a repellent. Blue serge figures largely...' They both laughed.

Adelaide asked if she and Victoria might leave the table. It had been a very nice meal, the kind which, installed in their own house, they would enjoy every day. Thomas also excused himself. Papa said, 'Well, Charlie, if you are quite sure...' Consent enough.

'I have work to do,' Mr Cornwall said, planning to avoid the company of Agnes, once so eagerly sought. He went to the library where the bottle of brandy stood, unopened. Mrs Cornwall went, as a lady should, to the drawing room. There had been a time when she had seen herself there, mistress of the house; Mrs John Vincent Cornwall, the new wife, with everything new about her. New decoration, new furniture; but circumstances had beaten her down and she was now glad to lie on the comfortable old sofa and wait for bedtime. Charlotte disposed of, and the bills about to be paid, however mysteriously.

Mr Cornwall went to the library and realised that Vincent's first excursion into the world of literacy had been made at the expense of a half-written report which began 'With a school of sixty and no more assistance than that afforded by a pupil-teacher, whose own spelling is notably defective, Mr Brown does his best. The earth closets, two in number, are not really sufficient to serve a school of this size . . .'

Below this reasonable assessment of the situation, Vincent had taken over with his Big A, his little a. Mr Cornwall took a glass of brandy in order to brace himself for the rewriting . . . And then the bell rang. Nellie answered it and hurried back to the kitchen.

'The parson and his missus,' she reported, pulling the kettle over what remained of the dying fire and then proceeding to prepare a tea-tray for two. 'I bet they're on the beg.'

'Sunday School Summer Treat,' Beattie said. 'Brook told young March, and he told his father, and he told Catchpole and he told me. Brook said he didn't mind lending his meadow and his kitchen so long as it was just the Sunday School. But last year it was the lot, church, chapel and downright heathens. They broke his fence and left gates open. Pigs rootling in the garden and cows all over the place. Never no more, at least so he said, according to Catchpole. I bet thass what it is.'

It was. In the library Mr Greenfield put his case over a glass of brandy. 'It would be a change of venue. I devoutly hope that next year, or perhaps the next, I shall be able to afford to take them all to Lowestoft. To see the sea is an experience which they are otherwise unlikely to ex . . . enjoy. In the meantime, your meadow, if you would kindly lend it, is nearer the village and has the benefit of *shade*. The meadow which Mr Brook has

33

always so kindly put at our disposal, has no trees.'

Mr Cornwall, in his present good mood, said that he would be glad to lend his meadow and his kitchen for the buttering of buns, his stove for the heating of hot water.

In the drawing room, over the tea cups—tea was *said* to have a finally cooling effect, but it took a little time—Mrs Greenfield, stout and well-corseted, after her walk along the lane on this sultry evening, was feeling the heat.

'If your husband does consent, Mrs Cornwall—I rather think he will because, after all, he is much concerned with the young—I shall be obliged to ask you a personal favour. Lady Frances ... she takes an interest, she always presents the prizes, but her zeal exceeds her strength nowadays. If she could take a little rest, between the races and the presentation of the prizes, here, in your quiet, pretty room ...'

Lady Frances, almost as old as Catchpole's mother, and markedly eccentric, had been one of those once fond of the first Mrs Cornwall. She had come soon after the daffodil-wood incident and been put off. Mrs Cornwall was not well enough to receive visitors. She had then gone abroad for eighteen months; learned on her return that poor Emily was confined to the house, and come again, determined to take her for a drive. On that occasion she had been admitted by 'that governess' and had seen Emily, in dressing-gown and slippers, her hair half up and half down. 'It is very kind of you, Frances. Very kind, but I cannot leave the house. Whenever I go out something disastrous ... It is not safe outside now. I must stay here.' Lady Frances had failed in her errand, but she had concerned herself quite unnecessarily, giving advice to Miss Gooch and Mr Cornwall, asking advice of the doctor. Agnes Cornwall had little doubt that the old busybody was largely responsible for sly rumours about the sick woman not receiving proper attention, being made of no account in her own house. And Lady Frances was to blame entirely for the social ostracism which had followed. If she had called, others would have followed.

'If Lady Frances wishes to rest and take tea here, she will be welcome.' Nothing wrong with the words. But the ungraciousness showed in the voice and Mrs Greenfield thought—What a pity; this could have been the thin edge of the wedge.

She changed the subject.

34

'My husband tells me that Charlotte asked him to sponsor her application to St Mark's. Do you think her health will stand up to such rigorous training?' More sidelong criticism!

'I had nothing to do with it. Even her Papa knew nothing until this evening, and then only because she wanted his signature. And there's nothing wrong with Charlotte that I know of.'

Not a ladylike expression, though hard to say why.

'I am not averse to girls adopting some vocation,' Mrs Greenfield said. 'They cannot all find husbands and to be a dependant is hard—especially in later life.'

'Charlotte will be independent enough when she is twenty-one. Their grandfather provided for all of them. All the girls.'

'Really. I was not aware of that. How very fortunate.'

'Three hundred a year each.'

Mrs Greenfield's eyes widened. Her husband's stipend was two hundred and forty, her own income twenty-five.

On the way home, in the long lingering light, Mr Greenfield said, 'He agreed to our using his meadow. What is more he gave me a sovereign towards the tea. We could have *iced* buns.'

'Or cherry cake. I wish I did not find her so uncongenial. She did tell me one very interesting thing. When she is twenty-one Charlotte will have three hundred pounds a year. The grandfather—that would be poor Emily's father—provided for all the girls. And the twins attained their majority more than a year ago. So why do they wear such extraordinary clothes?'

'Do they? They always look all right to me. They never *give*, though.' Long experience had taught him that the best givers were unmarried women of independent means. 'Maybe their father takes charge of it,' he mused. 'And who could blame him? He seemed to have a pocketful of money this evening.'

'I am inclined to think that perhaps the rumours about the bills are as ill-founded as those about ... other things,' Mrs Greenfield said, charitably. 'After all, that little boy was born a full year after the marriage. And as I said at the time, four young children, and a capable woman there in the house; it probably seemed the best thing. At the time.'

'I never held it against him,' Mr Greenfield said, truthfully.

Mrs Greenfield's mind shifted. She had no children of her

own; but she had nephews, sons of dear friends, young men embarking upon careers, presently to be lucrative, one hoped. A wife with three hundred a year . . .

'It is a pity about the twins being so . . . odd. They cannot be regarded as marriageable, can they?

'Not in a country which does not practise polygamy,' Mr Greenfield said, in his dry way.

She laughed: became grave again.

'I don't feel absolutely happy about Charlotte. She looks so delicate, and nursing, particularly in the early stages, is very onerous.'

'Set your mind at rest, my dear . . . I cannot remember the exact occasion, but not long ago. Some festivity in the Guildhall. She was carrying something, I think it was an urn and I said that it was too heavy for her and she said, "I'm stronger than I look." Which was true. She carried it without effort. Also, never forget the old saying—God fits the back to the burden.'

'Very true,' Mrs Greenfield said. So she set her mind at rest and went to bed happy.

Under the wide slate roof of Stonebridge House only Thomas went to bed positively unhappy, and since he fell asleep almost as soon as he lay down his unhappiness was of short duration. For all her ungraciousness over the matter of entertaining a decrepit, though powerful old woman, Agnes Cornwall felt that she had won, after all. Lady Frances had made the first move, belatedly and through a deputy, but a definite move. And Charlotte, that thorn in the flesh, was going to London. And the bills were to be paid. When her husband gave her another dutiful kiss and said, 'Go to bed, my dear. I have a lot of work to get through. Perhaps it would be as well if I slept in my dressing room,' she made no demur.

The twins were now certain that the beaded bodice would be ready by Sunday. 'We can go to bed now,' Adelaide said, when even by the westerly facing window the light no longer served.

'Yes, we can go to bed,' said the echo.

Nellie put her shining coin into the purse that held her inconsiderable savings and thought of asking time off on Wednesday, when the carrier's cart went into Bereham. There was still a lot of summer left and she'd buy sprigged muslin, a new straw hat—and, taking a leaf out of Nurse Ellis's book, some scent, lily-of-the-valley, if such a thing was to be found.

Beattie prised up the loose board in the floor of the cupboard where her few pitiable garments hung and slipped her two shining sovereigns into the mouth of the linen bag which contained her miser's hoard. A noble contribution. God bless Mr Cornwall. They could say what they liked, there weren't many like him. She placed the old flat-iron by her bed and was soon dreaming of Brancaster, of matching Fanny's half-crown a week, and gathering and selling cockles.

Charlotte looked about her small room, so often a refuge, soon to be abandoned. But what she treasured could be taken with her—the photograph of Mamma, so faded as to be almost indecipherable, the silver-backed hairbrush and hand-mirror which had been her mother's and should by rights have gone to the twins; but they were so accustomed to having everything in pairs, but at the same time matching, that they hadn't wanted them, the little picture of Vincent, painted by Thomas, very life-like though Vincent had refused to sit still. There was also a large, pink-lined shell, in which one could hear the sea roar. A few books ... She hoped that now that she was not going to be an expense to Papa in future, he would contrive to squeeze out enough money to provide a new dress before she went to London. Those she had were all three years old, part of her school outfit and she had grown a good deal since then. Skirts had been lengthened by letting down hems or inserting bands of material, but the bodices looked skimpy. And what about shoes? Her best pair had been clumsily resoled; her everyday ones resoled *and* patched. Would the provided uniform include shoes?

In her nightgown, she paused by a bowl of pinks that stood on her chest-of-drawers and took several deep breaths. Then she knelt by her bed and went through the now meaningless procedure of saying her prayers. This was a tribute to her mother's memory, paid faithfully every night and morning. She had lost faith in, and contact with, God during that time when Mamma was ill, unable to take part in family life, unable to go out. She had prayed passionately, then. 'Dear God make Mamma better. Restore her to us.' Mamma had died, and nothing that kind Mrs Greenfield had said about release from suffering, reunion in Heaven or accepting the will of God had made the slightest difference. Behind the feeling of having been badly let down there was nothing but a blankness. But Mamma had insisted upon the ritual, just as she had insisted upon washing behind one's ears and speaking pleasantly to one's inferiors.

At ten o'clock John Cornwall performed his evening routine —entrusted during his absence to Cook. He locked and barred the front door, barred the one at the end of the back hall which gave upon the drying yard and then went into the kitchen. Tiger's dinner, enhanced this evening by the giblets and neck of the fowl—stood ready in a chipped enamel bowl. He went into the yard and placed the bowl by the dog's kennel, at the same time unhooking the chain. Tiger knew better than to go through his 'I love you, please love me', with his master. As Mr Cornwall had explained, 'Tiger is not a pet, he is a guard dog. Fussing would just spoil him.' While the dog gulped down his dinner Mr Cornwall walked across the yard, past the carriage house, the stable and the woodshed and barred the tall doors which Catchpole had closed before he went home. He then returned to the kitchen and shot the bolts on the door.

These rather elaborate precautions in the midst of a wide area where there was little indigenous crime except poaching, were rendered necessary by the fact that Biddlesford was often pestered by gypsies. Beyond the church there was a large common which offered ideal temporary resting place for nomads. It was dotted with gorse and blackberry bushes which made excellent fuel; it was bounded on one side by the river, and it was less than a mile from the main road. The gypsies' depredations were sometimes exaggerated, but their evil reputation was not ill-founded. They stole fowls, linen from lines, a lamb once from the flock at Lane End Farm; and once every rose from Doctor Fletcher's garden. He and his gardener took enormous pride in the roses and one summer morning the trees were stripped. Later that day Mrs Greenfield had seen a woman, indubitably a gypsy, hawking roses in Bereham. But, as she said, there was nothing to be done about it; one could not positively identify the roses. One gang had made an attempt to steal a horse, Potter the butcher's, and might have got away with it had they known that this otherwise amiable animal simply would not back. It had never backed in its life; it had to be turned, in the rather narrow stable and led out, and then the cart had to be brought to it. The gypsies tried to back it out and the horse kicked and plunged about, so that Potter's attention was attracted. By the time he reached the stable the gypsies had vanished, but there was, on this occasion, what might be called circumstantial evidence against them, in so far as the butcher's horse was wearing a strange halter, and a dead donkey was left on the common. However, to take proceedings against them was hardly worth while; they all looked alike; they changed their names at will and could, as though by magic, conjure up any number of witnesses to swear that at any given time the suspect was fifty miles away. So decent citizens defended themselves as well as they could. Doctor Fletcher had indeed bought himself a dog to guard his rather vulnerable rose-garden, but he had not followed Mr Cornwall's stern example; he had made a pet of his dog which now slept across the foot of his bed and always accompanied him on his rounds in the gig.

Mr Cornwall's horses were well worth stealing; he had given a hundred and seventy pounds each for them; a gentleman was known by his horse-flesh. He might, when he set out on his labours, leave behind a household suffering mild penury and he might be bound for places reeking of old corduroys and unwashed bodies, but on his way, mounted in his gig behind either of his horses—'first-class style and manners and grand action'—he was able to revert to the wonderful days, eight years of wonderful days, starting with his twenty-first birthday, when money had been something to spend. Even when it was spent, some habits stuck; good horses, superb tailoring, a clean shirt every day and when, as he was sometimes obliged to do, he had to be away from home for as long as a week on end, always a first-class hotel.

Back in his library he looked at the clock, checked it by his watch; poured himself another glass of brandy and sat down to read what he had written since bidding Agnes good night. Lucid and succinct. Neither at Eton nor at Cambridge had he gained any very high academic standard—too many more fascinating things to do. But his mediocre degree had served him well when it came to seeking a job . . .

Still not quite half past ten.

He thought of his lucky afternoon. A bold bet; ten pounds on a rank outsider which had romped home at twenty to one. Maybe Fortune, so long frowning, or at best indifferent, intended to smile on him again.

Twenty minutes to eleven. Safe now? He hoped that Agnes

had taken some of the drops which Doctor Fletcher had prescribed as a sedative. He hoped she was sound asleep. He would soon know. If she heard him moving about, however softly, in his dressing room, she would call. He'd often thought that the less women deserved attention, the more they demanded it. If she were awake she would want the window opened, or closed, or a drink of water.

Again he was lucky. No sound from the bedroom. He stripped and put on his dressing-gown, heavy silk with velvet collar and cuffs, a relic of those carefree bachelor days, and his slippers, matching crimson. Then he stood and listened again and heard a very comforting sound, too slight to be called a snore, but the audible sound of a heavy woman, slightly drugged, fast asleep.

He took the few steps to the door of the nursery.

Rose was waiting for him. Hours earlier she had greeted him with words to which no listener could possibly have taken exception. 'I expect you are glad to be home, sir.' And he had said, 'I am indeed.' But their eyes had communicated, saying other things.

Eighteen years earlier a gaunt, work-bowed smallholder and his lean, leathery wife had produced this thing of beauty, this changeling child and had, in a moment of aberration, given her the right name, Rose, not Deborah, Miriam, Rachel or Rebecca, culled from the Bible. It was their only lapse. She grew up to be lovely and they both knew that in a female beauty was a snare, and led to temptation, which led to sin. They had combated it with all their might. Rose Ellis had always been most plainly clad; her naturally curly golden hair scraped back from her forehead, plaited tightly. They had kept her busy, ordered her comings and goings. They belonged to a religious sect, called the Children of Jerusalem, so severe that by comparison even the Methodists of the kind called 'Primitive' seemed to be a lot of loose-living hedonists. It was not a popular sect and the nearest meeting house, with its muster of twenty people, was four miles' trudge away.

They would have kept her there forever, meek and submissive; but there had been a series of small disasters which had wrecked their frail economy. One of the family, after the swine fever had carried off the pigs, and a fox had killed twelve laying fowls and the cow had succumbed to milk-fever, must seek.

40

some gainful employment. Matthew Ellis must stay, cultivate his ten acres and somehow by the utmost economy and faith in God, hope to restock his little farm; Charity, his wife must stay and feed him, wash for him, aid him in every possible way. It was Rose who must go, be thrown to the wolves, exposed to the wicked world.

But they had been careful. It was not until their landlord mentioned that a friend of his was looking for a nursemaid ... And even then caution had prevailed and questions been asked. Mr Cornwall had daughters older than Rose; another daughter and a son in their teens. He had been widowed, re-married and had, from this second mating, a little boy of four and a baby girl.

No danger? No danger!

And at Bereham, within what was regarded as easy walking distance, five miles, there was a little enclave of Children of Jerusalem. Rose's father had stipulated that she should have one whole free Sunday in a month in order to attend the meeting. Apart from that she needed no time off; idleness led to mischief. Her wages, five shillings a week, she was to send home. Neither parent had kissed her at parting; both had told her to be a good girl.

She had been a very bad girl indeed; quite possibly quite the worst girl in the world, for she knew better and had had the advantage of good upbringing. And she was not being bad for money. She was being bad for the sheer joy of it.

The first time she had expected to be struck dead. The Father of the Children of Jerusalem was very easily angered—look what had happened to Lot's wife, to the children who had jeered Elijah's baldness, to Ananias and Sapphira. However, no lightning had struck, no earthquake yawned, there was not even a voice from Heaven. Some punishments were postponed, however, and when she woke in the morning she half expected to be blind, or a leper. In fact she woke in perfect health, feeling very happy and, for the first time in her life, important. There would, of course, be Hell at the end. Once she startled her lover by saying in a tranced voice, 'So long as we burn together, I can bear it.'

She ran to him now and gave him the kind of welcome any man had a right to expect. Amidst the hugging and the kissing she almost purred. She said she had missed him so much, and that the two days he had been away had seemed like a month.

41

He said it had felt the same to him. The fact that they were obliged to whisper because of the two sleeping children in the room, lent the most ordinary statement a kind of intimacy.

He would have carried her straight to the bed, but she whispered, 'Put me down, darling. I want you to see it.'

It was a nightgown which she had made for herself—the first pretty thing she had ever owned. It was made of white lawn, very fine. At the yoke, at the waist and just above the flounce at the bottom there was something known as 'insertion' which could be bought by the yard; the insertion had slots, through which she had threaded blue ribbon. Mr Cornwall had himself given her the materials and on and off it had taken her a month to make it.

She had no real notion of how she looked in it because in the tiny space, nothing more than a cupboard with a window, which served her as a dressing room, there was only a small glass, very old and spotted. In it she could see the be-ribboned yoke, with her firm white neck rising out of it; by looking down she could see the ribbon at the waist, and the flounce. But she thought it was pretty; she knew that she was pretty—he had said so, often enough.

There was the usual nightlight, and tonight two ordinary candles. In their glow she postured; almost, not quite, innocently. The golden hair, released from the plait, turned about on itself like a snail and clamped to the back of her head with thick brown hairpins, now fell about her face and on to her shoulders, lively and shining. Her eyes sparkled, her lips, coral pink, were a little parted, moist from kissing, ready to kiss again.

'Like it?' she whispered. She loved him so extremely that she was trying to model her pronunciation upon his. She knew, humbly, that she could never attain that easy rise and fall, but she could avoid saying, 'Loike ut?' as once she would have done.

John Vincent Cornwall whispered, a little hoarsely, 'Come here . . .'

As the setting for a love scene the nursery at Stonebridge House was incongruous. Walls washed a pale cold blue, a Turkey carpet, once, if gaudy, gay and thick, now worn, faded, stained; curtains with all colour and much substance washed away. But it had advantages; if Amelia woke and whimpered,

42

or Vincent woke and shouted, Rose was there. 'Hush now' or 'Be quiet!' It served.

Vincent woke. He had a nasty taste in his mouth. Nurse had relented and given him a lump of sugar. She did that occasionally and although the sugar always tasted all right at the time when he woke his mouth tasted horrid.

His dream had been horrid, too. Big D, little d, D for dog, and there was Tiger, white teeth, flapping tongue. Nasty taste, nasty dream. But the faint steady glow from the nightlight almost reassured him. (Rose, obeying the order, 'Come here', had blown out the two ordinary candles. They had served their purpose.) Vincent could see the rails of his cot; and inside them he was safe from Tiger even if Tiger had somehow got into the nursery. Quite safe, except ... Something was going on in the room, something that linked with his dream. He reared himself cautiously and saw in the nightlight's faint but adequate light, a huge, hairy animal, on top of Nurse, killing her.

He screamed with all the force of his well-developed lungs. Yagh! Yagh! Then something even worse happened. The hairy thing left Nurse and came towards the cot, far, far more dangerous than Tiger.

Vincent screamed again. And then finding words in this extremity: 'Charlie! Char...' Something large and heavy and damp closed over his mouth, his nose, cutting off his cries. And his breath. Bearing him back against the pillow.

In the silence they listened, sweating. The screams had been enough to rouse the whole house. John Vincent Cornwall, thinking quickly, reached for his dressing-gown, girded it tightly. The child had had a nightmare and he had come, arriving first. That would be the explanation. He slipped his arm under Vincent and raised him, speaking soothingly, but rousingly, not troubling now to lower his voice. 'Vincent! It's all right. Papa is here...' Against his hand the shoulderblades felt limp as a dead butterfly's wings.

'He has fainted. Get some water.'

Rose had lived on a farm, seen dead fowls, dead pigs. She was a Daughter of Jerusalem and ever since Easter had expected punishment. Here it was.

She said, 'He is dead.'

The small face was waxen, the lips bluish.

43

'God! God!' John Vincent said in a terrible voice. He leaned against the corner of the cot and broke into harsh gasping sobs.

Rose said, 'Be quiet!'

For three months he had been her God; displacing the other. *Thou shalt have none other gods before me. The wages of sin is death.*

His death. They would take him away and hang him. And her punishment would be to live on, knowing what she had done.

Not if I can help it, she thought. She braced herself, and from somewhere strength, control and resourcefulness flowed in.

'You leave this to me,' she said. 'You do exactly what I say and it'll be all right.' He was not listening; he went on sobbing.

'Listen,' she said, taking his arm and shaking him fiercely. 'It was an accident. You don't want to hang, do you?'

'I deserve to hang...'

'Well, I ain't going to let you. You listen to me. Go and get into bed alongside her. You don't know nothing. You hear me? In the morning you behave ordinary, till you're told. Then you can cry all you want. But stop now and go and get into bed.'

There was great power in her and he was completely broken. 'Wh-what can you do?'

'Never you mind. The less you know the better. You don't know nothing. Remember that.'

When he did not move she said brutally, 'All right then. We'll tell them the truth. And we'll both swing.'

That remark did reach him. He raised his stricken face.

'Not you.'

'Oh yes. I was here.' Positive inspiration visited her. 'In fact I shall swear on the Bible that I did it.'

'You couldn't.'

'I would. And they'd believe me. Everybody knows I never liked him much. Now will you go. In the morning he'll just be lost. I know where to put him so he'll never be found. Now go.'

He went. She began, with a cold and deadly precision to carry out the plan which had slipped, fully detailed, into her mind.

Never having liked the child was a help to her now. She never had. Quite without knowing it the little girl who had

44

grown into a young woman was jealous of the little boy who was so beloved and so pampered, allowed to have his own way, and to answer back. Very different from the way in which Rose Ellis had been brought up. In addition he was demanding, occasionally defiant and always so ready with words. 'I shall tell my Mamma,' and harking back to some other nurse he had once had, the comparisons always in Rose's disfavour. She was thus constantly reminded that she was not a proper nurse at all and only held the position because she was cheap.

Her upbringing was also a help to her; no sentiment, no squeamishness was allowed to any Daughter of Jerusalem. It was the inner purity that mattered, not the soiling of your hands.

Most help of all was experience. When a pig sickened and died from some mysterious cause it was best not to say anything about it. And when Matthew Ellis's sty suffered its first casualty he had put the body into the manure heap; a reasonable action; it saved the bother of digging a grave and it contributed something to the heap. Charity Ellis had ventured a little protest. 'It'll stink.' She meant that to the permanent and not noticed manure-heap odour, something extra would be added. Her husband had replied that well inside the heap, where there was heat, flesh, bones, hide would be consumed in no time at all. In order to speed the process he had slashed the pig's belly, to let the blood out and prevent it blowing up.

The cot had two blankets, one red, one white. Having kindled one of the ordinary candles from the nightlight, Rose took the top blanket, the red one, and laid it on the floor. Then she lifted Vincent out. The cot had a drop side, but some time before Rose had come to Stonebridge House, Vincent had mastered the catch and the drop side was now fixed by an intricate system of knots. He had to be lifted out every morning, lifted in every evening. It did not surprise her that he seemed heavier now; live and dead weight were accepted facts.

She trussed him in the blanket with a sure, callous hand, opened the nursery door, listened. The house was quiet. She took the candle, the bundle and went down the back stairs which led straight into the kitchen. She went barefoot. Had she had slippers and been accustomed to wearing them, she would probably have put them on. In the kitchen she went to the dresser drawer and took out the implement which Beattie always referred to as 'my knife'. Rightly, since she had brought it with her. Honed on the stone doorstep it took a far sharper edge than Mr Cornwall, using his steel, could produce on the dining-room carving knife; and it had a point, very useful for coring apples or taking the deep-seated eyes from a potato. Nobody, not even Nellie, was supposed to use 'my knife'. Now Rose Ellis, parting the folds of the red blanket, used it.

Outside, in the drying yard, she did not even need a candle. What remained of the brief June darkness was illuminated by a lopsided moon and a multitude of stars. In the east the darkness was already lifting. The drying yard was almost entirely enclosed; a blank, windowless wall of the kitchen to one side of the door, the long disused laundry with its heavily cobwebbed window on the other; the gable end of the stable and on the opposite side the opening into the kitchen garden, with, just inside, the heap, a flat-topped pyramid. Its main component was the sweepings from the stable, but it also contained grass cuttings from the lawn and kitchen refuse. Tonight the heap, March's idol, wore on its flat crown the empty pea-pods and the strawberry hulls. They glimmered, pale.

Rose, with Beattie's knife, cut into the base of the heap, it cut rather like rich fruit cake. She made a kind of cave, placed the red-blanketed bundle in it, shovelled back with her hands the stuff that had been disturbed and patted the mound into shape. She was not in the least concerned that a healthy, extremely intelligent child had come to an untimely end. It had happened and she had done her best. Nor did it concern her that a child whose end, however untimely, should have been decently observed with full funereal paraphernalia, had been shovelled away, like a dead pig.

Back in the kitchen she was obliged to wash her hands and the knife; and in order to do that she must work the pump over the sink. It made a clunking noise, but if anybody should happen to notice, she had her answer. Master Vincent had woken and asked for a drink of water. She washed the knife and dried it thoroughly and put it back in exactly the position from which she had taken it. In the sanctuary which the nursery now seemed to offer, she was perturbed to discover that despite all her care her beautiful nightdress was ruined. There had been little blood, but some sticky drops and two smears were on the front of it, and the flounce—she had not noticed—had been in close contact with the manure heap. Yellowish and brownish marks and a distinct smell. A direct

46

connection. Sad as it was the garment must be sacrificed. She took it off, folded it small and stole down again into the kitchen. The fire there was dead and although there was paper, there was no kindling. Catchpole chopped sticks. In his daft, half-witted way, he was soft on Cook and liked every morning to present her with a bundle of kindling, as though it were a bunch of flowers, 'Here y'are, my dear.' Kindling was there, ten steps across the yard, but Rose dared not take those ten steps, because of Tiger; and she doubted whether paper alone could kindle a fire strong enough to consume a whole garment, damp with love's exudence, with the sweat of fear, with blood and the moisture that had seeped from the base of the heap. It did not occur to her to go out into the drying yard again and push the dangerous garment into the heap. All she could think of was fire, instantly consuming. And that made her think of the copper-hole, in the old laundry, just across the back hall.

Except in very poor and backward homes the copper—literally a vast cauldron, originally of copper but later made of baser alloys—set in brick, given a wooden lid and heated from below by a deep, narrow fireplace, called the copper-hole—had been relegated to the past. The modern cooking stove boiled and fried on top, heated the oven on one side and a full tank of water on the other. As a source of hot water the copper had been superseded. And so had the visiting washerwomen. Easier far to employ people like Mrs Whinney, who collected, washed, starched and ironed and delivered the fresh laundry back. The laundry at Stonebridge House had not been used for at least thirty years and the cobwebs which Rose had to break, once she had wrenched the rusted door of the copper-hole open, were almost as substantial as muslin. The parcel she thrust in was loosely twisted up in newspaper.

Some time tomorrow I will bring a few sticks and there will be a quick blaze and that will be the end of my beautiful nightgown. With that thought some regret did come. But Mr Cornwall would bring her some more material, and without Vincent to disturb her she would make a new garment in less than a month.

She slept as well as usual.

John Vincent Cornwall did not sleep at all. He lay and lived through the moment of tragedy again and again. Accident. Accident. But one that would never have happened had he been content, as so many men were, with a wife who had lost

47

her charm for him. His overriding emotion was remorseful grief, but he also felt fear and a doubt as to whether they had acted wisely ... Open conduct would have been better, send for the doctor, tell the truth. No jury would convict ... Would they not? It was murder, accidental, but murder linked with adultery and fornication, a fatal combination. Now and again he wondered what Rose had planned and was now doing: he thought she might intend to put the body into the water under the stone bridge, or hide it in Tutt Wood. *The body, it.* It was Vincent, his well-beloved, his favourite, the charming little boy who had mastered eight letters in one afternoon ...

He lay quite still except for a shudder that occasionally shook him. He must not wake Agnes. But she woke nevertheless, as the darkness gave way to dawn and the first bird chorus began. Still a little fuddled from the sedative drops, she seemed not to wonder at his presence here in the bed, after he had said he would sleep in his dressing room. When she stirred and turned over, he could move, too, and she said, 'John. Are you awake?'

He said, 'Yes,' in a thick-sounding voice.

'Could you get me a drink of water?' He was glad to move; there was a carafe of water on the marble-topped washing stand. When he gave her the glass she did not notice the unsteadiness of his hand, she did notice that there was enough light in the room to enable him to fetch the water without lighting a candle. She drank and said, 'What a bright moon.' She settled herself and soon slept again.

Outside the light brightened inexorably and presently the new day began.

2

Mrs Cornwall called 'Come in,' expecting Nellie with the morning tea.

Rose Ellis said, 'Good morning, madam, I've come for ... Oh, I thought he was with you. Master Vincent...'

John Vincent lay still and tense; the bad time was about to begin. Above the edge of the sheet he saw with one bleared eye, Rose, trim in the grey alpaca inherited from her predecessor, and a shining white apron.

'And why should you think that?' Agnes Cornwall asked.

'Because he is not in his cot, madam. I overslept a bit. I thought he'd woke early and called and you fetched him.'

'I didn't. I had a very restless night myself and slept until this moment...' More or less fully awake now, she reared on one elbow. 'If anyone heard him it would be Miss Charlotte. Or were you careless again and left a chair...' It had once happened; Vincent had climbed out of his cot on to a handy chair.

Rose said, 'Well, I might. I did move the chair to make way for the bath.'

'In that case he might be *anywhere*,' Mrs Cornwall said crossly. 'Go and look.'

In the doorway Rose met Nellie, carrying the morning tea-tray.

'Have you seen Master Vincent downstairs, Nellie?'

'No, I ain't,' Nellie said brusquely. 'Good morning, madam, good morning, sir.' She put the tray on the bedside stand on

49

Mrs Cornwall's side of the bed and went briskly away. Between seven and eight in the morning was one of her busiest times.

Agnes Cornwall poured a cup of tea and then nudged the inert form beside her.

'Your tea,' she said.

Now he must break cover and face whatever the day might bring—the most terrible day in his life.

He took the tea cup and said, 'Thank you.' Not his own voice. His wife, looking at him, sideways, saw that he looked unlike himself.

'Did you have a bad night, too? I did. I had a very bad night.' She had slept like a log through the . . . woken once, taken a few sips of water, slept again.

'I had a very bad night. Perhaps it was the heat,' he said.

'Tea will pull you together.'

Tap, tap on Miss Charlie's door; 'Miss Charlotte, is Master Vincent with you?'

'No, Nurse. I have not seen him,' Charlotte opened the door, 'this morning. Why did you think . . . ?'

'He's not in his bed, nor with Madam. Nor downstairs.'

Charlotte also remembered the occasion when Vincent had climbed from cot to chair. She asked the same question and was told the same lie.

'Then he's hiding again. I'll find him.'

Vincent had thoroughly enjoyed his former escapade and would be disappointed if this one drew less attention. So as soon as she had finished dressing she called Thomas, saying loudly, for Vincent's benefit, 'Thomas! Thomas! Vincent is lost again. Come and help me look for him.' Thomas, roused from sleep, yawning but good-natured, pulled on his dressing-gown, very old and far too small and pushed his toes into his slippers. They also were so small that they would no longer accommodate his whole foot, his heels protruded over their trodden-down, flattened backs. He then joined Charlie who was making a great pretence at hunting, calling 'Vincent! Vincent!' and whispering to Thomas not to look into the lumber room next to the nursery because it was there that the child had been found before, hiding behind the hip-bath.

Adelaide said petulantly, 'Such a noise. That is what we mean.'

'Yes, that is what we mean,' Victoria echoed. She also volunteered a remark. 'Addie, Saturday. Bacon *and* eggs.'

The food was always better when Papa was at home.

'In our house we'll have bacon and eggs every morning.'

'Every morning. Or kippers.'

'Or smoked haddock,' Adelaide said, naming the third of their favourite breakfasts.

Outside the lumber room door, so that Vincent could hear and laugh to himself, Charlotte said, 'Well, the only place I can think of now is the garden.'

Thomas had by this time had enough of the game. Once he was fully awake his overnight unhappiness had revived and he did not feel like playing. But he said, in the right voice and the right spirit, 'I must get dressed first. Don't forget the shrubbery, Charlotte.'

It was another beautiful morning, dew-drenched and sweet-scented, with a promise of heat. Idling away the five minutes which she estimated would be enough to satisfy Vincent's self-importance, Charlotte looked round and thought that this was one thing she would miss in London. But there would be compensations, high among which ranked company of her own age. Apart from a little less than three years at school, this was a thing she had always lacked, even in Mamma's time. There was a dearth of decent middle-class people with families in and around Biddlesford. And nobody could pretend that Addie and Vikky had ever been company for anybody except each other.

Catchpole arrived, a little late, he was supposed to be there at seven. He entered as he usually did, through the opening in the wall that divided the garden from the drying yard and in at the side door, unbarred by Nellie. He went through the kitchen where Beattie was using her knife to cut paper thin slices from a piece of bacon.

'You're late,' she said irritably. 'I had to get the kindling myself. Why you can't bring it in last thing before you go home is a mystery to me.'

'I always have brung it in, first thing,' he said mildly.

'That was when you kept better time,' she said, unplacated.

'Have to get my own bit of breakfust, now. The old woman is past it. Clean past it. It come a bit hard on a man. On his own, you might say.' He imbued the expression with a sly significance.

He was taking quite the wrong line with Beattie. Her plans for the future were made and they did not include looking after a half-wit, and quite possibly his ancient mother, in a clod cottage.

She said, 'Well, get along with you now.' Catchpole went into the yard, hooked Tiger to his chain and unbolted the yard door so that March, when he arrived, could enter the premises without going through the kitchen. He then shambled about getting the horses' first feed. But he saw Beattie come out and begin to rub her knife on the stone step.

'I'll do that for you if you like, my dear.' The offer was intended to make up for his unpunctuality. Beattie retorted unkindly, saying that when she wanted her knife blunted forever, she'd ask him to do it.

Charlotte opened the door of the lumber room next door to the nursery. It contained various trunks, valises and hat boxes, the twin to Vincent's cot—Adelaide and Victoria had had one each; a galvanised iron bath in which a few baby clothes, and some of Vincent's were soaking—Nurse did her own, and the children's washing—and the big hip-bath, brown on the outside, speckled black and white, like a bird's egg, on the inner. It was behind its high, shield-shaped back that Vincent had been found on the first occasion when he had escaped from his cot and there she expected to find him now. She leaned over it and said, 'Boo!'

He was not there. She had played the game too thoroughly, prolonged the hunt past a child's limited patience. But she could make up; could say 'Vincent, we hunted and hunted...'

She opened the nursery door and there was Nurse, fixing the baby's clean napkin. She said, 'Did Vincent come back?'

'Not here,' Rose Ellis said. 'I thought you were looking for him.'

'I was. I still am.' Poor Vincent, his little game had fallen flat.

Papa was in his dressing room. He had a case of razors with ivory handles, seven of them, one for each day of the week; delicate little letters, black against the white, spelled out the names of the days that made up the week.

'Papa, have you seen Vincent this morning? Is he in there?'

She nodded towards the door that connected the dressing room with the bedroom. Once Mamma's, once a happy place,

52

then a kind of sickroom, a kind of prison, the place where Mamma had died. Now Mrs Cornwall's bedroom.

Mr Cornwall said, 'No,' and with an unsteady hand moved the blade of the razor marked 'Friday' through the froth.

'Then I must look again ... Papa, this is Saturday and you are using Friday's razor. You have lost a day. You know what they say, "Lose a day and gain a friend".' Then she saw that above the half mask of white foam his eyes and what could be seen of his nose looked red.

She said, 'Hay fever again, Papa? What a nuisance.'

'Maybe,' Papa said. But the dread moment could not be dodged indefinitely. A little boy, four years old, big and strong for his age, had completely vanished ...

Agnes Cornwall said, 'For God's sake, tell me the truth for once. That money ... Did you win it? I thought so! And gypsies hanging about. They marked you. They've got Vincent. They kidnapped him somehow and as soon as a reward is offered, they'll bring him back. They'll say they *found* him. On the road. In a gravel pit.' That had been known to happen, but on a lower level. 'You get away in the gig,' she said. 'Never mind Lark and Champion, they *walk*. Get into Bereham, get the wagonettes out. They could overtake them in an hour.'

He thought—Poor Agnes! He thought—Poor wretched me! But he was glad to get away from her, to go on an errand, however futile.

'And whass all this about?' March asked Catchpole, referring to the manner in which Mr Cornwall, in the gig and the less manageable of the two horses had gone smashing past him, almost running him down in the lane.

'Little boy missing. Gone in the night. They think gypsies.'

'Don't talk daft. There ain't no gypsies. They went off, coupla days ago. Pea-picking at Lopham.'

'Then where is he? He seem to be gone?'

'Up to some trick,' March said. 'Artful little sod. I said last time what he needed was a good slap on the bum. And if he'd been mine he'd have got it, long time ago. Where've they looked?'

'All over the house. All over the garden. And he ain't in the yard. That I do know ...'

'What about the drying yard?'

'But I come through there, like always.'

53

'Did you *look*?'

'Why? Why should I? I didn't know then. I didn't know he was lost till they started yelling.'

'Little limb of Satan,' said March who had fathered four such, and belted them. 'I bet you a tanner he's in the one place they wouldn't look.'

He made for the drying yard, the one place where nobody had looked. Catchpole followed him. March, just inside the enclosed space halted, forgot about the lost child.

'Who been messing about with my muck heap?'

It wasn't everybody who could make one or who understood what he called the principle of the thing, which was to keep the heat in, the air out.

'Somebody been at it. And whass this?' This was about an inch and a half of blue ribbon lolling out from the place at the base of the heap at the point where disturbance had obviously taken place. He jerked at it and it resisted for a moment and then yielded, bringing with it something that looked like red flannel. Female, mucky stuff, and he'd told them and told them that anything to be disposed of in this way should be put on *top*. Irritably he pulled the red flannel and the cave that Rose Ellis had made, too soon disturbed, not given time to solidify, broke, flaked away and gave up its secret.

'Christ,' March said.

Catchpole turned away a little and was sick.

March felt worse than sick, remembering how often he had said, 'No' and 'Get out of my way,' and 'Be off with you,' and how often he had thought—and a moment ago to Catchpole said—that a good smack on the bum was what the child needed and would have had, had he belonged to him. He envied Catchpole being able to *be* sick.

'When you've done,' he said, 'go and warn them. I'll bring him in.'

The kitchen was full of the good smell of frying bacon and freshly made coffee; Beattie was not easily put out of her routine and she did not believe that the gypsies had made off with the child. Why should they? They had enough of their own.

Catchpole said, 'We found him.'

'I knew it,' she said, and went on gently ladling fat over an egg. All that fuss about nothing.

'He's . . .' Catchpole said, and could not bring out the next word. Stammering, stupid fool, she thought; late with the kindling and now disturbing her. She looked around, ready to give him some scathing words, a searing look. His face was greenish.

'Dead.'

'What!' She dropped the spoon into the pan.

'March is just bringing him in.'

She did not enquire what had happened. Time enough for that. She said, 'Not in here.'

March, carrying his dreadful burden reverently, was already within the side door. Catchpole stepped out into the back hall and opened the door exactly opposite that of the kitchen, the door of the old laundry.

'In here,' he said. March obeyed him and laid the dead child down on the long stone bench just below the window. Then he said, 'Poor little sod. What a way to end! Who could've done it?'

'Somebody should ought to fetch the doctor,' Catchpole said. Not that the doctor could do anything, but he remembered across the space of thirty years when his father had hanged himself in the shed. They'd sent for the doctor then. It was the right thing to do.

March, masking profound emotion with a show of indifference, said, 'I got work to see to,' and went off, leaving Catchpole, of all people, in charge. He returned to the kitchen. Nellie had by this time come back from setting the table in the dining room. She had shared Beattie's scepticism about gypsies and expressed an opinion that a child who could climb out of a cot—as Master Vincent had been known to do—could climb the front gate. She was quite positive that the master would overtake him in the lane; silly to bother about taking the gig, really. But when she heard the news she shared March's feelings, forgot how Vincent loved to steal up behind her and untie her apron strings, so that it fell and made her stumble and how he would run off with brushes and dusters, inviting chases she had no time for, calling, 'Ha, ha, *hee*, you can't catch *me*!'

She said, 'Oh no! Poor dear little boy. And whatever will Miss Charlie do?'

Charlotte had believed the theory about gypsies. What else could have happened to Vincent? She knew nothing about her father's spectacular win or her stepmother's idea that Vincent had been taken and held for ransom. What she did know, from hearsay, was that gypsies would steal anything, and, from the evidence of her own eyes, that they were cruel. They hitched skeletal horses and staggering little donkeys to caravans and lashed them along. Their dogs were cowed, and all bones. Their children like little old men and women. She could understand *why* any gypsy, given a chance, would snatch Vincent; until he was starved and prematurely aged, he would be an asset to any gypsy woman hawking linen pegs or tin kettles or bunches of flowers. What a beautiful little boy ... Attention drawn, the sixpence certain.

But this time whoever had Vincent in their clutches was in for a surprise. She knew a short cut ... A straight line was the shortest way between two given points, and any water, unless prevented, ran in a straight line. At the stone bridge she abandoned the lane, hopped over and followed the water to the point where it skirted the common—where there were no gypsies, nor any sign of their having been there for several days. The black rings where their fires had been already fringed by the quick summer-growing grass; what animal droppings there were were old, dried out. No gypsies here yesterday, last night, early this morning. So Vincent, where are you? My dear one, my darling, where are you? What has happened to you?

Thomas, once he had abandoned the game in which he had only involved himself in order to please Charlie, had been busy. His everyday boots, like Charlotte's everyday shoes, had been cobbled. On one of his the little short nails had broken away and he had to hammer them back. Not an easy job for a boy who had useless thumbs. His were absolutely useless, very thin, quite powerless, they lay across his palms, the tip of each thumb just touching the base of the little finger. It had, he knew, been a grief to the mother whom he could hardly, in any other context, really remember; what he did remember was her encouraging him to use a knife, a fork, a pen, a pencil between his first and second fingers. And no lesson, no encouragement had been wasted. He could use a knife and fork as well as anybody, a pen or paintbrush better than most. For most purposes his fingers had taken over the functions of thumbs, but hammering was a bit difficult and it took time. He had just made the boot wearable, put it and its fellow on and laced them both when Nellie came up and told him to run for the doctor because his little brother was dead.

Like Nellie he said, 'Oh no! How? Why?'

'We don't know nothing, 'cept that he's dead, Master Thomas and Catchpole say you should fetch the doctor.'

Low as he was in the hierarchy of Stonebridge House, Thomas had always ranked above Catchpole. Catchpole issuing orders?

'Where is my Papa?'

'Oh, he went off. He thought the gypsies took the poor little boy. He went to Bereham to tell the police.'

A bit of Thomas's mind, shocked, but still active, thought—How silly. The policeman at Ashworth has one of these speaking things. Wires and bells and mystery, but Police Constable Champion at Ashworth could have been in communication with the Police Headquarters in Bereham, far quicker than Papa could drive there. Another bit of his mind took another direction. How would Charlie bear this? But he was already in motion, running to fetch the doctor. Why? What could Doctor Fletcher do? Just before he came in sight of the green, the piece of his boot sole that he had just hammered on, came loose again and almost tripped him; he tore it off and flung it aside. The rough surface of the lane began to cut through his sock, and presently his foot. But he did not stop running until he burst in upon the old doctor who, having walked among his roses, was just sitting down to the sound good breakfast in which he believed as the only sensible way to start the day. Even when he had stayed out all night and did not get home until mid-morning, he still took his breakfast.

Thomas was momentarily speechless, gasping for breath. Never a strong boy; ordinary healthy boy shouldn't be so white after a brisk run on a lovely fresh morning. Shock?

'Sit down, Thomas, and get your breath. Calm down. Nothing's quite so bad as ...'

Thomas made a noise as though he were being strangled. Doctor Fletcher poured a cup of coffee, sugared it well and stirred it.

'There; try to drink that.' Thomas managed two scalding sips.

'My brother . . Dead.'

'Impossible!' the doctor exclaimed. He'd seen Vincent only a few days before, perfectly healthy child, but a bit consti-

57

pated. He'd prescribed a calomel pill. Surely not an obstruction of the bowel.

'What ailed him?'

'He was all right ... Then he was lost ... Nellie said something about Catchpole finding him dead ... In the drying yard.'

That made sense. Linen props could be lethal, and an active child could run into trouble with a clothes line. The word *Catchpole* started his mind on another track. Practically a half-wit who might just possibly mistake unconsciousness for death.

'We'll get along,' he said, breaking his own rule and abandoning his breakfast.

Out in the yard, too, he betrayed unusual signs of flurry. 'Harper,' he shouted to his handyman, 'get Flash harnessed,' and while that was being done, he himself pulled out the light gig. 'Hurry, man, hurry.' The ruined guard dog was, as usual, the first to get into the gig. 'Come on, Thomas, hop in. Now Flash, get going!'

Like every other gig-driver, the old man carried a whip; the vehicle would not have looked complete without it, but he had never been known to use it. There was no need, his horses knew every tone of his voice; when he said, 'Get going', they showed their paces.

Mrs Lark, the wife of the village constable, came out of the baker's carrying a fresh, warm loaf. Lark would soon be in for his breakfast and he enjoyed new bread. A childless couple, on constable's pay, could afford such small luxuries. It was the ordinary labourer with a large family who must eat stale bread because it was more filling.

'Why, Miss Charlotte!' she said, when they had almost collided. 'Whatever is the matter?' Out so early, no hat or gloves, her hair not pinned up and her bodice buttoned all crooked. And coming from the common. And looking so wild and ghastly.

'We've lost Vincent. Somebody said the gypsies ... So I went ... There's nobody there.'

'They left on Wednesday.' Lark had been glad to see the back of them. 'And I've never heard of gypsies stealing children, Miss Charlotte. Who said that?'

'I think, Papa. He went to Bereham to tell the police.'

'There was no need for that. Champion down at Ashworth

has one of those Bell things. He could've let them know.'
Resentment sharpened her voice; she was jealous of the prestige which the communicating system gave P.C. Champion: and also aware that in going to Bereham Mr Cornwall had bypassed Lark. When a child was missing, surely the first to be informed should be the village constable, the one responsible for all law and order.

'Perhaps Papa hoped to ... to overtake them,' Charlotte said.

'But they moved on Wednesday. And they went to Lopham.'

'Papa did not know ...'

'No, of course. Well, you mustn't upset yourself too much, Miss Charlotte. I'd say that when you get home you'll find him there. Children go wandering off. Generally they come back when they're hungry.'

If Vincent had not been stolen by gypsies; if he had climbed the cot side and then the front gate ... perhaps Lane End Farm to see the little pigs. Or even Tutt Wood. Perhaps in chasing after the vanished gypsies she had been wasting valuable time.

'I must get back. Good morning, Mrs Lark.' She began to run.

'If there's anything Lark can do ...' Mrs Lark called after her and without stopping, Charlotte called back, 'Thank you.'

Mrs Lark crossed the green and entered her neat cottage, to find her husband already there. He had been out in the night and was looking forward to his breakfast: home-made brawn and new bread. He had already made a pot of very strong tea.

'I rather think,' said Mrs Lark who always did her nagging in a pleasant manner, 'that you ought to look in at Stonebridge House. It may be a false alarm, but at least it would *look* willing.' She described her meeting with Charlotte.

Lark sighed. Susie was the best wife in the world, but she was inclined to urge. She was always on to him about making a bit more of himself; to stand up for himself. He was industrious and conscientious but entirely lacking in ambition, whereas she was crammed with it. She wanted promotion for him; wanted him to be moved to Bereham, where she would be back with the pavements and the streetlights and the other amenities that she had sacrificed when she married him.

'I might look in presently,' he said in his easy way. 'But I daresay he's found by now. Child like that couldn't have gone far and there's nothing dangerous in the lane.'

'There's always the river,' Mrs Lark said. Headlines! In the *Bereham Free Press*. *Police Constable rescues child*. That would draw attention. 'I think you should just go along.'

Lark moved restively.

'Champ'll be along in a minute. I promised him some peas. We got more than we can eat.'

'Never mind about Champion,' said Mrs Lark, now doubly anxious to get her husband on his way. She knew exactly what would happen if he didn't soon make a move. P.C. Champion would offer to go along with him, and he'd push himself forward, as usual, and get all the attention and whatever credit there was going. 'I'll give him his peas.'

'Make me a sandwich, then,' Lark said resignedly. He poured his tea into his saucer, blew on it and gulped it down.

As Lark left his house, Champion came out of the forge where he had obligingly been delivering a message. Ashworth had no forge. Ashworth, Champion's parish and his 'beat', began just beyond Biddlesford Common and stretched down to the main road. The two beats met in a number of places and the two constables had met with and parted from one another, some time earlier, in a rosy dawn, at one of their rendezvous, on the far side of Tutt Wood. Champion had said he had an errand to do in Biddlesford and Lark—it was typical of him—did not ask what the errand was, or offer to do it, but he had said, 'Look in and I'll let you have some peas.'

'Off again already?' Champion asked. 'Fire somewhere?'

Lark explained.

'I'll walk along with you,' Champion said, just as Mrs Lark had known he would. 'If he'd crossed the line it'd concern me. I might as well know.'

'Glad of your company,' Lark said, without knowing why he should be. Inside the lane, with nobody to witness the lapse from police dignity, he said, 'Better have a bite,' and broke his sandwich into two unequal pieces, of which he gave Champ the larger. Poor bloke, he never had anything home-made. His wife was a sloven who spent her time visiting her relatives. In Ashworth she had at least twenty.

They walked along in a companionable silence, broken only by a kind of verbal shorthand

Champion said, 'What d'you think?'

'False alarm. Susie did mention the river.'

'Might as well look,' Champion said. So at the bridge they halted and looked. The summer-depleted stream ran shallowly over brown pebbles and bits of water weeds. The banks were so hard and dry that even where Charlotte had jumped down and run, there were no traces.

'Couldn't drown in that,' Lark said, relieved.

'Not less he was held down,' Champion agreed.

'By what I heard he was missing, not murdered,' Lark said.

Catchpole received them, showed them the corpse, told them what he knew. Both men briefly regretted that enjoyable brawn sandwich.

'Doctor is up with Missus,' Catchpole said.

Lark said, out of profound depth of feeling, 'Somebody could have washed his poor little face.'

'Mustn't do much,' Catchpole said. 'Not till the police arrive.'

Lark would have taken that without protest, but Champion said, '*We are the police.*'

A statement nobody contradicted, a statement nobody could contradict; but even Champion regretted having made it. Because what could they *do*? What could anybody do?

Upstairs Doctor Fletcher dealt with three females, only one of immediate importance. He had viewed the body; definitely dead; no mistake or unwarranted panic on the near-village-idiot's part. A terrible crime, it was obvious, had been committed, but that would be dealt with by the proper authorities. He was committed to the living rather than the dead.

He had experience. When women were upset, you diverted either their minds or their bodies.

He started on Mrs Cornwall.

'Now, listen to me. If you carry on like this you'll lose your baby—the one who might take that boy's place. You've had a cruel loss, you don't want to double it. Get into bed, Mrs Cornwall.'

He spoke sternly because that was the only way, but he pitied her greatly, though he did not like her much. He held two things against her—the brisk efficiency, with something hard in it, with which she had treated her mistress at a time when the poor woman needed gentle, patient handling; and the

61

fact that some time later she had ignored Charlotte's decline in health so that when at last he did examine the child he found her suffering from a form of anaemia usually only seen in the very poor.

Having got Mrs Cornwall into the bed, which shook under the violence of her weeping, he turned to Charlotte in whom shock appeared to have taken the opposite—and more dangerous—form, a kind of stupor.

'Come now, Miss Charlotte. I understand that you wish to become a nurse. Here is a chance to show your worth. Go and warm some milk, sweeten it and add five drops, exactly five, of this mixture. See that she drinks it. Then plump up her pillows, tidy the bed, sponge her face. You must think about the little one on its way, you know.'

Charlotte did not speak; she nodded her head jerkily, like a puppet, and moving in the same unco-ordinated way, went out.

'As for you, Nurse, you must not neglect Miss Amelia. She is crying. She sounds hungry.'

'I was just about to feed her, sir, when we heard the news.'

In Rose the stoic qualities of a Daughter of Jerusalem had taken charge. There had been that one dreadful moment when she knew that her plan had failed; and then she saw that it was doomed from the start. Whatsoever a man soweth, that shall he also reap. There was no getting away from it. Be not deceived, God is not mocked. All she could do now was to take the burden of guilt upon herself and save *him*. Naturally, if lying and a profession of innocence could, in some way, save them both, it would be better. But the moment a finger pointed definitely to *him*, she would up and confess.

'They *are* dotty,' Nellie said to Beattie, referring to the twins, 'I always said so, didn't I? Eating away there as though nothing had happened.'

'Eat at their own funeral,' Beattie said.

'Me, I couldn't touch a bite.'

'Nor me. Tell you what I could do with, though. A good cuppa tea.'

Nellie made it, and thought of Lark and Champion who, not knowing what to do, were standing guard just inside the doorway of the laundry, their backs to the bench. Neither of them had ever had anything to do with a murder before; and they were now very glad that Mr Cornwall had passed them both over and sought help at a higher level.

'Though of course,' Champion said, without preliminary, knowing that Lark would understand, 'he only went to report a child missing. They may not think that worth coming out for. In which case I'll go home and use my Bell.'

'It'll be a rare upset for him, coming back to *this*,' Lark said, pitying the bereaved father.

Catchpole took it upon himself to break the news and John Vincent Cornwall's luck held in that the only witness of his reception of it was a man not over-bright at any time and at the moment completely flown with his own self-importance. Being sick had ended Catchpole's squeamishness and he was rather enjoying himself.

'Bad news, I'm afraid, sir,' he said, as Mr Cornwall alighted. 'We found him and he's dead. Murdered.'

A keener observer might have observed that though there was some shock, there was no surprise. The father did not say—Murdered! My God! How? He asked, 'Where?'

'In the muck heap, sir. He's stabbed.'

That *was* a surprise.

'Stabbed!'

'Clean through the heart, sir. I sent for the doctor. I hope I did right.' The praise he hoped for was not forthcoming. Mr Cornwall needed a drink more badly than he had ever needed one. He went into the kitchen, ignoring Cook and Nellie who jumped up from their tea-drinking and stood, staring at him with silent pity. In the back hall he ran into Lark who was bringing the teacups back to the kitchen. Behind Lark, in the laundry doorway, Champion. Police already!

But the sword did not fall. The dread words were not spoken.

'Speaking for both Constable Lark and myself, sir—Our deepest sympathy,' Champion said.

Mr Cornwall acknowledged this with a nod and went into the library, leaving the door open. He stood there, pouring brandy, in full view of the stairs, down which Doctor Fletcher, having seen Charlotte in action, pouring the exact five drops, was coming, there being nothing more that he could do here and a good deal that he could do elsewhere. He must get permission to perform a post mortem and he must go to Lopham to investigate something that *might* be cholera. He had had a report the previous evening that a large number of those dreadful gypsies were suffering in a way that made some of them quite unable to pick peas, and also made it highly undesirable that those still able to work should do so. Remembering his roses he had thought that given the slightest excuse he'd put the lot into quarantine.

He spared a few moments for Mr Cornwall.

'You've heard? My dear man, I cannot tell you how sorry I am.'

'It was a shock,' Mr Cornwall said. Lifting the glass in an unsteady hand, he drank.

'Your wife,' said the doctor, who had sedulously avoided any such encumbrance, such encroachment upon his comfortable life, 'took it hard, naturally. But she has her condition to consider. So must you. We mustn't let one loss lead to another.'

'Catchpole said *stabbed*.'

'Definitely stabbed. I must ask Mr Whymark for permission to make an autopsy.' It was easier to talk to a man, who, though obviously shaken, retained sense enough to know that brandy was a good cure for shock. 'There are puzzling features. So little blood; big healthy boy like that. And a kind of bruise about the nose and mouth. I am rather inclined to think that he may have been smothered before he was stabbed; in which case he would not have suffered. That is some slight comfort.'

For all his long experience Doctor Fletcher was, here, a bit out of his depth. He could remember one case of murder—a man who had set about his unfaithful wife and her lover with an axe and then gone to Lark's predecessor and given himself up. Simple. And once a poacher had shot a gamekeeper. The poacher had never been identified, but the gamekeeper's widow had been well taken care of. The cottage hers for life and a pension of five shillings a week. All her five children had suffered from that same form of anaemia—chlorosis—which had attacked Charlotte Cornwall. But they had survived, gone out into the world and done well. Apart from these cases, long ago, and Catchpole's father who had been mad for quite a long time, and a man struck by lightning as he sheltered under a tree, Doctor Fletcher's brushes with Death, the ultimate destroyer, had been undramatic. Little Vincent Cornwall's death was something extraordinary and very mysterious. It had indeed upset him although, well self-disciplined in a demanding profession, he had maintained an outward calm. Had it occurred to Mr Cornwall to offer him a glass of brandy, he would have accepted it. He was physically, if not consciously, missing his breakfast.

'I'll be back early this afternoon,' he said. 'The body should not be touched. I think Mrs Cornwall will sleep, and that will buffer the shock for her. Keep an eye on Charlotte; I never like it when females don't cry.' Mr Cornwall gave no sign that he was heeding these instructions, he emptied his glass, refilled it and drank again. Poor fellow, he needed what comfort he could find, but Doctor Fletcher felt obliged to issue a little warning. 'Go easy on that,' he said, indicating the bottle, 'it's a palliative, not a cure, you know.'

John Vincent Cornwall thought in dull misery—What cure could there be for my ill? An impulse which, if not whole-hearted, was sincere enough, made him wish that each gulp might be lethal. But far deeper and more fundamental was the instinct of self-preservation. It was in fact strong enough to constitute a barrier between him and the grief of bereavement, between him and the agony of remorse. The favourite child, dead and somehow safely disposed of, would have been a matter of unmitigated sorrow; the little body, discovered, its state a source of suspicion and of danger, was something else again. Almost, not quite, but almost a threat to be avoided, evaded, countered.

It was in this mood that John Vincent Cornwall confronted Superintendent Spender who had come to Biddlesford as fast as the police wagonette could bring him, simply because he was an extremely class-conscious man. All that Spender knew was that a child was missing; had that child been missing from a humble dwelling, or a gypsy caravan in the area, Spender would not have stirred, not because he was callous, but because the matter would have been too trivial for his attention and could be left to the police constables who were on the spot. And also because the poor tended to have large families, the last-but-one-baby shoved off when the last arrived, made prematurely mobile. Spender had come into contact with families where a four-year-old would hardly have been missed. But Mr Cornwall, of Stonebridge House, was a different matter; a gentleman, well known in the district; a man whose child had been missed immediately, missed before breakfast; a man whose child could have been kidnapped. There were people who would steal even the dogs of the well-to-do and then demand ransom money; how much more likely that, given a chance, such people would snatch a child. Spender felt that this was something he should look into himself.

The little body, mutilated and obscenely soiled, laid out on the laundry's stone slab, shook him to the core. Murder, no less. Murder done in the kind of house, the kind of family, upon which Spender had always looked, not with envy, but with wistfulness. His snobbishness had always been tangled with romanticism; hundreds of times he had passed such houses, large, solid, eminently respectable and his mind had visualised the life within or around; tea-tables set by glowing fires in winter, under weeping willows or copper beeches in summer, pleasant voices, nice manners.

That something like *this* should have shattered what for Spender was a dream world was a distinct shock, and when he faced Mr Cornwall in the library he was tentative, sympathetic, respectful. He invited the bereaved father to tell him what he knew and when that little was told, asked a question which showed in what direction his own mind was working and which at the same time gave John Vincent Cornwall's sharp intelligence a cue. He said, 'Sir, have you an enemy? Can you think of anyone who bears you sufficient malice to have done this?'

'No, Inspector. Like most normal people I have displeased others from time to time, but never to an extent which would warrant ... Occasionally I am obliged to write an unfavourable report about a school, or a certain teacher. And certainly some years back Brook, the farmer at the end of the lane, and I fell out over a right of way. Mere trivialities. I am more inclined to think ...' He paused and made a little deprecating gesture with an unsteady hand. 'It is hardly for me to offer suggestions.'

'Anything,' Spender said. 'Anything that would shed the least light.'

'Well ... Yesterday afternoon I won two hundred pounds at Newmarket races. I ask myself is it just possible that I was seen to collect it, and followed home by somebody who intended to rob me. Who, perhaps opened the wrong door and woke Vincent and ... and killed him in panic.' As I did, God help me! He shuddered, but went on firmly. 'Or kidnapping may have been the aim; again by somebody who knew that I had two hundred pounds in cash and then found the child not easily handled. He was ... he was only four ...' Grief for a second got the upper hand and he choked. 'But big and strong for his age.'

Not strong enough; all that vitality snuffed out like a candle. If I had not completely lost control. Any story would have pacified him. Or, if the worst came to the worst and Agnes *knew*, what matter? She could do nothing except scold.

Spender courteously waited for the moment of emotion to pass. The idea that the murderer had come from outside accorded entirely with his fantasy theory of life in such a house being orderly and pleasant, solid, respectable, far above crime level. Presently he said, 'The house is locked at night, sir?'

John Vincent Cornwall thought quickly. Nellie would be questioned and would say how she had found the doors. And to admit that for once he had forgotten to shoot a bolt or turn a key, on the one night when there was within the house something to steal, on the one night when murder had been committed within it would seem too much of a coincidence to be credible.

'Yes. Last night I locked up myself.'

'Who opens the doors in the morning?'

'The maid. She is down first.'

Nellie was positive that when she came down in the morning every door was locked or barred from the inside. Spender, though at heart a snob, was gentle by nature and to Nellie said, pleasantly, 'You know, when one does a thing every day one does not pay close attention. Or one day can be confused with the next. Can you be *positive* that *this* morning all the doors were bolted?'

'Yes. And I'll tell you why. When the master is away Cook do the locking up and the top bolts are a bit of a strain for her. She can't drive them right home like he do. This morning I had a right old tussle and I remember thinking to myself that even if I hadn't known he was home I could have told by the way the bolts was shot. If you see what I mean.'

'I see,' Spender said. His prejudiced mind still shied away from the idea that the crime could have been committed by an inmate of the house. After all, an intruder need not necessarily have used a door.

Spender had brought one of his own men with him,

Sergeant Hawes, a very bright, sharp young man. He now set him to work.

'Hawes, I want you to go round the house and see if there is any possible means of entry, other than a doorway.' With his habitual courtesy to those under him, Spender explained the theory he had adopted. He himself went up to view the nursery from which the child had been taken and to talk to the nurse.

Rose Ellis had steadied herself on the stoicism that was part of her creed. She had sinned, she must bear her punishment. She was capable of seeing a sort of justice in the fact that it was the blue ribbon which had betrayed her. Vanity was displeasing to God. Fortified rather than distressed by such thoughts, and strong in her determination to protect her lover to the utmost, to take, if necessary, all blame upon herself, she received Spender with composure.

His manner reassured her. Invited to tell him exactly what had happened that morning, she told him how she had overslept, waked to find the child gone and imagined him to have been taken by his mother.

'Somebody,' Spender said, but still gently, 'entered this room in the night and removed the child. You are a *heavy* sleeper?'

'I always sleep well. More than once Master Vincent has woke and called out and been took by his mamma and me not knowing.' That was a statement that could be checked, Spender thought. 'And I'd had a hard day,' Rose went on. 'It was so hot and the baby was fretful. And then Master Vincent got himself all dirty and had to be washed and changed.'

Spender seemed to accept her story. He walked over to the cot, saw that the window by which it stood opened out on to a bit of flat roof and saw a possibility. The child-snatcher need never have entered the room; simply have opened the window and reached in. But when he moved the cot and attempted to open the window from the inside—noting the broken catch as he did so, that possibility vanished.

'It had to be nailed up,' Rose explained. 'Master Vincent could open it, standing up in his cot. He did once and got out on that roof and give us all a rare old fright. Mending the catch wouldn't have done, he'd soon have mastered *that*. So Catchpole nailed it up.'

There was the other window, opening on to the stable yard, open on this warm morning, but below it the wall dropped sheer, no drainpipe, nothing. While Spender pondered this, Hawes arrived.

'I've found it, sir. Window in that old laundry place.'

It made complete mockery of all the locking and bolting of doors. It was, unlike every other window in the house, not a sash, but a casement, two halves, made of small leaded panes, opening outwards. At some remote time somebody, considerate towards the women who must work at tubs set on the stone slab and with the copper steaming away in the corner, but with the weather outside too cold to admit of a half window being opened, had had a smaller opening devised. Six of the little panes at the top of the right-hand half of the casement made to open on a hinge, how far open, how far closed, controlled by a ratchet device, long since rusted away.

'You see, sir,' Hawes said. 'That opens outwards. Anybody could open it, put his arm in and unlatch the whole window. Or half; half would be enough. Would you care for me to demonstrate, sir?'

'Yes,' Spender said. So Hawkes went out into the drying yard, prised open the inset window, reached in, swung half the casement back and climbed through, lithe and lively, on to that part of the stone slab not occupied by the body.

'And out the same way,' he said, standing beside Spender and pleased with himself.

'That's it, Hawes,' Spender said, aware of a deep, secret satisfaction. 'Somebody from outside.' As he spoke he turned to give Hawes a look of approval and saw him staring at the corpse, wide-eyed, slack-mouthed, as though this were his first encounter with death by violence. 'What's the matter, man?'

'That,' said Hawes, pointing a thick finger to the bit of blue ribbon which no one had noticed once it had served its turn. Doctor Fletcher, chiefly concerned to make sure that the child was really dead, had not observed it; nor had Spender in the bad moment when he realised that he had a murder case on his hands.

'Part of his nightgown, poor little soul,' Spender said.

'I doubt it, sir.' Hawes pulled at the end of the ribbon and it came away from the fold of the blanket in which it lay. 'Not attached to anything, sir.' They both stared at the length of ribbon, in places so bright, so glossily new, in other places soiled, a little blood, a good deal more of that vital substance that March called *juice*. Hawes waited for his superior to voice

69

the obvious conclusion and when he did not do so, said the words himself, 'Looks as though some female was concerned, sir.'

With an inward sigh and a sinking of the heart, Spender said, 'Yes. We shall need a female searcher.'

'Police Constable Lark's wife would be handiest,' Hawes said, trying to be helpful because the Superintendent whom he liked without respecting much, seemed suddenly so doleful. Why, Hawes wondered, far from comprehending what Spender felt about the length of ribbon which pointed directly to someone in the house. Would-be robbers or kidnappers did not go about trailing lengths of ribbon, nor did they take their womenfolk with them. So, if the ribbon were a valid clue ... And not only Spender's romantic snobbishness but his chivalry was revolted by the idea of any female being involved in such a hideous business. However, he was a trained man. He went quite briskly about, telling Lark to go and fetch his wife; telling Champion to dismantle the manure heap, keeping a sharp eye out for any other incongruous thing, telling Hawes to inspect every fireplace in the house for any sign of something being recently burned. If one of the five young women in the house had been concerned—he exempted the child's mother and the wrinkled, hobbling old cook—more than a blue ribbon must be involved.

Female searchers were not in great demand since few women committed crimes which needed intimate enquiry, so the pay was high—sixpence a search. When Lark plodded home and told Susie that she was needed, she briskly reckoned what she would earn. But the job meant more than mere money; it was a chance to be in on things, a possible opportunity to draw favourable attention to the name of *Lark*, and the satisfaction of that curiosity which women feel about other women's clothes.

Spender told her what to look out for; a garment unnaturally soiled, or showing signs of having been hastily washed; a garment with a matching blue ribbon upon it, or some evidence that such a ribbon had been torn away. He showed her the soiled piece, holding it himself, not expecting her to handle it; but Susie Lark was hardy.

'Excuse me, sir,' she said, and reached for it. Apparently oblivious to its state she studied it carefully, especially at the ends. Then she looked up and said with certainty, 'One thing I can tell you straightaway, sir. This wasn't torn off anything because it was never sewn on. It was tied round, or ... or slotted through something called insertion.' She looked again. 'And tied in a bow. You can see by the creases, here and here. There's other creases from where ... where it has been, but these are different. Where would you like me to start, sir?'

Consistent to his belief, Spender said, 'The nurse and the younger maid, Mrs Lark.' A new theory was forming and it concerned the question of *followers*. Either the nurse, not unpretty even in an unbecoming dress and with her hair scraped back, or the maid, comely enough in a bucolic way, could have become involved with some undesirable fellow.

'And what about Mrs Cornwall, sir?' Susie asked. Spender hesitated; his natural instinct was to spare the poor lady against whom there could be no shadow of suspicion; on the other hand his common sense told him that if an incriminating garment existed it might well have been hidden in a place where no one was likely to look.

'Yes, I am afraid you must look there, too. With the least disturbance possible.'

Rose Ellis accepted the search calmly. Her wardrobe was exactly what a girl in her first place of service might be expected to own. Of underclothes three of everything, relatively new, and all of cheap but hard-wearing calico. She had two of the grey uniform dresses, one on, one off, and a frock of her own, just as severe and in colour even duller. The only irrelevant thing in her possession was a bottle of scent on the shelf below the looking-glass which served her as a dressing-table; to Mrs Lark's unsophisticated eye it conveyed nothing, except that the girl liked a drop of scent, as she did herself, preferring violet to lily-of-the-valley.

Nellie, longer in service and under no obligation to send any part of her wage home, had a more interesting outfit, a real, rustling silk petticoat, for instance, and two pretty camisoles made of fine lawn and threaded with ribbon, but narrow, pink ribbon.

Surprise began when Mrs Lark surveyed the wardrobes of the twins. She had only ever seen them at a distance, chiefly in church and had always thought them smart and fashionable. Seen close to, their outer garments showed many signs of contrivance and at one point Mrs Lark thought for a moment that she had made a significant discovery. A red-and-white skirt with no matching bodice, but Adelaide explained, with hauteur, 'If it really is anything to do with you, we used the bodice to make a collar and cuffs for a dress that needed cheering up. You will come to it soon.' Their underclothes bore no ribbons —ribbon cost money—but were elaborately embroidered; all on such cheap, shoddy stuff that Mrs Lark could not help thinking that it was a waste of time and eyesight.

'I wish you would find whatever it is you are looking for,' Adelaide said. 'You are disturbing us. And all this has nothing to do with us.'

'Nothing to do with us,' Victoria said. And then she volunteered a statement of her own. 'Addie, it has, you know. We shall have to wear mourning!'

'You are right, Vikky. What a pity, with the beaded bodice practically completed.'

Mrs Lark left them to the contemplation of further contrivances and went down to Charlotte's room.

Charlotte sat at the foot of her bed, her arms folded on the brass rail and her head leaning on them. When she lifted her head the dumb, tearless misery in her face shocked Mrs Lark who explained the purpose of her errand with more apology and less briskness than she had used in other rooms. When Charlotte's person had been examined, Mrs Lark said gently, 'There, sit down again. You look as though you could do with a cup of tea. I'll get you one as soon as I've finished.'

Charlotte shook her head and then spoke for the first time.

'I have three of everything. Things I took to school. There is a list in the drawer.'

What Charlotte had taken to school was exactly the outfit with which girls were sent to service; the material the same as that of the nurse's clothes, the garments older and worn. Only on the nightdresses had any attempt been made to relieve the austerity—a single line of feather-stitching around the collars and cuffs. Washing had faded the blue of the embroidery silk. There were two nightgowns, clean and folded, in the drawer, and another, the one in use, lying on the bed, between the pillow and the counterpane. Mrs Lark said, 'Excuse me,' as she reached for it and shook it out; even pity did not make her perfunctory.

On Mrs Cornwall the carefully measured dose had had its desired effect; she did not stir when Mrs Lark tiptoed in. Perhaps this wardrobe was the greatest surprise of all since on Sundays Mrs Cornwall had always appeared to be well-dressed in an unostentatious way. To find only *one* silk dress, one silk petticoat, both well worn, and underwear not half as pretty and dainty as her own, shocked Mrs Lark, who had expected to find, here at least, silk, lace, chiffon. The Cornwalls lived in this large house, kept two horses, employed indoor and out-door staff; despite the whispers of bills left unpaid, Mrs Lark found it difficult to look upon the family as poor. Before she married Lark she had been in good service, a parlourmaid in a well-to-do household, and she knew that the gentry did not take bills as seriously as humbler people; they simply did not bother, knowing that any day they could settle their liabilities. Closing the door softly, she thought—Well, I shall have something to tell Joe tonight.

She had, however, nothing to tell the Superintendent. Hawes's search of Mr Cornwall and Thomas and their rooms had been equally abortive. Nor had Spender, now nose-down-to-trail in search of followers, been more successful.

He had begun with Rose Ellis, who, asked about followers, said with absolute and patent truth that she did not know what the word meant.

'Oh come,' Spender said, descending to flattery, 'a pretty girl like you. Surely you must have some men friends.' She faced him steadily.

She said, 'I am a Daughter of Jerusalem. Except for my father, and Brothers, at the meeting, and once when Mrs Saunders was ill and Mr Saunders came for the eggs, I don't think I have ever spoken to a man.' She added, painstakingly, painfully honest, 'At least, if Mr Cornwall says "Good morning" I say it too. And the same with March and Catchpole.'

As it happened Spender knew about the Children of Jerusalem, there was a little group of them in Bereham, about a dozen of them; fanatics, strictly adhering to about the bleakest creed in the world; but honest, absolutely honest and so law-abiding that if everybody in England suddenly became a Son or a Daughter of Jerusalem, he and every other policeman in the land would be out of a job.

He accepted what she said without the slightest reservation and went on to tackle Nellie who said, 'Followers? You mean am I walking out? Well, I ain't.' Having said it she realised that it sounded horribly like a confession to being undesirable.

73

'There ain't much chance, stuck away here, is there? I will say Bob March has looked in my direction and I've looked at him and he once walked me home, but nothing was *said*.'

'He is the son of the gardener here?'

' 'S'right. He's head horseman up at the farm. I think myself,' Nellie said, putting into words her own secret hope, 'that if the old man that had the job before would die or move away—Mr Brook is too soft-hearted to turn him out—then Bob'd have the cottage and he'd speak up. You can't, if you're decent, get married till you got a roof to offer. Can you?'

About her there was an honesty too, as patent as Rose Ellis's, though less plainly labelled. But Spender's mind was bound to consider any possibility; a young strong man anxious to 'speak up', lacking the roof that would justify his doing so; the girl ripe, perhaps showing signs of growing impatience.

'When did you see him last?'

'Tuesday. Or could it be Wednesday?' This was Saturday and the days before, before this disastrous and horrible day, the days ran back, as indistinguishable as beads on a string. 'Anyway,' Nellie said, 'we met by accident, I'd gone a walk in the lane to get a breath of air and Bob said he was off, with Mr Brook to the South Norfolk Show with a coupla horses ... That must have been Tuesday. I remember now, he said it'd take a full day to get there and the Show was Thursday and Friday. He should be back tonight, being Saturday. But not ...' she gave a gulp, 'not what I was looking forward to. I know I spoke against him, time and again, he was such a mischievous . . And I can't help remembering; once when he'd untied my apron strings, and I didn't know, I walked into it and fell and chipped this tooth, see? I said, "You little imp of Satan!" And now when I think of him laying there . . .'

Her eyes filled and spilled over. With a sense of desolation Spender abandoned his theory about followers so far as she was concerned.

It was now lunchtime and there was a certain comfort to be derived from a sticking to routine, observing the timetable that was the day's skeletal shape. Beattie put the coarse-fibred, but tenderly cooked piece of beef on the pretty flowered dish and Nellie, having washed and drained a lettuce, went and set the table.

Thomas, extremely hungry, and ashamed of his hunger, looked in on Charlotte for the fourth time. He said, awkwardly,

'Charlie, couldn't you eat just a *little*? I know it's awful, but starving ourselves won't do any good.'

She lifted her head slightly and shook it, as she had to Mrs Lark's offer of tea.

Even more awkwardly Thomas said, 'I know it's awful ... but he had had a very ... happy life, Charlie. What life he had ... I know it's awful, but he'll never be sick or unhappy, or old.'

The loss was too new, the sorrow too raw for her to find any comfort in this crude philosophy. She made no response and Thomas, feeling extremely guilty, went down to the dining room where Adelaide, having waited for Papa to arrive, had taken up the carving knife. One day, when she and Vikky were in their own house she would be obliged to carve and she needed practice. She carved very well, neat, even slices.

To Spender food was completely unimportant. He had on occasions gone twenty-four hours without it and felt no deprivation. And when he did eat he did not care what. His landlady in Bereham, her best efforts unremarked, declared that if she cooked an old boot he'd eat it. Hawes was different. Before joining the police force he had spent a little time in the army, where, if you were treated like a dog, you were, like most dogs, regularly fed. Hopefully, he now mentioned to Spender the fact that, coming through the village he had noticed a tidy little inn, the Jolly Sailor, the sort of place, he thought, where a man might get a bite.

'You go, Hawes, if you're hungry. Take the wagonette. We didn't bring the horse a nosebag, did we?'

'No, sir. We'd no idea then.'

'Fodder him too. I'm going up to the farm, just to check ... I believe the girl but best to make certain.'

This exchange of remarks between the Superintendent and his sergeant took place in the space, under an archway where the front hall and the back converged. The library, the lair into which John Vincent Cornwall had retreated, was near-by, the door open. He now came into the doorway and said, 'Superintendent, if your sergeant is going into the village, would you have any objection to his undertaking a small commission for me?'

'Most certainly not,' Spender said obligingly.

'I'm out of liquor. If you could bring me three bottles, Sergeant. Brandy if it is available, otherwise whisky.'

Hawes who did not share Spender's reverence for his betters, accepted this errand with ill grace and went out through the kitchen where Nellie was repeating to herself, 'Didn't I always say they were dotty? Pulling in to the table as though nothing had happened. Me, I couldn't touch a bite.'

'Me neither,' said Beattie. 'Tell you what, though, I could do with a cup of tea.'

Susie, Lark and Champion shared the tea, hovering about a little uncertainly. Clothes had been searched, the manure heap dismantled—and not so much as a button found—but Spender had not dismissed them before setting out for the farm. The tea drunk, the men went and sat on the shady side of the yard, smoked a pipe each and had a little nap. Susie sat with Nellie and Beattie and was there when Rose Ellis brought down the nursery tray.

All morning Rose had regretted that as soon as she found favour in the new god's eyes she had severed her casual links with the kitchen. All morning she had longed to go down, hang about, know what was being said, how people felt. The tray, so recently a cause of discord, gave her an excuse to enter the kitchen and she would have lingered over a cup of tea, had she been invited to do so. She was not. Her reception was definitely hostile. Nellie broke off what she was saying to remark, 'Well, wonders'll never cease,' in a nasty voice as Rose put the tray on the dresser and when Rose, undaunted, said, 'I could do with a cup,' Beattie said, 'It's all gone.' Her recent uppity behaviour had alienated them, and, now that they were recovering from the shock, they were beginning to see that she was in some degree to be blamed for the tragedy. When she turned and was on the stairs which led out of the kitchen, but still well in earshot, Nellie said, 'Sleeping like a pig while that poor little boy was done to death!' Beattie chimed in, 'Ah. There's nothing in my room that I'm *paid* to look after, but d'you think anybody'd get in there and me not wake?' It was the first expression of an attitude soon to be general.

One of a row of bells that hung over the door into the back hall jangled sharply.

'Missus,' said Nellie, and scampered upstairs with more than usual alacrity; a few seconds later she ran down the front stairs and into the library and said breathlessly, 'Sir, the mistress wants you.'

It was the moment that John Vincent Cornwall had been

dreading, knowing that it was as unavoidable as death. He had drunk what was left of the brandy and the despised sweet brown sherry, but he was not nearly drunk enough to face Agnes with equanimity. It was not inconceivable, he thought, as he climbed the stairs, that she might make an accusation very near the truth; she could hardly have forgotten *their* clandestine love-making. She was capable of putting two and two together.

In fact she had done so. She had woken when Mrs Lark closed the door behind her, and had lain, thinking, a little confusedly at first and then with painful clarity. She had put two and two together and made them into the wrong answer, but oddly enough, the one which John Vincent himself had concocted and which Spender had seemed to accept. It was very strange, strange to the point of unreality to hear her say, with intense savagery, 'You are to blame for all this. You went racing yesterday, didn't you? That's where you got the money for the bills so suddenly. How much did you win?'

He said, 'Two hundred pounds.' For a moment he relived the moment, in another world, another life, Cookstown breaking away, a length, two . . . the scent of trampled grass, the sun hot on his back, the feel of the money in his hand, just when he needed it, the thought—Whenever I'm in a real corner something turns up.

'And then what did you do?'

'I went to the hotel where I'd stabled Romper and left the gig.'

'And stood treat to all and sundry!'

'Not quite that; but yes. A win of that sort . . . I ordered champagne.'

'I knew it! Throwing money about like a drunken sailor. I can see exactly what happened. Some thief followed you home and broke in. Went to the wrong door . . . I shall never forgive you; never. Quite apart from the fact that you promised me never to bet again.'

The whole situation was so ludicrous that he felt a crazy desire to laugh. He felt the hysteria mounting, held in check by an awe that was almost mystical. That Agnes should have hit upon the very explanation which he himself had offered; it was almost as though thoughts blew about, infectious as measles. One must be careful what one thought. Doubly careful of what one said. What he said, at last, beating back everything except

77

the instinct of self-preservation, was, 'He was my son, too.'

She said, 'Let that be your punishment.' She looked at him and realised that she had hated him for years, had begun to hate him during that waiting time when she did not know whether he would marry her or not, and then, when he did and the hatred might have died down, quenched by gratitude, disappointment had fanned the flame again. The insecurity which —once married—she had thought ended, had clamped down, worse than ever because there was no hope, with him gambling, drinking and at home penny-pinching. Out of her hatred she said, 'Doctor Fletcher said that I must think of this child. I want a poached egg and some tea.'

Doctor Fletcher was now back, armed with the magistrate's permission to perform an autopsy and on the whole relieved to find that the gypsies at Lopham were not suffering from cholera; they had simply eaten too many green peas.

Spender was back too. Mrs Brook had confirmed Nellie's statement; Bob March had gone with her husband to the South Norfolk Show.

'The child,' Doctor Fletcher reported to Spender, 'was, as I suspected, dead, asphyxiated, before he was stabbed. That accounts for the absence of blood. He was killed by pressure, I should say from some soft substance, applied over his mouth and nose. He was then stabbed by some instrument with a sharp pointed blade, broadening, I should say, towards the handle. It went in more easily than it came out. Whoever did it had to twist the knife and there is a slight injury to one rib. I should say that a man struck the blow. To withdraw the knife must have taken considerable force. And that is all I can tell you, Superintendent. Except that the poor little fellow should now be properly laid out.'

Over the laying-out, Susie Lark came into her own. She offered to do it, after Nellie and Cook and the nurse had squeamishly refused. Spender said, 'Thank you, Mrs Lark,' and she hoped that he would remember the name. Doctor Fletcher said, 'It's a good thing you're here, Mrs Lark.' All very well for them! It was sad, a distasteful job, but she had undertaken it and she did it well, making up for the unpleasantness by being extraordinarily bossy, ordering people about, asking for this and for that.

By some unspoken consensus of opinion Vincent was laid

out in the old laundry on the same slab to which he had been taken. Had he died of some childish ailment or from an ordinary accident, he would have been taken into the guest room; as it was, it was as though what had happened to him was so vile that he, the victim, must share the crime's ostracism from normal life. However, when Mrs Lark had draped the stone slab with a damask tablecloth and refused the first pillow cover and sheet that was offered, saying tetchily, 'I want real linen and a pillowcase with a frill if you can find such a thing in this house,' she was able to regard the work of her hands with some satisfaction. The little boy, except for the faint discoloration around the nostrils and mouth, might have been peacefully asleep. His freshly washed hair, still damp, formed a golden halo. As she stepped back to view the whole with self-approval, Mrs Lark bumped into Charlotte who had entered noiselessly, her arms full of flowers, all white, all sweetly scented, roses, the few last sprays of mock-orange, pinks and stocks. They were no whiter than her face.

Without speaking she seemed to offer the flowers to Mrs Lark who, sharing Doctor Fletcher's theory about the value of having something to do, said, 'No, Miss Charlotte. I've done my part. You give him the flowers.' She watched while Charlotte placed them around the pillow, along the sheet so that the little face lay in a flowery frame. Then she said, 'That's beautiful. He looks like a little angel. And that is how you must think of him, you know. A little angel, in Heaven.'

That seemed to break the stony barrier between grief and tears and Charlotte broke into bitter sobbing. Mrs Greenfield had offered much the same kind of comfort when Mamma died and Charlotte, younger then, and only recently disillusioned about God, had tried to imagine her mother, restored to health, enjoying the freedom of Heaven, after the close confinement to one room. She had been unable to do so or to persuade herself that Mamma's spirit was near her. Mrs Greenfield had said something about the dead acting as guardian angels to the living whom they had loved. Occasionally, locked in the cellar, Charlotte had pondered this statement, finding it hollow. If guardian angels existed they were powerless, and being powerless, they must be very unhappy. How would Mamma feel if she knew how her children were being treated? Far better to be completely dead and know nothing! On the other hand, she had had during that troubled period some dreams, extraordinarily vivid ones, in which Mamma appeared, very young and gay, against backgrounds of extreme beauty. Sometimes she was near and real enough to be touched; at other time she was at a little distance, but waiting for Charlotte, inviting her to join her. It was from a dream of the latter kind that Charlotte had once waked to find herself out on the landing, face to face with Cook who had a flat-iron in her hand.

In the case of Vincent even the poor comfort of thinking of death as a release was denied her. As Thomas had said, Vincent's brief life had been very happy. A favourite child, handsome, healthy, intelligent. Sobbing against Mrs Lark's kindly offered shoulder Charlotte did for one second entertain a questioning thought—Could the happiness have continued? The scene on the landing on the previous afternoon came back; Mrs Cornwall was quite capable of being unpleasant even to her own, and she was jealous. If Vincent had lived, headstrong, wilful and tactless . . . The thought slid away. Charlotte sobbed and Mrs Lark patted her, forgot that she was Miss Charlotte and said, 'There, there, my dear. Have your cry out. You'll feel better now.' Presently she suggested the inevitable cup of tea. Charlotte again refused and, still crying, though less violently, went up to her room.

In the hot sunshine of the late afternoon Spender and Hawes sat in the police wagonette and considered their complete lack of progress. Hawes considered that Mr Cornwall had behaved, not only peculiarly, but badly. In this huge house he had put no room at their disposal, given no thought at all to their material needs, used him as an errand boy.

'Nothing,' Spender said, 'ties in with anything else.' He sounded defeated. Hawes had been mulling over some thoughts which, if they did not tie in very firmly, made some sort of sense and opened a possibility to which Spender seemed blind.

He said, 'May I tell you what I think, sir?' He knew Spender's weakness and guessed that his next words would not be welcome. 'I reckon he did it.'

'Mr Cornwall?' Spender asked in a shocked voice. 'The child's own father!'

'The doctor said it took a man's strength. So far as we know there was no other man here last night. We do know he was.'

'It's unthinkable, Hawes.'

'Well, is it? I don't say he set out to do it. Could have been an accident. By all accounts the boy was a bit obstreperous. Women put up with that sort of thing. Men don't. Look at this, sir.' Hawes lifted his always carefully draped cowlick of hair and showed an old, seamed scar. 'My old man did that. I was about seven and I cheeked him so he fetched me a clout and knocked me over and I hit my head on a pig trough. Concussed I was for two days. Now, supposing I'd been dead. Think he'd go running to the police saying "I've killed Alf!" And him with my mother and five others to think of. No, he'd have shovelled me away and made a good job of it, too.'

'Mr Cornwall sought police aid immediately.'

'Yes. For a *lost* child. One he thought'd *never* be found. I don't know whether you've noticed it, sir, I did. *We* haven't been made very welcome here, treated more like enemies. If you ask me he was willing enough to have us hunt a lost child, but didn't take too kindly to us when it turned out to be a murder investigation.'

'I think too much importance should not be attached to his manner,' Spender said. 'He is, naturally, very much distressed. And the child was not *struck*. He was suffocated.'

'I know. He could have been yelling and screaming and his Dad says "Stop that!" and clamps down on him and holds on a minute too long. They all say he was big and strong for his age, but he was only four. He'd go out like a candle.'

'What about the stabbing?'

'An after-thought,' Hawes said. His education had been scanty, but he had learned to read and read a lot and so widened his vocabulary. 'Meant to be taken as a red herring because it was done in cold blood. A man can knock a boy down, or stop his breath by accident, not deliberate. But the stabbing was deliberate, something no father would do, or so it would *look*. If you see what I mean, sir.'

'It is an argument, Hawes. What about the ribbon?'

'Ah,' Hawes said. 'I've thought about that, too. Somebody helped, afterwards. The boy wouldn't be much use—did you notice his hands, sir? One of the girls then. And for my money it'd be the nurse. Not related and built like a pony, very strong, an employed person, bound to take orders.' Both in the army and in the police force Hawes had gulped down the aloe-brew of taking orders against his inclination. Obey or be busted!

'There is absolutely nothing to connect the nurse. Mrs Lark

made a very thorough search, you know . . .' Spender's mind struggled feebly, unwilling to accept, unable quite to reject. But he could at least, indeed he must, approach the person who so far had been protected by her condition and her bereavement. Mrs Cornwall . . .

The sight of Spender in her bedroom rang an alarm bell in Agnes Cornwall's mind. Nobody could possibly suspect *her*; did they think that John had done it? Spender's gentle, courteous questions seemed to point that way. In reply she said she had retired first, leaving her husband to lock up; that he followed her as soon as he had done so and came straight to bed. She repeated what she had said about having a very bad night. 'In fact I hardly slept at all.'

'Yet you heard nothing unusual?' There was a faint hint of you-can't-have-it-both-ways in the smooth question. Awake enough to give a man an alibi . . .

She said, 'This house is much older than it looks. Floorboards creak, the panelling cracks. I knew that the baby was cutting teeth and might need attention in the night. My youngest stepdaughter has been known to walk in her sleep. I heard no noise for which I could not easily account. *At the time.*'

Spender, because he wanted to believe, found it easy to believe that Mr Cornwall had retired at about a quarter past ten and slept like a log until disturbed by the nurse's entry in the morning. Hawes was more sceptical.

'Any woman will alibi her bread-winner,' he said.

'Hawes, in any investigation a preconceived theory can be dangerous. This of yours has a certain ingenuity about it, but it has no backing that I can see. To adhere to it might well blind us to the truth.'

That came well, Hawes thought, from the man who had started off with, stuck to, a preconceived theory—that this was an outside job, must be an outside job, simply because Mr Cornwall was a gentleman and gentlemen did not commit acts of violence, even by accident. However, Hawes was experienced enough to know that a man did himself no good by running counter to authority, so he said no more.

Mrs Lark sent Lark to look upon her handiwork. Earlier in the day, staring at the body, Lark's emotions had been mixed, shock, uncertainty as to the correct procedure; now this had clarified into pure rage. Lark had no children, but he was fond of them and now, gazing upon the child he thought—By God, I should like to have five minutes alone with the chap what did this! Such immediate satisfaction would never be his, but there was justice, there was law. Standing there Lark remembered that Susie had not found what she was hired to hunt for—a female garment, connected with the blue ribbon, and thus with the crime. Nor had Hawes, given the job of examining every fireplace, found any trace of such a garment having been burned. Would Hawes, a townee, have thought of the copper-hole? In any case there'd be no harm in looking. Lark looked, plunged in his hand and found the parcel.

As he blundered out of the laundry he could hear Spender's voice in the library whose door stood half-open. Rapping in passing, Lark hurried in and said, 'Sir, I just found it,' and deposited on the top of the handsome desk the parcel which now looked, and smelt offensive. As he laid it down the edges gaped. 'In the copper-hole, sir.'

One would have thought it impossible for Mr Cornwall to look worse, but he did, his pallor turning green, his reddened eyes before he put his hand over them, bulging with horror. This reaction seemed natural to Spender who said aloud what he felt Mr Cornwall must be thinking, 'It looks as though there was an accomplice. In the house.'

A few seconds before Lark came bursting in, Mr Cornwall had produced a quite feasible explanation of the ribbon. Vincent he said loved anything pretty and often insisted on taking a new acquisition to bed with him.

Now Lark had spoiled it all and in a peculiarly shattering way; for even in its present state it was obvious that such a garment had not belonged to the nurse or the maid. One of the young ladies. Small wonder that the father wore a look of death.

Mr Cornwall had suffered a pang of memory. The smooth, rose-ivory flesh just glinting through the fine lawn, the gay ribbons, the provocative bounce of the frill. 'Like it? I made it for you.' God! God!

But sharper was the fear. He, carrying out Rose's instructions, had bought all the materials for this garment from the best shop in Bereham. And he had done it openly, a man with a wife and three daughters. The bolt of lawn, the card of insertion, the spool of ribbon were all in the shop at this minute.

With a fierce effort he pulled himself together. Spender was murmuring about being afraid that it looked like one of the young ladies being involved after all. Dry-lipped, Mr Cornwall said, 'It should not be difficult to decide which one.'

'By the fit?' Spender asked, thinking of those matching twins; thinking almost with relief that they seemed dotty enough to do anything, just the kind of young ladies who would take up with rogues.

'No. If we might have a word alone together, Superintendent. And if the constable could refrain from mentioning his find just at the moment.'

'That understood, Lark? Wait outside.'

'May I offer you a little brandy?'

'Thank you, no, sir. Never drink on duty.'

John Vincent Cornwall helped himself and drank. 'It certainly is not my place to suggest anything to *you*, I know that. But a thought did occur to me.'

'Yes, sir?'

'That,' said Mr Cornwall, indicating the parcel but not looking at it, 'was obviously placed where it was with the object of burning it at the first opportunity. If nothing were said of the discovery, whoever planned to burn it might still make an attempt to do so.'

'It'd be a quick, sure way of finding out,' Spender agreed.

'I myself would keep watch. I can't hope to sleep. First my poor child. Now this which makes me fear that someone close to me ...'

'It would be too painful a task for you, sir,' said Spender, unaware that he had been pushed past the moment of decision. 'I couldn't allow you to do it. I'll watch myself.'

A suggestion to be resisted.

'I am inclined to think that it would be better for you to drive away, rather ostentatiously. The idea is to lull the ... the culprit into a sense of false security.'

'Yes, I see that.' Spender was willing to make the experiment, but it must be conducted under police supervision. And he had just thought that he was collaborating with a man whom Hawes suspected. 'The locals can keep watch. I'll send them home now, they can get some rest and come back at a quarter to ten when Hawes and I leave. I will explain to Lark.'

This was not what John Vincent Cornwall had planned, but it was half-way.

84

Before Lark, ordered to keep his mouth shut, carried the parcel back to where he had found it, Spender's mind, still wriggling away from the unacceptable, had offered him the suggestion that even a poor girl, entangled with a bad man who made easy money by robbery or kidnapping, might have received a gift above her station. Earlier in the day he'd been put off by the nurse's statement of her creed—even Children of Jerusalem had been known to lapse—and by the maid's current hopes regarding young March—she'd been in other places. He gave them both another and even stricter going over and learned nothing of importance.

Mrs Lark, Lark and Champion walked along the lane and only Champion was moderately happy. Lark felt positively disloyal because he was bound to keep a secret from his wife and his best friend, and Susie was angry because her pride in her good work and all the interesting things she wanted to recount about the clothes at Stonebridge House had been engulfed in her perennial grudge—the shameful way in which village constables were treated. She said, 'I've always said it and I'll say it again. The constable always gets the thick end of the stick. You were both up half the night. They weren't.'

Lark said nothing. Champion said, 'Beats me what the idea is. Do they reckon whoever did it'll come back and do it again? Mucking about most of the day and now up all night when the answer's there as plain as the nose on your face. I been keeping my ears open. That little boy was a tattler. March said so, so did Catchpole.'

'Granted he was,' Mrs Lark said. 'In fact the cook and the maid both said the same. Would that account for his being killed?'

'If he'd found out something his dad or his nurse didn't want tattled about,' Champion said. 'And not so far to look. I remember things. There was goings on, or so they said, when *this* Mrs Cornwall was governess and the other one was poorly. Ruled the roost the governess did. Then he married her and just now *she's* poorly and that nurse, out of that uniform and with her hair loose ... I can see just what happened, a bit of the old slap-and-tickle and the boy saying, "I'll tell my Ma ..." '

Susie said, 'Champ, you want to be careful what you say. That's libel.'

85

'Slander,' Lark said. She asked what the difference was and he told her exactly and Champion said, 'Well, anyway, it was only between *friends*.'

The word cut Lark who could think of only one way to ease his feeling of guilt towards Champion and that was to invite him to share the beef pudding which Susie had pulled to the back of the stove before she left to be police searcher. 'Spare you a bit of a walk, Champ,' he said. Champion accepted the invitation gladly and in reply to Susie's enquiry as to whether his wife would worry, replied that she wouldn't even notice any absence of his less than a week in duration. When they had eaten, the men went to rest, Lark on his own bed, Champion on the slippery horsehair sofa in the parlour. Susie promised to wake them in good time so that they could have a wash and brush up and a good cup of tea to sustain them. While they slept she made fourteen pounds of strawberry jam.

Thomas came into Charlotte's room, where the dusk was gathering, clutching between his left hand and his chest a little tray on which stood a glass of milk and a plate holding a chicken sandwich.

'Charlie, I know it's awful. I know how you feel. But you can't live if you don't eat. Charlie, what'd I do if anything happened to you? There'd be nobody.'

'I don't feel like eating, Thomas. Thank you all the same.'

'I made the sandwich. At least I put it together. I remembered that you liked salt, Charlie. Do please try.'

His pathetic earnestness was touching. She took a bite which tasted of nothing, and then another which was better. He watched, pleased, and when the sandwich was consumed said, 'Does your door lock?'

'I don't know. Why?'

'I'm going to lock myself in. I'd advise you to, too. I'm nervous.'

'I don't think you need be. Nobody would break in here again.'

They both accepted implicitly that the crime had been committed by an outsider; to them, as to Spender, though with better reason, it was inconceivable that anyone inside this house, their home, could possibly have done so vile a deed. They talked quietly. Thomas had moved about during the day, hovering unobtrusively, and now that Charlotte was prepared to pay him a little attention he passed on things which he had overheard.

Across the landing Adelaide and Vikky had already set about the mammoth task of providing mourning for themselves, and for Charlotte, out of what was left of the black they had worn for their mother and anything else that they could contrive. Mrs Cornwall was all right, her Sunday wear in summer was a black silk pelisse, in winter a black cloak with a sealskin collar. Exercising considerable ingenuity, reserving the best for themselves, and working as one entity they insulated themselves from the household tragedy.

Nellie, like Thomas, was nervous. At frequent intervals during the day she had reminded Beattie that she had always said, hadn't she, that this was not a *good* house; that she'd always felt nervous in it. She spoke again about giving notice and Beattie said it'd be daft to do it too soon. Might give people ideas. Finally, when they were breaking their fast with more tea and some toast, Nellie said humbly, 'Would you mind if I slept with you tonight?'

Beattie greatly valued the privacy of her bedroom, cook's status symbol, she said rather grudgingly that Nellie could sleep in her room, on the floor though, and on her own mattress. She then said that she intended to do her feet.

'But, Cook, this is Saturday,' said Nellie who, what with the shock and all the questioning and people in and out all day, badly wanted to go to bed and escape by sleep's door, yet dared not go up alone. Beattie's feet were always done on Sunday afternoon. They were feet that had suffered every ill-usage known outside China; shoes too large, shoes too small, shoes with wrung-over heels, too much standing, too many stairs. They had retaliated valiantly with corns, bunions, dropped arches, hammer toes and ingrown toe-nails, a pad of calloused skin on the sole of each foot, thick and hard as a hoof. But an hour's soaking did wonders and Beattie's knife, sharpened up on the stone door-step, always served her as a chiropodist's tool.

The knife had, naturally, attracted a good deal of attention during the day. It conformed exactly to Doctor Fletcher's description of the murder weapon; but Rose had cleaned it, so promptly and thoroughly that even under the police magnifying glass, wielded by the sceptical Hawes, it had said nothing.

Tonight Beattie did not, as she usually did, lay the knife

beside her before pouring hot water into the chipped footbath and adding a handful of salt. Noting the omission and anxious to placate, Nellie said, 'Don't you want your knife?'

'Not tonight. Tell you the truth she don't seem like my knife no more, handled so much by other people. She was my knife. Give to me when I was a young mawther, the second place I was at. About fifteen I'd be. As you know, I never let anybody touch her.'

Stripping off her coarse footwear, testing the heat of the water with a toe, lowering her feet cautiously, the old woman knew that something much darker than mere handling had alienated her from one of her most prized possessions. She did not analyse the feeling closely, she was sixty and had kept alive by minding her own business, which was to sell her labour and do the job she was paid for. She'd never had time or the inclination to be fanciful and even now, feeling an aversion to her knife, she drew no conclusions. Let other people, people paid to do it, do that.

Nellie said, 'How about another cup of tea?'

'I could do with it,' Beattie said. 'Use the other kettle. I want that one,' and she tipped, as was her custom, a little more hot water into the cooling footbath. She thought that at Brancaster, when she got there, if she got there, the salt water would not be hot, it would be cold, but that wouldn't matter because her feet would be free, every step cushioned by soft sand, smooth, smooth as silk except for the little pockholes, smaller than a pea, under which the cockles lay.

She almost drowsed, rousing now and again to take a sip of tea, or to add a little more hot water, and little dreaming what she was doing to her employer whom, on the whole she liked and would not willingly have incommoded.

The police wagonette had rattled away. Mr Cornwall had a few minutes to do what he had to do and he could not do it while the kitchen door, immediately opposite that of the laundry, glowed yellow, and sent to his painfully acute hearing the sound of two gossiping women's voices. Damn them to hell, they were always making for bed by half past nine, except on a few special occasions when they stayed up, *as a favour*. Everything else within the house was all right; Agnes, under sedation again, sound asleep.

He strode into the kitchen. He said, 'You girls should be abed, you know. It's been a long ... a long horrible day for

88

everybody.' For nobody so long or so horrible as for me, the child's father, self-condemned, trying to avoid a more dangerous condemnation by a hair's-breadth. By a matter of minutes now.

At his entry Beattie had lowered her skirt so that her knuckly knees were hidden, but there were her thin, rope-veined shanks, the distorted feet, somewhat exaggerated by the refraction of the water. Quite uncharacteristically, in his muddled, frightened, near-frantic mind, the thought struck—One day to me too, if I live . . . It was literally the first time that he had ever entertained the thought of age for himself. That he should do so now was the measure of the breach which the tragedy had made in his self-complacency.

The desperate attempt to behave with control which had made him address them as 'girls', an expression carried over from happier times, failed him suddenly.

'Get off to bed, both of you. It's nearly ten o'clock.'

'Five minutes fast, sir,' said Beattie, glancing at the clock on the mantelshelf.

'Never mind that. Get along.' His voice was now high and unsteady and he gestured as though they were animals and he their drover. Her feet insufficiently soaked and insufficiently dried, Beattie hastily put on her slippers, stooped to take one handle of the footbath. Nellie reached for the other. She was not always so punctilious about helping to clear up after this operation but tonight was different.

'Leave it. Leave it,' Mr Cornwall shouted. 'Clear up in the morning.'

Flustered, Beattie took up her footwear and the candle and led the way towards the stairs. And even there she stopped, thinking that having been done out of one comfort was no reason why she should miss the other, 'Bring the tea, Nellie,' she said in a hissing whisper. Then, in a muted, half-frightened voice she said, 'Good night, sir.' Nellie repeated the wish. Mr Cornwall muttered 'Good night,' and went towards the door. He was just outside it, half-way between it and the laundry door when he heard the pre-agreed signal, a tap on the library window. He hesitated, tremulous with indecision. Should he keep Lark and Champion waiting for just those few seconds that it would take him to dash in and snatch the parcel and conceal it about his person? Or wait till morning? And then, every detail complete, a far better plan slid into his mind and he hurried to admit them.

Even on tiptoe the men's heavy boots sounded loud on the black and white tiles. Mr Cornwall led the way into the kitchen and, in striking contrast with his manner during the day, concerned himself with their comfort. He apologised for not being able to offer them beer to cheer their long vigil, but he produced a bottle of whisky and two tumblers and drew a jug of water from the pump. 'Or you can drink it neat if you prefer.' Lark muttered something about being on duty, but Champion, oppressed by Lark's mood, his silence, said he thought one drink wouldn't hurt, this being a sort of extra special duty.

Catchpole's sister down at the Jolly Sailor kept no great store of spirits but she had sent what she had, one bottle of brandy, into which Mr Cornwall had made considerable inroads; and three of whisky. Mr Cornwall poured generously, added the minimum of water and the two men, feeling a little embarrassed by being waited on by him, sipped as though taking medicine. Champion was accustomed to beer, Lark drank it seldom, because Susie made such good home-made wine out of dandelions, cowslips, blackberries and elderberries. Neither man was accustomed to spirits.

'Drink up,' Mr Cornwall said, 'because I shall have to leave you in the dark. You must sit with the door open and a light would warn . . .'

He then played his master card. Addressing Lark, he said, 'Constable, it might be as well if you checked that the . . . the article is still where you left it.'

By night, in the light of a single candle the laundry was an eerie place. Without glancing at the slab, Lark crossed to the copper and made sure and then hastened out, conscious of a funny feeling at the back of his neck.

'It's there all right, sir.'

'And you closed the door, so that if it is opened you will hear?'

'I did that, sir.'

He went away and left them. It was not quite dark in the kitchen; the light of moon and stars seeped through the window and both men, accustomed to night beats, had well-developed night-sight. The scrubbed deal top of the table was a pale lake, Lark a solid promontory on one side, Champion on the other.

Champion said, quietly, but with anger, 'Now, what's all this you know and I don't?'

Lark said, miserably, 'D'you reckon we ought to talk?'

'I reckon you'd better,' Champion said nastily.

Lark told all, adding that he had had no intention of keeping Champion in the dark, he'd meant to tell him as soon as they were alone.

'Why not in the lane then?'

'Getting dark. You never know who's behind a hedge.' Champion accepted that and was further mollified when Lark whispered, 'I wanted to ask you, Champ, what to *do*. I mean, if it works. The Super didn't say arrest or apprehend exactly. He said catch. 'S'been worrying me.'

'You needn't worry, Larky. We shan't catch anybody. Not with *him* in on the trick.' Even to himself he could not explain what the object of the vigil might be, but it was not the one given to Lark, of that he was certain.

The church clock struck eleven. 'Six hours to go,' Champ said and settled himself more comfortably. He'd got the better chair of the two, the one Beattie used; it had arms, a high back, a thin red cushion on its seat and another at about neck-level. He put his feet on the table and relaxed. Lark, in Nellie's uncushioned, upright chair, heard it strike twelve. The next thing he heard was movement near him. Susie? Morning already?

Champion said, 'I don't know about you, but I could do with a pee.' He spoke in a normal voice and Lark said, 'Sshh.' Champion rose and went towards the door that led to the yard.

'Not that way. Dog. Have your leg off,' Lark said.

He was himself aware of his bladder's need. Staying awake all night wasn't like being asleep where these things were concerned. However, believing as he did in the value of what he was doing, Lark was against moving about. Champion, convinced that he was being hoaxed said 'Please yourself,' and made for the other door, into the back hall, out by the door into the drying yard, and Lark followed. Modestly they turned away from one another. The moonlight which had served Rose Ellis drenched the yard and Lark thought it was bright enough to show him the time on his watch. He drew it out and squinted. It must be the light. Or his watch had stopped some time yesterday afternoon. It couldn't be!

Back in the kitchen Lark whispered, 'If we stood behind the

door and I struck a match for a minute, could you tell us the time, Champ?'

Quite unperturbed by the answer his watch gave him, Champion said, 'Five to four. We're getting along. Not long now.'

Since he had never taken the vigil seriously his only feeling about the flight of time was relief that it had passed so quickly. He knew he had slept, but what did that matter? His suspicions centred around Mr Cornwall and the nurse and neither of them was likely to go near the laundry with two constables keeping watch in the kitchen. Lark, however, was appalled.

'We musta been asleep, Champ.'

'You speak for yourself, old boy. I never closed my eyes.'

'You should have woke me,' Lark said humbly. 'I'm wholly sorry, Champ, leaving it all to you.'

'I'd have woke you if there'd been cause. One awake was enough. And if I was you I shouldn't mention it. Blimey, I couldn't half do with a cup of tea.'

'And a pipe,' Lark said, needing comfort.

Outside the window the light strengthened and warmed. At five o'clock Mr Cornwall, as he had promised, came to relieve them.

Champion reported for both.

'Not a sound all night. We kept sharp watch and nobody came nigh nor by.'

'Then the evidence will still be there. Would you look?'

Lark went and came back looking deeply distressed. He felt that by sleeping he had failed the poor little old chap who lay there, dead, and he now suspected that Champion had not been as alert as he claimed.

'It's gone, sir,' he said.

'Well, it was an experiment and it failed,' Mr Cornwall said. Champion who had suspected something fishy all along and genuinely believed that though he had been dozing he would have heard anything there was to hear, looked puzzled and angry.

'I don't see how it could have been taken. With us sitting here.'

'It seems to have done so. I expect you would like to be off now.'

Lark said, 'If it's all the same to you, sir, we'll wait for the Superintendent. He said he'd be early. About seven, he said.'

'As you wish.' Mr Cornwall opened the door into the courtyard, re-tethered Tiger and opened the big gates, ready for Spender's arrival. His mind had taken another step away from his guilt, away from his bereavement, hard sharp thinking left little room for emotion.

He went back into the kitchen and Champion said, 'Would it be all right if I made us a cup of tea?'

'Perfectly all right, if you can get the stove going.'

Mr Cornwall went away and Champion, accustomed to fending for himself since his wife was so often out, made tea. Added to, it was rather weak and tepid, but quite drinkable when Nellie came down to begin another day.

Spender was very punctual; he had had a bad night, had in fact slept far less than Lark or Champion. Once out of Mr Cornwall's compelling ambience he had realised what he had done, collaborated with someone outside the Force, moreover someone whom Hawes, for one, suspected. He'd taken an unjustifiable risk. If the experiment succeeded, all would be well; if it had failed . . . Perhaps worst of all was the thought that he had not taken the sceptical Hawes into his confidence.

The experiment had failed.

'Lark, you are absolutely positive that both of you, or one of you, was awake all the time?'

Lark told his lie not very convincingly, 'Yes, sir.' Champion was more positive. He'd heard every chime of the church clock. 'And there's another clock, somewhere in the house, sir, that chimes, five minutes after the church one. I noticed it every time. And the dog was a bit restive. He seemed to know we were there and kept clawing at the door. Keeping awake is part of our job, sir. P.C. Lark and me kept awake and nobody came nigh nor by.'

Yet the incriminating garment *had* been removed. The experiment had failed. Spender said, weakly, 'Well, all right. I rather think that the less said about this the better. You know how the public is. They don't like us; they're only too ready to blame us. If this got out they'd say you'd both been asleep.'

Lark who knew he had been, Champion who even to himself would admit no more than an occasional nod, knew how critical of the police the public was—except when it needed help. Finally, trudging along the lane even Champion admitted that though the experiment had been a bit of foolery, the less said the better. Lark agreed.

But the pretty, obscenely soiled garment had existed, had offered its mute evidence and disappeared. The one man concerned in the case who, had he been fully informed, was capable of seeing what had happened, clear as a map, clear as a plan, knew nothing because Spender could not bring himself to tell Hawes.

As it was, all that Hawes could do, after another futile day of poking about and asking questions that led nowhere, was to say to his superior who was obviously taking this case hard, 'Well, sir, we must look to the inquest. People often break down in a formal atmosphere ...'

Something inside Spender shuddered. He dreaded the inquest. By the time it was held—on Monday—the crime would be more than forty-eight hours old and his investigation had led nowhere. The one piece of concrete evidence which he had held in his hands was lost. Only on one point was his mind steady; it was an outside job. At one point he even considered the subject of gypsies. A batch of them had been in the village until Wednesday, could have made themselves familiar with the outside of the house, at least; gypsies frequented race-courses and would do anything for money. Then, what about the nightdress?? Explain the nightdress to yourself, Spender! Well, gypsies stole things from drying lines and it was just possible that a man, bent on robbery or kidnapping, could have worn a long white garment over his clothes so that in the dark he might be taken for a ghost. Spender's imagination, except in the area where it was stultified by his will, was active enough. He could almost see a swarthy fellow entering by the laundry window, failing in whichever crime he planned; stuffing his disguise into the nearest hiding-place, the body into the manure heap. Then why come back to take the garment? Because, washed and bleached it might fetch half-a-crown?

With a mounting sense of guilt because he still could not bring himself to mention the nightdress, Spender tried out the gypsy theory on Hawes who after a moment of silent stupefaction said, 'I hope to God *not*, sir. In that case we might as well go home. I never knew anything to be pinned on a gypsy unless he was caught in the act. They're all alike to look at, they're all named Lee and they can all call upon fifty kinsmen to prove that they were on the other side of the country at the time.'

94

Hawes looked at Spender speculatively. 'I suppose, sir, you have thought over my theory.'

'I have indeed. I still don't think it holds.' It could not, it must not, because if Mr Cornwall were guilty, then Spender had made himself an accessory after the fact. That was blunt truth. He had aided the guilty man to dispose of vital evidence. Wearily, Spender considered the possibility again. To reach the copper-hole in the laundry Mr Cornwall would have been obliged either to pass the open kitchen door, or let himself out at the front one and go round to the laundry window. Lark and Champion, unless they were sound asleep, must have heard him on the stairs, in the hall, at the door. They must have . . .

As much to convince himself as to show a willingness to consider Hawes's theory Spender said, 'The question of *when*, comes up. Put all the statements together and you have a minute-by-minute account of the poor child's last hours.' He ran through it from the return in soiled clothes to the being put to bed in the usual hour, in the usual way. 'So when, Hawes, could what you call an accident have occurred?'

'All right then, sir.' Hawes abandoned, though only temporarily, his suspicion of Mr Cornwall. 'That leaves the nurse. She could've lost her temper with him. She entioned the hot day, the baby being fretful, the boy coming in all mucky. She's a strong girl. Lived on a farm till five months ago—country people do put peculiar things on muck heaps. And I don't take to the idea that she slept through whatever happened . . .'

'It's very unlikeliness makes it sound possible, don't you think? It would have been so easy to have concocted a more credible story.'

On this Sunday morning when at midday the yews and the tombstones in the churchyard cast hardly any shadow at all, the man whose duty it was, 'tapped' the jury. He had plenty to choose from, for an unusually large number of people had attended church that morning. There was the primitive need to huddle together in the face of disaster: there was curiosity as to whether any of the stricken family would be present. None was.

'Inquest tomorrow at eleven at the Jolly Sailor. Mr Cornwall's poor little old boy.'

3

ON MONDAY MORNINGS ADELAIDE PERFORMED HER ONE regular household duty. She stood in the lumber room next to the nursery and listed the items to be sent to the wash, as Nellie placed them in the big wicker basket. They never dawdled over this task and this morning worked more quickly than ever because Adelaide was anxious to get back to her sewing and Nellie had to change before she went to the inquest to give evidence about the locks and bolts.

Mrs Whinney, worn, bent, always in a mouse-like scurry, and her big, raw-boned bad-tempered daughter, came as usual to collect the basket at half past ten. In summer, by this hour, they had done a day's work, the wash known as 'The Rectory' was already on the line; 'The Doctor' was in the copper. The Whinneys never knocked, they walked straight in and up the stairs to the waiting basket. This morning, as they went through the kitchen, Mrs Whinney glanced as usual, at the clock and said, 'Oh dear; five minutes late. We shall be behind all day.' Had either Beattie or Nellie been about Carrie would willingly have spent another five minutes discussing the catastrophe, but the kitchen was empty.

Back in their steam-filled kitchen, Mrs Whinney took a copper stick and began dredging 'The Doctor' into a tin bath to await mangling while Carrie checked 'Stonebridge'.

She said sharply, 'There's a nightdress short.' Without looking round Mrs Whinney said, 'Have another look. Folded in with a sheet or something.'

'There's still only three in the basket, four in the book. And you remember that time when they kicked up such a shindy about one of their shirts getting in with The Rectory? I'm going straight back and tell them about this.'

'Oh, Carrie! You can't. Not today. Poor things, it's a wonder they got a wash together at all.'

'That's all very well,' Carrie said harshly. 'You dropped dead, or I did, they'd expect their wash back, wouldn't they?'

Carrie's naturally irascible temper, inherited from her father, was inflamed by the conditions in which she worked, hot water, hot irons, and usually her mother refrained from any argument with her. Now she said, 'Well, just wait till they've got the inquest over, poor souls. And give me a hand with the mangle.'

'I shall go across the minute I've had my dinner,' Carrie said, and vented her vast, general discontent with the world by turning the mangle's handle so violently that her mother was obliged to say, 'Here, Carrie, steady up a bit. You nearly got my fingers.'

The coroner for the district was a doctor who had not liked his profession and had retired from it when an aunt had, quite unexpectedly left him a house and a modest competence. To him it was plain from the first that the public room at the Jolly Sailor could not possibly accommodate the crowd who wished —and had a right—to attend the inquest. So he adjourned it to the nearest possible place, the Old Guildhall.

Drama seekers were disappointed. Even mortal wounds lost impact when described in strictly medical terms and, contrary to Hawes's theory about the formal atmosphere breaking people down, all the evidence given was exactly in line with the statements taken by Spender. Rose Ellis described how she had missed the child; Nellie how she had found the doors, March and Catchpole how they had found the body. Spender confined himself to strictly routine statements.

A juryman held his hand up, like a child in class asking for permission to leave the room.

Doctor Lomax said, 'Yes?' The man stood up and said, 'I'd like leave to ask a question, sir.'

Doctor Lomax said, quite genially, 'We are here to ask questions, and if possible to answer them, Mr er—er . . .'

'Dodman. Wheelwright,' the man said; and that was modest of him. He had a flourishing business, he made wagons, tumbrils, even gigs. 'What I, what we, want to know, sir, is why no member of the family has been called.'

'Because none of them had anything to add to the statements they had already made, Mr—er—Dodman.'

'But then, with all due respect, sir, neither did anybody we *have* heard, so far.'

'There was also,' said the coroner, 'a natural wish to spare their feelings.'

'With murder done you'd think their feelings would be wishing to get to the bottom of it,' Mr Dodman said.

The crowd gave vent to a wordless sound of agreement and somebody from the rear of the room said, 'Where's his father?'

'I shall not tolerate interruption,' Doctor Lomax said sharply. 'Now, Mr Dodman, which members of the family would you wish to have called?'

'All of them, sir.' As Mr Dodman sat down another juror stood.

'Ridgeway. Farmer,' he announced himself. 'If I might say so, we'd get a better idea if we knew the lay of the land. We'd like to take a look at the scene of the crime.'

'Very well. We will adjourn to Stonebridge House.'

A few women whose husbands ate at home at midday and liked their meals on time, drifted away. The rest of the crowd trudged along the lane and into the grounds of the house, infuriating March by treading on the lawn and the flowerbeds. Doctor Lomax, who knew Mr Cornwall slightly, and who shared Spender's belief that gentlemen did not kill their own sons, apologised for intruding upon the privacy of the family in their hour of grief, but privately he thought the man would have been wiser to have shown a more co-operative attitude. Only jurors were admitted, and they were sent round to the back door. Studying the lay of the land included a good long stare at the nursery, by the standards of most of them a sizeable room but not big enough, surely, for the nurse's story to be true.

Doctor Lomax waited for Mr Cornwall to offer a room in which the inquest could be continued, but no such offer was made, so the family's statements were taken in the kitchen. Everybody thought that Mr Cornwall looked ill, Miss Charlotte even worse, and that the twins were very peculiar, never

98

saying *I*, always *we*. Nothing that was said cast the faintest
light on the mystery and the verdict might just as well have
been given earlier in the Guildhall. Murder by person or per-
sons unknown.

As the crowd began to disperse, Carrie Whinney crossed the
lane with the washing-book clenched in her water-wrinkled
hand. Beattie and Nellie had just taken possession of their
kitchen again. Carrie wasted no time.

'There's four nightgowns down here and only three in the
basket,' she said.

The inquest had refocused Nellie's attention upon the subject of it, and she had cried again. She said with less than her
usual spirit, 'I know I put four in, Carrie.'

'You didn't. You couldn't have done. Mum and me took the
basket straight home and there was only three. And I know
whose is missing. Miss Charlotte's; with the feather stitching.
You either go get it or have this book altered.'

'I picked it up outside her door and I put it in with my own
hands.'

'You calling me a liar?' Carrie asked.

'You calling me one?' Nellie demanded, her spirit reviving.

Beattie said, 'Shut up. I've had damned well enough for one
day. People clumping in and out and not knowing what to do
about lunch. You two want a row about a nightgown missing
go and settle it in the yard.'

From the doorway Hawes said, 'What's all this? A nightgown missing you say?'

'Four in the book and three in the basket,' Carrie said.

'But I put four in. I know I did.'

'*Very* interesting,' Hawes said. 'Stay right where you are.'
He went to find Spender.

To Spender Nellie said, 'I stood here. Miss Adelaide stood
there. I said "Four nightgowns" and she wrote it down. The
last thing was the tablecloth and I put it over and tucked it in
all round. Then Miss Adelaide went upstairs, and so did I to
tidy up for the inquest. No, half a minute, I didn't go straight
up because Miss Charlotte came down and stood at the bottom
of *them* stairs and asked me to fetch her a glass of water. She
didn't want to go across the landing because there was a man in
the hall.'

'What man? Did you see him?'

'No. I sort of looked but I didn't see nobody and I was in a hurry, see?'

'You fetched the water?'

'Yes. Miss Charlotte took a sip and then went up the stairs carrying the glass. I followed her up.'

'Did you happen to notice the time?'

'Half past ten on the dot. I know because there's a chiming clock in the hall and it struck half past and I knew I'd have to hurry to tidy myself and get to the Guildhall.'

Mrs Whinney was also positive about time because she had looked at the kitchen clock and seen that she and Carrie were five minutes late. So it looked as though the laundry basket had been unattended for five minutes; quite long enough for some-one to lift the tucked in tablecloth and abstract a garment. But who? But why?

Spender's mind wrestled with something as difficult as moulding quicksilver into a ball. Driven to it he must admit that there was some connection between the pretty, soiled garment that had been the subject of his ill-fated experiment and the disappearance of a totally different garment. What connection? And it was no help to have Hawes, unaware of the pretty thing's being found, saying, 'But sir, isn't it obvious? One of them is a garment short. Or was. Honestly, sir, I suspect the nurse. You may remember that Mrs Lark mentioned the similarity between Miss Charlotte Cornwall's nightwear and the nurse's. And the nursery door is about four steps away from the room where the laundry basket stood.'

'Mrs Lark also said that the nurse had the three of every-thing with which such girls are sent out into the world.'

Hawes had, in his short army career, faced many kit parades and knew all the tricks. The quickness of the hand deceived the eye. And once again, fighting blind, Hawes was very near the truth.

On the evening of that dreadful Saturday—far worse than the Friday when she thought she had managed well, Rose had waited for Mr Cornwall to come to bed. She knew nothing of Lark's discovery, nor of the vigil being kept in the kitchen; she was prepared to go down and burn the nightdress herself as soon as she had told her lover how very, very sorry she was about the oversight which had led to the discovery. Taking the baby for an airing in the perambulator during the afternoon she had collected sufficient dry, brittle twigs to make a good blaze. It would be the work of a moment.

She was obliged to wait for hours, and when he did come up the stairs he came so stealthily that only an ear tuned by love and anxiety would have heard him. He was lighting his way, not with a candle, but with a lantern whose almost closed shutter emitted the merest thread of light and could be darkened in a second. He did not see her, walked almost into her as they met at the stairhead, gave a great start and then recoiled. She reached towards him.

Before she could speak he said in a tense whisper, 'Police downstairs.'

In a matching whisper she said, 'Oh darling, I am so sorry. All my fault. I'm sorry.'

'They found the nightdress, but I have done away with it.'

There again she had failed him. She said again, 'I am sorry,' and tried to embrace him, but he recoiled again, so that her clutching hands only reached his upper arm. Among a hundred other thoughts and feelings he was conscious of a sharp revulsion.

'What will happen? Darling, I shall take all the blame. All of it.'

Their night conversations, their love-talk had always been conducted in whispers, and even at this moment the whispering lent a spurious intimacy. He freed himself of her hold and said, 'Stick to your story. Don't vary it by one word.' He went on and she turned back into the nursery.

He was angry with her. He had not accepted her apology or her offer to take the blame; he had pushed her hands away; he had not even said good night. She sat on her bed and tried to bring her mind, shallow to begin with and completely untrained to the process of thought, to bear upon this new aspect of the situation. He had told her to stick to her story; she could do that, it was in fact the easiest thing to do; but she needed to do more. She needed to find some way of diverting suspicion.

Her thoughts never veered far from the nightgown; *they* had found her nightgown and he had done away with it. So they would know one was missing. It seemed to her that the loss of another nightgown might possibly cover up, or be confused with, the loss of this one. She was still feeling rather than thinking and was ruthlessly regardless of what consequences her plan might have; and when, on the Monday morning, heart thudding, hands shaking, she lifted the tucked-in table-cloth and removed a nightgown, she did not discriminate but simply took the first to come to hand. Back in the nursery she found the garment a temporary hiding-place under the mattress of the baby's crib. She was quite calm and controlled again when she went to the inquest and stuck to her story, as she had been told to do.

Once the inquest was over the victim could be buried and public attention switched to the funeral. Here again John Vincent Cornwall acted with a lack of diplomacy. Whatever theories were held—and they were many and various—pity for the child was general and there was not a woman in the village who would not have stripped her garden for flowers to line the grave, or strew upon it. But the old grave-digger said he had no orders, and Catchpole—now no longer dependent upon his sister Sally for his beer—said he knew nothing. He continued to know nothing until Wednesday when he informed a shocked audience that there was as much mystery about the funeral as there was about the murder. The little coffin had been placed in the back of the gig and covered with what looked like a velvet tablecloth. Then Mr Cornwall, in black, and Master Thomas, with a black hat and arm band, had mounted and driven away. 'Miss Charlotte was the only one to see him off. She'd made him a tiddly bit of a wreath.'

The general opinion was that the child had been shuffled away and feeling against the father hardened; it was felt that real sorrow expressed itself in elaborate ceremony. And why the mystery, a secret kept so close that even Catchpole did not know the gig's destination. In fact only Mr Greenfield, helpful with telegrams, knew that. He had sympathised with Mr Cornwall's wish not to make a public show of the funeral and had arranged with a fellow clergyman in a village eighteen miles away to take charge.

On that same Wednesday Rose's father, Matthew Ellis, was cutting his patch of oats. He took no papers, had no time to gossip, and on the whole avoided the company of the ungodly, one of whom, a neighbour, was not ill-pleased to be able to come and shout across the fence, 'That girl of yours seem to hev got herself mixed up in some nasty business.' He told what he knew. Matthew gave a grunt of acknowledgment, turned and left the field. He hung his scythe on its accustomed hook and went upstairs. His wife hardly noticed, she was, as always, busy and she had been trained not to ask questions. However, when he came down dressed in his meeting clothes, worn black suit, new black boots and a kind of flat-topped bowler hat, she did venture, 'Where you going?'

'Fetch the girl home.'

'Rose! Why?'

'Bad company,' he said and walked out.

He reckoned that the walk would take him between four and five hours, but he had reckoned without his boots which were new and stiff and not yet broken in. Discomfort impeded pace, so he sat down and took them off, his thick home-knitted stockings, too, and stuffing the stockings into the boots and tying the laces of the boots together, he slung them round his neck. He had spent most of youth barefoot and found it no hardship to tread the thick soft dust of the road, or the grass of the verge. He stopped twice to beg a drink of water, and when he reached Biddlesford he had to ask where the house was. At the stone bridge he dabbled his feet and resumed his footwear—doubly painful now.

Nellie answered the front door bell and Matthew Ellis said, 'I want to see Mr Cornwall.'

'You can't. He's gone to take . . . to take his poor little boy to be buried.' Like the inquest, the funeral day had revived sentiment; Nellie had been crying and was ready to cry again.

'Then I'll see my daughter. Rose Ellis.'

'Oh!' Nellie's mood changed. Miss Hoity-Toity who couldn't carry trays and slept like a pig. 'If you'll round to the back, I'll send her down.'

Face to face with his daughter Matthew said, without preliminary, 'Get your things together and we'll be off.'

Rose was ashamed. He *looked* decent enough, quite as respectable a parent as either Nellie or Cook—all agog in the kitchen—could have produced, but so gruff, speaking to her as though she had been his dog.

'I can't. I can't leave without giving notice.'

'Man can't look after his own child can't look after mine. Get your things.'

Rose looked about, a little wildly and saw, inside the open woodshed, a cavern of shade and the sawhorse on which Catchpole sawed logs, the block upon which he split kindling.

103

She led the way to it. She said, 'Sit down a minute. You've had a long walk.' He took the sawhorse, glad to get his weight off his feet, but when Rose sat down on the block he said, 'I don't want no argument. Go get your stuff.'

'But there's still the little baby. And Mrs Cornwall is expecting again. I can't just leave. And if I did, it would look bad. People would say I'd had something to do with it and was running away.'

She had never argued with him, never opposed his will. In homes ruled by a Son of Jerusalem men were paramount. But, unpractised in argument, he had an answer, 'No harm can come to the righteous. Get your things and come along.'

Back to the wretched little smallholding; to isolation; away from the new god, away from joy forever and forever. She still thought, she felt in her bones that once this horrid thing was done with all might be, *must* be as it had been before. That hope and the realisation that her father, the old god's representative and mouthpiece, had no longer the power to awe her, even in his meeting clothes, gave her strength and ingenuity.

She said, 'If I went off now, when they're in such trouble, it'd give every Daughter of Jerusalem a bad name.'

In the whole of England the Sons and Daughters numbered two thousand four hundred and four. Their reputation must be protected.

Matthew said slowly, 'There is that.' He looked at his daughter, paying her, for the first time, real attention. Plain dress; hair scraped back.

He shifted ground.

'You go to meeting regular?'

A lie would not serve; the Children of Jerusalem were a close-knit community, a Brother from Bereham would tramp twenty miles to preach at Lowestoft, and the other way round. And there were the big regional gatherings.

'No. I couldn't. Being a nurse isn't like any other sort of job. You can't leave children alone.'

'You can take them. They can't start too young. We *carried* you, from the first. And a place this size'd have a pram, surely.'

She had won! She said meekly, 'I never thought of that.'

'Then think of it now.' He felt his spirit uplifted. In the oatfield he had felt a direct inspiration, almost a direct order— Go and rescue a weak Daughter of Jerusalem from the contamination of the world. But he had been, and he was willing to admit it, mistaken in his errand. Rose was not weak, she was staunch, though neglectful and his real errand had been to call her back to the path of duty. God did move in mysterious ways!

He said sternly, 'You see to it,' and stood up and his feet screamed. Rose stood too and he allowed himself a gesture of affection, a touch of his hand, hard as wood, on her shoulder. 'God keep you,' he said.

Outside the gate he sat down and removed his boots and stockings and loped away.

The papers, alerted by some mysterious means—the *Daily Banner*, for instance, had given an account not only of the inquest but described Stonebridge House in some detail— began to make some caustic comments. A child had been foully murdered, and nothing done. There was no libel, no direct accusation. One comment: 'We have seen a reward of a guinea offered for a lost dog.' And questions: What were the police doing? How did the magistrates feel? Would a poaching offence have been dealt with so tardily?

Cut to the quick, Mr Whymark, Mr Gooderam and Sir Richard Barlay consulted together, over Sir Richard's port.

'I did offer a guinea when Phoebe was lost,' Mr Whymark said. 'And I got her back. But how the *Daily Banner* got wind of that, beats me.'

'I object to the remark about poachers,' said Mr Gooderam, well known for his severity with poachers. 'Dammit, there's no comparison. No comparison at all.'

Sir Richard said, 'Personally, I think it is a case for Scotland Yard.'

Almost like calling in the man on the moon. Specialists, an outgrowth from the old Bow Street Runners, and, like them, available for hire.

'A bit expensive,' Mr Whymark said.

'Well, surely poor Cornwall . . .' Sir Richard faltered. 'I grant stringing up the fellow wouldn't give him back his boy, but surely, this must hurt him as much as it hurts us. To bring the crime home . . . a sort of satisfaction. I must admit that I had wondered why he hadn't offered a reward.'

Mr Gooderam said, observing codes of conduct, 'Strictly between ourselves, he couldn't afford it. I happen to know. He

105

rents Stonebridge House and is frequently in arrears. And in debt all over the place, butcher, baker, candlestick-maker.'

'You astound me,' said Sir Richard. 'I always understood that he had private means...' He brooded, decided upon a gesture.

'This,' he said, tapping the paper, 'must be stopped. It ridicules us all. Bad policy. A man from Scotland Yard shall be hired, and I will make myself responsible for the charge.'

'That is extremely generous of you, Sir Richard,' Mr Whymark said. Mr Gooderam said, 'Most generous.' And then added, 'If you could get Fowler...'

Mr Greenfield had, all through these trying days, been only too well aware of the disability that had been such a handicap. In his church, in his pulpit, in his robe, he was one man, out of them another. Professionally he could speak, with confidence, of the life everlasting, of the spirit returning to God, its Giver and Maker, he could even say such things as 'Safe in the arms of Jesus'. But face to face with a person whose loved one's spirit had returned to its Maker, and who was safe ... Somehow words always failed him, stuck in his throat ... Lucy could always produce the right word and on the whole he left the comforting of the bereaved to her. But he was not a careless shepherd to his flock and he realised that feeling was mounting against poor Cornwall. He felt it his duty to point out that if the whole family could possibly appear at morning service it would look well. He intended to speak, from the pulpit, words of comfort and reassurance.

Adelaide and Victoria had worked miracles of contrivance: for them the week, which had dragged tediously for everyone else, had seemed all too short.

Sunday was a warm day though overcast and thunder-threatened. Catchpole drew up at the churchyard gate, Thomas hopped down from his perch and wrestled with the carriage door; Mr Cornwall alighted and offered his arm to his wife. The twins followed and Charlotte and Thomas fell in behind them. The path that climbed up between the yews was lined with villagers; farther back some stood on tombstones to get a better view. At the sight of them John Vincent Cornwall set his teeth and regretted accepting the rector's suggestion. In any case it no longer mattered about making a favourable impression. He had a very shrewd idea that this would be his

106

last Sunday at liberty. Tomorrow an Inspector Fowler, a man who was said never to fail, would take over from Spender; and the magistrates irked by the accusation of inertia had arranged to hold a more thorough examination of Rose, *in camera*.

Somebody said, 'Murderer!'

A woman said, 'Poor soul! She's going to have a baby.'

'Kill that, too, most likely!' There was some coarse laughter as well as some shushing sounds. The people of Biddlesford were no better, no worse than those elsewhere; there was a minority who, had bull-baiting been legal, would have enjoyed it. Baiting a man was just as exciting.

'What about the insurance?'

Very few people there understood insurance or how long it took to collect on a policy, but the story of Wainewright, who had poisoned for the sake of insurance money, had reached even this remote place and was remembered. And nobody could deny that bills long owing had this week been paid.

'Couldn't even bury him decently!'

Through the mounting antagonism and noise the family advanced, staring straight ahead or with eyes downcast. Just outside the porch a young man, more affected than most by the scene, stepped into the path right ahead of Mr Cornwall and made faces and noises. 'Yah! Yah!'

John Vincent Cornwall's natural arrogance came to his aid.

'Out of my way, you *lout*!' he said, elbowing his tormentor aside and helping Agnes into the porch. The lout danced and yelled, 'See that? Kill me for twopence.'

The church door stood open, Mr Cornwall heaved Agnes in, turned, saw that all the family was inside and said sharply, 'Thomas, shut the door.' Thomas did so.

Mr Greenfield, robed and ready in the vestry, heard the noise and came out. He paused by the pew where his wife, just arrived, knelt, her gloved hands peaked before her face. 'My dear, you are needed,' he said, and swooped on to the back pew where Mrs Cornwall sat in a half-fainting condition, with Mr Cornwall looking more angered than distressed, with the twins wearing their this-is-nothing-to-do-with-us expression and Charlotte and Thomas on the verge of tears.

Agnes Cornwall, so far shielded even from gossip, had been shocked by the evidence of hostility, but something within her had joined the accusers—they spoke with her voice. He was to blame and she would never forgive him.

'To the house by the north door,' Mr Greenfield said.

The few people in the church, in their usual places, saw Mrs Cornwall, supported on one side by her husband, on the other by Mrs Greenfield, go out by the door which gave directly upon the rectory garden.

Mr Greenfield saw them go and regretted that his carefully prepared sermon would not be used to comfort them. He went to the west door and flung it open and said with even more authority and in a more carrying voice than he ordinarily commanded in the pulpit, 'Those of you who wish to worship God, in the proper spirit, may come in. Those who do not, leave the churchyard. At once!'

Almost all of them went in; a congregation greater than at Christmas, Easter or the Harvest Festival. When he stood up in the pulpit Mr Greenfield administered less a sermon, than a scolding, an extempore tongue-lashing which was greatly enjoyed by everyone except by one old woman so deaf that she had to keep her eye on her fellow worshippers in order to know when to stand, sit, kneel.

Across the garden, in the rectory, Mrs Greenfield was kindly competent. Smelling salts, a glass of cold water for Mrs Cornwall, a little brandy for Mr Cornwall and how about a cup of tea for the rest?

'It is very kind of you,' Mr Cornwall said. 'But we must get back. My wife should be in bed. Thomas, fetch the carriage. Tell Catchpole the rectory gate.' He longed to get home; his stock of liquor had been replenished and he intended to drink himself into the state of non-caring which had enabled him to survive this horrible week.

While they awaited the arrival of the carriage, a short space of time, since on Sunday mornings it was housed in the yard of the Jolly Sailor, Mrs Greenfield snatched the opportunity to speak to Charlotte who looked, she thought, terribly ill. She had nothing new to say, nothing that she had not said to a child bereft of her mother and torn with grief. Excess grief a sign of lack of faith. Resignation to God's will. Actually Mrs Greenfield was qualified to speak; a born mother she had been childless; she had prayed, urgently but futilely. Every time she went into the village she saw women with more children than they wanted, more than they could feed. She saw children who were neglected, a few positively ill-treated—in which case she took action. ('Mr Potter, you really must tell your assistant that if he

108

beats his little boy again you will *sack* him. Unless I have this assurance from you, I shall be obliged to withdraw my custom. And if I do, a good many others will follow my example.') Mrs Greenfield had done what she could, borne what she must and was now resigned. She even had the good sense to realise that resignation could not be communicated and she parted from Charlotte with the old threadbare promises; God knew best and Time would heal.

When the family arrived home there was a hired cab standing to one side of the drive and a man at the front door, in the act of ringing the bell.

Fowler!

Mr Cornwall said to the four young people whose mother Agnes Cornwall was not, 'Look after your mother,' and himself advanced towards the man on the step.

'Mr Cornwall. My name is Fothergill. Of Fothergill, Ampton and Fothergill.'

'Ah. Young James?'

Turn the clock back. Fothergill, Ampton and Fothergill had been the trustees for John Vincent Cornwall, an orphan. The Trust had paid his school fees, the best preparatory school on the south coast, and then Eton. It had arranged for his holidays, not with tutors exactly, but with young men who taught him to shoot and ride, read a menu, know his wines. When he was twenty-one the Trust had been wound up and he had been handed what had then seemed a fortune. He could remember the very day, when, emerging from the musty office where he had signed his name about twenty times, he had seen a little boy, very small-faced and shy, waiting. And Mr Hugo Ampton had said, 'This is my nephew. Young James. He is about to start school.'

John Vincent Cornwall had given the boy a sovereign, in his exuberant mood tossing it, 'You'll need some tuck,' he said.

In a just world such generosity should have endeared John Vincent Cornwall to James Fothergill forever, but the little boy had been too sunk in misery to be grateful. Their paths had not crossed again, but in the last two days old Hugo Ampton had been showing an astounding interest in the Cornwall case, and as a result Mr Fothergill was here instead of overlooking the preparations for one of his elegant little supper parties in his elegant little house in Essex Street.

But it was not his deep exasperation at being forced into this

109

unsavoury affair which made him avoid the hand which Mr Cornwall extended as he said, 'Young James.' He managed to do so by stepping aside while the rest of the family walked into the house. A good deal of Mr Fothergill's thinking was strictly rational, but his frustrated artistic temperament occasionally broke out in hasty, instinctive judgments which, though they might sound ludicrous at the time, were almost invariably proved right by the course of events. 'I wouldn't touch it. The man's a crook,' he once said of a man of the utmost respectability and impeccable reputation, two years later to be exposed as a swindler on a huge scale. Uncle Hugo had long since ceased to say, 'Nonsense, my boy,' though he still joked about James's hackles. Mr Fothergill's hackles were active now, so he avoided the handshake, and when Mr Cornwall, making no introductions, led the way to the library and offered a drink, Mr Fothergill said, quite untruthfully, that he never drank until evening.

'My uncle, Hugo Ampton, is very much concerned about you, Mr Cornwall. He feels that you need legal advice and representation.'

'That nobody could deny,' said Mr Cornwall, pouring brandy for himself.

'You have not sought it elsewhere?' If not, why not?

'No. It never occurred to me that a lawyer could do anything at this stage of affairs.'

'We have our little uses. For example, when your nursemaid is examined *in camera*, you would not be admitted to the hearing. I should be. Shall be,' he corrected himself, facing the fact that he must be involved. It had been his hope to find Mr Cornwall so well legally represented that he could go home. 'I understand that no reward has been offered. The omission seems to have attracted unfavourable comment. My uncle Hugo . . .' somehow, by the repetition of that name Mr Fothergill managed to give the impression that he was disassociating himself. 'My uncle Hugo suggested a thousand pounds.'

'Frankly, Mr Fothergill, I don't possess such a sum.'

'My uncle Hugo had foreseen that possibility. He said that he would put up the money.'

Mr Cornwall was astonished, but no more so than Mr Fothergill had been when his uncle had made this most uncharacteristic offer. Outside strict limits, laid down by his consideration for his own comfort and well-being, Hugo Ampton always looked at both sides of a penny before relinquishing it.

'That is extraordinarily generous,' Mr Cornwall said.

'I will see to that.' And although Mr Fothergill's manner remained remote and cold, Mr Cornwall had the heartening feeling that now somebody was on his side, that he was being looked after. As indeed, in a way he always had been. Always in the past, whenever he was really up against things, something had turned up. In the extremely mixed feelings which he had entertained in the past eight days there had been an element of this-cannot-be-happening-to-*me*. The knowledge that old Hugo Ampton, only vaguely remembered across the years, had been concerned, had sent aid, was particularly cheering after the hideous scene in the churchyard. Presently, after a little more talk, and another brandy, he felt sufficiently restored to suggest that Mr Fothergill should stay to lunch and meet the family. Mr Fothergill excused himself. The driver of his cab, he said, had not been overjoyed at being hired for such a long journey on Sunday morning and Mr Fothergill had promised that he should be back in Bereham in time for his Sunday dinner.

Chief Inspector Fowler had travelled down from London on the same train as Mr Fothergill, but he did not arrive in Biddlesford until much later in the day, having had a long, long talk with Spender who could not conceal his relief at being superseded. Fowler's genial, hearty manner enabled him to conceal his contempt for a man who, on the spot from the start, had been so ineffectual. Spender made no mention of the experiment that had failed and as Fowler drove, in a gig, let out by the week on a drive-yourself contract, the only garment that he knew about was Charlotte's missing nightdress. But Fowler had followed frailer clues over colder trails and notched up, if not quite a hundred, at least ninety per cent of successes. He enjoyed an international reputation; he had been hired to solve mysteries in France, Belgium and Holland—all very difficult because of the language barrier, but all successfully solved. He believed, and experience had proved him to be right, that once you had *motive* you were home and dry. Every crime ever committed had some motive behind it, sometimes a motive which sounded mad, too far-fetched to be considered. Fowler attributed his outstanding success to the fact that for him nothing that any human being did was too incredible to be considered—allied to an infinite capacity for taking pains.

He drove into the yard of the Jolly Sailor and Sally Awkwright gave him a warm welcome. She liked big, hearty men. Her husband had been big and hearty when she married him and she had taken delight in feeding him. He was now eighteen stone of inert blubber, too idle even to talk. And she was a naturally garrulous woman, her talk restricted by the rule that in an inn you must *listen* to everything, but not *say* much because you might appear to be taking sides and thus, pleasing one customer, offend another. She was very happy to let Fowler the little parlour that adjoined the bar and the low, beamed bedroom above; very happy to serve up a piece of steak, a brown shell over a pink succulence, with onions, new potatoes and fresh peas; very happy to chat.

She said, 'It never was what you could call a *happy* house. Poor Mrs Cornwall—that is, I mean, the first one, was never strong and went into a decline. A bit touched in the head. Then she died and after a bit he married the governess. And she never was nice to the two youngest. Miss Adelaide and Miss Victoria, well, they were old enough to look out for themselves, but the two others. By all accounts they had a rough time.'

This was the kind of gossip which could yield most fruitful results, and often had, but it must be checked.

'In what way, Mrs Awkwright?'

'Well, four–five years ago there was a maid there. A nice girl. Maggie her name was and tell you the truth I set my eye on her for my brother. He ain't all that bright—in the head, I mean—but he's decent and a good upstanding girl like Maggie could have been the making of him. So I had hopes and I asked her here, a good few times—her time off.' Kindness, hospitality, all wasted! Sally Awkwright had for a few weeks seen her old mother, her not wholly capable brother safely delivered into Maggie Simpson's hands. 'She left, all of a sudden. She said she couldn't stand the ill-treatment.'

'Who ill-treated her?'

'What, Maggie? Nobody ill-treat *her*! She could stand up for herself. No, it was Mrs Cornwall being so hard on Miss Charlotte and Master Thomas. Boxing their ears. Locking them in the cellar. Maggie couldn't stand it. So she left. Took off and went to Lopham and got married. Did right well for herself, too.'

112

'Whom did she marry, Mrs Awkwright?'

'A farmer called Peabody. And the funny thing is he grows peas. Acres and acres.'

Motive? Vengeance upon the woman who had been unkind. Add the loss of the nightgown. Consider the age—sixteen, dangerous in both sexes since it combined maturity of body with immaturity of mind, and in the female was often linked with a tendency to hysteria.

When Mrs Awkwright had served a dish of stewed gooseberries and custard, followed by cheese, she cleared away and went out, closing the door behind her. Fowler opened it a little. Eavesdroppers might hear no good of themselves, but they often heard interesting and useful things about other people.

Talk in the bar centred naturally around the rumpus in the churchyard, a good deal of it concerned with whether Mr Cornwall had deliberately struck young Briggs or merely shoved him out of the way. Catchpole, one of the few who had not been present at the scene, said he had to admit that Mr C had a nasty temper when roused; and he had something to add to the general pool of knowledge—the arrival of a real proper toff at Stonebridge House that morning. 'Come off the London train. I know because he come in a cab and when I'd put the carriage away I nipped round and had a word or two. Couldn't find out who he was, though.'

'Family, sounds like.'

Mr Cornwall had his defenders as well as his detractors, and when the argument grew heated and several people spoke at once, Fowler could distinguish little. Out of one such confusion of noise a voice—it was Catchpole's—said, 'Well, she weren't then. She was as right in the head as you or me.' A great roar of laughter greeted that remark. '. . . real pleasant lady, that one was,' the same voice said. 'Passed the time of day whenever she met you. Used to call on our old mother, regular, didn't she, Sally? Ma right missed her when she was locked up.'

'She never was locked up.'

'Locked in, then.'

'Bill Catchpole, you stood just where you're standing now and told us about Tutt Wood and the children nearly dead with cold.'

'Did I now? Well, you can't remember everything.' That, in fact, summed up Catchpole's state, his memory was very selective. There had been a time immediately after his father's

113

suicide when he could not remember anything, not even the making of the gruesome discovery.

At the evening's end Mrs Awkwright came to offer her guest a nightcap. Anything from the bar, tea, cocoa? Fowler said he would take tea, if she would take a cup with him and over the tea she translated the half sentences, the allusions, even the laughter, into a nugget of useful information. The first Mrs Cornwall had not been quite right in the head; her eldest children, twins were a bit odd, though nobody had really noticed until now quite how odd they were; her son had something wrong with his hands and there had been a time when Miss Charlotte's health had been poor.

'And what about the children of the second marriage? The little boy, so tragically dead.'

'Oh, he was beautiful. Ever so good-looking.' Like Mrs Greenfield, Sally Awkwright was childless; unlike Mrs Greenfield she knew why. 'Funny thing,' she said, 'only Friday; I mean not this Friday, that Friday, I was cleaning the window and saw him coming out of Fiske's—that's the shop, with Miss Charlotte. And he did look lovely, so lively and sort of ... coaxing. And then, the next thing I heard ...'

Out at Lopham, in a fine old Tudor farmhouse—just the kind of place to which Fowler hoped one day to retire, over a table spread with cloth starched to crackling rigidity and from behind a silver teapot, Maggie Peabody, born Simpson, said, 'Yes. I left. I'm funny that way. I never could bear to see an animal, leave alone a child, ill-treated. There was nothing I could do. Not there. It's different here, anybody rough, even with pigs, and they hear from me! That poor little girl ... You see she just would *not* call her stepmother "Mamma". That was really what started it all. You see, the second Mrs Cornwall thought that as soon as the ring was on her finger she'd slip into the first one's place. I wasn't there at the time, but I do know that she didn't. And every time Miss Charlotte wouldn't say "Mamma" this Mrs Cornwall went angry and she'd stand that poor little girl facing the wall with her hands on her head. Did you ever try that? Well, I did, just to see how it felt. Ten minutes and I was ready to drop. Miss Charlotte did drop, more than once. She'd drop where she stood. And the same with the cellar. One time she was down there a day and a night,

114

without sip or crumb. And I never knew her to make a complaint or shed a tear. But I couldn't bear to stand by and do nothing. So I left. And I was right glad to hear, in a roundabout way that she'd gone to school.'

'Where, Mrs Peabody?'

'Now let me think. It was hearsay; I may have got it wrong ... It was a bit of a way back. But I'll catch it ... Yes, Miss Barker's, over at Thorden. May I give you another cup?'

Quite unintentionally Mrs Peabody had presented Fowler with a character who fitted into his mental picture; tough, resilient, shedding no tears, voicing no complaint, but quite capable of thinking—One day! At Miss Barker's he found a very different character described, but he knew that human beings were capable of duplicity and that circumstances could affect behaviour.

'Charlotte was very happy here and popular with everybody. We were all so sorry when she left.' Miss Barker looked at him with faded, periwinkle blue eyes ringed with the white of old age. 'She was so good with the little ones. Some are homesick at first, you know. She'd tell them stories and make them laugh.'

'Was she clever?'

Miss Barker considered that and said judicially, 'She was naturally intelligent. She was very backward when she arrived. I understood that her stepmother—who had been the family governess—had had charge of her education. One could only conclude that she was a bad governess. Charlotte made such progress in such a short time. When I first read of this dreadful thing my first thought was how deeply Charlotte would feel it. She was much attached to that poor child. Her dearest possession, indeed one might almost say her *only* possession, was a little picture of him. No, that is incorrect; she had a photograph of her mother.'

Fowler then asked about friends. Miss Barker explained that the school was dispersed on account of the summer vacation. But Charlotte's best friend, Lilian Headstone, lived in Thorden; a day girl, not a boarder. She directed Fowler to Lilian's home.

In the pleasant, prosperous-looking villa Fowler found himself confronted by a talkative woman and a pretty lively-looking girl who, as soon as Charlotte's name was mentioned, became hostile and defensive.

115

'Charlotte was my *friend*.'

'Yes dear; we know.' Something in Mrs Headstone's manner informed Fowler that the friendship had not been fully approved. 'That is why Inspector Fowler wishes to talk to you.'

Lillian's expression said very clearly: Let him talk!

'I'm trying to get a bit of background, Miss Headstone.' Fowler turned on his smoothest, most persuasive manner. 'Anything you could tell me about her home. Her family.'

'I never went there. I never saw them.'

'Lilian, dear, you *could* tell the Inspector what Charlotte said about the holidays.'

'What holidays?' It was interesting to see that this gently-reared Miss had the old lag's way of stalling.

'When you said you were so sorry for her, dear.'

'So I was. She said she wasn't looking forward to the holiday; her home wasn't like other people's.'

'Did she say why, Miss Headstone?'

'That was all she said.'

Helpful again, Mrs Headstone said, 'And there was the dress.'

'What dress?'

'The red one.'

Exasperated, Lilian said, 'There wasn't a red dress. All Charlotte said was she needed a new dress but she didn't think she'd get one. But *if* she did she'd ask for red because then she could be sure of not getting it. She hated red. I thought that was sad. But she didn't. She laughed. Charlotte isn't like anybody else. She even laughed about not getting anything for her birthday. She said not taking notice of birthdays was a sure way of keeping young.'

'What was her attitude towards her little half-brother?'

'She adored him.'

'Lilian, really. I heard her say, once when you brought her home for tea, that he was a monster.'

Lilian gave her mother a dark look.

'What Charlotte said exactly—she had just been home for a holiday—was that he had grown into such a monster that soon she wouldn't be able to lift him any more.'

Something at the back of Fowler's mind said: Ah!

Mrs Lark proved difficult. She refused absolutely to be

116

shaken from her statement that on the Saturday morning Charlotte had three nightdresses. 'Two clean, in the drawer and the one she'd worn on the bed.' Yes, she had examined that one carefully; when she did a job she did it thoroughly. No, she had not mistaken some other garment, a chemise, say, cunningly folded to *look* like a nightdress in a drawer. Susie realised that her flat refusal of every suggestion Fowler made wasn't enhancing the name of Lark; but it would have been positively damaged by any admission that she had been careless, or mistaken. And it wouldn't have been fair.

Nellie also stuck to her story. She had collected the things for the wash and put four nightgowns in the basket. Fowler made a little test. Standing where Charlotte was said to have stood, he asked Nellie to run down and fetch him a glass of water. There was, he found, ample time for the garment to have been removed during her absence. Charlotte's excuse for not wishing to cross the landing seemed to have no substance; nobody else had seen the man in the hall; nobody had admitted him to the house.

Bit by bit the picture built up and in his talks with Charlotte Fowler observed a composure unusual in a girl of sixteen. He also thought that her posture, sitting very straight, head high on an exceptionally slim neck, indicated pride. She was the kind who would feel humiliation very keenly, but be too proud to show it.

The magistrates' examination of Rose Ellis led nowhere. She, too, stuck to her story, credible because of its very incredibility, the kind of thing that nobody would have invented. Curiously, although Rose had turned away from her father's stern old God, she still had faith in His rules. As her father had said, 'No harm can come to the righteous,' and although, with attention so much centred on the nightdress, Miss Charlotte might seem to be *threatened* she was in fact safe because she was innocent.

The innocent were safe; the wicked were punished.

Rose Ellis was taking her punishment.

Night after night, waiting behind the half-closed door.

The house drowned in sleep. Mrs Cornwall's sleep audible. But always he put her away, unresponsive to her hands, her lips. She blamed the liquor that she could smell on him. It was in the Bible: Wine is a mocker, strong drink is raging. But it was in her that need raged and desire was mocked. In her narrow bed, once the centre of joy, now deserted, she grieved, now and again clutching at a little comfort from the thought that though on the fatal night she had not managed as well as she thought, since then she had managed better; outfacing policemen and magistrates, and disposing very cunningly of the stolen nightdress. Two sizeable portions of it were now neat patches on bed linen; the rest she had cut into tiny pieces, the size of a postage stamp, some of which were carried away by the river, running full and swift again after the rains, some trodden into the quagmire of Mr Brook's pigsty. As the second week aged it seemed to Rose that she had succeeded in diverting suspicion from herself and from him. And since they must suffer in the life hereafter, punishment in this world should not be unduly prolonged.

As it became obvious, within the house, that suspicion centred about Charlotte, John Vincent Cornwall also told himself that no real harm could come to her. He based this argument not on God's law, but on English justice. He also told himself that if, by some fantastic chance she should be in any real danger, he would confess all. There were moments when, either very drunk, or coldly sober, his sense of self-preservation failed and death seemed preferable to life as he was leading it now. It had been a hideous moment when Agnes, after a long session with Fowler, said, 'I am beginning to believe that he thinks Charlotte did it.'

Avoiding her eye, he said, 'Absolute nonsense. Why should she? She loved him. And how could she? She could hardly lift, leave alone carry . . .'

'Mad people sometimes do things they wouldn't and couldn't do in their right minds.'

'Charlotte isn't mad.'

'Why not? Her mother was. Towards the end she didn't know Sunday from Monday.'

'An entirely different thing. Emily suffered from softening of the brain. She was never violent.'

'Not in *your* presence! Several times with *me* she was very truculent. And strong. Look at the twins. They're cracked. Thomas is afflicted. Why should anybody expect Charlotte to be ordinary?'

'Is this the sort of thing you have been saying, to *him*?'

'Why not? And moreover if she did it I know why. I

scolded her that afternoon and she gave me one of her looks. Vicious ...'

And John Vincent Cornwall knew that it was useless to go to Fowler—as in similar circumstances he could have gone to Spender—and try to argue and explain. Not that there *was* any explanation of the missing nightdress. To Mr Cornwall that was as inexplicable as it was to everybody else—except Fowler who, as he put this and that together, thought he knew all.

Outside the house, since Fowler was not only busy but seen to be busy, an arrest was momentarily expected. And most people thought that the person to be arrested would be Mr Cornwall. By a process almost as mysterious as the operation of tom-toms in an African jungle, bits of genuine information spread alongside rumour. The magistrates had had a session with the Inspector and he had applied for an order to arrest which had been granted. However, even Sally Awkwright, in such close contact with Fowler, still giving him the best of food, superbly cooked, could not say when the arrest would be made. For that the village must depend upon its own observations. The arrival of extra police and a closed cab gave the signal. A crowd began to gather in the lane, and but for March, would have invaded the garden again. March had what he had lacked on the day of the inquest—strong police support—and no unauthorised foot trod his lawn or flowerbeds. So the watchers stood on the opposite side of the lane, where the steep bank formed a natural grandstand.

Finally a policeman, one of the strangers, came out of the house and walked to the cab, opened its door and stood waiting. Scarcely breathing, the crowd watched. Next, Inspector Fowler and Miss Charlotte. Nobody else. As they walked towards the cab the house door closed behind them. Carrie Whinney spoke for all when she said, 'Christ! Not Miss Charlotte!' There was a hissing groan. Few in the crowd had ever had much contact with Charlotte; those who had, people who lived in the lane, or kept shops in the village, liked her for the same reason that Catchpole had liked her mother. She had a pleasant way with her. People to whom she had never spoken, had seen her playing with Vincent, or taking walks with him. There were the old stories, largely spread by Maggie Simpson, that in earlier years she had been roughly treated. Added to all this was the fact that Doctor Fletcher had mentioned 'Considerable force'. Her naturally fragile look had been lately increased by grief, by lack of sleep, lack of appetite. 'She could hardly carry a cat, poor little soul, leave alone that great bouncing boy,' a woman said. Vincent had been displaced as an object of pity. And in the minds of most people, indignation against the assassin, known or unknown, had been transferred to Fowler.

His first awareness of this—since he was impervious to hisses and groans—came when he returned from Bereham after seeing Charlotte into gaol. After an unusually long wait for his evening meal, Sally Awkwright put before him a very small mutton chop, villainously overcooked and instead of the new potatoes and peas, straight from the garden, an old greyish potato, boiled almost to mush. There was no gravy, no mint sauce, no red-currant jelly; nor did the setting of the table indicate that there was pudding to come. Alongside the cruet was a plate bearing a small, old, cracked piece of cheese and two biscuits. Something else was lacking, too. She did not speak. He looked at her, genuinely puzzled and saw her lips set in a hard, grim line.

Poor old girl, something must have upset her; probably that fat husband of hers, a man so indolent that if a customer in the bar asked for anything that demanded his heaving himself to his feet, he would say, 'Just a minute. Maggeee!'

Fowler said, genially, 'Is this all I get?'

He wasn't local, but he was police and it didn't do for anybody who kept an inn to fall out with *them*. So caution warred with disgust and made her say, 'Yes. I'm sorry. I'm busy.'

Apparently she remained busy for the rest of his stay in Biddlesford. At that table he never again had a truly edible meal.

While Fowler gnawed his charred wood chop, food was being discussed in another place. Mr Fothergill, in this week, had not been exactly idle, but his activities had been limited. Now that Fowler had moved, he could move too and the first thing he did was to visit Charlotte. To him, the sophisticated London lawyer, her arrest had been as much of a shock as it had to the village people. Fowler had talked to him, willingly and amiably enough, but not openly, and always implying what was true enough, that between civilians, even lawyers, and police officers there was a great gulf which must be respected until some third person became to the lawyer *my client* and to the police officer *the accused.*

Now Charlotte had been sufficiently accused by Fowler for a warrant for her arrest to have been issued, and Mr Fothergill, jumping a little ahead of any formal instructions, regarded her as his client.

The room she occupied was a very small one, with one high window, barred. It contained a narrow bed, a kitchen table and a chair, a jug and ewer on a stand. Nothing else. No shameful, malodorous bucket in the corner—something which Mr Fothergill had dreaded. Until the moment when his uncle Hugo had said, so urgently that Mr Fothergill had feared that unless his wishes were complied with he might have a stroke, 'You must get down there, James,' Mr Fothergill had never had anything to do with crimes, criminals or gaols. The firm of Fothergill, Ampton and Fothergill, from cramped, shabby offices within ten minutes' walk of Mr Fothergill's home dealt with trusts, wills, estates. They were 'money lawyers'. But Mr Fothergill had read, widely if superficially, and knew a little about conditions in gaol which varied widely from place to place. He had dreaded that bucket. But, although it was not there, and although the place looked to be scrupulously clean, there was in this narrow room the faint, sad smell of a zoo cage. And on the table there was a coarse pottery dish containing a hunk of meat, bloody red where it was not fat, and some mashed potato into which the redness had seeped. A wound and the bandage. He hastily averted his eyes.

Charlotte said, 'In these cages the animals are fed at five o'clock, Mr Fothergill. Isn't it disgusting? I will put it away.' She lifted the plate and set it on the floor.

'In the circumstances,' he said, 'food from outside can be sent in to you. I will arrange for this to be done at once. From the Rose and Crown where I am staying.'

She said, 'That is very kind. But truly, Mr Fothergill, I am not often hungry now.' She linked her fingers, looked down at them and then up, into his face. 'What is going to happen to me now? Can you tell me that?'

He could and he did. He tried to speak comfortingly; a magistrates' court—it might be a pure formality, and he would see to it that she should be, in that court, defended by the best obtainable barrister. She listened and seemed to understand the difference between a solicitor and a barrister, and when he had explained she said, 'Thank you, Mr Fothergill. But the cleverest barrister in the world could do little for me unless the man in the hall could be found. I know,' she said, and the delicate hands, usually so passive, linked and wrestled, 'nobody believes that there was a man. Nobody else saw him and everybody thinks I made him up as an excuse for not crossing the landing and sending Nellie down to fetch that glass of water. But I saw him. He was there. He got in somehow, the same way he did on that night .. And he came back and he stole my nightdress, so that I should be blamed. As I have been, since nobody believes me.'

'I am inclined to,' Mr Fothergill said, trusting his instinct. 'What was he like? Did you see him clearly enough to describe him, Miss Charlotte?'

'Nobody else bothered to ask me that. He was not very tall, thickset though. He wore glasses, and a green suit. Oh yes, and he had a notebook, at least something that looked to me like a notebook, in his hand.'

Mr Fothergill found himself obliged to say, though he said it gently, 'The maid, Nellie, absolutely denies admitting anyone to the house that morning.'

She said in a voice which, coming from an older person and speaking on a lighter subject, would have been called 'dry', 'Nobody *admitted* the murderer either, Mr Fothergill.'

'So far as we know,' he said, cautiously.

'I know exactly what happened. Papa was followed home, by a would-be thief. The house is not locked until dusk. When Papa locked up the thief was already in the house; in the old laundry, I should think. Nobody ever went there. Then something went wrong ... At least, Vincent woke. It may well be that for that some blame attaches to me.' She lifted her hands and pressed them to her head. 'I taught him too many letters; I took him for a walk in the heat; I let him eat a *whole* chocolate bar. And it was because of me that Mrs Cornwall was angry and spoke crossly to him. He was always a light sleeper and sometimes woke, screaming. I think the events of the day combined ... Vincent woke and the man did what he did.' Her voice faltered, but she pressed on. 'That man was no ordinary thief. He had sense enough to re-enter the house and bolt the door. He waited in the laundry again, until Nellie opened up in the morning. Then he walked out. And he did not go far, Mr Fothergill. He was a fairly local man. By Sunday at the latest, he knew that Vincent had been ... been found. So he did the same thing again and on Monday stole my nightdress to make it look as though I ... And he succeeded! I tried to explain this to Inspector Fowler. He seemed almost ... amused. He thought I had invented it all. Do you?'

It left a good deal unexplained; the piece of blue ribbon found with the body, for one thing: but for a girl of sixteen, in a state of distress, it was a piece of close, rational reasoning. Mr Fothergill realised, with a sense of shock that, but for his instinct, he, like Fowler, might easily have found it too glib, too explicit. As it was he could only think that at least at the magistrates' hearing she would have no opportunity to expound theories and display a liveliness of mind which could well be mistaken for cunning. At the back of his mind, as he thought these things, that extra sense was at work and he did not answer her question. Instead he asked one.

'You say the man in the hall wore a green suit, Miss Charlotte?'

She said, 'Yes. That is one thing I can be sure of. It was green.'

A green suit, spectacles and a notebook spelt out *reporter* to Mr Fothergill, now that he came to think about it. An ordinary man might wear green tweed when shooting, wishing to merge into the background of greenery; but reporters were not ordinary men; they were a race apart. They gloried in their freedom from ordinary conventions, they had no respect for privacy. Assume then, for a moment, a reporter ...

Accustomed to examine any assumption with criticism—even his own—Mr Fothergill's mind checked. The man was seen on the morning of the inquest, about fifty hours after the discovery of the body, and one of the intervening days had been a Sunday. Did that allow time for the news to have reached London? A local man then.

He said, with almost fatherly solicitude, 'Miss Charlotte, you find yourself in a very unpleasant position, but you must try not to worry. Try to eat and sleep properly. And I think ... some occupation ...' His voice trailed off somewhat vaguely. How did young ladies of sixteen occupy themselves? 'Do you care for reading?'

'Very much.'

'Then I will see to it that you are supplied with reading matter. And,' he glanced at the bed, 'any small comfort that is allowed. And I shall use my best endeavour to trace the man in the green suit. I may not see you tomorrow, as I am obliged to go to London, but I shall look in on Friday and hope to find you well.'

Fortunately for Mr Fothergill all his errands could be performed in a small area. Having had a word with the governor of the gaol, he went to his inn and ordered meals to be taken to Miss Cornwall, and then found, not a bookshop exactly, but a newsagent's and tobacconist's which ran a small lending library from which he ordered three books, 'of a light, entertaining nature, suitable for a young lady', to be delivered. The charge was twopence a volume for a week, and Mr Fothergill paid another sixpence to ensure their delivery that evening. He then moved to the office of the *Bereham Free Press*. A pimply youth whose main duty, apart from sweeping up occasionally, was to accept and sort advertisements and announcements, had on this early Wednesday evening just cleared the spikes on which he filed such orders. The dead-line was five o'clock on Wednesday, and as he rose, lackadaisically, the boy reflected that if this toff had anything to insert this week, he'd missed the boat.

'I wish to speak to your editor.'

To the boy a mythical figure; it was eight years since the owner and editor of the paper had set foot in these premises. From his half-invalid seclusion of his home on the town's outskirts he maintained, however, tight control of his business, annoying the boy by invariably refusing a rise in his wretched pay, and infuriating Mr Sawyer, who did all the work, by blue-pencilling his editorials. 'Dear me, Sawyer, this would never do. It might lose us an advertisement.'

'You'd better see Mr Sawyer first, sir,' the boy said. He opened a hatch and called, 'Somebody to see you, Mr Sawyer.' Mr. Sawyer used an uncouth word and emerged from a door alongside the hatch.

Short, thickset, wearing a green suit, wearing spectacles.

'I think,' said Mr Fothergill, concealing his satisfaction, his near-awe, his surprise, 'that it is you, Mr Sawyer, whom I wish to see.'

In a cramped and incredibly cluttered little office Mr Sawyer said, with jaunty pride, 'Yes, I was there. First on the spot. Had to go out to cover the inquest and thought I might as well take a look round. Give the readers a bit of background. They like that.'

'Who admitted you to the house?'

Mr Sawyer laughed. 'Admitted! Me! They'd as soon admit a tramp. Of course it was different when the *big* boys were around, specially the chap from *The Times* . . No, I just walked in. Had a good look round. I suppose you didn't see my report. Headline: *Mansion Murder*, that's another thing readers like, a bit of alliteration. I described the chandeliers, hall and drawing room; Turkey carpet on the stairs, marble fireplaces, white in the drawing room, black in the dining room . . . As a matter of fact,' a glint of false modesty, 'it was *my* description the *Daily Banner* used, practically word for word. I've got a kind of arrangement with them, anything of more than local interest—fr'instance, if it *had* been cholera with the gypsies—I send a telegram. I'd already done that, of course, soon as I heard myself. Full report was too long for that, it had to go by post and as I say, they used it, chandeliers and all.'

It never did to show impatience. Mr Fothergill listened and then slipped in his vital question.

'Did you see anyone, Mr Sawyer?'

'Not at first. I was back in the hall, wondering how much further I could go without being booted. I'd have risked the stairs I *think*, but I could hear a voice now and again. Upstairs, away to the right. Then a young lady—I didn't know who she was *then*, of course, this was *before* the inquest, and to tell you the truth I don't know now whether it was Miss Adelaide or Miss Victoria—came on the landing and went up the top stairs; and she'd no sooner gone up than Miss Charlotte—of course I didn't know who she was, either, but I do now—came down and stood at the bottom of the top stairs and sort of leaned against the wall and spoke to somebody I couldn't see, again out of view to the right. I had a kind of idea that she'd spotted me, as a matter of fact. So I faded into the shade of the grandfather clock. And quick! I couldn't get to the door and outside without showing myself, full view. And I couldn't move while she stood there. So I watched.'

'And then what happened, Mr Sawyer?' Mr Fothergill spoke calmly, though his heart had quickened and his breath shortened a little.

'Well, she stood there, and whoever she'd spoken to—it was the maid actually—came into view and crossed the landing and vanished. I've got the hang of the lay-out now, and I'd say she went down the kitchen stairs. Anyway she was back in no time

125

at all, with a glass of water. She handed it to Miss Charlotte and then they both went up the top stairs.'

'In what order?'

'Miss Charlotte first; the maid behind her.'

'While the maid was away, did Miss Charlotte move at all?'

'Not an inch. If she had, I'd have moved, too. To tell you the truth, the way she leaned against the wall and held the banister, she looked a bit ill. She didn't manage the stairs very well, either. The maid seemed to be holding her a bit.'

'So they went upstairs. What did you do then, Mr Sawyer?'

'Well . . .' Mr Sawyer hesitated; jauntiness and self-satisfaction fell away, leaving a professional, almost apologetic for his professionalism. 'This may sound daft to you. But I'd got so far . . . The point is . . . well, I know they say morbid curiosity, but it stuck in my mind that the poor little boy would be laid out in one of the bedrooms and if my luck held, as it had done, I might just . . . So instead of making for the door *then*, I waited a bit; three, four minutes . . . It's Mr Rayner—owner and editor—who'd mind if there was any sort of rumpus, if you understand me; he's old, he's old-fashioned. It was thinking of him made me cautious. So I waited. And then, before I'd made up my mind to risk it, the washerwoman and her daughter were on the landing and went out of sight, as I told you, to the right, and came back with the laundry basket. And they'd no sooner gone than Mr Cornwall was on the stairs, coming down.'

'Did he see you?'

'No fear! He went into the library. And by that time I had realised that between getting a possible view of the corpse and a place at the inquest I must choose the inquest. So as soon as the coast was clear I let myself out as I'd let myself in.'

Mr Fothergill drew a long deep breath.

'Mr Sawyer, would you be prepared to swear, *on oath*, that while the maid was away, fetching a glass of water, Miss Charlotte did not move from the foot of the stairs? And that, having retired with her glass of water, she did not come down again until the washerwomen removed the basket?'

'Isn't that just what I've been saying?' Mr Sawyer asked, using the patient gritty voice which Mr Rayner knew so well. 'That's the truth, as I saw it with my own eyes.'

Mr Fothergill drew a long, deep breath and said, 'Thank you, Mr Sawyer,' very heartily, as he entertained an uncharacteristic thought—That's spiked Fowler's gun! Later, in the slow train to London he warned himself against premature jubilation. Mr Sawyer's story had reeled out, glib and whole; would it stand up to cross-examination? To a re-enactment of the scene? Exactly how clear a view was possible to someone, himself hiding, from the shelter afforded by the grandfather clock?

'It's about the worst way it could have gone, James,' Hugo Ampton said. 'Woman in the case always attracts a lot of attention. Is she pretty?'

'I don't know.'

'Don't be so damned silly.' The old man vented his anger with events upon his nephew. 'Don't tell me you've reached your age without knowing whether a gel is pretty or not. If she is the publicity will be trebled.'

'She's not pretty in *that* way. In fact it's rather difficult to describe her. Beautiful hair, a kind of auburn colour; beautiful eyes, smoky grey. That's about all, but there's a . . . a grace. And great dignity, for one so young and rather small.'

From under thick, frosted eyebrows the old man shot a sharp look.

'Well, it's happened and must be faced. And as I said— Edison. Not a first-class legal brain, but a man who can move himself to tears has no need for great acumen. If your Mr Sawyer can swear that he did not sneeze and bury his face in his handkerchief, or stoop to tie a shoe-lace . . . then that knocks hell out of Fowler's nightdress theory. But it's all a great pity. And this I must say, James. If you had investigated your Mr Sawyer earlier the arrest might never have been made. Fowler seems to me to be slipping, but he is not yet so senile.'

'That is easily said,' Mr Fothergill retorted with some spirit. 'I have been occupying a very anomalous position. Until Fowler showed his hand . . . I first heard of Mr Sawyer's existence at precisely half past five this afternoon. I had his statement well within the hour.'

'Yes, yes, I know. Still it is all a great pity. Even if Edison does have the magistrates blubbering, the harm is done.'

'To the poor girl, yes. A most unhappy experience in what from what I gather has not been a very happy life. So far. But . . . Well, this may sound a strange thing to say, but she has

127

great character. This afternoon, in circumstances where most young women would have been hysterical, or lachrymose, she first essayed a little joke and then gave me a completely calm and reasonable explanation of the crime. As she saw it, of course. Quite obviously, in associating the man Sawyer with the murderer, she was mistaken, but she could not know that. And I have been thinking . . . You know, Uncle Hugo, if the magistrates decide in her favour, as I hope and pray they will, the main mystery, the crime itself, the abstraction of the night-dress, remain unsolved.'

'I pray so.'

Mr Fothergill had had no dinner; he had accepted a glass of brandy and this, working on an empty stomach, gave him Dutch courage enough to ask, 'Why? Don't you want to see justice done? A child was killed, Uncle Hugo. Fowler, the best man, at least supposedly the best man, has made what I believe to be an error and hope will be proved to be. What I should like to know is why you were interested in the first place, why you sent me there, told me to stay there, why in fact,' said Mr Fothergill, his hackles all abristle, sensitive as antennae, 'you want John Vincent Cornwall *protected*.'

The ruddy colour in the old man's face receded, leaving his face the colour of unbleached linen, streaked with red veins. For a second or two James Fothergill feared that he had pro-voked the fit, the stroke, the inward collapse which overtook all old men, sooner or later. But Hugo Ampton rallied and said, 'That, my boy, I can't tell you. So you will never know. It was a sacred trust. I gave my word, fifty years ago when the boy was in swaddling clothes. I said: *So long as I live, no harm shall come to him*. And so far I have kept my word. And intend to keep it.'

'Even if . . . even if he were the guilty person?'

'Have you the slightest evidence, James, for making such a postulation? It is the equivalent of my saying to you: If I were a pretty girl with four hundred a year, would you marry me? Could you answer such a hypothetical question? No. And I can only answer yours—pointing out, by the way, that neither Spender nor Fowler ever even hinted at it—by saying: Yes! If John Vincent Cornwall were guilty, I should still feel it my bounden duty to protect him to the best of my ability.'

'You amaze me,' James Fothergill said.

'From time to time I amaze myself, James. I never even liked

128

him. But I gave my word and I tell you frankly that if he were now where his daughter is I should be talking about accident, provocation, even insanity. Or, more likely, I should be organising his escape from the country. There are no lengths . . .' He broke off for a moment and brooded. 'A sacred trust is a sacred trust. Not that he hasn't been a damned nuisance to me all along; feckless, reckless, profligate. He was comfortably provided for, spent money like water, married a wife with a bit of money, lost her and married a penniless governess. And now this. Oh dear, dear.'

'Is he any kin to you . . . to us?'

'No, he is *not*,' Hugo Ampton said vehemently. 'If he'd been my second cousin's second cousin I should have walloped some sense into him long ago. Now, short of using thumbscrews, James, you'll get nothing else from me, so stop trying.'

'I'll see Edison in the morning,' Mr Fothergill said.

'I'll see him. He owes me a good turn or two.'

Mr Fothergill had intended to spend the night in his own bed, but now, deprived of any excuse for staying in London, he felt the pull of Bereham, of one small cell in Bereham, growing stronger and stronger; so he went to his own house and ate a makeshift meal while his man packed him some more clothes and then he rode back to Suffolk on the earliest, worst train of all, the one that stopped to deliver mail and daily papers at every station.

4

'MAY I JUST SPEAK TO PAPA?' CHARLOTTE ASKED, AS ES-
corted by the governor, she entered the crowded Guildhall, now
transformed into a courtroom.

'You may indeed. Come back to *this* table.'

She crossed to the one where Papa sat, with Mr Fothergill
and Mr Edison.

She had not seen Papa for ten days. He had once come, Mr
Fothergill had told her, but inside the gaol had broken down
and been unable to complete the visit. Now she thought that he
looked extremely ill, worse even than when she last saw him,
his face fallen away into greyish folds, semi-circular lines as
definite as scars under his eyes and much more white in his
hair. Poor Papa, to have lost one child in such a cruel way, and
now to be so worried about another. She kissed him. His face,
for all its collapse, felt curiously hard, almost mummified. She
said, 'Papa, you must not worry about me. I did not do it, so I
shall be all right.' She went back and sat at the table beside the
governor. From there she could see that Papa had put his stony
face in his hands and for the first time it occurred to her to
wonder whether Inspector Fowler had talked him into believing in her guilt. Fowler seemed so certain, had produced such a
closely-knit story that sometimes it was almost enough to make
one doubt oneself. She sat very straight and folded her black-
gloved hands in her lap and thought—I must remain calm. It
will soon be over, and all the stories, not only the Inspector's,
will be heard.

There were three stories which could not be shaken. Linked together they made a sequence as close-knit as Fowler's, and directly contradictory to it. Mrs Lark was absolutely sure that she had seen three nightgowns in the prisoner's room; two completely clean, one showing nothing but signs of a week's ordinary wear. Nellie was equally positive that she had collected and packed four nightgowns, that she had tucked the tablecloth well over the basket; that she had taken less than a minute to fetch the glass of water and, returning with it, had found Miss Charlotte exactly where she left her and had then followed her upstairs. Nellie was the only person who seemed still to regard Charlotte as a person. Everybody else said *the prisoner*, Nellie never used the term. Mr Sawyer's story, and he was not to be budged, either, confirmed Nellie's. Yes, he admitted, he was behind the clock, but his view was not impeded, though anybody looking down from above could not have seen him, the top of the clock would have been in their way. No, he had not for so long as a single second taken his gaze away from the upper landing.

Charlotte listened to it all and thought that it was rather like a merry-go-round; one of those which in another world, another age, had spent an evening on the common; the little wooden horses, white, black, brown, dappled, going round and round and up and down as the man turned a crank which also activated a hurdy-gurdy organ. Question and answer. Face after face. The face, rounder and redder, of a maid named Maggie, one of the many who had not stayed long; and who now, saying nothing but what had been the truth, seemed to have gone over to the enemy. The implication was obvious; Mrs Cornwall had been so cruel to the prisoner that hatred, and a desire to be avenged had resulted. And that was offset by Mrs Fiske from the shop. 'The prisoner never came in without buying him a chocolate bar. Often with her last penny.' Fancy Mrs Fiske noticing that!

But the real jolt came when Lilian Headstone was called. Even Charlotte forgot for a moment to maintain composure. Lilian, so gay, so fortunate, the apple of her widowed mother's eye, dragged into this!

The jolt that Lilian administered to Charlotte was as nothing compared with the jolt her story gave Fowler.

Lilian knew that her mother had never approved of her friendship with Charlotte; there were so many other nice girls

131

at Miss Barton's, girls who could return hospitality, girls with elder brothers. Lilian knew that on Fowler's first visit she had displeased her mother by her attitude; and after all, they had to live together. So she had recanted. She had shrugged, 'All right; have it your own way.'

Now, in this solemn place, Lilian recanted again. No, she had never once heard the prisoner express any animosity against her stepmother. And Yes, the prisoner had doted upon her little half-brother, always had his portrait standing by her bed, together with that of her own mother; had spent a lot of time making a jigsaw puzzle for him, pasting a picture on cardboard and cutting it into small pieces.

The Cornwall case was now of national interest and all the big daily papers were represented, either directly or indirectly. One reporter wrote that Inspector Fowler 'roared for the nightdress, as Othello for the handkerchief'. And as the hot day dragged on it became more and more obvious that apart from that missing garment there was nothing to connect Charlotte, more specifically than anyone else in the house, with the crime. The mystery remained, but when Mr Edison, well-briefed by Mr Fothergill, had finished with Nellie, the idea of an intruder lurking in the old laundry had been fairly firmly implanted in everyone's mind.

The roundabout stopped at last and Mr Edison began his final speech with a quiet statement. 'We are not here to enquire into the fate of a garment, lost in the wash.' He made it sound such an ordinary occurrence, as indeed it was. A thing that almost everyone had experienced at some time: from Sir Richard Barlay who could remember losing a shirt because a laundry maid had burned it with a too-hot iron and afraid to confess, had hidden it, to the humblest man in the hall whose wife, tipping suds into the river, had sent one of his socks on its way to the sea.

Lost in the wash. Mr Edison was holding to two of his self-made rules. You began with something that everyone could *understand* and ended with something everyone could *feel*. With tears in his eyes and in his voice, he denounced the error which had placed an innocent young girl in such a position, a position which might well have disastrous results upon her future. He begged the magistrates not to compound that error, but to return her to her home, to the family from which she should never have been torn. When he sat down and un-

132

ashamedly mopped his eyes, many others mopped theirs, or blinked rapidly.

The magistrates retired to the little room behind the platform, used in happier occasions for the making of tea and the buttering of buns. They were soon back with a verdict which pleased everybody but the prosecution, and Mr Edison and Mr Fowler who recognised it as a compromise. There was insufficient evidence to justify committing Charlotte Cornwall to the Assizes; but her father, John Vincent Cornwall, must enter into a bond to produce her for trial should any further evidence be forthcoming, or forfeit three hundred pounds.

To the crowd this was understood to be acquittal and they gave noisy evidence of their approval. Public indignation against Fowler took the form of a shower of stones and horse-dung as he drove away; and then, more hurtfully, in angry letters to the Press.

Four hundred solid citizens demanded his instant dismissal. He forestalled that by tendering his resignation. He had, he said, always wanted to farm and it would be silly to leave it too late. In fact, for him it was already too late. Mary Tudor, Queen of England, told that Calais was lost, remarked that when she died the word *Calais* would be found written on her heart. Fowler could have said the same of *Charlotte Cornwall*. More than his failure, more than the obloquy heaped upon him was the ridicule. He was dead within a year.

Thirty-four ladies expressed their sympathy for Charlotte by sending her nightdresses, all very beautiful and not a blue ribbon on any of them. Actually haberdashers noted a slump in the sale of blue ribbon.

Nineteen men wrote and made her offers of marriage.

And the day came when she said to Papa, with her slightly crooked, sad smile, 'Perhaps I should have accepted the least crazy-sounding one. Nobody else seems to want me.'

Not St Mark's, a polite rejection. Neither of the two hospitals that operated similar training schemes. Not even the three orphanages, short of staff, short of funds, which Mrs Greenfield had suggested. Each rebuff was like another blow on a bruise; it said: We do not think that you are to be trusted with children! Unfair, unfair. But you could not blame the people.

When she made her remark about nobody wanting her, her father, grappling bemusedly and drunkenly with his own problems, said, 'Charlie, why worry? You've got a home. And you mustn't mind Agnes. Women in her condition get queer ideas. Take no notice. It'll blow over.'

For him the worst seemed to have blown over. After the infallible Fowler's stupendous failure, interest in the case seemed to have died. With every day, with every drink, Vincent receded into the past, a shallow-rooted love dwindled and died. But he had to live with Agnes. And with Rose. Rose, coaxing, urgent. Once, aware of what he owed her, he tried. A dismal failure; impotent as a mule. And from her, coarse daughter of the soil, no flicker of understanding, no memory of the last time; no idea that for him the nursery was a haunted place.

She said, 'It's the drink. Give that up and you'd be all right again.' He knew, only too well, that with her he would never be all right again.

He had another bother, too. He would have liked to apply to the Board of Education for a transfer but was doubtful of the wisdom of drawing attention to himself. Except in the church-yard nobody had ever accused him, and it now seemed possible that nobody ever would, but he knew how many people felt, and he dreaded the opening of the new term when he would have to emerge into the world again and face the unspoken doubt in the eyes of school-teachers, the stares and the sniggers of the mannerless young. He wished with his whole heart that he could get away from it all, away from the house that he hated, away from Rose with her hungry, reproachful look; away from Agnes who insisted on saying, again and again, 'If she didn't do it, why did they arrest her?' and who had forbidden Charlotte to go near the nursery, ever.

Soon after the end of the August vacation, still called by its rural name—*the Harvest Holiday*—toothache added itself to Charlotte's other miseries. None of the old, tried, domestic remedies served. The tooth must be extracted. Mr Cornwall who knew that he must resume his duties somewhere, and soon, said that he would make a visit to a school in Bereham that afternoon, and take her to the dentist.

This would entail their being alone together for the duration of the drive and John Vincent Cornwall had not been at ease with his daughter since the tragedy. Her vast, unfeigned grief had reproached him, even in those early days of bereavement when he shared it. He was now aware that he had ruined her life.

134

On this afternoon Mr Cornwall drove Romper, the friskier of his two horses and livelier than usual from lack of exercise, so he was able to concentrate on driving as an excuse for not talking much. Charlotte held her aching jaw and reflected that physical pain was a kind of antidote to mental woe; in the end one just *became* a toothache. When Romper steadied down, Mr Cornwall did break silence.

'What I should really like to do, Charlie, is to send you abroad for a bit. But frankly I can't afford it. Also, I'm not sure about this ridiculous bond. There might be difficulties about your leaving the country.'

'Something will turn up, Papa. Don't worry.'

A scheme of a kind was already forming in her mind and once she was rid of this tooth, she intended to give it serious thought. Mr Fothergill had taken leave of her very kindly, taking the hand she offered in both his and looking into her eyes with great earnestness.

'If there is ever anything I can do for you, Miss Charlotte, in any way at all, I beg you, let me know. I take my holiday in August and shall be in Scotland, but this address will always find me.' It was his home address. 'And when you come to London'—this was before St Mark's refused her—'please get in touch with me. I should be delighted to show you London . . . take you to a theatre, or a concert.'

She had thanked him warmly and smiled and he had thought how, given a little happiness, she would be charming; and how pleasant it would be to contribute to that happiness.

She intended to write to him, her only contact in the wider world and ask his assistance in finding employment of some kind. In a shop perhaps, or as a maid.

Outside the dentist's, Papa reined in, and then, succumbing weakly to the wish to postpone facing his own ordeal as long as possible, asked, 'Would you like me to come in with you?'

'Oh, no, Papa, thank you. Not unless you could have it out for me.' There was just a hint there of something he had always liked about her.

'I'm sorry I can't, Charlie! All right then, I'll put the gig into the Rose and Crown. You wait for me there. I shan't be long.'

'I have several errands.'

Parsimonious as they were, the twins could not ignore the fact that their mourning clothes were very makeshift and

135

would, in any case, one day need to be replaced by half-mourning; they needed a few little samples of cloth to brood over, and the latest edition of *Style and Fashion*, excellent value for fourpence. Nellie wanted stockings, six handkerchiefs and a bottle of scent. Even Cook had a commission, some grey knitting wool with which to refoot some of her stockings, so much mended that she attributed, quite rightly, some of her foot discomfort to them.

Bereham was fortunate in having a proper dentist. He had come some years ago and hired a small portion of the ground floor of a widow's house; a passage, which served as waiting room, and a disused scullery which became his surgery. He advertised 'swift, painless extractions'; the first adjective was apt, he could whip out a tooth in two seconds, the second was less applicable; as his landlady said, 'If you don't hurt them, Mr O'Bryan, why do they shriek so loud?' At a shilling an extraction, and with no competitor nearer than Bywater, he had prospered, but his patients still waited on a wooden bench along one side of the dismal passage, the latest comer taking the space nearest the door, and everybody moving up one place as those waiting at the far end accepted the invitation, 'Next please.' Once dealt with, his patients were ejected through another door; those waiting were not discouraged by seeing others emerge looking pallid, pressing blood-stained handkerchiefs to their mouths.

Charlotte took her place at the end of a fairly full bench, and had moved up three times when the door opened and a woman came in, holding the hand of a little boy with a swollen face. She looked at Charlotte, stiffened, tightened her mouth so that it seemed to be lipless, and then took the place at the very end of the bench. The kindly old woman who had explained to Charlotte the ritual of moving along, now explained it again.

'You could lose your turn if somebody came and took them places.'

'I don't want to sit next to a murderess.'

The horrible word rang out. Charlotte began to tremble inwardly, smitten by a feeling of something she had not experienced when she was arrested, or when she made her appearance before the magistrates.

'That's Charlotte Cornwall, that is,' said the mother, making protective gestures towards her child. As though I were a wolf, Charlotte thought.

And as though she were a wolf, or a rabid dog, they all began to talk as if she could not understand. A big man, a farmer by the look of him, said, 'Come, come, Missus. You marn't say that. They let her off.'

Hubbub broke out. Somebody said, 'It wasn't her. We know who it was.' Somebody said, 'What about that night-gown. We never heard the last of that, did we?' Somebody said, 'There's no smoke without fire.'

Inside his scullery-surgery the dentist heard the noise. He said, 'Rinse,' and flung a rotted, long-fanged bicuspid into the bucket, and, forceps in hand, opened the door into the passage. Occasionally somebody did try to dodge the strict rule about order of precedence and there was noise, like this, which he must quell.

'What is going on here?' he asked sternly.

The farmer, her friend, took Charlotte by the arm and said, 'You'd best take this young lady next.'

Mr O'Bryan hesitated. He took the man to be Charlotte's father, and he was a big man, looking very belligerent. There was a drill for this, too.

'By appointment?'

'Yes,' the farmer said, and gave Charlotte a little push.

'Very well.'

So far as the dentist knew she was out of line, and looked to be the kind of young woman who would shriek, or, worse still, need the administration of smelling salts, a waste of time. So he dealt with her swiftly, ungently.

He said, 'Rinse,' and she pretended. The half-empty glass had red marks around its rim. Mr O'Bryan only gave it a rub and a re-fill at about every sixth patient.

'That-will-be-a-shilling-and-you-go-out-by-that-door,' he said, thankful that she had not screamed, or fainted. Then she surprised him. She said, 'Thank you very much. It feels better already.' That was true. It still hurt, but in a different way.

He was unused to thanks and could not be gracious.

'It was a nasty abscess. Swill it out well with hot salt water,' he said.

Charlotte went into the lane on to which the dentist's rear exit gave and leaned against a fence. In the ordinary way she would have mopped herself up—she had brought three hand-kerchiefs and gone about her errands. There was no shame in having had a tooth extracted. But the scene in the waiting

137

passage had shattered her. In any shop—indeed in any place—somebody might say, *That is Charlotte Cornwall, that is*. Leaving all her errands undone she walked back to the Rose and Crown, and unable to face the room set apart for females awaiting their menfolk, sat down on an upturned barrel in the yard. Mopping away, not only at the blood but at the greeny-yellowy pus which the extraction had released, she knew that there must be another question for Mr Fothergill. What were the legal procedures for changing one's name? Did it cost anything?

Mr Cornwall, his horse stabled, his gig accommodated, had gone into the bar of The Rose and Crown and given himself a quick bracer, two double brandies.

It was his misfortune to have chosen to make his first issue into his professional and public life at the school ruled by David Williams, a lifelong abstainer from spiritous liquors. In a poor quarter of Bereham, where the men drank because they were hopeless—and thus increased the hopelessness of their condition, Mr Williams had laboured and contrived and achieved results. Not without a lot of hard labour and cost to himself. More than once, many times in fact, he had provided some little barefoot boy with a pair of boots, begged or bought, and the boots had been pawned for the miserable twopence or so which would provide the boy's father with a pint of beer. Furiously, Mr Williams would buy other boots, or redeem those pledged. He formed a Temperance Society which met on Tuesday evenings and all but the most stupid boy in his school knew that if he wished to keep on Mr Williams' sunny side, enjoy the privilege of being a monitor, get into the cricket team or have a good testimonial when he left, he must join the society and profess a horror of strong drink.

Into this atmosphere Mr Cornwall walked, reeking of brandy.

Mr Williams thought—I shall write to the Board and complain, it is not right, so it is not, for those who are set above us and full of criticisms, to give such a bad example.

Mr Williams was a man who kept his promises, even those he made to himself. And he wrote with his natural Welsh fluency . . .

Not wishing to distress Papa, Charlotte did not mention the incident in the waiting room. She simply reported that the extraction had not hurt much. The homeward drive was made in silence. John Vincent Cornwall was thinking again of a transfer. He had misread the expression of shocked disgust in Mr Williams' eyes and misinterpreted his changed manner. If, in every school he entered . . . Quite intolerable!

When they reached home they entered by the kitchen door and Mr Cornwall went straight to the library and the brandy while Charlotte paused to explain her failure to do the errands: 'I didn't feel like going into shops.' Nellie and Cook understood. Would Addie and Vikky? Not that it mattered. Everything was so horrible, a few complaints could hardly make it worse.

As she reached the top landing, Thomas, who had obviously been waiting for her, emerged from his room. He had now been a pupil-teacher for four days and learned that his fear and dread of the job in no way measured up to the reality. Charlotte braced herself to listen once again to his account of how awful it was, how awful Mr Macferson was, how awful, collectively and individually, the children were. But this afternoon instead of saying, 'Oh Charlie, I can't bear it,' Thomas said, 'Mr Greenfield came into the school this afternoon and gave me this to give to you. From Mrs Greenfield.'

It was quite a thick packet.

'Let's see what it is,' Charlotte said.

It was a thick, glossy brochure. 'Homelands,' it announced. 'The School that is also a Home.' There was also a letter in Mrs Greenfield's meticulous copperplate hand. It was quite a long letter, but Charlotte perused it in a flash. Then she said, breathlessly, 'Oh Thomas! Isn't it marvellous? Mrs Greenfield has found a place for me. With a distant relative of hers. I shall be a pupil-teacher too, helping with the little ones in the morning and having lessons with the older girls in the afternoon. That is, Mrs Greenfield says, if Papa consents. I am sure he will.'

'It sounds a nice place,' said Thomas who, while Charlotte had read the letter, had idly looked through the brochure which promised proximity to the sea, spacious grounds, individual tuition when needed, modern sanitation, shared bedrooms but no dormitories. Music and French were extras. Holidays were observed, but provided for when the real home was out of reach. The brochure had been aimed at a certain audience, even to the mention of the bracing east-coast air. 'A bit different from my place,' Thomas said grudgingly. Then his better nature took the upper hand and he said, 'I'm glad for you, Charlie. But I'm going to miss you. I shall be alone now. Who can I talk to?'

To whom shall I make my complaints? Upon whom shall I lean for the comfort and cheer?

Charlotte said, 'In a year you'll be at the Pupil Teacher Centre. You'll make friends there, Thomas. And after that, Training College. Then, I tell you what, you get a headship in a nice little country school and I'll come and keep house for you until you marry.'

With a flash of precognition Thomas said, 'I never shall.' But, as usual, Charlotte had made him feel better, setting a term, a year, as a limit to his present misery, and holding out some hope for the future which he hoped would take a different shape from that which she had outlined. The idea of being another Mr Macferson in another Biddlesford was utterly repulsive. Still, Charlie meant well, and she had somehow reminded him that there was a future, a long, forward-reaching time in which almost anything could happen.

He said, 'I do hope you'll be happy, Charlie.'

'I think I shall, thank you, Thomas.'

And it augured well. Mrs Greenfield wrote that her cousin by marriage, Mrs Armitage, to whom the school belonged, had been 'fully informed'. (Mr Greenfield had insisted upon that. He had met Viola Armitage once and had not been much taken with her, but when his wife, after the second orphanage had professed itself able to function without Charlotte Cornwall's services, had said, 'What about Viola?' he had said, 'It would be necessary to be absolutely honest with Viola, my dear.' It was necessary to be honest even with those one faintly disliked. So Mrs Greenfield had been honest. And her cousin by marriage had been honest too, writing back that she was fully prepared to offer a home to the poor child, but she did think that a change of name was advisable).

Papa, tackled at just the right moment, almost genial, said, 'No difficulty. There's no law against using any name you like. I could write you a cheque, Charlie, made out to Little Miss Moffat, and if you endorsed it thus it would be valid.'

'Then I think I shall choose *Burns*, Papa. Mamma's maiden name.'

PART
TWO

I

IN THE MELLOW, LINGERING LIGHT OF A SEPTEMBER afternoon, Homelands seemed to fulfil the promises of the brochure. Only the narrow lane and a few low bushes separated it from the beach. The drive, lined with laurels and rhododendrons, hinted at spacious grounds, and the house itself was imposing, red-brick with grey stone facings, several gables, two little turrets, balconies in front of french windows on the upper floor. It had been built twenty-six years earlier by a very rich brewer whose delicate wife had briefly benefited from a stay in the bracing east-coast air at Lowestoft. There had been no time to test whether permanent residence in the area could halt her decline. She died just as it was completed. He had never wanted to see it again. It was not everybody's house; too large, too much exposed, rather more than half a mile from the village of Gorston-on-Sea, three miles from Lowestoft. It had stood empty, its price cheapening, a godsent bargain, almost a gift to Mrs Greenfield's cousin by marriage when she came along looking for a suitable property in which to establish her school.

Inland it had been a warm day, but here the wind, straight off the sea, blew chilly and strong. It lifted Charlotte's hat as she stepped from the cab which had brought her from Lowestoft.

The driver said, 'Two shillings, miss.' He had delivered young females of all ages upward of six at this imposing doorway, and could not decide whether this passenger was pupil or teacher. Rather small and young for a teacher, but with a manner that suggested that she might be older than she looked. Not much luggage, he noted, carrying the two bags, neither of them heavy, to the step. When she paid the fare, with sixpence added, she said, 'Thank you very much,' and gave him what he thought a very sweet smile. Something made him say, 'I hope you'll be happy here, miss.'

Charlotte thought—If only you knew. I am prepared to be happy anywhere. I am beginning a new life; with a new name. I must remember to answer to my new name.

She rang the bell and the door was opened by a trim parlourmaid in black and white.

'I am Miss Burns.'

The hall was high, lighted by a lantern window in the roof. Some of its panes were coloured and cast shapes of red and blue and orange light on to the tessellated floor, on a white-painted staircase that ran up to a gallery, on to a white marble statue in the centre and two black ones, bearing lamps. Several pieces of furniture and some decorative objects had been in the house when the brewer was bereaved and he had never wanted to see them, or even to think of them again. The statue was of the goddess of Health.

'Miss Burns, madam,' the maid said, opening a white panelled door upon a room that gave the impression of being all rose-coloured, a warm, pretty, sweet-scented room. Near a cheerful little fire, on a rose-brocaded chaise-longue, Mrs Armitage reclined. She offered a slim white hand, and a sweet, welcoming smile.

'My dear, I'm afraid you've had such a tedious roundabout journey. Do sit down. No, wait. You may find it rather warm. Take off your hat and your jacket.' As Charlotte did so, Mrs Armitage said, 'Tea will be here immediately. Before it comes, while we are alone together, I have just one thing to say and then the subject will never be mentioned again. My cousin has told me everything and believe me, I deeply sympathise with your sorrow and all the trouble you have borne. I have divulged nothing, even to Mrs Osgood, and I never shall. I just hope that you will put the past completely away and be very happy here.'

'Your accepting me has already made me very happy, Mrs Armitage. I am extremely grateful.'

They smiled, while taking stock of one another. Mrs Armit-

143

age must once have been very pretty, Charlotte thought. Age had silvered her fair hair to a delicate primrose shade, and her skin was like tissue paper, lightly crumpled and then smoothed out. She had heavy white lids over eyes the colour of a harebell. Her rather wistful look, her soft, plaintive voice and her filmy black dress, with touches of white at neck and wrists, made her seem like a widow.

Mrs Armitage regarded Charlotte with approval; obviously a lady; rather small for sixteen, but composed, almost sedate in manner. Even her clothes were pleasing. Mrs Greenfield had taken charge of the new outfit which no one could deny was needed, and she had banned black. Charlotte's jacket and skirt were a soft dove-grey, her blouse of crisp white piqué.

The maid came in with a laden tea-tray which she placed on a round table, well out of Mrs Armitage's reach. Outside the open door there was the sound of footsteps, firm, heavy. A woman entered, fairly tall, fairly stout, plain.

'Augusta, this is Miss Burns, about whom I was telling you. Charlotte, this is Mrs Osgood, my partner and my friend.'

Mrs Osgood put out a large, hard hand, said, 'Good afternoon,' in a voice which, though coarse, was friendly, and sat down by the tea-tray. The service was of silver, highly polished, the cups frail and beautiful. There were tiny savoury sandwiches and two kinds of cake.

Mrs Armitage enquired after Mr and Mrs Greenfield and being answered went smoothly on. 'I am sorry to say that I shall not be able to keep exactly to what I promised my cousin. I'm afraid you will get very few lessons this term. The junior mistress whom we were expecting let us down at the last moment and I shall not try to engage another before Christmas. Any teacher unemployed once a term has started, simply is unemployable. So, with Miss Lamb singlehanded she will need more help from you than was foreseen.'

'I shall be very glad to help in any way I can.'

'French you shall have. Mamselle spends a whole day here on Thursdays.'

'Staff, both sorts,' Mrs Osgood said, 'is a bother in a place like this. Young teachers like somewhere to go in their time off. And women who should be in kitchens'd sooner gut herrings.'

Gut was not a drawing-room word, and Charlotte looked with covert interest at the woman who had used it. Mrs Osgood was well-dressed—plum-coloured silk, a cameo brooch on the high stiff collar, a gold chain for the watch tucked into her waistbelt.

'But we manage, Augusta,' Mrs Armitage said, almost lightly. 'With a little goodwill and flexibility . . . Mrs Osgood is really matron and housekeeper, but she has also been cook . . . Augusta, how long? Time does fly so.'

'It's two years. But I don't mind cooking. Given somebody to peel vegetables, I enjoy it. And there isn't the waste you get with a hired woman.'

'As for me,' Mrs Armitage said, 'I undertook the teaching of music,' she glanced at the gleaming rosewood grand piano, 'in addition to all the clerical work.' Her gaze shifted to an elegant, breakfront bureau. 'After all,' she said, 'we contend that Homelands is a home rather than a school, and in one's home one lends a hand.'

Charlotte said, 'I expect—at least I hope—that Mrs Green-field did tell you that I have never actually *taught*.'

Except for Vincent, big A, little a, A for apple, in the beech tree's shade! Put that thought away. This is a new life.

'That may be an advantage. The young ones need only the simplest instruction. They come to us from India and other places where the climate is unsuitable for children over six, and the educational facilities non-existent. Many of them have been much spoiled by servants. They learn to read and write, and to behave. For a year or so that is enough.'

Mrs Osgood said, 'Miss Burns, if you won't have another cup, I'll show you your room and then take you along to Miss Lamb.'

It was a nice room; and nearby there was, wonder of won-ders, a bathroom and a water closet. The brewer had built well and had employed a very go-ahead architect. The brochure's mention of modern sanitation was no idle boast; under the roof of the house that he had intended to call New Place—new hope, new life, new health—there were as many bathrooms and water closets as there were in many a fair-sized town.

'These are the school stairs,' Mrs Osgood said, leading the way to another staircase, its paint a more utilitarian brown, its steps covered with linoleum and edged with metal. Across a kind of lobby. Into the classroom, spacious, pleasant. It had once been the billiard room, planned but never played in.

Thirty faces, mainly young, but some not so young, turned and stared as Mrs Osgood, followed by Charlotte, entered.

145

'Miss Lamb, this is Miss Burns, our new assistant.'

Miss Lamb stood up. She gave the impression of being badly put together, large, knobbly joints connected by almost skeletal bones. Even her face with its prominent cheekbones, high bony forehead and teeth over which the pale dry lips seemed only *just* to close, had a starveling look. But her eyes were brilliant, green and clear between dark lashes that matched the plentiful, untidily bundled up hair.

She said, 'How do you do, Miss Burns. I am indeed very glad to see you.' A third handshake. 'Oh, thank you, Ella.' A girl, gracious, how tall, how beautifully dressed, how old-seeming, had risen and brought a chair.

'Now,' Miss Lamb said, 'would you like me to reel off the names, or would you prefer to come to them gradually?'

'I think ... gradually.'

'Very wise. This is plain needlework, make and mend. I combine it ...' Miss Lamb looked at the pile of exercise books and the sharp red pencil which she had laid down in order to welcome Charlotte. 'Thirty,' she said, 'is a small class—I once had sixty—but the varying ages make it hard. While you try to deal with one group, the others must write, and it makes a frightful amount of marking. Do excuse me ... Frances, will you find the dictionary and look up the word "receive".' Miss Lamb looked back at Charlotte and said, 'I hold that a mere correction is water on a duck's back. Makes no impression at all. Once it is looked up it makes some impact.'

Miss Lamb did some more marking and Charlotte sat, conscious of an atmosphere. Extremely quiet and courteous, very different from that of any plain sewing class at Miss Barton's, where such classes were gossiping sessions. 'May I have the scissors, please, Constance?' 'Florence, would you mind passing me the white cotton?' And all the voices, however young and treble, had a kinship with Mrs Armitage's, quiet, soothing. The tall girl who had brought the chair said, 'Excuse me, Miss Lamb. Table girls.'

'Goodness me. Your watch must be fast, Ella.'

Ella's watch was a pretty thing, pearls and turquoises suspended from a pin like a bow. Miss Lamb's was a battered little silver one, hung on what looked like an elongated shoe lace.

'You are right, Ella. Table girls! Oh dear me, half the evening gone. Frances, if you are still under the delusion that in the

146

word *receive* the i precedes the e, you will never find it.'

Four girls—their age, Charlotte judged, about twelve—had risen. 'Valerie,' Miss Lamb said, 'look to the salt.' As the four girls went out a very appetising scent of onions drifted in.

Miss Lamb marked three books, looked up, and said, 'That will do girls. Pack up.' There was movement, but no noise, none of the this-is-the-end-of-class commotion which Charlotte remembered from Miss Barton's. The girls moved away and presently gathered again in the dining room, the room that had been planned to accommodate a housekeeper and a few servants of a superior kind, ladies' maids, gentlemen's gentlemen. Now two white scrubbed tables ran, lengthwise. There were little posies of late-flowering scabious and knapweed and a few autumn berries set along the centre of each table and they, with the lamps, brought in from the schoolroom, gave an almost festive air.

Miss Lamb said, 'Ella, you are deposed. Miss Burns will take the junior table.'

The tall girl said, 'Miss Lamb, I welcome the deposition. As you know, I was never very good at fractions.

They both laughed and very soon Charlotte saw the allusion. On the dish before her lay a kind of elongated dumpling, to be divided among the fourteen girls at the junior table. And myself! she thought. Admittedly she had had tea, but the dumpling smelt inviting.

It tasted as good as it smelt; a plain suet roly-poly, made not with jam but with onions chopped small and fried golden brown. Everyone received a slice about an inch thick. As in the classroom the standard of manners was high. 'Would you like salt, Veronica?' 'Thank you. Would you?' 'Sophie, would you mind passing the water jug?' There was some quiet conversation. Charlotte learned a name or two; admired the little posies, answered one question, put politely: 'And where is your home, Miss Burns?' She almost replied 'Biddlesford', and remembered just in time that the village name was as infamous as her own. 'Oh, a little village you would never have heard of,' she said.

The table girls collected the plates and the forks and carried them into the kitchen. Movement became general, a drift back to the classroom.

'After supper,' Miss Lamb said, 'the girls do what they choose. It would be an opportunity for you to learn names.'

Ella approached and said, 'Miss Burns, would you care to play whist?'

'Thank you, Ella. I do not know how.'

Ella, with an experienced hostess air, said, 'Another time perhaps. We should be delighted to show you.'

Within a few minutes everybody was busy, or at least occupied. Two games of whist were in progress and at the other end of the age scale there was a dolls' tea party going on. In between girls wrote, read, painted, did embroidery.

Charlotte moved about. Drawn to the youngest group she accepted imaginary tea in a cup the size of a thimble and said, 'Delicious. I hope you will invite me to drink tea with you again.'

'Tomorrow we shall have cherry cake.'

She moved on to a little girl, sitting apart, busily writing.

'I am doing my letter. I write a little every day.'

Such of the letter as could be read ran—'It Has terned veree Kold heer if you could send me some heet and I could send you some Kold we should be orl right i shall ask the wind deer mamma deer Papa if a wind blos Kold on you it is from me with a Kiss . . .'

'And what is your name?'

'Sophie. Sophie Wrenn.'

'And where is this letter going, Sophie?'

'To Calcutta, Miss Burns.'

'And how long have you been here?'

'A month, nearly . . .' Suddenly tears brimmed. At Miss Barton's there had been little homesick creatures. Charlotte said with feeling—not that she had ever been a homesick school-girl, in fact only too glad to get away, but she knew what it was to have lost a whole way of life, to yearn, to hunger and remember, 'Sophie, it gets better. In about another month you'll feel at home here.'

At half past seven Miss Lamb tapped the end of her red pencil on the table and said, 'Junior bedtime. And please remember your teeth. Miss Burns and I will come and say good night in just ten minutes.' The fourteen under-twelves packed up whatever they had been using and went quietly away.

Again the brochure had not lied; there were no dormitories. In one huge room seven narrow beds, in another five, in another two. Miss Lamb looked into each room and said briskly, 'Good night, girls,' and the girls in the beds said, 'Good night,

148

Miss Lamb.' In the room where only two beds were occupied
—one by Sophie Wrenn, Sophie reared up and said, "Miss
Burns . . .' Then as Charlotte approached, she held out her
arms, 'Miss Burns, please kiss me good night . . .'

'And that,' Miss Lamb said, 'is something to beware of. You
must not mind my saying this, I have learned by experience.
The really young ones are looking for somebody to take the
place of their parents. Absolutely understandable. And the
older ones . . . Ella Smythe, for example, are looking for something else. It is extremely unwise to allow any *physical* contact.
If only for the simple reason that it makes it somewhat difficult
to correct or admonish a child with whom one is on . . . well,
intimate terms. That is why most parents are such failures.'

Charlotte said, 'I'm sorry, Miss Lamb. I shall not offend you
in that way again.'

Miss Lamb said, astoundingly, 'Good God! You didn't
offend me. You simply obeyed a law of nature—cuddle the
young. But in a place like this . . . Never mind. You'll learn.
Senior bedtime is a quarter to nine. Lights out at nine. After
that I make a cup of tea in my room and if you care to come,
and don't despise condensed milk, you'd be very welcome.'

Miss Lamb's room was almost a replica of Charlotte's, but
cluttered. She had to move some books from the chair on to
the bed before she could say, 'Do sit down.' She then knelt and
took from under the bed her tea-making apparatus. A tin tray;
a little spirit stove, a tin kettle, a tin of condensed milk, another
tin, masquerading as a tea caddy, two thick cups with no
saucers and one teaspoon that looked as though it were made of
lead. While the kettle boiled and the tea stood for a moment,
Miss Lamb said, 'I still can't believe it.'

'What?'

'That you're really here. I could easily persuade myself into
thinking that I owe Mrs Armitage a public apology. All last
term, all through the holiday—I spent the holiday here, as do
most of the girls, and it suits me, having no home to go
to—there's been talk of an assistant whose arrival was imminent. When this term found me still on my own I thought—
Mythical as the unicorn! But here you are.' Miss Lamb's eyes
became even brighter. 'I had so many plans, improvements,
ideas, and all I could do was to muddle along.' She poured the
black brew, stirred in enough condensed milk to make it the
colour and almost the consistency of mud and handed it over.

149

'I'm sorry I can't offer you a biscuit. But frankly, there have been so many things to buy. There wasn't even an atlas in the place when I arrived, and the dictionary was so ragged as to be quite useless. I spent the whole of my first term's salary before I had it. Books on credit.'

'I should have thought . . .' Charlotte began.

'So did I. I asked of course. Mrs A said she would look into the matter. Nothing happened, so I asked again. And then she was somewhat displeased and pointed out that my predecessors had never complained about the equipment.' She laughed, not sourly, merrily. 'Judging by what the girls didn't know, and *still* don't know, I was coming to the conclusion that my predecessors were mythical, too. Still, we shall begin to make headway now. If you stay.'

'Oh, I hope to. Like you, Miss Lamb, through the holidays, too. I *have* a home, but my mother is dead; my father married again and there is a second family. Of course, you may not find me very useful at first. I have never taught.' She remembered some of the things about which Thomas complained. 'I may not even be able to keep order.'

'Have another cup. Order. Now that is one thing about which there is no difficulty here. None at all. Everybody's behaviour is modelled on Mrs Armitage's. You must have noticed, quiet courtesy, consideration for others.'

Was that meant sarcastically?

'I thought they all seemed extremely well-behaved.'

'Phenomenally. You see, they all adore her. And there is another reason, too. An almost totally farinaceous diet. You will feel the effect yourself. I did, within a fortnight. I had to say to myself—Mary Lamb, are you going to be downed by a dumpling? Paralysed by porridge? I fought it off. It can be done. So if you find inertia encroaching, do not despair, you will *not* be dying on your feet.'

'I shall rely on you, Miss Lamb, to remind me of that. In about a fortnight's time.'

'In a fortnight's time,' said Miss Lamb, her mind back with its preoccupation, 'I hope we shall have been able to do something about these wasted evenings. That everlasting whist, that interminable dolls' tea party. With so much marking I could never organise what is needed—some communal activity. I have some ideas, though. But now you must get to bed. You've had a long journey and new faces and places can be exhausting.

150

Good night. I hope you sleep well.'

Charlotte went to bed and had time to reflect only upon one thing before she slept. Miss Lamb had once, only once, referred to Mrs Armitage as Mrs A, and because she and Thomas had used a similar curtailment for Mrs Cornwall, she deduced that Miss Lamb did not much care for Mrs Armitage. Charlotte had liked her very much. But she liked Miss Lamb, too. And even Mrs Osgood had seemed quite friendly. Charlotte's last thought was one of deep gratitude to Mrs Greenfield.

2

BREAKFAST WAS PORRIDGE, PLENTY OF IT AND PERFECTLY made. It was served, not with milk and sugar as at home and at Miss Barker's, but with salt. There was an urn of tea, very lightly milked, and with the tea there was sugar, of that very cheap kind the colour and texture of sand.

Immediately afterwards Miss Lamb stood up with a little dogeared notebook in her hand and asked briskly, 'Excuses?'

Four or five of the elder girls raised their hands. Miss Lamb consulted her book and said, 'Muriel, it is a biological impossibility unless there is something seriously wrong with you. Is there?'

The girl, blushing, said, 'No, Miss Lamb.'

Those excused stayed indoors, so did the four table girls, different ones from last evening's, who stayed to clear and wash up. The rest trooped into the yard.

'We do a few exercises now,' Miss Lamb said to Charlotte.

'Shall I come?'

'You must please yourself, Miss Burns. Exercises are very good for the lungs and the bowels.'

Charlotte went. Miss Lamb behaved like a lively, conscientious sheepdog dealing with a flock of slow, reluctant sheep. As she gave such an order as, 'Feet astride, *jump!*' she performed the action. Pins fell from her hair, her blouse came out from her waistbelt. After the exercises there was a game. Then everybody went in to make her bed and do her share of sweeping and dusting. Classes began at a quarter past nine.

152

'I drafted this for you last night,' Miss Lamb said and handed Charlotte a rudimentary timetable and a list of the fourteen girls who would be her charge. Alongside each name was a terse—but Charlotte was to learn—amazingly accurate comment on each girl's attainment and potential. Despite the muddle in which she said she had lived, Miss Lamb had missed little.

The morning with a fifteen-minute break at a quarter to eleven, sped away.

Lunch was rice, again plenty of it and beautifully cooked, served with very powerful curry sauce.

In the afternoon they went to the beach where again Miss Lamb tried to generate energy. A game or two, and then a shell hunt. Who could find most? Who could find the most unusual?

'One thinks of children *disporting* themselves on beaches,' she said breathlessly. 'But of course their clothes are all wrong. And those four languid young ladies are not a good example.' She looked with mild irritation at Ella and three other much senior girls. 'Mind you, I am sorry for Ella Smythe. She's well over eighteen now. She should have gone home a year ago. But I suppose it *is* difficult to keep up the illusion that you yourself are thirty and the toast of the garrison with a grown-up daughter around. And by the way, if Ella tries to confide in you, Miss Burns, as she did in me, don't for God's sake *pity* her. She has morbid moods. So tell her she's lucky; admire her belongings. Her parents will send her anything except the one thing she wants, leave to go home ... How many, Sophie? Eighty! Dear child, you can't count so far, yet. Ella, I'll ask you and Angela, Felicity and Florence to help the young ones count their shells.'

Back in school a cup of tea and a thin ginger biscuit. Lessons again. Supper—vegetable pie; peas, onions, carrots under a thick brown crust of mashed potato. Then the do-what-you-like period.

Sophie Wrenn at least was not wasting her time. She was adding to her letter.

'I have put something about you, Miss Burns. Would you like to see?'

'A new teecher came yessterday. She is nice. She kissed me goodnite and she is yung. She can touch her tose. on the beech I picked up aty shells. Miss lamb said I couldn't count to aty

153

but you can if you do it in tens.'

'You have absolutely the right idea about letters, Sophie. You do find something to say. But your spelling is all your own. And your use of capital letters. I'm not suggesting that you should alter anything you have written so far, but if you like to come to end of the table, I'll try to explain a little.'

Against the well-modulated noise of the whist game and the dolls' tea party and a game of Lotto, Charlotte tried to explain, not only the spelling of *toes* and the use of capital letters, but something that seemed to be of more importance at the moment.

'Sophie, I kissed you good night yesterday. I can't do it again, because, you see, things must be fair and I should end by having to kiss everybody. And that would take too long. Do you see?'

A child who could discover for herself the reckoning of eighty by tens, was no dunce. Sophie pondered and then nodded.

'Yes. You might have to kiss Julia. I see. I couldn't myself.' Charlotte looked along the table to the face of the child against whose name on the list Miss Lamb had written, 'Congenital idiot but amiable.' It was a simian face with red-rimmed eyes, an almost bridgeless nose and a loose-lipped blubbery mouth.

'We all have to wear the face we were born with, you know, Sophie.' How very teachery I sound!

'Yes. So we do. I know what. I'll give her my best shell. She didn't get any. Miss Burns . . .'

'Yes?'

'Tonight when you look in will you make a little sign to me, please? Just to show that if there weren't so many of us . . .'

'I'll wave my hand,' Charlotte said.

In saying that things must be fair Charlotte had unknowingly voiced one of Mrs Armitage's axioms. It was not fair that some girls should be provided with ample pocket money while others had little and some none at all. So Mrs Armitage impounded it and would hand a little back for any specific expense, like a new toothbrush, and spent the bulk of it on things that could be enjoyed by all. In the same way, because the younger children's letters must be inspected before dispatch, everybody's letters must be put on the console table outside Mrs Armitage's door unsealed. By the end of a term everybody knew what was likely to be deemed unsuitable and Mrs Armitage confined her attention to the letters of those who had not yet learned the basic rules. Sophie Wrenn was one of these.

'Ah, Sophie, come in. Pull up that stool, dear, and sit beside me. I want to talk to you about that lovely long letter of yours. Would you like a chocolate? Now . . . I think this is your third letter, is it not?'

'My first real one, Mrs Armitage. I have been writing this all the time. I wanted to send a nice long one.'

'On the whole it is a very nice letter. But there are things in it which I don't think your parents will be happy to read. Let me see . . .' She leafed through the pages. 'For instance, that you are very homesick and cry yourself to sleep every night.'

'I did at first. I wrote that a long time ago.'

'Then I don't think it very kind to mention it. I know you are young, but not too young to understand that a letter should give pleasure. And then . . . umm, umm, umm, yes, here we are, so much about being cold. Naturally anybody coming from Calcutta is bound to find England chilly. You mention the cold several times. It sounds so complaining. Your parents chose to send you to this healthy, bracing spot. And I do think that it would distress them very much to read that you are always hungry. I'm afraid I don't understand that at all. Have you missed a meal?'

'Only the first day. I *do* eat what is put before me. But I am still hungry.'

'That may be because you are not accustomed to English food, Sophie. I left India twenty years ago, and I still miss the fruit. But missing things is not quite the same as being hungry, is it? There are so many pleasant things in your letter.' Mrs Armitage glanced down at it again. 'You like Miss Burns, I see. So do I. You enjoy the beach, you have made two friends, gathered wildflowers and collected shells. *Don't* you think it would be rather nice if you wrote this letter again, leaving out what would make your parents unhappy and keeping in what would please them?'

Sophie took her time, but after some thought said, 'Yes, Mrs Armitage.'

'Church parade tomorrow,' Miss Lamb said, over the Saturday evening cup of tea. 'Best bib and tucker. My trouble is that

I have no best. Mrs A does actually make an inspection and I know she deplores me.'

And her clothes were, by almost any standard, deplorable. Her everyday wear was a dark blue blouse which had four buttons; three were the originals, grey-blue mother-of-pearl, the fourth was made of white bone. All the buttonholes had gaped from long usage and been hastily cobbled together. With this she wore a grey skirt, with on its front a large patch of some material not quite a match in colour and of a different weave. Charlotte had wondered about that until Miss Lamb explained airily, 'It wore out at the back, where I sat, so I simply turned it back to front. I didn't think the patch would stand the strain.'

She owned another blouse, a dark brown one and a skirt of lighter brown. She had an outer garment, black, that defied description, not a pelisse, not a jacket, not a topcoat, not a cloak. Her shoes were not only cobbled, they were patched, and her one hat, greenish in colour, looked as though it had been put through the mangle.

On this Saturday evening Miss Lamb said, 'However, let us not brood over my sartorial deficiencies. You, Miss Burns, will more than compensate. What I want to talk about now is the communal effort. I *think* a play, with a part for everybody. *A Midsummer Night's Dream*. Plenty of characters; that play within the play; the people of the court; the fairies ... The wings ... wire and butter muslin, quite cheap. We'll think about that later ... But something in which everybody could join ... Ella Smythe as the Duke, she has the most splendid dressing-gown ... What do you think? You know the play?'

'Not the *play*.' Miss Barton had in fact banned Shakespeare; rather coarse! 'I know the story. From *Lamb's Tales*. Miss Lamb, I only this moment realised ... Mary Lamb ...'

'No relation to me, God be thanked. Poor woman, she died raving mad. You know, if we really put our backs into it we could have this little play ready by Christmas. It would do something to enliven that vacation. The summer one dragged, despite the good weather and a picnic or two that I arranged. Now the winter is closing in.'

Winter closed in. Dark at three o'clock in the afternoon; scarcely less dark at eight o'clock in the morning. And cold. Often so cold that even Miss Lamb's sturdy spirit failed and the morning exercises were performed in the classroom and the afternoon walks abandoned. 'We'll have rehearsal,' she said.

There were colds and coughs and chilblains, all dealt with in a pragmatic manner by Mrs Osgood; crude cod-liver oil, bitter quinine and an ointment compounded of lard and mustard. None of her remedies were a hundred per cent effective in a medical way. On another level they worked marvellously, a cough was preferable to a tablespoonful of cod-liver oil, a snuffle concealed better than one treated with quinine, and as for the chilblains, far better ignore them than to have inflamed, swollen fingers and toes further irritated by the mustard ointment. Only the most innocent and trustful went more than twice to the little dispensary, once planned as a dressing room. Alongside this desire to avoid Mrs Osgood's ministrations, ran the interest in the play. In this sphere Miss Lamb had succeeded in inculcating some central motive interest.

'I think,' Charlotte said over the tea one evening, 'it is because everybody really wishes to be somebody else. It's a kind of . . . escape. I mean, take Ella, while she struts about, being Duke of Athens, she can forget that really she is a girl, too old to be at school.'

'You know, Miss Burns,' Miss Lamb said, handing up the cup of mud, 'I do thank my God for your being here. There could have been a million, and not one so intelligent . . . no, wrong word, percipient and understanding. So easy to work with.'

'I'm grateful for you, too,' Charlotte said warmly. 'You have made what could have been a difficult time for me so easy. And such fun!'

Close friends as they had become, they always addressed one another formally and had exchanged no confidences; Charlotte knew that Miss Lamb had no home; Miss Lamb knew that Charlotte had a home to which she did not wish to return. Except with the bookseller in Lowestoft, who gave credit, Miss Lamb had no communication with the outer world. Charlotte wrote and received a few letters. Those she wrote were always addressed to Mrs Greenfield, those she received always postmarked Bereham. This rather complicated arrangement, the result of Mrs Greenfield's determination that there should be no obvious link, caused Charlotte to write less frequently than she would otherwise have done. It seemed to place a burden on Mrs Greenfield's good nature.

Thomas's letters were uncheerful; he hated the school more

every day, he hated Mr Macferson, at home there was no one to talk to. On one occasion he wrote, 'The new baby has come, it is another girl, it cries all the time. There is some talk of Papa being moved, but I don't think that will do me much good. I suppose I shall be left here and sent to board with the Macfersons. Then I couldn't bear it and should run away.'

Answering his letters called for much discrimination. To tell him that she enjoyed teaching, liked those for whom and with whom she worked would simply emphasise the contrast between her lot and his. She could write, 'At least, Thomas, in a day school you have Saturday and Sunday free. Miss Lamb and I get alternate Sunday afternoons, but usually we don't bother because there is nowhere to go and nothing to do.' Then she reflected that Thomas's free time must be equally blank. 'Thomas, dear, could you make me a little watercolour of our house? We were happy there once, weren't we? And if Papa is to be moved I may never see it again.' She tried to make jokes. 'When I come to keep house for you, Thomas, we shall be able to live on twopence a day. I now know five different sorts of dumpling.' She described Sophie Wrenn's spelling. 'She writes so much, where other girls do a page, she does four, such a great deal of my marking is concerned with her. Deer tomas iff wun day my spelling goes pekuliah you will no it is katching.'

She always sent a covering letter to Mrs Greenfield. In such letters she could say how happy, how fortunate, how grateful she was. And she was always careful to emphasise the fact that she had French lessons every Thursday, and that Mamselle said that her accent was improving.

Mamselle was the daughter of a solid Norfolk yeoman farmer whose only foolish action had been to fall in love with and marry the French governess from 'up at the Hall'. She was looking for a home and for independence and believed that, once married, she could change him and his way of life. She failed and turned into a shrew. When her daughter was born she was christened Marie-Josephine, but her father never called her anything but Mary. She was brought up to despise the farm and everything about it, including its owner. She grew up completely bi-lingual, she and her mother always conversed in French when they were alone—and often when they were not. Mamselle's mother died when her daughter was fourteen and a kind of peace descended on the farm. John

158

Finch adored his daughter and would give her anything. Marie-Josephine had learned not to ask for any but material things. Let him call his midday meal dinner and sit down to it in his shirtsleeves if he wished to.

Marie-Josephine was not bad-looking and her father was well known to be a 'warm' man; she could have married many times over, but she was not prepared to accept any man of the kind who was prepared to propose to her. She was twenty-eight and past her prime, when accident brought Mrs Armitage and her together. Mrs Armitage had been obliged to exert herself and escort two girls to the junction at Norwich; Mamselle had been to the city on a shopping expedition. They shared a railway carriage back to Lowestoft. Mrs Armitage, though poor enough to be obliged to keep a school, represented everything that Marie-Josephine had been trained by her mother to value; Marie-Josephine was to Mrs Armitage another stroke of that same luck which had given her Homelands so cheaply.

Old John Finch was told that Mary had met a lady in the train and had been asked to lunch and to spend the day with her on Thursday. It became a weekly arrangement. Well, he was all for it, especially since Mary now seemed so much more settled and contented. But you couldn't, he protested, go on taking hospitality week after week; how about asking Mrs Armitage to supper? Marie-Josephine had an answer to that. Mrs Armitage did not go out much, she was rather delicate and frightfully busy. Then next time Mary went to Gorston she must take something. How about a nice brace of pheasants? A joint of fresh pork? A ham? A hare?

Mamselle had her own conveyance, a plump shiny pony and a miniature gig, largely made of cane work. Driving this at a spanking pace, anxious to get back to her idea of Heaven, she would arrive at Homelands, offer her oblations, and spend the morning in spritely French conversation with those girls whose parents paid extra for that tuition. She found time to glance through the exercises she had set on her former visit, and to set some more. She then had lunch with Mrs Armitage and Mrs Osgood in Mrs Osgood's room. No meal except afternoon tea was ever served in the rose-coloured room, partly because Mrs Osgood's room, the original dining room, was nearer the kitchen, and partly because Mrs Osgood had brought with her to Homelands a very large solid dining table and an ornate sideboard. It was also a fact that Mrs Osgood never felt really at home in the drawing room.

After lunch came the joy. Occasionally Mamselle would take Mrs Armitage for a little drive; occasionally Mrs Armitage would play the piano for Mamselle; occasionally they played cards. Often they just talked.

More than once Mamselle had mentioned the fact that when her father died she would be very well-off, that she would sell the farm and buy a house in sunny Provence. To such remarks the beloved one never made the right, the direct response, because, pleasant as it was to be admired and worshipped and given things like hothouse flowers in the middle of winter, adoration could become burdensome, and sometimes Thursday afternoons seemed rather long.

One day Mamselle was forced into the open. '. . . that is what I have always meant to do. Until I met you, Viola. Now I know that I should never be happy, even in Provence, unless you came, too.'

'My dear, that is a very nice thing to say. I appreciate it. But . . .'

'But what?' Mamselle asked, betraying the possessive, aggressive quality which lay only just beneath the surface of adoration.

'Well, to be frank, you would be rich, I should be poor. You would be in your spiritual home, I should be an exile. You have been coming here for four years—is that right? Four years, and although I attend all your lessons, I still know hardly any French. I seem not to have the knack. Too old perhaps.'

'But you would be with me,' Mamselle said. 'I would look after you. And alone with me, surrounded by other French people, you would quickly learn.'

Alone with me. What a dreadful prospect.

'And don't talk about being old, Viola. It's simply that this awful climate is bad for your health. In Provence . . .'

'My dear, there is one little thing,' Mrs Armitage said, mistress of the situation as, she knew, she could never be in Mamselle's house in Provence. 'Do you think you could remember not to call me Viola in front of Mrs Osgood. I use her Christian name, I know. She does not use mine. It is one of those small things which enable us to keep our relative positions. A thing that is very important when two women have to live and work together.' For a second the pretty harebell colour in Mrs Armitage's eyes took a different, harder, tinge.

'Did I make a slip?'

'Twice.'

Mrs Osgood said, 'Straight up against the edge of the door,' and measured every girl. Later the miller weighed them. The rhyme ran, 'There was a jolly miller and he lived by himself and a jolly man was he.' The miller at Gorston did not live by himself; he, his wife and children filled a whole pew in church on Sunday mornings; but jolly he certainly was. 'Oops-a-daisy,' he cried, lifting them, beginning with the smallest, on to his scales. 'You're a little tiddler; haven't seen you before,' he said to Sophie Wrenn. He said, 'My my, you've grown. Break my scales next time, you will.' He said, 'You're quite a young lady now.'

Standing a little apart, writing down the weights in a little book, Charlotte noticed how the girls responded to his hearty masculinity, an element missing in their conventual lives. The little ones tended to cling to him. One said, 'Weigh me again, Mr Miller.' But Ella Smythe, very elegant in a sable trimmed cloak, sulkily refused to be weighed. Miss Lamb who had been through this process before, could visualise a blank left on Ella's report. Her parents would not notice, or care, but Mrs Armitage would.

'Oh, come on, Ella. Miss Burns and I intend to be weighed.'

Nine stone seven pounds for Ella. Eight stone two pounds for Charlotte. For Miss Lamb a grunt of disbelief. 'Must have got stuck. Will you try again, miss. Well, it don't *seem* right, but it *is*. Seven-two, and I was always led to believe that bones weighed heavy.'

Charlotte knew what was wearing the never-too-plentiful flesh from Miss Lamb's prominent bones. To a degree it was the play, planned to use up idle hours and to bring seven-year-old Sophie Wrenn and eighteen-year-old Ella Smythe together. Nothing more. But Mrs Armitage had thought it a fit subject out of which to make an occasion, just a small invited audience and a buffet supper, useful social experience for the girls. The other thing was the reports which Miss Lamb took very seriously indeed. 'Last term, Miss Burns, I was so busy. I did not even know that reports were *required*. I did them in a great hurry. Trite phrases . . . But this term we can do better.'

So they had done better and when 'Height' and 'Weight'

had been filled in, the reports were submitted for Mrs Armitage's scrutiny.

There came an evening when the maid—not the one who had admitted Charlotte, her name had been Sarah, this one was Eva—padded in and said, 'Miss Lamb, Madam would like to see you after supper.'

Sarah and after her, Eva, constituted a frail and tenuous link between the two very different sides of the house. The maid in current employment at Homelands did nothing—except for carrying a message or two—that she would not have done in private service in a house occupied by two ladies. She ate, as the saying was, 'as family', which meant she ate well on the less choice portions of the dishes which Mrs Osgood prepared for herself and for Mrs Armitage. She was required to do nothing, except to prepare vegetables for the pupils, and she was housed in a pleasant little room on the ground floor. But it was a lonely life, its loneliness emphasised by the communal life that went on behind the invisible barrier. Few maids stayed long.

Miss Lamb said, 'Thank you, Eva,' and just before leaving immediately after supper for her interview with Mrs Armitage, she said to Charlotte, 'It may be about the *wings*.'

It was not about the wings. Charlotte, having seen everyone to bed, had the little kettle on the boil when Miss Lamb came in and threw the thirty reports on to her bed and said, 'All to do again!'

'Why? What is wrong with them?'

'Lack of tact. Lack of sensitivity,' Miss Lamb said grimly. 'Away in the hot, humid outposts of Empire loving parents wish only to know that little Emmeline has grown, put on weight and is making good progress.' She gathered the scattered report forms and brooded. 'God, and we tried so hard ... And I still think that Cecilie Burke's parents should know that she is number blind and will count on her fingers if she lives to be a hundred. It's like being colour-blind, but more of a handicap. Is it so cruel to tell them? And over Ella Smythe I had been so subtle. "Now has no competition." "Would benefit by seeing something of the world." Offensive? Insensitive?' She looked at Charlotte with eyes which were a little too bright.

'Drink your tea,' Charlotte said. 'Miss Lamb, you must not take it too much to heart. Remember your head.'

Miss Lamb suffered from headaches, not frequent, not regularly, but quite incapacitating when they did occur.

'I certainly can't afford a headache with all these to do again in time for the mail to the hot humid outposts.' She drank some tea and recovered a little. 'I suppose in a way she is right. Quiet courtesy and consideration for others! Back to "making good progress", and "very promising". Ella's parents will doubtless be delighted to learn that she has benefited greatly by her prolonged stay. But to write it will make me vomit!' She drank more tea and recovered still further. 'One good thing emerged from this interview. The wire and muslin for the wings can be provided from the Pocket Money Fund. I was beginning to think I should have to ask for an advance on my salary.'

Nobody had French on the following Thursday; Mamselle drove Mrs Armitage into Lowestoft and treated her to the best lunch obtainable; a good lunch, though Mamselle criticised the food as being only fit for farmers and spoke of the small, wonderful restaurants which, according to her mother, flourished in France, even in villages.

On her return Mrs Armitage gave the parcels of muslin and wire to Eva to carry to the schoolroom, and also sent a message that she would like to see Miss Lamb after supper.

The evening was spent in contriving wings; the play was to be performed in eight days' time, because thirteen girls were going home for the Christmas holiday.

From this interview Miss Lamb returned looking less upset than bewildered, and later, in her bedroom, instead of sitting down, she remained standing and said, 'Miss Burns, please be honest with me. Do you see anything wrong with my appearance?'

'I think you are thinner.'

'My clothes,' Miss Lamb explained, and without repeating the question, went on. 'I know I am shabby, but I am not in rags and I am clean; I simply cannot afford new clothes. Even at Gummage's; even with discount. It seems that Mrs Armitage, while buying the muslin, looked round on my behalf. She discovered a really pretty, well-made dress for fifteen shillings, a cloth coat and skirt for a pound, an overcoat for twenty-five shillings. Work that out, deduct the five per cent that the philanthropic Mr Gummage allows if Homelands is mentioned and you can see what I am expected to spend.' She laughed. 'I am not going to do it, just for the vicar's benefit. I said so, quite

163

frankly. In any case I owe that poor bookseller over three pounds and my shoes need mending. What do you think she then suggested?'

'Raising your salary,' said Charlotte, who knew that Miss Lamb received five pounds each term. Most maids had twelve pounds a year and some kind of uniform.

'You'll be the death of me! No. She suggested that as Ella and I are much of a size, Ella should lend me a dress for the party.'

Look at it one way and you could see the affront; look at it in another and one could see that the proposal could even have been prompted by a certain kindliness. Miss Lamb's least worn skirt, the brown one, was now spattered with ink spots which nothing could remove.

'I told her that it would be fatal. Ella and her little clique take a bit of managing, in a quiet way; once start borrowing . . . However, I compromised. I shall conceal the worst of my deficiencies behind the buffet table where the turkey will be the centre of attention.'

Mamselle's father had very happily promised to give one of his best birds, a twenty-five-pounder.

The play, in fact the whole party, was a great success. It was attended by the vicar and his wife, the doctor and his niece and Colonel Jepson J.P. with the lady euphemistically known as his housekeeper, and of course by Mamselle. In and around Gorston-on-Sea there was a shortage of what Mrs Armitage called gentlefolk; the area had neither the scenery nor the climate to attract retired service people, and the nearest really large house was the Hall, six miles away from which John Finch had chosen his bride. It was a countryside of John Finches, in fact, all good worthy people no doubt, but . . . In the past one or two of them, ambitious for their daughters and well able to afford the fees, had approached Mrs Armitage with a view to sending their girls to Homelands. The drawbacks were obvious, an inculcation of envy in those whose homes were far away; a parent within visiting distance if a girl had a cold, the introduction of that thick country accent, one of the things which in Mamselle, when she spoke English, grated upon Mrs Armitage's ear.

So the audience was small, but very appreciative; the vicar playing tit-for-tat, invited the Homelands girls to a carol service on Christmas Eve, an innovation.

After that the girls who had relatives, or friends of parents, departed. And there was Christmas.

Thomas sent Charlotte the picture of Stonebridge House for which she had asked. It was a good picture in a way, like and yet unlike. He must have drawn it, or studied it, from the far side of the lane, for the picture included the leafless copper-beech, every branch ending in tendrils that seemed to be reaching ... Papa sent a sovereign and best wishes for Christmas and Thomas's letter brought some information. Papa had been moved. At the end of the spring term, in April, he was to go to London. 'Papa,' Thomas wrote, 'is not pleased about the place itself, though he welcomes the move. And so do I. Nothing has been said about my staying here and boarding with the Macfersons which I did so dread. In fact, Papa, speaking of the house that he is going to look for during the Christmas holiday, spoke of a room for me. So I am looking forward to the move. Nothing could be worse than here.'

3

NOTHING COULD BE WORSE THAN HERE, JOHN VINCENT
Cornwall thought as he moved, in his hired cab through a part
of London that he had never seen or envisaged. Street after
street of fundamentally charming little Georgian terraces from
which sixty, seventy years ago prosperous merchants had set
out for the City. The centrifugal movement making itself evid-
ent everywhere, even in such a backward country town as Bereham, had scattered the decent families and now every house had
its ground floor occupied by some shabby little shop, its upper
floors divided and sub-divided into dwellings which, if not
quite so horrible as the rockeries of the East End, were inde-
scribably dreary, the paint and plaster flaking leprously, windows broken, windows patched with paper or cardboard.

Swarms of children, John Vincent Cornwall observed, as the
cab rattled on towards the house he had been recommended.
'Quite a select area, sir. A quiet square, near Islington High
Street.' Swarms of children, not at the moment his concern,
but soon, after April, to be. Ragged, dirty, numerous. Mr
Cornwall realised that when the summer term in this dreadful
area to which he had been transferred, opened, his nose would
be assaulted by something worse, much worse than the smell of
country corduroy. He hastily averted his eyes from the sight of
an old woman, a scarecrow thing of long grey hair and rags,
relieving herself in the gutter.

God! Did I deserve this?

St Lawrence Square, if not precisely select, was battling for
respectability. It lay in the shadow of a church which, with

166

what was obviously the rectory or vicarage, occupied one side. For the rest it was made up of tall, narrow, grimy-grey houses, built in pairs. There was a tiny, blighted garden in the centre of the square and in *its* centre a statue of some sort, white with birds' droppings. A well-polished brass plate announced a doctor's residence; a board stretching across the façade of two adjoining houses read, *St Lawrence Private Hotel*. In the ground floor window of another house, black on white was the word *Apartments*.

An outpost of Hell, he thought, prepared to inspect the fourth house that day. His choice was so limited. It must be reasonably near the centre of his new district; it must be fairly spacious, within his means, and vacant by April 30th. A house vacant now, in January, would have to stand empty, with the rent being paid and its windows probably being broken by hooligans. On the other hand he could not defer the search until April because that would mean paying another quarter's rent on Stonebridge House. And nobody, not even Agnes, could complain that St Lawrence Square was not respectable.

As he followed the present occupant, a very depressed woman, from room to room, he reckoned in his mind: twins, Thomas, nursery, *us*. It was clear that within this narrow house—the best he had seen so far—he would be obliged to choose between having a dressing room and having a study. There was, of course, no stabling; every stable within two square miles of where he stood had been made into makeshift dwellings. In any case, only the wealthy could now afford to keep a horse in London. There was an oblong of garden at the rear of the house, a desolate space crossed by a linen line upon which the depressed woman had hung a few depressed-looking articles. Look beyond the garden and there was the churchyard with some lurching gravestones.

'It's a family house, you see,' the woman said. 'But the family's gone now. My youngest boy and my youngest girl got married last summer. They had a double wedding. So now it's too big for us, you see . . .'

What John Vincent Cornwall's essentially egocentric eye saw was himself, here in this outpost of Hell, going out—given Agnes and Rose going gladly out—to catch a horse-bus in the main street. Life a long, grey, ugly avenue leading on, darker and more hopeless, to the grave.

Why don't I cut my throat?

Men *had* done it. Castlereagh had done it. One firm stroke with the bared blade. But it took courage. With a start and a blink he realised that he lacked courage; and with another start, that the hopelessness of his present situation might on this grey day, in this grey place, be slightly over-exaggerated. He had been in seemingly hopeless situations before. The right horse, the right card, the right woman, and indeed with Spender and Fowler one might even say the right *man* had come looming up. He was capable of vast self-pity and of a despair which touched rock-bottom and then rebounded. It was a fact that his application for a transfer had not resulted, as he had hoped, in a move to Cornwall or Westmorland; it was a fact that the rent of the horrid house in St Lawrence Square amounted to as much as he now paid for Stonebridge House, and for the services of March and Catchpole, the upkeep of two horses, a gig and a carriage. It was a fact that he had taken one look at the hideous path that led to the grave, and shuddered away. And yet at the very core and centre of him, there was that nub of faith the result of a sheltered childhood; the stupid little voice that said—*This cannot be happening to me. Somebody must do something.*

Agnes took his news that he had found a supremely suitable house with the right spirit, but with the wrong words. 'I shall be very glad to be gone from here. This house has brought me nothing but misery.'

Nellie said, 'Oogh, sir, I couldn't go to London, much as I'd like to see it. But you see, Bob March and me . . .' It had come about, what she had hoped for.

Cook said, 'Well, I'm sorry to say it, but I'm too old for any move but the last, sir. What with one thing and another . . . I was reckoning about money . . . but now I think I'd better go while I've got the use of my feet.'

Mr Cornwall received their giving of notice with equanimity. Perhaps in the anonymity of London it would be possible to manage with a parlourmaid who could cook, and a daily woman. Any small economy in the household would enable him to take a cab instead of the horse-bus; would enable him to dine out. He intended to spend as little time in that depressing house as possible.

'We don't want to go and live in London, do we?' Adelaide asked.

'No, we do not. And this baby is noisier than the other one.'

'Papa will be displeased. I think we shall have to wait for an opportunity.'

It came on a windy day in March. Papa had taken Mamma to London to view the house and to decide what curtains, carpets and furniture from Stonebridge House could be fitted in at St Lawrence Square.

'I think today is the day,' Adelaide said. They dressed warmly and took the linen bag which contained their hoard.

'You must hold this, Vikky, because I shall be driving,' Adelaide said.

In the yard she called 'Catchpole!' in the authoritative voice which she could assume at will. Catchpole, who had been enjoying a nap in the woodshed, emerged from that retreat.

'Harness the gig.'

'Whaffor?'

'We wish to go to . . . to take a drive.'

'In the gig?' Catchpole asked, unbelievingly.

'And we want Romper. We wish to go quickly.'

It was no concern of Catchpole's, whose term of employment was to end in April, but he had never known Miss Adelaide to take the reins and felt obliged to say, 'Romper, he take a bit of handling. He don't like bits of paper.'

'We can drive Romper,' Adelaide said grandly. And indeed there was a certain competence in the way she took the reins and drove through the gateway and negotiated the turn into the front drive. And in any case, Catchpole reflected, Romper wasn't absolutely fresh, having made the journey to Bereham and back once that day, taking the master and missus to the early train. Catchpole's thoughts reverted to the hope that at the end of April Sally would give him a job around the pub; with a husband too fat and too idle to move she needed a man about the place.

It was true that Romper did not like bits of paper, but the antics he indulged in over these, heaps of stones by the roadside and a few other objects were more playful than vicious. A piece of paper did blow across the road once—it was the last remnant of one of the reward posters which had been tacked to a tree-trunk—and he danced a bit and shied away from it. Adelaide handled him in a way that gave him confidence in her, bearing on the rein to pull him straight again and speaking sternly, 'Don't be silly, Romper.'

They arrived in fine style at the Rose and Crown and Adelaide said, in a businesslike fashion, 'We cannot tell how long we shall be. It may take an hour.'

So far there had been nothing about the outing that two ordinary young women might not have undertaken. But as they crossed the Market Square and turned by the Corn Exchange, fantasy took over completely. Vikky reached out for Adelaide's hand and said, breathessly, 'Isn't it exciting,' and Adelaide, playing echo for once, agreed, 'Very exciting.'

Iron posts, linked by chains, stood at each end of Exchange Lane, closing it to traffic. It was paved across its narrow width and contained a baker's shop, a cabinet-maker's business and several small pretty houses. Outside one of them, years and years ago, Adelaide, walking with Mamma and Vikky had halted and said, 'Look! Just like our dolls' house.' The simile was so apt that Mrs Cornwall had been encouraged to think that whatever there was that was slightly odd about the twins was being outgrown.

'So it is, Adelaide, how clever of you,' she said, and they had halted for a moment and stared for the first time at the elegant little red-brick frontage, with a fanlight over the door, a window on each side downstairs, and three above. Since then it had figured in their dreams, sleeping and waking.

'Here we are,' Adelaide said and rang the bell.

'Yes, here we are.'

The door was opened by a thin, worried-looking woman who made no attempt to conceal her disappointment.

'Oh. I thought it was the doctor . . .' She looked past them to the end of the lane. No doctor! She returned her attention to the twins. Begging for some good cause or other, most probably.

'We've come to buy your house,' Adelaide said.

Mrs Gedge thought—Well, they might have waited until the breath was out of his body! Almost simultaneously she thought—Maybe it's more saleable than I *realised*. There were drawbacks to Exchange Lane; the baker rose at unearthly hours and rattled his pans; the cabinet-maker's chief trade was with coffins and often he hammered far into the night.

'It isn't my house,' she said, 'not yet. It's my father's. And he's so ill . . .' She looked again towards the posts. 'Oh, there he is!' The doctor came through the space between the end post and the wall of the first house, and she ran towards him.

'Oh doctor, he's so poorly. Moaning . . .' She led him in, shut the door and left the twins outside.

'We could have white paint,' said Adelaide, eyeing the house whose present paint was brown and very old.

'And crumpets for tea every afternoon,' said Vikky, looking into the baker's window.

They waited patiently and with a kind of deadly tenacity. One aspect of their oddity, one which their mother had done her best to correct, was their complete absorption in their own concerns, an almost callous disregard for anything or anybody outside themselves.

After a quarter of an hour the doctor emerged, saying to the woman in the doorway, 'I think it is unlikely that he will regain consciousness, Mrs Gedge. Should he do so, send for me.'

Adelaide moved forward at once. 'We want to buy your house.'

'But I told you. Couldn't it wait? Till tomorrow, at least. Come back tomorrow.'

'That is quite impossible. The gig will not be at our disposal tomorrow,' Adelaide said firmly.

'Well, I suppose there's no harm in just talking . . .' It would be hers as soon as the old man was dead, and she'd earned it : sending him in farm produce that she could ill-spare, having him out for Christmas, grumpy as he always was, and for this last dreadful fortnight . . .

There was a nasty sick smell in the house and the room into which the woman led them was dingy, all brown again where it wasn't black and far too full of over-large furniture. Again Adelaide thought of white paint and of how, with the window cleaned and nice lace curtains . . . But she was conscious of the smell and wanted to get away from it. Vikky would be feeling the same, so she simply said, 'How much is it?'

'I don't really . . . Excuse me a minute. I must just listen . . .'

She went to the foot of the stairs, visible from the sitting-room door. Painted white and with a *blue* carpet, Adelaide thought.

Mrs Gedge stood irresolute. No sound from above. Unlikely to regain consciousness. She thought of her husband and her six children being looked after by Gracie, only twelve. She was needed at home. And selling a house took time, she'd have to show people over herself, or pay someone to do it. On the other hand she had never bought or sold a house in her life and had

171

so little to go upon, except that Fred had once said that painted up a bit he reckoned this one might fetch two hundred and fifty pounds, and they could do with it.

She went back and Adelaide repeated her question.

'I don't really know, except that my husband did once say it was worth . . . three hundred pounds.' You could always come *down*!

'We could afford that,' Adelaide said.

'Yes, we could afford that.'

'And we have it here.' Adelaide produced the bag.

There was something almost frightening about being pushed into a major transaction at such speed, Mrs Gedge thought; something almost frightening about the two ladies, popping up from nowhere and pressing so hard. She said nervously, 'But you can't just buy and sell a house like a loaf of bread. There's the lawyers . . . and . . . well, papers and things.'

'We have a very good lawyer. His name is Watkins and he lives in Bristol. But this is nothing to do with him. He only sends us the money. Besides, letters take time. We have to do this today.'

Vikky felt that Addie needed support, so she said, 'Yes, to-day. Because of the gig.'

The trouble with the world, the twins had always known, was that it was full of stupid people. Like this woman who couldn't make up her mind whether she wanted to sell or not. They always knew exactly what they wanted.

'It's real money,' Adelaide said. She untied the string that fastened the neck of the bag and spilt out the money on to the brown plush tablecloth. It had its effect on a woman to whom a half sovereign was real money and a whole one a rarity. Yet this shining pile did not seem real, none of this business seemed real.

'You can try it, if you like,' Adelaide said with gracious condescension. But not one of them knew how to test a sovereign. Then Adelaide surpassed herself. 'The bank would know. They could tell you that it is real money.'

Mrs Gedge turned her harassed eyes to the ceiling.

'I can't go to the bank, not with him dying up there.'

Already the one who had most to say was counting. Making little shining golden towers, ten coins in each. Mrs Gedge watched fascinated, yet frightened. She felt so *alone*. Until her marriage her father had always told her what to do; now Fred

172

always told her. At this critical moment she needed a man's support and advice. She said, 'Excuse again,' and went and listened by the stairs. Then she came back, took a sovereign from one of the heaps and said, 'I shan't be a minute.'

She ran across to the baker's.

'Mr Frewer, please. I've got two ladies wanting the house. Cash on the table.'

'You're lucky,' he said. 'How much?'

Some obscure instinct which she had no time to examine, made her say, 'Two hundred and fifty.'

'You're *lucky*. With the roof the way it is. I told your Pa twenty times, if I told him once, the roof'd fall in on him if he didn't do something. They seen the roof?'

'Oh yes.'

'Then you take it before they change their minds.'

She held out her hand where the sample sovereign stuck to the sweat.

'Is it a good one?'

The baker knew how to test a sovereign. He bit it, rang it on the counter and said, 'Good as gold.'

During her brief absence, Adelaide said, 'It smells horrid, doesn't it. It must be thoroughly scrubbed out.' She scooped the spare money back into the bag. 'There is plenty left for paint. And for scrubbing.'

'Very well,' said Mrs Gedge, hurrying back. 'I'll take it.'

'Vikky,' Adelaide cried, 'it's our house!'

'Yes, it is our house.'

'We must go now. I said about an hour,' Adelaide rose and made for the door. Vikky followed. They were gone as suddenly as they had come and Mrs Gedge realised that she did not know their names; that they had not asked for a receipt for their money, or made any arrangements about taking possession. It could have been a dream, except for the money, fifty pounds more than Fred had expected even when the place was painted, fifty pounds more than she had told the baker. Then she knew why she had asked more than Fred had said, and told the baker less than she had been offered. Of the two hundred and fifty pounds she would never see a penny; Fred would take it all and spend it on the hungry, unprosperous little farm. But she would have fifty, a secret nest egg. She would have to be very careful and cunning, dribbling it in to the housekeeping money so that it was not noticed, but what a help when one of

the children needed something. When Gracie was married ...
Having listened once more at the foot of the stairs, Mrs Gedge
took off her corsets, and out of a ragged old tablecloth made a
series of small pockets inside them; into each pocket she sewed
a sovereign. When, her sewing completed, she mounted the
stairs and looked in, she saw that she had merely forestalled
inheritance by about an hour.

Adelaide and Victoria shared, as they had always shared
everything, a sense of jubilation.

'We did it.'

'Yes, we did it.'

'Papa must not know. Not until the last day. Then I shall
say that we are not going to London.'

'He will be angry,' Vikky said, making one of her rare con-
tributions.

'Yes; he will be angry. But he cannot do anything. We have
bought the house and paid for it.'

Even now their relationship was so close as to need few
words. Romper, headed for home, moved more briskly. The
wind blew shrewdly. On such an afternoon as this there would
be drawing of curtains, a heaped fire and crumpets for tea.

Vikky said, 'or savoury toast,' and Adelaide understood
immediately.

'And no crying babies,' she said.

Then it happened. Romper shied partly from fun at stone-
heaps, at bits of papers, steam-rollers, a rat scurrying, a frog
hopping across the road. But he had a real if irrational dread of
perambulators. In his reaction to them there was no element of
playfulness at all. And about the one which came out of an
opening into the wood on the left-hand side of the road along
which he was going at a spanking pace, there was something
more than usually terrifying. The old woman to whom it belonged had been gathering fallen branches and twigs. She was
deaf and did not hear the clatter of hooves. But before coming
on to the road, she looked left, right, saw the gig, the horse's
nose almost within arm's reach, and pulled back to let it pass.
Too late for Romper. Terrified he reared on his hind legs,
like a circus horse, jumped away to the other side of the road
where the grass verge ran up steeply. The right wheel of the
gig mounted the bank and the gig canted. Victoria was thrown
clear, into the road, breaking her neck. Adelaide, gripping the

174

reins, fell sideways and lay parallel to the dashboard. Entangled in the tilted shafts, the left-hand one broken, its sharp end piercing his smooth hide, Romper kicked himself free, breaking a leg in the process, battering Adelaide to death among the splinters of the gig.

'Lovely and pleasant in their lives and in death not divided,' was the text of Mr Greenfield's sermon. Nobody could know that they had died at the peak of happiness, but everyone with the slightest knowledge of them agreed that to die together would have been what they would have chosen for themselves. Sympathy and hostility being self-perpetuating emotions, those who had pitied Mr Cornwall over Vincent's death now pitied him more, and those who had thought him guilty of a crime thought the accident a judgment on him. Romper had to be shot, the gig was smashed, a loss to Mr Cornwall, but that was made up to him by the money found in the linen bag, to which, as next of kin, he was entitled, since the twins had died intestate. What had been their income reverted to the trust funds now accumulating for Charlotte. The household would miss the regular two pounds a week and the house in St Lawrence Square would now be too large, but it was too late to do anything about that, and Mrs Cornwall had rather taken to the district, if not to the house itself. A freckling of small green leaves on trees and bushes and an outburst of daffodils in the central garden had improved the look of the square; she would have neighbours, she could go shopping. Rose could push the perambulator round the square or into the garden.

Mrs Gedge, with the funeral arrangements to make and the mess that poor Gracie had let things get into to clear up, never even heard about the accident, and had she done so would hardly have made any mental connection. Her husband was pleased that she had sold the house in its unpainted state, for the sum which he had in a moment of optimism, mentioned. And for cash! As she had foreseen, he took charge of it, and of the fifty pounds, found in a box when her father's bed was moved. What she obtained for the furniture, three pounds for the lot, he generously allowed her to keep and in the following months it never occurred to him to think that it was a singularly elastic three pounds. The key of the house she left with the friendly baker, and when, the house cleared and partially cleaned, she left it, her responsibility towards it ended, she tacked a little notice on the door: 'Key at baker's.' Nobody claimed the key. The roof of the pretty little house fell in. 'Just as I said,' said the baker, not without a certain satisfaction. The house stood and quietly rotted. A dolls' house whose owners had outgrown it.

4

It was possible, Charlotte discovered, to feel a slight
sense of shock but no bereavement. The twins had never
seemed real, never quite sisters. In the most miserable time of
her childhood, ears boxed, stand in the hall with your hands on
your head, into the cellar you go! they had ignored her plight
entirely. She bore them no resentment; they could not be
judged by ordinary standards because they were not quite ordinary. When she read Thomas's letter, telling her the news, she
did think—How sad, but they died together. And then she
thought of their clothes; many of them contrived and a bit odd,
but some—articles not subject to fashion and the itch to contrive—sound and good. Particularly she thought of their cloaks.
In London trees were putting out their leaves and daffodils nodded. At Gorston-on-Sea a wintry wind still blew.

She wrote, not to faithful Thomas, but to Papa who, apart
from his Christmas gift, had ignored her existence, a fact
which she found quite understandable; what with one thing
and another, all the work he had to do, so much writing, and
the move, and now *this*. She said that she was sorry to hear
about Adelaide and Victoria . . . 'It must have been a dreadful
shock for you.' She found herself wondering—What on earth
made Adelaide think she could drive Romper? 'Dear Papa, I
hope you will not think this unfeeling of me, but it is as one of
my pupils says, "verree Kold here". If Addie and Vikky were
not wearing their cloaks on the day of the accident, could they
be sent to me? Thomas, I am sure, would see to everything

177

except the packing, which Nellie could do.'

To Thomas she wrote, after explaining about the cloaks, 'and anything else either warm, or pretty . . .' And to Mrs Greenfield who might well find herself somewhat involved, 'I do hope that this will not be too much bother, dear Mrs Greenfield. We do so need stuff for our plays. As I told you, at Christmas we did *A Midsummer Night's Dream* and we are now planning to do *The Merchant of Venice* at the end of the spring term. I cannot think that Adelaide and Victoria would mind our using some of their clothes, but I do realise that the dispatching of whatever Nellie packs and Thomas brings will impose a burden upon you when next you or Mr Greenfield go to Bereham.

Adelaide had not worn her cloak on that fatal day; she knew that she needed her arms free. So Vikky had not worn hers either. So there they lay on the top of the hamper; one dark blue, one crimson, both collared and edged with fur.

Charlotte said, giving Miss Lamb a sidelong look, 'I did ask somebody to send me a few things for the play . . . But I think this, and this,' she shook out the two cloaks, 'are a bit too good . . . In fact I would like to wear one, if you would wear the other.'

'What splendid garments,' Miss Lamb said without envy or greed. 'How generous.'

'Which would you prefer, Miss Lamb?' Oh, please choose the crimson . . . Adelaide's? Victoria's? They were so much of a muchness that I never made any clear distinction. And whichever Miss Lamb chooses, the one left to me will be a kind of hair shirt, worn as a penance, because I have deceived *her*, so honest . . . so almost saintlike.

'Well,' Miss Lamb said, 'if it is really all the same to you, I'll have this one.' She chose the crimson. 'Oh, how warm! You are absolutely right, Miss Burns. One thinks of the Forest of Arden as temperate . . . What else did your very kind friend send?'

The year moved along; a month late spring reached Gorston-on-Sea and Charlotte and Miss Lamb could hang up their cloaks. On John Finch's farm the pullets began to lay with such zest that one day Mamselle brought more eggs than Mrs Armitage and Mrs Osgood could possibly eat while they were fresh, so instead of a few grains of scrambled egg scattered on slices of toast, everybody had a whole egg, fried, for supper.

Thomas wrote. 'Dear Charlie, really the most marvellous thing has happened. I can't remember if I told you, but Nellie wouldn't come. Nor Cook. So Papa said that if I did a lot of what they used to do, and Catchpole, I mean carrying coal and chopping sticks, and help down the steps with the pram, etc. etc. I could do that and not be a pupil-teacher which I never wanted to be, but go to art classes at an evening school instead. So I said I would. And there is a master, Mr Sylvester, who likes the way I draw. He said something about my being like Blake, but needing experience. So I go four evenings a week and except that I still miss you, Charlie . . .' An obvious by-thought which she could match. 'I am happy for the first time in my life. So is Mrs C. A lot of women around here play whist and she has taken to it. Papa isn't home much and I don't think Nurse Ellis likes London. So that is all my news for now . . .'

May, pleasantly warm on the east coast, was hot in London. In the West End, once John Vincent Cornwall's stamping ground, roads were swept, the horse-droppings and any other debris taken away and the water-carts went their round, sprinkling, laying the dust. London on a May morning, swept and sprinkled . . . But this was a different place. Horse-droppings and even more disgusting things lay where they fell and dried in the sun and were powdered by passing wheels so that the very dust stank, and water-carts were rare. The crowded horse-buses stank, the overcrowded schools stank. Also London teachers were lacking the deference which—at least until the disaster—the rural ones had shown to Her Majesty's Inspector. Several of the head teachers were graduates and they were all damned Radicals, with no respect for anything or anybody. They were unamenable to suggestion and resentful of criticism. In his own manner there was nothing left of the bonhomie which had made him popular in Suffolk; everyone with whom he had to do considered him gloomy and disagreeable. Mrs Cornwall's growing circle of friends, most of whom had never spoken to him, thought that he looked disagreeable and stuck up into the bargain.

As hideous day followed hideous day, he lost his inner certainty that it was all too horrible to be true, that this simply could not be happening to him. It was true, it was happening, and would go on, and on. He reached a point where he needed the fortifying glass of brandy before he could face the day; and on the morning when the post brought him a square white envelope of very superior quality, with the familiar embossed seal of the Board on its flap, he imagined that it contained his dismissal. At first sight the letter did not reassure him. It simply requested him to call, at his earliest convenience, to discuss a matter of some urgency. His first impulse was not to go; they could dismiss him—that was their right, but he did not intend to submit himself to a scolding. Then, looking at the letter again, he saw that it was not signed by the official who dealt with such matters as appointments and dismissals in the inspectorate. And why a matter of some urgency? If they felt that he was no longer fit for his post, they could suspend him at a moment's notice. A faint curiosity began to stir. He'd go, this very morning. He went back upstairs and changed into clothes that were not permeated by the school smell. He'd go, and if it turned out to be, after all, a face-to-face lecture, he'd simply walk out.

He was cordially greeted. 'Ha! Cornwall. Very good of you to come at once.' A firm, friendly handshake and invitation to be seated, to have a glass of sherry. Then a rather tentative approach, 'The idea may not appeal to you at all, but we've gone into it thoroughly and you appear to be the most suitable, indeed in the circumstances, the only suitable chap we could suggest. I'll put it briefly . . .'

Put briefly what it amounted to was this. Uttahpore, one of the remaining independent states in India, had lately come under the rule of a rajah with very enlightened and progressive ideas. He wished to inaugurate an educational system and had—very sensibly—applied to the Board to assist him in this worthy scheme. He asked the Board to send him a Director of Education. Like the twins, the Rajah of Uttahpore knew exactly what he wanted and what he wanted was rather rare. A man from a public school, from either Oxford or Cambridge, yet with a thorough knowledge of education at a primary level.

'Uttahpore!' John Vincent Cornwall said. 'That rings a bell somewhere, but for the life of me . . .'

'The Rajah mentions that he himself enjoyed the benefits of an English education. At Eton.'

'That's it! We used to call him Bunjo. He fagged for me.' And a dirty little tyke he was in those days, too.

The remuneration was lavish; ninety thousand rupees a year, a house in the capital as a permanent residence, accom-

180

modation in rest houses near each school that was planned. Servants and horses provided. 'He who rules must have grandeur.'

'Would you think about it, Cornwall?'

John Vincent Cornwall had already thought. The prospect filled him with ecstasy and yet somehow he was not really surprised. It was *bad* luck that surprised him—and God knew he had had enough of that in the last year.

It was easy enough to convince Agnes that Uttahpore was unfit for a white woman. Actually old Bunjo had written that the Director could bring his family should he wish to do so; the plains of Uttahpore were hot in summer, but there were hills . . .

A rupee was worth roughly one and sixpence; ninety thousand of them was pretty near seven thousand pounds; Mr Cornwall could afford to be generous to Agnes; rent and rates paid by banker's order and a thousand a year for housekeeping. She had tired of him as he had tired of her. She thought that with his gloomy presence removed she would be much like the spinsters and the widows around her, and with a thousand a year, better off than most. She gave absolutely no trouble at all.

Rose was very different. She said, 'Take me with you. You must take me with you . . .' She had clung, like a little bulldog to the one hope that had made life endurable for her. One day, if only he'd stop drinking, joy would be renewed. Country born and bred, she detested the city and had missed the comforts she had enjoyed at Stonebridge House. But hope had supported her.

'I can't, Rose. You could not live in the climate.'

'If you can, I can.'

'My dear, it is quite impossible.'

She said, 'You could take me if you wanted to.' A sudden, almost frightening change came over her face. 'I only came to this horrible place to be near you and now you are going away. You won't, you know. If you do this to me, I shall go to the police. I shall tell the truth, the whole truth and nothing but the truth,' glibly the parrot phrases fell.

Everything, he thought, always in the balance, good luck, bad luck. With everything arranged, his passage booked. Now this!

Feeling sick, he made the last, desperate gambler's move.

181

'Very well, Rose. Run along. You will find a policeman in the High Street.'

Eye challenged eye in hatred as once eye had challenged eye in love. And he won. Rose said brokenly, 'I can't. You know I can't. Once I thought if we burned together in Hell, or hanged together ... And I would have hanged for you. Everything I did, or said, was for you. And now ... and now ...' She began to cry.

'Rose,' he said, 'Rose. Even if what happened had not happened, parting was bound to come. You're young. You're pretty. One day you were bound to be married, while I ...'

I. Seeing Bunjo again, sunshine, horses, polo, tiger shooting, work well within my scope. He said, 'Rose, it was lovely while it lasted but we both knew that it couldn't last forever. Don't cry.'

Rose cried on; she cried herself out. Then she got up and foraged about and found a card left by a visiting Daughter of Jerusalem, who had called one day at the house when Rose had been out with the double-burdened perambulator, lifting Amelia out to take some staggering steps under the soiled, but still sweet-scented lilac bushes of the garden in the centre of the square.

The card said that the Children of Jerusalem met on Sundays at seven o'clock, at 24 Cumberland Street, Bethnal Green, over the fishmonger's shop.

The shop was shuttered and its door was locked, but there was another narrower door on to which was tacked the fellow of the card which had been left in St Lawrence Square. Rose opened it and found herself in a passage, lined with crates and the rush baskets in which individual orders were delivered. The whole place smelt strongly of fish. There was a flight of steep stairs and at the top of them a room, exactly like every other room in which the Children of Jerusalem met. With a sudden feeling of coming home, after long absence, Rose slipped into place on a narrow wooden bench to the left of the room. Sons sat on the right; Daughters to the left. On this evening there were six Sons and, including herself, eleven Daughters.

A far less egoistic person than Rose Ellis might have been forgiven for feeling that the whole meeting had been designed to fit her need. The doleful, unaccompanied hymns both dealt with the cleansing quality of the Blood of the Lamb; the

182

preaching and the prayers would have led an uninformed listener to believe that gathered in this upper room was a collection of the worst sinners in the world. Every word seemed to apply to her who had committed sins of the flesh, sins of the spirit and never properly repented until now. It seemed to her not sufficient that the false god, first by withdrawing his favours and then by deserting her, had inflicted suffering upon her; she must punish herself. She must do something to show how penitent she was.

As was usual, the Brother in charge stood at the doorway and said, 'God keep you,' to each member. He had noticed the new face and to Rose he also said, 'We hope to see you next Sunday, Sister.'

She shook her head slightly. 'I am a member of the Lowestoft community and I am going home tomorrow.'

Back to meek submission, to gruelling physical work, an eight-miles trudge each Sunday. What better proof of penitence could she give? She was sorry for all her sins; she would show that she was sorry, and God would eventually forgive her and bring her safe to Heaven. The substitution of one hope for another was easily accomplished by her shallow, single-minded nature.

5

AT HOMELANDS, AS IN ALL SIMILAR ESTABLISHMENTS, THE summer term was the best of the year. The afflictions of the winter vanished, walks on the beach became a pleasure. On two consecutive Thursdays Mamselle brought strawberries enough for all; and then she brought raspberries and the luscious yellow gooseberries called Golden Drops.

'Anything *fresh*,' Miss Lamb said, 'that is what we all need. And I still think that the suggestion I made last autumn, fresh herring or sprats once a week, was in essence sound.'

'Did you make that suggestion?'

'I don't report all my failures, Miss Burns. I failed on that occasion. Naturally, I approached Mrs Osgood first. I told her that what she calls "cold sores", you remember, at the sides of the mouth, were in fact evidence of a mild form of scurvy. She pooh-poohed the idea. I shall have to try again next term. With more confidence, now that everything is going so well.'

Academically things were going well. Cecilie Burke still could not count—she never would, but Sophie Wren could now spell any but the most unusual words—and could look them up in the dictionary. The books upon which Miss Lamb had expended her salary—readable classics like *Jane Eyre*, *Wuthering Heights* and *Vanity Fair*—had coaxed quite a number of non-readers into the fold. And a certain impediment—something that Miss Lamb had been aware of without being able exactly to name it except by saying 'those languid young ladies', and 'Ella and her clique', had been removed when

Angela, Florence and Felicity had left at the end of the spring term; immediately after the perfomance of *The Merchant of Venice*.

Miss Lamb said, 'In a way I am glad; glad for them and glad for the school. That rather look-down-your-nose attitude towards school was contagious. But I am sorry for Ella, absolutely stranded now.'

Two other girls, not in the highest age group, had left, one because her parents were back in England, in Cheltenham where she could attend a day school; one because her parents could no longer afford the fees, though they did not say so. Had they done so they might have strengthened Mrs Osgood's hand. She had always argued that a reduction of fees was the one way to combat the decline.

Homelands had in fact started with twenty-two girls, almost all of them daughters of Mrs Armitage's friends, or of friends of her friends. It had grown, reached its apogee with a hundred girls, and on that comfortable plateau had remained for some years, with a cook in the kitchen, hired girls making beds and waiting at table.

The decline had set in, partly through competition, similar establishments opening on the milder south coast; partly through Mrs Armitage's friends and the friends of her friends getting too old to provide the supply of girls, and partly because a whole generation of Homelands girls went about saying things like, 'Oh, I was happy enough and of course I adored Mrs Armitage, but . . .' But Gorston-on-Sea was very bleak, quite the coldest place in England and so remote . . .

There it was. Five girls had left at Easter and only one—and she, as Mrs Armitage said, was 'suspiciously *dark* though her name couldn't be more English'—had arrived.

Mrs Osgood said that she had said it before and she would say it again, the fees must go down. Mrs Armitage said, as she had said before, that to lower the fees would be to fall into the second grade, and that would be the beginning of the end. 'My dear Augusta, we are simply going through a bad patch. It will pass, I am confident. If we hold on and make every possible economy.'

As always when arguing with Mrs Armitage, Mrs Osgood found herself at a disadvantage, always bound to look back to the beginning when outwardly their circumstances had been almost identical. Both widowed, both possessed of a little, a

185

very little money, both back in England since both had had sense enough to know that India was no place in which to be poor. At first sight Augusta Osgood had some advantage, she was a trained nurse, she was employable. Apart from having charm, some social contacts, engaging manners and an ability to play the piano, Mrs Armitage had nothing, except her little, very little money. Left to herself, Mrs Osgood would have hired herself as a private nurse, probably to some querulous, incontinent old patient. She had had enough of hospitals, with all the rules and regulations. Left to herself Mrs Armitage would have become companion-housekeeper, at the beck and call of some spoiled old woman. Combining their assets, and blessed by phenomenal luck in their search for a suitable house, they had both lived well and comfortably for almost twenty years. Even now they enjoyed spacious and comfortable surroundings, the services of a maid and—a thing of value to them both—independence. Apart from this common desire to be answerable to nobody, their natures differed and complemented one another almost as exactly as their talents. Mrs Osgood found it no more of a hardship to do the cooking than Mrs Armitage found it to teach the piano and deportment, and to write charming letters. Neither could have done the other's job, and neither interfered in the other's sphere. But Mrs Osgood had been aware from the first, not only of the social gap between a colonel's widow and the widow of a stationmaster, but of the fact that, left to herself, Mrs Armitage could have hired a matron, while she, left to herself, would have found it difficult to find another Mrs Armitage. That was one reason why, when economy seemed advisable, the cook had been the first to go. By assuming this duty and doing it so well and so cheaply, Mrs Osgood had entrenched herself still further.

She now said, 'I can't see any other economy that we could make. Can you?'

'Well,' Mrs Armitage said plaintively, 'I suppose I could dispense with my little tea parties.'

Twice a week four girls took tea in the drawing room, taking it in turns to play hostess, mastering the art of pouring tea and making pleasant conversation at the same time. The teas were always delicious, a break in a dull routine, and from them stemmed the adoration for and imitation of Mrs Armitage.

'That wouldn't save much,' Mrs Osgood said bluntly.

'Those little buns with a bit of cherry on, four a penny at the baker's, I can make at half the price. It's going to take more than that. We're down to twenty-six and that's the lowest we've ever been. And I still think . . .'

'I know what you think, Augusta. As a matter of fact, if I do anything about the fees it will be to increase them.'

This rather fruitless discussion, though it was to bear results, went no further because the front door bell rang very loudly.

Eva scurried across the hall and a voice, clearly audible in the drawing room, said, 'Mah name's Colin Campbell. I want to see Mrs Armitage.'

He was rather over six feet tall, had flaming red hair, the weathered skin of an outdoor man, the clothes—tweed jacket, breeches, highly polished buskins of a farmer of the more successful kind. Mrs Armitage summed him up instantly, a second generation member of one of those Scots families who had moved into East Anglia and done very well. He would have a little girl whom he would wish to place at Homelands.

'And what can I do for you, Mr Campbell?' she asked gently, while her mind raced. Down to twenty-six; local girls might be the solution, though parents in the vicinity were a nuisance.

'I don't quite know. But you seemed to be the one to start with. I've fallen in love with one of your young ladies.'

Surprise widened the harebell-blue eyes.

'Miss Ella Smythe is her name. It's my intention to marry her if she'll have me. Subject to her parents' consent, of course.'

'Mr Campbell, have you ever spoken to her?' What has been going on, unknown to me?

'No. I was at the miller's at Gorston and I saw her then. Folks laugh about love at first sight, but it can happen. It did to me. So I spoke to Miss Finch.'

Who on earth was Miss Finch? Oh, of course, Mamselle!

'My land runs alongside John Finch's. So, as I say, I spoke to Mary, and she told me Miss Smythe's name, and yours. Then, on Sunday last, I drove over to church here, though Ah'm Presbyterian mahself, and took another look to make sure. And now I am sure. Has she parents?'

'She has. They are at Agra. In India.'

'No sense in troubling them until we know how Miss Ella

feels about me. Would you, in loco parentis, so to speak, give me permission to ask her that?'

A man of some education. Even the Scotchness of his pronunciation was variable.

'I could do that.'

'Maybe I'd better give you some account of myself. I am twenty-six years of age. I own Priory Farm, at Greston, six hundred acres and I've another, three hundred, at Overton. I think I may say I have a good name in the district. I owe no man a penny and I've never been one for the women. In fact I never noticed one much until that day in the miller's. John Finch would speak for my character, and Thorley's Bank could tell you I'm sound.'

Absolutely sound, Mrs Armitage was sure of that. A fine upstanding direct young man. Mrs Armitage found herself liking him. And what a chance for Ella. There were other aspects, too. The fact that a girl had made a good, if not splendid, marriage straight from Homelands was not a thing one could mention in the brochure, but word would spread. Mrs Smythe would spread it with the utmost satisfaction and delight. And from Gummage's five per cent discount on a wedding gown, bridesmaids' dresses, a trousseau. The Smythes would not stint.

'I think perhaps you had better see Ella,' Mrs Armitage said.

When Ella entered, the young man stood up, Mrs Armitage noted with approval; and though one would not have thought that his red-brown face could have shown a blush, it did.

'Ella, dear, this is Mr Colin Campbell, who is a neighbour of Mamselle's. Mr Campbell, Miss Ella Smythe.' Ella was blushing, too, and Mrs Armitage said, with exquisite tact, 'Ella, would you like to pour us all a little sherry?' By the time she had done so Ella had regained her composure, and, trained by many, many lessons on deportment in this very room, made some light remark about the wonderful weather. The doting look in the young man's eyes was really quite touching. As soon as the sherry was drunk Mrs Armitage made an excuse to leave them together.

'Well,' said Miss Lamb, 'it's the best thing that could possibly have happened to Ella; and the preparations for the wedding will enliven the holidays.' The wedding was fixed for the first week in September, with the harvest safely in. 'But in a way I wish she could have left school first. It rather puts ideas into the heads of the older girls. And she flaunts that ring so much that I warned her that if she didn't look out she would become left-handed.'

Charlotte laughed and then felt rather guilty. This was the last Saturday of June, by day, if not by date, the anniversary of Vincent's death. She knew it was silly to pay attention to anniversaries, a dead person was no more dead on one certain day than at any other time of the year. Just as no person was more alive on a birthday. Still, she had felt rather sad all day and now was glad when Miss Lamb rattled on about netball, a game she intended to introduce as soon as the new term opened. She had ordered the posts from the village carpenter, the iron rings from the blacksmith. The nets would be made from a bit of old fishing net. 'Perfectly adequate. The ball is the problem. I really think that that should be provided from the Pocket Money Fund. I am prepared to pay for the posts, and shall do when I am paid on Tuesday. I shall also mention the football then. One can but *ask*.'

'I wish I could help more,' Charlotte said.

In a different way Miss Lamb was quite as tactful as Mrs Armitage. Never, by word or by look, had she asked why Charlotte should be here working unrewarded except by her keep and a bit of French conversation each week. Papa had sent a sovereign at Christmas, and another with a short letter which informed her that he was going to India and that if she needed anything she could ask Mrs Cornwall. It seemed to Charlotte very unlikely that Mrs Cornwall would give her anything, even if she asked. So she hoarded that sovereign carefully. Yet one could not really think—as one was sometimes tempted to do—that Papa had been a bit casual. In his own way, with all that he had to do, leaving for India so suddenly, he had remembered her. Proof of that lay in her left-hand top drawer. A letter from Mr Fothergill.

Dear Miss Charlotte,

Until this morning, when your Papa called in at the office, to make arrangements about that bond, which I think it most unlikely will ever be needed, I did not even know where you were. I gathered that you had not come to London. Your Papa tells me that you are well and happy and busy, as indeed I have been myself. You may have read of the Comedine business in which my firm was deeply in-

189

volved. It took me to both North and South America, trips erroneously regarded as holidays since they involved long sea voyages. But I am back in London now, and likely to remain here, since my uncle has gone into semi-retirement. If in any way—quite apart from that bond which I always regarded as nonsense, I could be of any service to you, please do not hesitate to call upon me . . .

Charlotte had read the letter and thought again that Mr Fothergill was extremely kind. She wondered whether, when she was penniless, it would be possible to ask him to go along to St Lawrence Square and wrest another sovereign out of Mrs C. It was just a possibility.

Tuesday, the last day of June, dawned clear and bright and rosy red, the kind of morning which those connected with the soil, or the sea, knew by experience or hearsay to be no good omen of fair weather. Inland they said, 'Red sky at morning, shepherd's warning,' on the coast they said, 'Rosy at seven, black by eleven.' The day had darkened steadily and in the evening, when Miss Lamb had gone to her interview with Mrs Armitage, and Charlotte prepared to make tea, the sky was purple, over a hushed sea, the colour of pewter.

'Well,' Charlotte asked, not looking up from the tea-making, when Miss Lamb entered, a little earlier than she had expected, 'how did it go?'

When Miss Lamb did not immediately answer Charlotte was reminded of the evening when Miss Lamb had brought back all the reports that must be done again. So she looked up and saw Miss Lamb much more upset than she had been on that occasion. Speechless. She tottered to the bed and laid upon it the shabby old reticule from which almost all the beads had fallen away, lacking that stitch in time, and five gleaming sovereigns dropped from her clenched left hand. Her always pale face was the colour of paper and her green eyes blazed.

'What happened, Miss Lamb? What happened?'

Miss Lamb attempted to speak; she opened her mouth. Her lower jaw shook convulsively and she put up both her thin hands and pressed it into position, into steadiness. Then between her teeth she said, 'She sacked me.'

There was what Miss Barker had explained as the *pathetic fallacy*, the poetic notion that Nature shared man's misfortunes

190

and moods. And it was true, to the extent that the threatening purple sky sagged. The room darkened. The little kettle boiled over and the flame of the stove hissed and died as Charlotte said, 'Oh no!'

The sensible, practical streak in her, said, 'Make the tea.' And she obeyed. Miss Lamb sat, holding her jaw, looking in the purplish light like somebody dead.

'Here,' Charlotte said, 'drink this. And tell me all about it.'

Tea, hot and strong, that had never before failed as a restorative, failed now. Miss Lamb tried to take the cup, but her extended hand shook so violently that she withdrew it again and propped her jaw; and when Charlotte held the cup to her lips, though she tried again, all that resulted was a clatter of teeth on the cup's rim and some splashes on the front of her blouse as the liquid spilled.

Was this a stroke? All that Charlotte knew about strokes was that one was supposed to be responsible for the distortion of old Mrs Catchpole's face, and that Miss Lamb often used the word somewhat lightly, saying, 'She almost had a stroke,' or 'I almost had a stroke,' or 'This will give her a stroke.'

The vibration which shook Miss Lamb made the brass knobs on the bedstead rattle.

'I'll fetch Mrs Osgood,' Charlotte said.

Miss Lamb shot out her hand and siezed Charlotte's sleeve. She said, 'No. No. All right . . . in a minute.' She fought for control and failed to attain it. Her face seemed to break up in a frightening way, the lower half seeming to laugh, while her eyes filled and shed tears that splashed down and joined the tea marks. 'Ha-ha-ha,' Miss Lamb laughed as though she had been told some hilarious joke, and mingled with the laughter were the sobs and the tears of unbearable grief.

Hysteria! The cure was a smart slap across the face, but to strike Miss Lamb was unthinkable. So Charlotte sat down beside her and put her arm around the thin, shuddering body, saying, as though to a child, 'There, there. Have a good cry. But don't laugh, Miss Lamb, please don't laugh.' After a moment or two during which the purplish light darkened and some rain flung itself against the window, Miss Lamb said, 'I really am sorry. It was the shock.' She sat up straight again and mopped her face.

'Absurd of me,' she said. The rigor had passed, and the hysteria, but her eyes looked wild.

'Try the tea now,' Charlotte said and poured a fresh cup. 'What happened? Did you have a row?' Could the word *netball* have sparked off a scene?

'No. There was nothing. No warning. She paid me. And before I had even time to put the money away, she dismissed me. She put the money in my hand and said she had come to the conclusion that I was not suitable for this post.'

'How could she say that? Why, you're the best teacher ... What did you say?'

'Nothing. I was unable to speak. Had she taken up the poker and struck me ... But there it is. She said I could stay until I found a post, but that I cannot do. I must leave at once. All my plans ...' she said, in a voice of great pathos. Then she gathered her forces and said, 'Miss Burns, you are very young for such a burden, but promise me ... Try to carry on. If I have given you any guidance, if you follow it, my time here will not have been entirely wasted.'

'But I couldn't possibly ...' Charlotte said and stopped short. Useless to say that to Miss Lamb. 'You sit quietly and drink your tea. I shan't be a minute.' A single impulse carried her out of the room, along the corridor, down the private stairs and to the white-painted door where she halted, drew a long breath and ran her hands over her hair. One must not appear distraught.

Mrs Armitage reclined on her sofa. On the long table behind it there was a great bowl of roses.

'Do come in, dear. What a dreadful evening. I can hardly see the cards.' She was engaged in one of her complicated games of Patience, the cards pale against the green baize of the card table. Rain was now lashing at the windows, and the wind was crying. 'Do sit down. Forgive me; you shall have my full attention in a minute.' Without haste she placed two cards and then looked up.

'I have just seen Miss Lamb.'

'Yes.' The word hovered between acknowledgment and enquiry.

'She is greatly upset. Mrs Armitage, I felt compelled to come and ask you in what respect she is unsuitable?'

'You may *ask*, Charlotte. I am afraid I cannot give you an answer. Unsuitability is very difficult to define.'

'But there must be some reason. She is such a splendid teacher. So clever. So devoted to the girls.'

'I agree. Entirely.'

'Then what did she do that was wrong?'

'Wrong? Nothing that I know of.'

'Mrs Armitage, you must have some reason. Whatever it is I must say that I think you are making a terrible mistake.'

'Possibly.' In this strange light the pink roses looked lurid and Mrs Armitage's harebell-blue eyes like aquamarines. She aimed straight at the heart. She said, 'Like everybody else I am liable to make mistakes. I have more than once taken a decision which other people would regard as mistaken—if they knew about it.'

What had not been said rang loudly in the silence.

'I see.'

'A mere fault can be remedied, an offence forgiven,' Mrs Armitage said. 'I have run this school for almost twenty years, Charlotte. I think you should trust my judgment. I did tell Miss Lamb that she could stay here until she found a suitable post. She left me rather abruptly, before I could add that I am prepared to give her a testimonial which will assure her a post in an establishment to which she will be entirely suited. If you would tell her that I should be grateful. Good night, my dear.'

Miss Lamb was not in her room. She had drunk none of the tea. The shabby old reticule, the five sovereigns lay on the bed together with the sodden handkerchief. Perhaps she had gone to what was politely referred to as 'the end', a place to which it was very ill-mannered to admit that you, or anybody else ever went. But after waiting two minutes Charlotte went and searched. She looked into every bedroom. Conscientious to the last, Miss Lamb would have answered any call.

Downstairs, perhaps, collecting the books which were, with her few clothes, her only worldly belongings.

Not there. Not anywhere in the house. Guilt fell, heavy and cold. I left her, when she was in no fit state to be left.

She tore open the front door and ran out. The wind gave its final cry and flung the last handful of rain at her, the evening lightened as she ran. 'Miss Lamb!' 'Miss Lamb!' The laurels in the drive glistened; the beach when she reached it stretched away to right and to left, the colour of honey, lapped by the sea which, as the storm blew inwards, brightened and frisked.

Why think the worst? She ran back into the lane where the puddles were just the colour of the tea which she and Miss

193

Lamb had drunk together so happily, so many times. In the garden patch before the first cottage an old man was replacing the pea-sticks which the wind had loosened. No, he said, he could swear nobody had gone by. Yes, he would have seen, he knew what a summer storm could do, he'd been looking out so that the minute the rain stopped, he could repair the damage the wind had done. 'Wanted to save my peas,' he said. *Could* he have been too intent upon his peas? Charlotte ran on, a woman with a drenched sack over her head, met her. 'Excuse me, please, did you see anybody in the lane?' 'No. I been to the shop and I was caught. I waited in the doorway but it didn't stop, so I borrowed this bit of a sack and set out. Surely yes, miss; if there'd been anybody to meet I'd have met them. I met you, didn't I?'

Drenched by that last fall of rain, her hair, like Miss Lamb's, half down, Charlotte broke into the rose-coloured, rose-scented room again and gasped out, 'Miss Lamb has drowned herself. And it is my fault.' Then something happened that had not happened for years, not since those times when she had stood with her hands on her head in the hall at Stonebridge House; a spinning darkness.

'Lay flat.' Mrs Osgood's voice. Scent of roses overlaid by the horrible stench of burnt feathers.

'A fine fright you gave us all.' That was Mrs Armitage.

The world settled and steadied. She found her voice.

'Miss Lamb drowned herself.'

'Charlotte, you have absolutely no reason for saying such a thing. Miss Lamb *left*. As she was perfectly entitled to do.'

'But she didn't take anything. That was how I knew . . .'

'Don't go rearing about,' Mrs Osgood said. 'Lay flat.'

'She didn't take anything. Her money, her reticule. On the bed,' Charlotte said. 'And it was raining . . .' She thought of the cloak hanging on the door, the outdoor shoes under the chest-of-drawers.

'So it was. And you've got yourself a soaking,' Mrs Osgood said. 'I'll make you a hot drink and put a hot water jar in your bed.'

Charlotte said, 'I am to blame. I left her. I should have known.'

'My dear child, this is absolutely ridiculous. You are upsetting yourself and everybody else over nothing.'

194

I am upsetting Mrs Armitage. I am on her sofa.

'I gave Miss Lamb notice,' Mrs Armitage said gently. 'I made a point of offering her a home while she sought another post. She chose to leave at once. And did so. Why you should assume that she drowned herself, is quite beyond my understanding. As is the fact that you blame yourself. Quite absurd.'

'She was so terribly upset . . . Quite unlike herself. Hysterical. I should not have left her. Mrs Armitage, we must do something. Tell the police.'

'It seems to me that you are hysterical, yourself, Charlotte. Miss Lamb is a fully responsible adult. She chose to leave at once. That was her right. Possibly she wished to avoid saying goodbye.'

'If she left like that, she would have taken her money at least. And how could she have left without walking either on the beach or along the lane?'

'By the field path of course. She probably has friends at Overton.'

'She hadn't a friend in the world.'

'If that is true, it is significant. Less than an hour ago you asked me what I meant by saying that she was unsuitable. Would you not agree that a woman of thirty-five—that was the age she gave me—a woman who has held various posts and not acquired a single friend, is somewhat of an oddity?'

'She never thought about anything except her work. And,' said Charlotte, reverting stubbornly to her argument, 'she would have taken her money and changed her shoes.'

'I can see that you are not in a state to be reasoned with. I shall ask Mrs Osgood to give you something to make you sleep. Everything will look quite different in the morning.'

Mrs Osgood returned, and taking Charlotte by the arm said, not unkindly, 'Come along, Miss Burns. Bed's the place for you.'

She helped Charlotte upstairs. In the corridor she halted outside Miss Lamb's door and said, 'I suppose it isn't possible that you missed her somehow and that she is . . .' She tapped on the door and called Miss Lamb by name. Then she opened the door. The money, the reticule and the tear-soaked handkerchief had gone from the bed, so had the cloak from the door, the outdoor shoes from under the chest-of-drawers.

'You must have been mistaken,' Mrs Osgood said.

'I swear I was not. She was sitting *there*. I was hardly gone a minute and when I came back everything was here, except Miss Lamb.'

'Maybe you're muddling what you saw one time with what you saw the other. People do do that. Or maybe she was in the building when you ran out and came back and collected her thing. Anyway, they've gone, you see. Now come along, your drink'll be getting cold . . .'

For the first time in her life Charlotte entertained a fleeting doubt of her own sanity.

The girls took Miss Lamb's sudden disappearance quite calmly. The elder ones were accustomed to mistresses coming and going; the younger ones had been in her sole charge for only a short time. She had not been popular with everybody, always brisk and sometimes sharp in her struggle against inertia. Sophie Wrenn said, '*You* won't go away and leave us, will you, Miss Burns?'

'No, dear. I shall stay.'

Even had she been free to leave, she would have stayed, because now Miss Lamb's last words had taken on the nature of a sacred charge. How inadequately her own education had prepared her for the task before her, and how much she had depended upon Miss Lamb, was borne in upon her by little things. The carpenter and his son delivered the netball posts with the iron rings already attached. They offered to plant them for her. How far apart? She was obliged to confess that she did not know. She had never known that such a game existed until Miss Lamb said its name. 'Maybe the other young lady . . .' the carpenter suggested. 'Miss Lamb is no longer here.' Vanished without trace. There was no rumour of a dead woman having been washed up by the sea. Charlotte told the carpenter that she would try to find out. How? From whom?

Then there was the matter of one of the things—healthy and educational—that Miss Lamb had planned as a holiday occupation; a huge relief map of the world to be made in the sand above the tide level. Big enough, she had said, to allow many girls to work on it at once, and all to proper scale. The one available relief map in the school said that one inch equalled sixteen hundred miles. How did one translate that into a map at which a dozen girls could work?

One thing that Miss Lamb had not planned was a rehearsal for the wedding. 'Of that I will take charge,' Mrs Armitage

196

said. She did so, very thoroughly; a proxy bridegroom, best man, giver-away; a real bride and bridesmaids; so many ushers, so many relatives of bride and groom. No Homelands girl need ever be at a loss at a wedding.

Finally came the wedding itself with Doctor Bowen to give Ella away. Her parents, free of the haunting thought that Ella could not be a schoolgirl forever, had provided lavishly. It was a splendid, and very pretty wedding, a great credit to the school, with so much food that several girls, including a bridesmaid, became very bilious. Wedding fever, as Miss Lamb had foreseen, ran through the school, from the senior girls, discussing what dress, what bouquet they would choose when their time came, to the little ones substituting a dolls' wedding for a dolls' tea party.

Then the autumn term began, bringing two new girls from Ceylon, who did not even know their alphabet.

'And I am so sorry not to have found you an assistant, Charlotte dear. I have tried all the agencies. I have even advertised.' I don't want an assistant; I want someone like Miss Lamb, to take charge and tell me what to do. Why, oh why, did you dismiss her? 'But I think we can manage,' Mrs Armitage went on. 'I shall do my best to help you. Music and French have always been extras, but I think that if we said nothing, about fees, I mean, I could slip in a few more music lessons, and Mamselle can chat as easily to a dozen as to six. That would relieve you, would it not?'

Unhappily Charlotte realised that between her and the elder girls, some as old as, and several taller than, she was herself, Miss Lamb had always stood like a rock. Quiet courtesy and consideration for others was still the prevailing rule, but it did not preclude some behaviour which Miss Lamb would not have tolerated. When Charlotte asked, before the morning exercises, 'Excuses?' a lot of hands went up and she had not the assurance to repeat the remark about biological impossibility. Ground thus lost could never be recovered and morning exercises, so good for the lungs and the bowels, very gradually became something that those under the age of thirteen did, albeit unwillingly, and those older shamelessly dodged. The do-what-you-like period after supper reverted to what it had been before Charlotte's arrival. As Miss Lamb had been, Charlotte was overwhelmed by the marking, made necessary by the fact that while the newcomers were being taught the alphabet and

197

initiated into the mystery of C-A-T, cat, the others must be occupied. Marking compositions, marking exercises, marking sums, while the now-oldest four played whist and the youngest held dolls' weddings and some in-between wrote or read or simply sat about and talked, Charlotte was conscious of failure. There was a letter from Thomas.

Dear Charlie, you know how my boots always were. Well, they were that way again last week and Mr Sylvester noticed and asked me if my father was unemployed. So I told him and he said that if I didn't get a new pair, after he had written to Mrs C, he would write to Papa, or to that Rajah. When Mr Sylvester gets his temper up he isn't afraid of anything or anybody. He did write and I got new boots and also trousers; they don't match but they are long enough . .

Thomas had obviously found a friend and she was glad. But sometimes she felt that she was the loneliest person in the world. Between her and Mrs Armitage and Mrs Osgood there was something that she tried not to think about.

Lonely, already half-defeated, she pressed on. There must be another play, another communal effort for Christmas, abandoning the whist, the dolls. But which? Miss Lamb's success in combining the stories in *Lamb's Tales*, and the original texts, had led Charlotte to think that the communal effort must be another of Shakespeare's plays, but was she capable, as Miss Lamb had been, of selecting and discarding, welding a kind of patchwork into a whole? And then of choosing characters, avoiding any cause for envy, inspiring enthusiasm, and liveliness without noise. She doubted it, but she must try. Every evening, by candlelight, she sat up in bed, with *Lamb's Tales* and Miss Lamb's battered Shakespeare and some bits of odd paper and a pencil and did her best.

Miss Lamb returned as abruptly as she had left. There she stood, wearing the blouse with the odd button and the skirt with the patch, studying the bits of the play upon which Charlotte had been working before she blew out the candle. Stunned, unable to speak for a moment, Charlotte watched her smiling when something met with her approval, frowning when something did not. When she found her voice Charlotte said, 'Miss Lamb! Oh, where have you been? How could you leave like that? I have been so worried!'

Miss Lamb looked up and made a silencing gesture. Of course, it must be late; one must not make a noise. Making no noise, Miss Lamb beckoned and turned towards the door. Pushing her feet into her slippers and snatching up her dressing-gown, Charlotte followed.

She had not been in Miss Lamb's room since that June evening. No effort had been made to clear it; her worn hairbrush and cheap bone comb lay on the dressing-table beside a little dish holding hairpins, books lay just as she had left them on the top of the chest-of-drawers. The dust was thick everywhere.

Keeping her voice low, Charlotte said, 'Now tell me. Where have you been? Why didn't you tell me? I thought something terrible had happened to you.'

Miss Lamb did not reply. She seemed to be looking for something among the books. She found it, a thickish notebook with a mottled cover. She held it out to Charlotte with a smile. Charlotte took it and then said, more urgently, 'What is wrong? Why won't you speak to me? Can't you speak?'

She had, not long before, just after the start of the term lost her own voice and Mrs Osgood said no wonder, hollering about in the yard every morning. But even without a voice one could mouth words, give some indication of a willingness to speak. Miss Lamb did not and a terrible fear fell upon Charlotte. A ghost! Safe in the dormitory at Miss Barton's, other girls within arms' reach on either side, Charlotte had enjoyed a ghost story as much as anyone. This was different, a chilly fear in the heart. Yet she remembered someone saying that though ghosts might not speak, they liked to be spoken to. In a tremulous, strangled voice she said, 'I miss you. All day. Every day. I never realised how good you were to me . . .' Miss Lamb gave no sign of having heard. She was dead; drowned; a ghost, and Charlotte knew that she could no longer maintain self-control. She was going to scream . . .

Waking in her own bed when the senior girl whose turn it was tapped on her door—at Homelands there was nothing so unhomelike as a clanging bell—Charlotte knew that she had had an exceptionally vivid dream. One might almost say a nightmare.

Its source was readily traced—her daily need for Miss Lamb's guidance and support; her worry about reducing *As You Like It* into a short play suitable for girls to perform; and her conviction that Miss Lamb was dead. A very vivid dream, one of those that last on, colouring the waking hours.

It was only when she was half dressed that she saw the mottled notebook lying on top of the papers which represented her own poor efforts at drama-writing, and realised that something more than mere dreaming was involved. That book had not been there when she went to bed. She picked it up, cautiously, as though it were red-hot.

It was Miss Lamb's version of the play. There in her small but legible hand, everything that was needed to keep the gist of the story, the beauty of the language while reducing it to something that could be performed by children, with the minimum of scenery and within the space of an hour. There was even a cast, with girls' names, some marked with a question, against each character.

Standing bare-armed in her petticoat and corset cover, Charlotte remembered that in the dream Miss Lamb had handed her the book, in the deserted, dusty room along the corridor—the room into which, waking, she would never willingly have entered. But the book had not moved itself! She had fetched it in her sleep.

She had once walked in her sleep, long ago. She knew that because Cook had found her, waked her, put her back to bed. But this was different; Miss Lamb had seemed so real. And the mottled book was real. And so exactly what she needed that one might call it an answer to prayer, had she ever prayed about it, which she had not. Her prayers were a parrot repetition of 'Gentle Jesus', and 'Our Father which art'.

Now, without ever even having heard the word, she became a spiritualist after a fashion. If Miss Lamb were dead—as she had always believed—somewhere enough of her had lived on to make her do this, to make some kind of contact. And at night, after the routine prayers, there was almost a cosiness in the thought that some essence of Miss Lamb was somewhere and could be communicated with. As the days shortened and it grew colder and she struggled with the impossible task of holding to Miss Lamb's standards, Charlotte found herself more and more inclined to direct her last conscious thoughts towards Miss Lamb. If you are there, if you can hear me ... Miss Lamb, I thank you for the mottled book. I hope that wherever you are, you are happy ... I hope you understand that I am doing my best ...

And if something of Miss Lamb still existed somewhere, what about Mamma? And Vincent? Miss Lamb, if wherever you are you should meet ... say that I love them still. A thought to sleep upon. A thought that occasionally provoked another—I must be going dotty! And that thought recoiled. Miss Lamb, you were always so sensible, help me to be sensible. You managed, help me to manage.

6

CHARLOTTE HAD HER CURIOUS EXPERIENCE IN THE LAST WEEK of September. Almost at the same time and as the crow flew a mere twenty miles away, something happened to Rose Ellis.

Charlotte had lost Miss Lamb at the end of June and had struggled on. Rose had re-entered the fold at about the same time and was, if anything, lonelier and certainly more miserable.

Her parents had welcomed her back. The pig sickness had vanished and the sty was full. There was the harvest to get in; potatoes to be dug out, put in sacks to be sold, or into clamps to be stored. Rose's hands, softened by gentle usage, blistered. The blisters broke and left raw places exposed, and they festered. 'Salt,' her mother said, not unkindly, 'it's a good hardener. Take some dry and rub it in, or hold your hands in the brine tub.'

On the last week of September, a time when every Brother of Jerusalem, whatever his business, could stop and take breath between summer and winter, the Children of Jerusalem held what they called a *Gathering Together*. They would not use the Popish word, *Pilgrimage*, not the Anglican one, *Harvest Festival*, nor the Methodist one, *Camp Meeting*, yet every repudiated word did apply. The Gathering Together was a pilgrimage, in that many people walked on foot twenty miles; it was a Harvest Festival because each man brought, in money or kind, a proportion of what a year's sedulous labour had given him, and it was a Camp Meeting because from Saturday

202

noon until Sunday evening people ate and slept as they could. It was great grief to Matthew Ellis that he had not enough pasture, or a large enough barn for the Gathering Together to be held at his farm. This year it was held on the border of Suffolk and Norfolk, on the property of a man who had once made a joke. 'Anybody ask me if I farm in Suffolk or Norfolk, I say it depend which way the wind blow.' His name was Bosworth, and despite the fact that his land lay on a sandy, perilously heath-like belt—once he had had to plant peas three times because topsoil and seed peas had blown away—he was prosperous. He had exactly the vast meadow, the vast barn needed; he had a wife, a good Daughter of Jerusalem, willing and well able to provide hospitality for the special speaker and the 'Meat Offering' at midday on Sunday.

To this gathering, the brightest event of the Children of Jerusalem's year, Rose walked in misery. Mental because despite her repentance, her submission, her labours and her pains, God had not turned towards her as He had once turned away at the moment when she had given herself to her lover's embrace. She had then actually felt the wrench; and over the fishshop she had felt the promise of forgiveness and reunion, but that promise had not been fulfilled. Physical misery because in mid-August she had hurt herself, tipping a pail of swill into a pig trough. Her mother called it a stiff neck and had given it a good rub with horse linament which, because it was a most effective counter-pain, seemed to bring relief for a little time. Her father said that swinging a scythe would loosen her up. It had failed to do so. The pain grew worse; sometimes it invaded her left arm; there was a prickling in her fingers, like pins and needles, but lasting longer. It eased when she lay flat in bed and when she supported her head with her left hand, and her left elbow with her right. In this posture she set out to walk fifteen miles. Burdened as he was by the sack of potatoes that was part of his 'offering', her father found her pace too slow.

'Step out, girl. Swing your arms and step out.' Her mother felt that she had done her duty to Rose by carrying both baskets, one containing the apples and eggs that made up the rest of the offering and the other the provisions for their simple needs. Rose tried stepping out but the pain increased, so she reverted to her hunched posture. The pain was doubtless part of her punishment.

'We don't look out we shall miss the opening,' Matthew Ellis said. 'Brother Wilson is a powerful speaker.'

They were in time. They deposited their produce in the open cartshed to await the sale which always followed the opening and which was in its way a form of barter, though articles were paid for, the money going into the general fund. Some town-dwelling Brother would buy the potatoes, some Sister without hens or apple trees the eggs and the fruit. The Ellises would go home with a sack of flour, some seed corn and probably something in the haberdashery line.

Brother Wilson, though nobody realised it yet, was something of a maverick though he had been born into the faith and believed in it absolutely. He had once been a blacksmith, but had abandoned that calling in order to become a permanent preacher, the thing that God had plainly created him to be. He had a voice that could make itself heard in Hyde Park against raucous competition, and the kind of rough-and-ready humour which could turn a laugh against hecklers. He had boundless energy, magnificent health and a magnetic personality. He was far more handsome than he needed to be and although his preachings dealt with the stark creed of the sect, he was at heart a kindly man.

On this occasion, at the end of a rousing and inspiring speaking, he issued his usual invitation; anybody with a problem would find him in Mrs Bosworth's parlour, ready to listen. 'I can't promise help; only God can give that, but some things benefit by a good talking over.'

It was, he knew, far easier to unburden oneself to a virtual stranger.

Rose, sitting on the grass, holding her chin, pressing very slightly to the left, thought—I'll go. I'll tell him everything—except about the murder, I didn't do that—and I needn't mention any names.

Most people had gone to the sale, but there were several who had taken advantage of the invitation and she had to wait for a bit.

'Sit yourself down, Sister,' Brother Wilson said, and cast a vastly experienced eye over her. The prim collar was too loose around her neck, the front of her bodice hung in slack folds—she'd lately lost flesh, and everything about her told of a deep dejection. He guessed he was about to hear a familiar tale. In love with a man who was not a Son. Well, sometimes a young

204

man could be talked round, and this was quite a pretty girl, apart from looking so wretched; sometimes prompt marriage to a Son was effective.

'Tell me about it,' he said.

She startled him by saying, 'I've lost God.'

'Well, the one thing you can be sure of is that God has not lost you. If He had you wouldn't be here. You wouldn't feel any loss.'

'I've been very bad,' Rose said. Suddenly the impulse to tell him everything weakened. It didn't, after all, seem a very nice thing to confess to somebody who was looking at her with interest and kindness. He might be shocked; disgusted.

'You don't look old enough to have done anything very bad,' he said. He doubted whether she would know what a bad woman really was; the children of the Children were strictly supervised.

'I did. I did a very bad thing. When I did it first God turned His face away from me. I felt it happen. I didn't mind so much then. But afterwards I was sorry. I was truly sorry, and I was punished. I thought God would forgive me and take me back —like the Prodigal Son. But He didn't and I just feel worse and worse. When I pray there's nobody there.'

The statement had an almost poetic ring. And it expressed a state of mind not common with the Children of Jerusalem. For them God was always there, even when disapproving.

'I think God is testing your faith. The greatest test of all.' One to which Christ Himself had submitted. 'You take my word for it, God is there; He knows all about you, what you did and how sorry you are. You just hold on to your faith, and believe and pray. And whatever the bad thing was that you did, don't do it again. Then one day you'll know, you'll feel in your heart . . .'

For some reason he faltered. Under his gaze her expression changed, became in fact quite awful in its utter despair. Far from comforting her he was making her feel worse. Silently he prayed : God help me to help her. And as he did so he noticed her curious posture.

'Why do you sit like that?'

About this she could be completely frank. He got up and stood behind the chair on which she sat.

'Sit up as straight as you can, and let both your arms hang down.'

205

Although he now no longer worked with his hands regularly, he often took casual jobs. The five shillings a week that he drew from the General Fund was insufficient for his needs, especially in winter and in the Midlands where even the most faithful Brother had no bed to offer. His hands were still hard and very strong; yet they were gentle as they explored, up to where the hair grew on her neck, down to the now prominent shoulderblades under the grey bodice. When they *knew* and conveyed what they knew to his mind, he acted swiftly and confidently. Rose felt a sharp pang of pain and heard a noise like a bundle of twigs being broken.

It was a terrible thing to think at this moment, but the pain reminded her of the moment when she had ceased to be a good girl.

'Now,' Brother Wilson said, stepping back. 'How is that?'

She moved carefully at first, turning her head from side to side, a thing she had not been able to do for weeks. She stood up, moved her arms.

'It's like a miracle,' she said, turning a different face, shining eyes, upon him.

'It is,' he said. 'That was God, working for you, through these hands of mine. You remember that if ever you're tempted to think again that He is not there.'

His own faith was absolute. That night, kneeling by Mrs Bosworth's best spare bed, he thanked God heartily that a simple little girl had been given proof of God's love and care for her. That one wrench, slipping a misplaced bone back had done more than a thousand words, however well chosen.

'Where you been?' Matthew Ellis asked rather petulantly. 'We been waiting for you. This here is Sam Parsons, come to break bread with us.'

Except for Rose's absence, the ritual of the Gathering had been observed. One of its purposes was the arrangement of marriages. The begetting of children to be brought up as Children, was one of the duties, and Matthew Ellis had had his eye on Sam Parsons for a long time. Sam was a thin, brown boy with shy brown eyes. Looking at Rose Ellis he considered himself lucky, unbelievably lucky. He was bound to accept his parents' choice for him and they had chosen this pretty thing, with lovely blue eyes and a glint of golden hair under the little white hat. And although she did not take much notice of him—as was right, girls should be modest—he noticed that she ate daintily, a thing which further commended her to him, for he had a squeamishness about such things.

In a few covert glances Rose summed him up and made unfavourable comparisons—not with John Vincent Cornwall, that false god who had first led her into sin and then deserted her, but with her new god.

Sunday dawned. The Sisters had slept in the barn; the Brothers in the open. There was a faint haze, akin to, but not quite like the haze of a summer morning; a hint of autumn. There was the morning meeting at which Brother Wilson spoke again, part of his speaking inspired by his experience with Rose. Consider Job, he said, and he warned the Children of Jerusalem not to confuse mere physical afflictions with the wrath of God. He was certain that Rose had confused them, thinking—I must be wicked to have suffered so.

After the speaking came the Offering of Hospitality. Mrs Bosworth had offered her best; cold chicken, ham, a pink, succulent sirloin, a huge salted silverside of beef. The Parsons and the Ellises ate together, their tacit bargain made. When at one point Sam got up and said to Rose, 'Will you have some more chicken?' Mr Parsons thought that he would *speak* to Sam. Once you started waiting on women you were done; they'd come to expect it; begin as you mean to go on.

The meeting began to break up; most people had some distance to go and almost every Brother, even those self-employed, must be ready for work on Monday morning. Brother Wilson must set off, too. But before he left Mrs Bosworth had said that he must have a cup of tea. So, having shaken so many hands and said, 'God keep you, Brother,' 'God keep you, Sister,' until his tongue felt stiff and the smile seemed like a mask fixed to his face, he went back into the parlour of the house, where his knapsack, already packed, lay on the horse-hair-covered sofa. And there Rose Ellis was waiting for him.

Well, it did happen. He knew a man whose knee went out of joint so often and was such a handicap that he had been obliged to show him how to wrestle it back into place himself.

'Cricked again?' he asked, thinking—I shall not be this way again for a year at least; maybe I could show her father . . .

'No. I'm all right . . .' She hesitated only a second. 'Take me with you. Brother Wilson, please, please, take me with you.'

It was not unknown for a boy, a young man, to be so affected by the speaking as to make a somewhat similar request —Let me be your disciple. Females had far more consciousness of home, of place. In the course of a year Brother Wilson tramped thousands of miles and he had seen few women committed to the life on the roads. Those who were were always with a man. He had never seen a woman tramp alone.

'I can't do that. How could I? I live rough. I doubt if I shall see a bed again until I get to Leicester.'

'I don't care. I'm as strong as iron. If you knew what I've been through. I'd sleep in a ditch, so long as it was with you . . .'

He said, 'Now, now! You mustn't say things like that. Just because I mended your neck.'

'I love you,' Rose said. 'I love you. You must take me with you. I'd be your servant. I wouldn't want nothing except to be with you.'

He had not lived to be thirty-five without attracting attention from women, but none had yet been so direct as this. So young, and yet . . . He remembered how she had summed up the dark night of the soul—When I pray there's nobody there. There was something about her, a force, a passion.

'That's silly talk,' he said. 'By tomorrow you'll see how silly it was. You run along now.' He was embarrassed.

Rose said, 'You never seen me properly.' She had come prepared for this. Her hair, not pinned up this morning, was simply bundled into the little white hat. With one hand she twitched off the hat, with the other she ripped open her bodice. The beautiful hair cascaded down over breasts which though less full than when John Vincent Cornwall had fondled them, were enticing enough.

The man was appalled, less by her action than by his own response to it. He could have taken her, there and then, in the prim parlour, with its horsehair furniture, its plush cloth, the bunch of pampas grass in the fireplace. He was only a man. But he was God's man.

He said, 'Dress yourself, Sister.'

His voice lacked some of its usual substance.

From the shadow of the tumbling hair her eyes glinted and narrowed.

'If you don't say you'll take me with you, I'll scream and say you did this to me.'

208

Evil! No. No, one must not think that. Momentarily possessed perhaps.

He was about as different from John Vincent Cornwall as a man could be, yet he handled the threat in identical fashion.

'Scream away. Sister Bosworth will be the first to hear you.'

The idea of Sister Bosworth seeing her like this! She had barely time to button her bodice, scoop her hair up and cram on her hat before Sister Bosworth was there, with the tea-tray. To her vast disappointment Brother Wilson picked up his knapsack and said, 'Thank you, Sister; but I can't stop. There's a mite of business I have to see to. Sister Ellis here could do with a cup. God keep you both.'

Rose's father and mother had collected what they had bought at the sale and were looking round for Rose.

'I'd like a word with you, Brother Ellis. I intend to have word with a few Brothers who have children of marriageable age. You have a daughter?'

'I have. Looking round for her now.'

'May I ask, have you chosen a husband for her.'

'Just fixed it with Brother Parsons.'

'When for?'

'We reckoned the spring, when the planting's done.'

'Could you make it sooner? I'll tell you why. We're a small community. We need new members. If you come to think of it, fix this marriage and one or two more I have in mind, let's say before the bad weather sets in, and by the next Gathering Together we might have a new Son or Daughter or two. See what I mean?'

'Brother Parsons agreeable, I got nothing against it. He ain't gone yet. He was hitching up. I'll have a word.' Brother Parsons was one of those who could afford a horse and cart.

Brother Wilson, keeping his word to himself and to his God, had a word or two with the fathers of other marriageable Children. Matthew Ellis had a word with Brother Parsons. They, and the boy were standing together when Rose appeared.

'Where you been? We been fixing for you and Sam here to get married. Monday fortnight.'

She knew that something was lost and gone forever. The capacity to worship, born in her and part of her nature. God; Mr Cornwall; God; Brother Wilson. She would never know it again; this thin, dark, shy boy could never inspire worship in

209

her. In fact the boot was on the other foot now. But they all seemed to be waiting for her to speak, so she said, 'All right,' and looked at Sam. A tendril of hair had escaped and fell, curling, beside her face. She gave him a smile that pierced his heart. He thought of the rhyme that other children, not Children of Jerusalem, sang to a game. Something about, '. . . will you be mine? You shall not wash dishes nor tend to the swine. You shall sit on a cushion and sew a fine seam and feast upon strawberries, sugar and cream.'

Striding out on the first lap of his journey to Leicester, Brother Wilson thought that, under God's guidance, he had managed well. St Paul had said that it was better to marry than to burn. And Sister Ellis had been burning with a flame that had not left him entirely unscathed.

It was as well that Rose's marriage took place when it did, for that year winter came early and severely. The November fogs were accompanied by frost, a combination that defeated even Mamselle. On two Thursdays she did not come to Homelands. There were no French lessons, and no exercises and no walks. No church even. 'Go breathing this in,' Mrs Osgood said, 'and everybody'll have bronchitis.' The self-enclosed little community turned in upon itself and Charlotte was grateful that there was the play. Copying out their parts, learning them, holding little rehearsals in various corners kept the girls occupied while she marked and marked or prepared lessons for the next day; not quite twenty-seven separate lessons, but almost. Even the two little newcomers had run off in diverse directions. One had mastered the alphabet with ease, the other seemed as blind to letters as Cecilie Burke was to numbers. She was reduced to the old device of delegation. 'Sophie, you now write and spell so well. Instead of doing a composition this morning, do you think you could help Dorothy?' 'Evelyn, every single sum of yours is right. Wonderful! See if you can explain to Kathie and Brenda.' Sometimes turning this way and that way she felt quite dizzy.

At the end of November the first snow fell and that cleared the air. There was a succession of bright, cold days. Mamselle's pony, his shoes properly roughed, clattered in briskly. She brought a goose which made a splendid meal for Mrs Armitage and Mrs Osgood; what they could not eat at a sitting flavoured and speckled one of the ubiquitous dumplings, and the fat from it enabled Mrs Osgood to fry heaps of bread and mounds of potatoes.

Day followed day, there was the play, the buffet supper, an exact repetition of last year's event except that Miss Lamb was not there, and that the vicar did not extend an invitation to the carol service; in fact he doubted, he said, whether there would be one; a particularly bad kind of cold, accompanied by a cough of a most distressing nature had laid half the village low.

There was Christmas.

Thomas wrote and sent her a parcel containing a sovereign and a light, lacy wool scarf. 'The money is from Papa, through Mrs C,' he wrote. 'The scarf is from me, I thought it might help when it is veree Kold. Mr Sylvester is showing some of his pictures in the New Year, and says that if he sells any he will take me to Paris at Easter. He thinks I should see some of the great pictures there. Wouldn't that be wonderful—Mr Sylvester says . . .'

Surprisingly, Mrs Armitage also gave her a sovereign.

'As a present dear. Just a token of gratitude for the splendid way you are managing. I thought you might like to buy yourself some new shoes. Mamselle would drive you into town on Thursday, I am sure. I will take charge of the girls.'

Mamselle regarded this arrangement with small favour, hustled the fat pony into Lowestoft, hustled Charlotte through her shopping which included the shoes, some tubes of paint for Thomas and some things from the chemist's. She bought a large supply of cough lozenges—almost everyone was coughing now, and three large jars of a cream guaranteed to cure chilblains in three applications. 'We must get back,' Mamselle said, hovering impatiently. 'Poor Mrs Armitage will be exhausted.'

7

JANUARY, HAVING COME SMILING IN WITH A FEW MILD DAYS,
settled down to savage frosts and icy winds. Mrs Armitage had
her fire, Mrs Osgood had hers, but the only heat on the school
side was provided by a single paraffin-stove. It was inadequate,
even in the schoolroom where it spent most of its time, yet it
was missed when the table girls carried it away into the dining
room. There it had hardly any effect at all before being carried
back again. Chilblains and what Mrs Osgood called cold sores
proliferated. The chilblain cure which Charlotte had bought,
and in the proper spirit, shared with everybody, though it
smelt nice and was not painful to apply was quite ineffectual.

In her own fashion, Mrs Osgood was conscientious. She
applied the remedies in which she had faith and she kept a
sharp lookout for any cold or cough that might show signs of
turning into something more serious than a nuisance. She had
once owned a clinical thermometer, but it had been broken and
she had never bothered to replace it. She used her own test,
knuckling her hard hand she applied it to the patient's neck.
Her rule of thumb seemed to justify itself; despite the snuffing
and the coughing nobody was really ill and the sickroom
remained unoccupied.

Half-way through January, Charlotte caught a cold so heavy
that she thought it advisable to join the queue outside the little
dispensary.

'I'll dose you first, Miss Burns,' Mrs Osgood said cheerily.
'Then you can set a good example.'

Charlotte swallowed the crude oil without grimacing, but five minutes later, being terribly sick in one of the cubicles at 'the end' she thought: What an example! Her stomach, resentful even of fat meat, had completely revolted.

Coming out of the cubicle she found Sophie Wrenn vigorously spitting into a washbowl.

'Have you been sick, Sophie?' Sophie ran the tap, wiped her mouth and smiled.

'I don't swallow it,' she explained. 'I just hold it in my mouth until I can spit it out. It tastes horrible, but it is better than feeling sick. You should try it, Miss Burns.'

'I think I shall have to,' Charlotte said. 'Don't tell anybody though.'

Delighted, the child said, 'A secret, just between us.' She added solemnly, 'Mrs Osgood once held Kathie's nose to make her swallow.'

Two mornings later, Mrs Osgood's keen eye spotted more than the symptoms of a heavy cold in Sophie Wrenn; she knuckled her neck and gave her a little push into the dispensary, beyond which the sickroom lay. 'A day in bed for you,' she said. 'Sylvia, fetch Sophie's nightdress, dressing-gown and slippers.'

Mrs Osgood's own bedroom, the dispensary and the sickroom formed what had been the guest suite on the architect's plan. The dispensary had been the dressing room and opened into both bedrooms. All three rooms had doors on to the corridor and the dispensary door was only open during sick parades.

Mrs Osgood's attitude towards a heightened temperature was simple and direct; bed, isolation, a fluid diet and more quinine. The temperature usually dropped within twenty-four hours, sometimes within twelve; another day in bed and then a test question, 'Would you like a nice poached egg?' Anybody who could eat a nice poached egg was well on the way to recovery. The young had great resilience.

That evening, with supper over and the do-what-you-like period begun, Charlotte collected two or three books and went up to visit Sophie, entering the sickroom by the door on the corridor. Sophie was awake, her eyes overbright and her cheeks flushed.

'I thought I'd just peep in, Sophie, to ask how you felt.'

'Ill all over. But it was kind of you to come, Miss Burns. I hope *your* cold is better.'

'Much better; though I tried your trick, Sophie.' The child's dry-looking lips smiled.

'That's our secret. Isn't it?'

'Yes. Look, I wondered if you'd like a book. I hope you haven't read all these.'

'That was very kind, Miss Burns. Actually I don't feel like reading just now.'

'Perhaps tomorrow; when you feel better.'

Charlotte put the books on the bed table, where a candle in a pretty china candlestick stood beside a glass of some semi-transparent, greyish liquid.

'That is barley water,' Sophie said. She broke into a fit of coughing, a prolonged, rattling cough which differed from the prevalent one. It carried Charlotte back across the years to the time when, after being lost in Tutt Wood, Thomas had been so very ill, and to add to the misery Miss Gooch had said that Mamma could no longer be trusted to take her own children for a walk. A sound of profound misery.

When the spasm was over and Sophie lay limply against the pillows, Charlotte said, 'How about a drink, now?' She held the glass and supported Sophie while she drank.

Sophie said, 'Thank you. Miss Burns, I do love you.'

Miss Lamb would not have approved of that! But to a little girl, bereft of her family, what could one say except, 'I love you, too, Sophie. Now have a good night's sleep and be better in the morning.'

'Must you go? Kiss me good night, please. Nobody would see.'

Charlotte kissed her. Despite the barley water her lips were dry and hot, the hands that clutched, burning.

'Come and see me again.'

'I will. I'll come tomorrow. Good night, darling.'

Quite possibly laying up trouble should Sophie ever need to be corrected.

Miss Lamb, I don't doubt your wisdom, but I just could not help myself . . .

When the sickroom was occupied Mrs Osgood slept with the door between her bedroom and the dispensary ajar and though she was a heavy sleeper she was twice disturbed in the night by a cough that she admitted she did not like the sound of. She gave Sophie a drink and found another pillow so that she lay higher. In the morning, since Sophie's temperature remained stubborn, Mrs Osgood said, 'I think I shall ask Doctor Bowen to have a look at the Wrenn child. She sounds bronchial to me.' She spoke rather crossly. Parents paid medical charges so the thought of the expense did not irk her; it was the feeling of having failed, of being obliged to call in, for a precaution, an amiable old dodderer who would be in a position to tell her what to do. She hated being told what to do and one of the reasons why her partnership with Mrs Armitage had been so successful was that Mrs Armitage so often said, 'You know best about that, Augusta.'

She said it now. Eva was dispatched to fetch the doctor.

Mrs Osgood's faith in herself and her remedies and her dislike of taking directions made the doctor's visits rather rare at Homelands and a sign that somebody was very ill indeed. In the mysterious way that whispers have of spreading, this whisper spread and the girl named Dorothy whom Sophie had helped with her spelling, broke into tears and said, 'Miss Burns, is Sophie going to *die*?'

'Of course not. She just has a very bad cold.'

Doctor Bowen arrived, used his stethoscope, his thermometer and sounded Sophie's chest with his fingers.

'There is some congestion,' he said. As he spoke he could see his own breath like steam on the air of the frigid room. The child, well tucked up in bed under a fat pink eiderdown was warm enough, but he knew from long experience that breathing cold air was bad for bronchial conditions. To his mind that was proved by the fact that old people creeping down for comfort and warmth to the kitchens of poor houses often did better, when bronchial, than those better attended, put to bed in unheated rooms. Steam from the kettle, steam from the pot. Warmth and humidity. The ideal was of course an open fire, and kettle on a trivet. But this room had no hearth, so he said, 'An oil-stove, Mrs Osgood. And a pan of water on it. A tablespoonful of Friars' Balsam to a pint of water.'

Mrs Osgood thought that if warmth and humidity had any healing value a lot of men whom she had nursed in India would now be alive. Oddly enough Doctor Bowen admired her; he would never forget the time when a measles epidemic had struck the school and she had been indefatigable. Nor could he forget the time when, under and around the nail on the middle finger of her right hand she had developed a terrible whitlow, brought it to him and said, 'Lance it. If it had been on my other hand I could have done it myself.'

'And I would suggest a little veal broth.' His faith in veal broth was absolute and he forgot—he was seventy-eight—that he had told Mrs Osgood how to make it several times before. While he said, 'You take a knuckle of veal . . .' she thought—And where do I get a knuckle of veal?

There was a butcher in Gorston, but, partly from policy—he might well think how little meat to so many mouths—and partly because the butcher in Lowestoft was much cheaper, Homelands had never patronised the local man. Every Saturday a wild-eyed boy, driving a wild-eyed horse, delivered to the school bones for the making of stock, a pound or two of the cheapest meat, some sausage meat and the choice joint of beef, mutton or pork that made the errand just profitable. He took the next week's order. This was Wednesday, even if Mrs Osgood had wished to obey the order 'Take a knuckle of veal', it would have been impossible for her to do so until Saturday week. As she listened Mrs Osgood thought that Sophie would have what the rest would have, good soup, made of bone stock, onions and potatoes.

Having repeated himself about the veal broth, Doctor Bowen said something that rang an alarm bell in Mrs Osgood's mind. He said, 'I think I'll look in this evening.' Out of his bag he took half a dozen little sweets, gelatine, flavoured with eucalyptus. They had no therapeutic value, but children liked to be given something and they liked to suck.

Outside on the corridor Mrs Osgood said, 'Is she *so* poorly?'

'I think she should be kept an eye on. Not much resistance there.'

'Could you give me some idea when you will be here? Not that I want to tie you down to time, Doctor, but I am rather busy. We are without a cook at the moment and I have the evening meal to attend to.'

'I shall be here at six,' he said.

At a quarter to six Eva took away the stove from the schoolroom. At five minutes past six Doctor Bowen found the stove, the open pan, the water just bubbling and the smell of Friars' Balsam on the air, exactly as he had ordered. And of the patient he could say, 'She seems to be holding her own. I'll look in tomorrow. Would eleven suit you, Mrs Osgood? I think I men-

tioned veal broth. You know how to make it? You take a
knuckle of veal . . .'

The stove was back in the classroom by half past six, and
everybody was pleased to see it.

'I have been waiting for you, Miss Burns.'

'How are you, Sophie?'

'Better, I *think*. How is your cold?'

'Very much better.'

'I am glad . . .' A spasm of coughing interrupted her. Better?
It sounded worse.

'Perhaps you shouldn't talk, Sophie.'

'It isn't talking . . .' she drew a laboured breath. 'I didn't talk
all day. Miss Burns.'

'Yes, darling?'

'The doctor said the stove and I was better then . . . I don't
think Mrs Osgood quite understood . . .' she coughed again. 'I
don't think he meant just to warm his hands over, though he
did. I think he meant for me.'

And of course he did, Charlotte thought, remembering
when Thomas was so ill, a fire burning day and night and a
steam kettle on the trivet.

She stayed for a little while, kissed Sophie good night again
and promised to look in next evening. Then she went downstairs slowly, planning how best to approach Mrs Osgood;
it would not do to say that the child had mentioned the
stove.

Mrs Osgood's room was quite unlike Mrs Armitage's; the
prevalent colour was a dark reddish brown and there was a
good deal of brass about. The fender was of brass, and Mrs
Osgood, sitting in a stern-looking armchair, had her feet on the
fender and her skirt turned back to her knees. Her shanks were
thinner than one would have expected in a woman of her size,
and her calves were knotty with varicose veins. She was drinking whisky and water.

She said, 'Well, Miss Burns?' in a not very welcoming voice.
After the meal which Mrs Armitage insisted upon calling
'dinner', she felt she had earned the right to sit down and be
undisturbed. She did not ask Charlotte to sit down.

'I have been thinking about Sophie Wrenn, Mrs Osgood.'

'Yes?'

'When my brother was a little boy he was once very ill. He

217

had a cough that sounded very much like Sophie's. Our doctor found a splendid way of relieving it. May I tell you?'

'If you like.'

As Charlotte spoke of the fire and the steaming kettle, Mrs Armitage's expression hardened. Somebody else telling her what to do!

'I don't agree. There's fashions in doctoring like everything else. You wouldn't send a child with a cough out into a fog, would you? To my mind a steam kettle is just bringing fog indoors.'

'My brother recovered.'

'When blood-letting was fashionable,' Mrs Osgood said reasonably, 'people recovered. In spite of, not because.'

'It might be worth trying . . . *We* could manage without the stove for a day or two, Mrs Osgood. We could wear our overcoats.'

'If I had twenty stoves,' Mrs Osgood said, 'there wouldn't be one in the sickroom longer than needs be.' Charlotte seemed unwilling to take that for an answer and go; she stood behind one of the upright dining chairs, gripping its back with her chilblained hands. 'When I come into the schoolroom and meddle with you, Miss Burns, then you can meddle with me. Until then I'll thank you to mind your own business.'

I'll thank you was one of Mrs C's expressions and Mrs Osgood said it in the same harsh, near-derisive way.

'I see. Good night, Mrs Osgood.'

'Good night.'

Outside the door Charlotte stood hesitant; then she crossed the hall and tapped on Mrs Armitage's door.

Mrs Armitage listened more graciously than Mrs Osgood had done, but when Charlotte had finished she said, 'My dear, I couldn't possibly interfere. Mrs Osgood is vastly experienced and I trust her judgment absolutely. And with good reason. In the almost twenty years during which she has had charge of the girls' health here, we have never had a fatality. We had a most frightful outbreak of measles and on one occasion a new girl from Malta arrived suffering from what Mrs Osgood said was typhoid. It would be as much as my place is worth,' said Mrs Armitage with a smile, 'to question anything in her department.'

'I see. Good night, Mrs Armitage.'

'Good night, Charlotte dear.'

Mrs Osgood was a good nurse. She kept her eye on the time. Presently she stood up and went to the ugly sideboard and foraged about in a drawer. She found what she wanted; an ordinary postcard, pierced by two holes joined by a loop of string. Carrying it she went into the kitchen, filled a stone hot-water jar, warmed some milk. She administered the dose of Doctor Bowen's medicine exactly on time, followed it with her own dose of quinine; stood over Sophie while she drank the milk; settled her for the night. The knuckle test informed her that the temperature had not dropped.

When Charlotte passed the sickroom on her way to bed the card with its ominous message, NO VISITORS, hung on the knob of the door.

At a quarter to eleven next morning the stove was taken upstairs and this time was away so long that Charlotte thought it possible that Mrs Osgood had been persuaded to change her mind. The classroom, never warm, chilled perceptibly, and Charlotte found herself looking at the splendid fireplace. Why should it not be used? A fire need cost nothing—she had long since realised that economy was a house rule—the beach was littered with driftwood. Imagine a blazing wood fire, heating the whole room.

Miss Lamb had said, in another connection, that she did not report her failures. That was true. She had suggested the gathering of driftwood for a fire in the schoolroom and been rebuffed. Mrs Armitage had replied that it would not look well for the girls to be seen scavenging; also the grate would have to be cleaned; also it was quite unnecessary.

Ignorant of this, Charlotte made her plans.

The oil-stove's long absence was due to Doctor Bowen having been delayed by an emergency call and by the time he took over the examination of a patient who seemed worse rather than better, despite splendid nursing, it was noon. In front of Sophie he spoke cheerily.

'You're doing well. You'll be up and about in no time.' He left her some more sweeties. But outside on the corridor he spoke gravely to Mrs Osgood and used the words bronchial pneumonia; but he added that they were doing everything that could be done.

The afternoon, though bright, was so cold that the drift-wood was gathered with an unwonted display of energy. It was all taken from the beach above the ordinary tide level, stuff thrown up by stormy seas; the dry salt and the frost rime shone white on the bits of broken boxes, barrel staves and some pieces of timber of a more substantial nature.

When everybody had collected as much as she could carry, they hurried back to the house.

'We'll light it before tea,' Charlotte said, 'then it will be warm to come back to.' She had never actually laid or kindled a fire, but this, her first attempt, was successful. The paper blazed, the smallest, driest pieces of wood caught fire, sparking, crackling, the flames from the salt-impregnated wood burning blue and orange. A good fire, but kindled beneath a chimney that had never been used, and consequently never swept, since it was built. Birds had nested in it, and the leaves of many autumns clogged it. The smoke went up a little way and billowed back into the room, greyish-yellow, bitter-smelling. Everybody began to cough. Coughing herself Charlotte said, 'Go into the dining room.' She stayed to take off some of the wood which had not yet caught fire, and to open the window.

Eva was in the drawing room, closing the rose-coloured curtains. She saw the smoke billowing out of the schoolroom window and said, 'Oh, ma'am, the schoolroom's on fire!'

Mrs Osgood was in the kitchen, counting out the thin ginger biscuits and waiting for the kettle to boil. She heard the commotion in the dining room; unusually noisy, surely, and at least ten minutes too early; and then she smelt something which she took to be the result of the oil-stove having been dropped. She snatched up the heavy rug which lay in front of the cooking range. She and Mrs Armitage arrived simultaneously at the scene of the conflagration, Mrs Armitage coming in from the hall, Mrs Osgood by way of the dining room, where Charlotte stood trying to quell panic. By this time the smoke was so thick that Mrs Armitage and Mrs Osgood were hardly visible to one another, but they could both see that the room was not ablaze. In fact in the ornate grate the fire was already almost extinguished.

'No need to damage the rug, Augusta,' Mrs Armitage said from behind her handkerchief.

They went together into the dining room where several girls were crying.

'There is no need to fuss,' Mrs Armitage said, addressing

everybody. 'The classroom will be unusable for at least an hour and everything in it will be filthy.'

Mrs Osgood saw the perfect opportunity to retaliate upon Charlotte for her interference of the previous evening. She looked straight at her as she said, 'Smoke seeps. If it gets into the sickroom'—the sickroom was immediately above the classroom—'it could kill a child breathing with such difficulty.' She turned and went out. She had spoken spitefully, but she had said what she believed and was prepared to open the sickroom window. However, in this house the ceilings were well-plastered and sound, the floorboards closely dovetailed. Smoke had not penetrated.

Still ignoring Charlotte, Mrs Armitage took charge.

'Really, I am very disappointed with you all. Making such a fuss about nothing. What would you do in a genuine crisis? Panic and cry? Most of you, I must remind you, when you leave Homelands will be going to places where you will be required to set an example.'

Having been stern, she relented. 'Now we will have tea. Miss Burns, if you detach yourself from those clinging hands and go to my room you will find a tin of biscuits in the right-hand side of the chiffonier. After tea the classroom must be cleaned. There will be smuts on everything . . .'

There were smuts, or a thin filming of greasiness on everything, and Charlotte, feeling guilty, undertook the nastiest job, washing down surfaces with hot soda water. It had a very detrimental effect upon her chilblained hands, and when at the day's end, in obedience to Eva's murmured message, she presented herself in Mrs Armitage's room she tried to keep them out of sight.

'You think I am about to scold you, Charlotte,' Mrs Armitage began, almost playfully. 'Well, I am not. What I am going to do is to ask you, please, next time you wish to introduce an innovation, to consult with me beforehand. That is all.' She regarded Charlotte whose face did not lighten, as it should have done, at this magnanimous speech and whose posture was in some way different. 'You still look troubled. What is wrong?'

'I am worried about Sophie.'

'Oh, naturally Mrs Osgood's remark worried me, too, but she assured me that there was no trace of smoke in the sickroom. Although the rooms are above one another, the windows are not.'

221

'I was not thinking of that, Mrs Armitage. You see, last evening I just looked in to say good night to her and I promised to do so this evening. But no visitors are allowed. I'm rather afraid that she will think that I have deserted her.'

With the slightest touch of impatience in her voice, Mrs Armitage said, 'Well, I am afraid there is nothing that we can do about that except to hope that the notice will be removed tomorrow. You must try not to *worry* so much, my dear. It does no good and it creates an unhappy atmosphere.'

Charlotte was still worrying, however, as she stood outside the sickroom door on her way to bed. She hoped that Mrs Osgood had explained the situation. It was too late now even to open the door and wave and call, without going in. The child would probably be asleep. So she sent a thought: Good night, darling. Sleep well and be better in the morning.

Huddled in her bed she had one of her now almost nightly sessions of communication with Miss Lamb.

I made a proper mess of that, didn't I? I should have known that if it could have been done you would have done it last winter.

I still think that Mrs Osgood is wrong about the stove, don't you?

That notice was put there simply to deter *me*. The girls never visit there.

Oh, Miss Lamb, I do miss you so much. I have nobody with whom to talk things over.

Then—it seemed almost immediately—there she was; looking exactly the same, wearing the same old clothes.

'Miss Lamb. Just when I needed you most. I know you can't speak to me. Could you make some sign? When I think about you, when I talk to you in my mind, does anything get through?'

The unanswerable question. Miss Lamb gave no sign. She made that same beckoning gesture and as before led the way to her old room. This time she ignored the books and went on and indicated the tray of tea-making gear under the bed.

'I know. I do miss the tea. But I could never make it or drink it alone. It would be so *sad*.' She imagined that this time Miss Lamb had come back in order to remind her of the comfort to be found in a cup of tea. And then she understood.

'Of course! Oh, Miss Lamb, how clever of you . . .'

Mrs Armitage stirred, unwillingly opened her eyes and was astounded to see not Eva with her morning tea, but Augusta, looking ghastly and holding a candlestick in an unsteady hand.

'What is it? Worse? Dead?'

'Come and look. I thought you should see . . . Before I touched anything.'

'Augusta, you know . . .' Mrs Armitage shrank back against her down-filled pillow. 'I'm not much good . . .'

'Come and look,' Mrs Osgood repeated grimly.

She knew, having lived with her for almost twenty years, that Mrs Armitage affected to be too sensitive to face unpleasant scenes, just as she affected to be too delicate to make any real exertion, but she had no fear that what she was about to see would make her faint or scream or fall into hysterics.

Mrs Armitage pulled on her blue velvet dressing-gown and pushed her toes into feather-trimmed mules.

'This is what I found,' Mrs Osgood said; and she made no distinction between the dead child in the bed and the little stove whose fuel had outlasted the water in the kettle which was now a lop-sided half-melted lump of tin. The room smelt strongly of burnt metal and scorched Friars' Balsam.

Mrs Armitage seemed slow of comprehension. She could see that Sophie was dead, but she did not immediately see the significance of the little stove. She actually said, 'What is it?'

'It's the stove Miss Lamb used for making tea. Miss Burns put it there. She was on at me yesterday about a stove and a kettle. The fumes killed Sophie. And in twenty years I never had a death.'

'Well, we have one now. Thank God the doctor had been attending. This must be cleared away, of course, and no mention made of the . . . mishap.' She was showing the fortitude and level-headedness which set such a good example, and even Mrs Osgood began to rally. Mrs Osgood was genuinely shattered, and furiously angered, but she could see the point in Mrs Armitage's remarks, and was for once willing to take directions.

'Find a box, Augusta. Put the whole thing in it and put it under my bed for the time being. I'll open the window for a minute. What time is it?'

'Getting on for seven. The smell woke me, you know. I had a broken night the night before. Tonight she *was* better. Not a sound. So I slept well, and the smell woke me. Twenty years,'

Mrs Osgood said bitterly, 'and I never lost *one*.'

'You mustn't brood over that, Augusta. It is a very proud record, even so. Find a box.'

A box was ready to hand. It had contained a dozen bottles of the cod-liver oil, separated by cardboard partitions. Setting out the five remaining bottles on the shelf of the dispensary, Mrs Osgood saw the state of her Friars' Balsam bottle. She did not believe in its being used as Doctor Bowen had advised, but she always had some on hand, for cuts.

Coming back with the box, she said, 'She must have poured half a bottle into that little kettle. That alone would have been enough ... She must be raving mad.'

'We'll deal with that side of it later,' Mrs Armitage said. 'Tell me, Augusta—you know about such things—if the fumes were responsible, would there be anything to show?'

'Not without opening her up. Except perhaps . . .'

Closing the flaps of the box Mrs Osgood went to the bed and examined the dead child's nose. To be on the safe side, she used her own handkerchief, which came away unsullied. 'She *was* getting better. She hadn't coughed once since the last dose.' In her way she cared.

'Come along, Augusta. I think Doctor Bowen had better see her as you found her—at six o'clock. But there is no reason to disturb him before eight, poor old man. I'll close the window. You put that box away and I'll rouse Eva. Since we're up early we might as well have our tea early.'

Charlotte woke, remembering only that she had dreamed about Miss Lamb again. On the former occasion there had been the mottled book to prove that she had followed the beckoning figure; there was no such concrete evidence this morning and she was left with only a hazy impression that Miss Lamb regretted the disuse of her tea things. That waking thought was quickly edged away by her memory of yesterday's mistake; of the spiteful way in which Mrs Osgood had spoken; of Mrs Armitage's mild, but unmistakable reproof, and of the fact that she had not seen Sophie. Well, perhaps today things would be better; the notice removed from the door. She realised that she was not feeling very well herself; her cold seemed worse, heavy and thick; and her fingers were so stiff and swollen that buttoning clothes was slow and painful.

Breakfast was one of the more popular dishes, mounds of

224

potatoes that had been par-boiled, sliced and fried. It was possible when eating this, as it was not on porridge days, to sniff with less envy the scent of fried bacon coming from the kitchen.

Talk at table was always quiet, but positive whispering was frowned upon. To whisper was as rude as to point. This morning, however, there was whispering, finally a girl near Charlotte said in a normal voice, 'Is it true, Miss Burns, that Sophie Wrenn died in the night?'

Charlotte dropped her fork.

'Oh no! Who says so?'

Everybody looked at her own immediate informant; a girl at the farthest end of the senior table said, red-faced, 'I did, Miss Burns.'

'And how did you know?'

'I heard Mrs Osgood telling Eva to go to the doctor's and to tell him . . .'

Several girls began to cry, some because they had been attached to Sophie, some because death is a matter for tears, some simply affected by the tears of others.

Choking back her own tears, Charlotte said, 'It is sad. But Sophie was very ill . . .' Here, in midwinter, she could smell again the scent of the white summer flowers, hear again Mrs Lark's voice. Conscious of the utmost falsity, she said, 'Perhaps it is better to be an Angel in Heaven than to be so ill.'

In most minds the words made a link with something overheard: a blessed relief: at least his sufferings are over: she is in Heaven now.

And Miss Burns was setting a good example; after that first uprush of tears, evoked by the thought—And I didn't even say good night to her! Charlotte had become stonily calm. After a minute she tapped on the table and said, 'I am sure that Mrs Armitage would disapprove of too great an exhibition of grief. And not eating your breakfast will do Sophie no good and you a great deal of harm.'

Mrs Armitage had used almost the same words, certainly the same argument, when Mrs Osgood said she didn't feel like having any breakfast at all. An argument as old as human bereavement, and sound, since food is comforting.

The morning exercises had been discontinued, so as soon as the meal was finished the girls dispersed, to make their beds, to talk in small groups, some to cry again. Charlotte went, cold fury in her heart, to Mrs Osgood's room where both partners were about half-way through the breakfast which, as Mrs Armitage had pointed out to Augusta who must cook it, was necessary to support them through a sad day.

Since seven o'clock Mrs Armitage's subtlety and tact had both had full exercise. Augusta had been so very angry that, once she had swallowed a fortifying cup of tea she had announced her intention of going along to Miss Burns's room and having it out with her.

'Augusta, I think that would be rather unwise. For one thing we have no positive proof that she is responsible.'

'And who else would have done such a thing?'

'A girl. Perhaps one who had seen a steam kettle being effective. Naturally I shall enquire, and administer a rebuke. But later. It would be a little awkward, do you not see, to have on the one hand, Doctor Bowen coming in to certify a natural death and on the other an accusation against Miss Burns, or some other person, of having been, through a foolish act, however well-intentioned, the direct cause. Do you see? Let us get the formalities disposed of. Then we can find out who it was who in the middle of the night, entered the sickroom, took the Friars' Balsam from the dispensary; and all without waking you. With the door open . . .' It was far from being an accusation of having been unwatchful, so sunk in leaden slumber, but as Mrs Armitage noted with some satisfaction, it gave Mrs Osgood something to think about. And Mrs Osgood had thought. Frying the mounds of potato slices, crisp and brown on the outside, floury within, and then making the usual good breakfast for herself and Mrs Armitage, she had had plenty to think about. She *knew*, let Mrs Armitage say what she liked, that Miss Burns was to blame: to blame for the only death in Homelands for twenty years and for the sullying of a proud record.

In Charlotte's mind Sophie's death was linked with Vincent's because she had loved them both. Vincent had been foully murdered and nobody had been punished. Sophie had been killed, less horribly, but nonetheless *killed*, and Charlotte knew how, by whom.

In the confrontation which Mrs Osgood had planned in other circumstances and been persuaded to postpone, Charlotte, entering the room without the preliminary knock, said, 'You are to blame, Mrs Osgood. If you'd done what the doctor said . . .' She could say that now, since Sophie was no longer there to be shielded, 'Sophie would have stood a chance. I begged you . . . I said we'd sit in our coats if she could have the stove. She's dead now because you are so pig-headed.'

Her entry and her launching into the accusation had taken both women by surprise. Now Mrs Armitage said, 'Charlotte!' in a tone sharp enough to check even the half-distraught. Mrs Osgood made a peculiar sound, mid-way between a whoop and a snort, almost a joyful sound.

'Ho! You dare come here and say that to me! You and your stoves! You killed her with your stove!'

'What stove?'

'That gimcrack little thing you used for making tea.'

'What has that got to do with it?' Mrs Osgood was too angry to notice the complete amazement in Charlotte's voice and face, but Mrs Armitage's gaze, ice-blue this morning, suddenly became intent.

'I'll tell you what it has to do with it,' Mrs Osgood said furiously. 'You put it there, with a pint of water and enough spirit to boil it ten times over. The kettle boiled dry and melted, with half a bottle of Friars' Balsam in it, too. The fumes were enough to kill anybody, leave alone a sick child.'

Charlotte looked towards Mrs Armitage as though seeking denial or confirmation and Mrs Armitage said, 'I am afraid that that is what happened.'

Charlotte said, in a horrified voice, 'Oh no!' and put her hands to her face. From behind them she said brokenly, 'If I did it, I did it in my sleep.'

Mrs Osgood made that peculiar noise again. 'In your sleep! That be hanged for a tale. You did it . . .'

'Augusta, *please*. Charlotte, sit down. The damage is done now and no amount of mutual recrimination will help in the slightest.' She leaned over and opened one door of Mrs Osgood's sideboard and took out a cup and saucer. She poured coffee and sugared it well. 'Here, drink this and pull yourself together. Mrs Osgood and I have had quite enough to distress us for one day.'

'Twenty years and not a single death,' Mrs Osgood said.

'Charlotte, drink that cup of coffee.'

Mrs Armitage had maintained control. She had also offended Mrs Osgood by taking into use a cup, one of six, that had never been used but were, like several other unused things, profoundly treasured. Charlotte reached for the cup, it jarred against the saucer, the coffee slopped and she abandoned the attempt.

She saw the disbelief in Mrs Osgood's hard brown eyes and was reminded of Fowler.

'It is possible that I did it. I have walked in my sleep . . . and done things of which I have no memory afterwards . . . Last time there was a book. And it is true that Miss Lamb . . .' She broke off, hovering on the verge of understanding.

'You can leave *her* out of this. *You* killed Sophie Wrenn as surely as though you'd strangled her with your hands.' There was something about that last phrase, something backward-reaching and so horrible that reason must refute it.

'We cannot be sure of that. But I shall ask Doctor Bowen. I shall tell him everything and ask him whether Sophie died because she did not have what he ordered or because I did what you say I did.'

In the crimson room, scented with the odour of fried eggs and bacon and coffee, there was a little silence. Then Mrs Armitage said, 'About that, Charlotte, I would advise you to think again. If Doctor Bowen has the slightest reason to doubt the cause of Sophie's death, there will be an *inquest*.' She weighted the word with a slight pause. 'At inquests very awkward questions are apt to be asked. Such as *what else you may have done in a state of somnambulism*.'

Mrs Osgood, in ignorance of the matter to which Mrs Armitage had referred, was astonished by the effect the words had. Charlotte cried, 'Oh no!' again in an even more horrified voice, and instead of putting her hands to her face, put her arms on the table and dropped her head upon them, not crying exactly, but shuddering and making little whimpering sounds.

'Despite the extreme inconvenience, I think a day in bed,' Mrs Armitage said. 'If the butcher's boy would take a message to Mamselle, I think she would come to our aid.'

Another bad corner turned. Far away a mother and father would grieve and wonder. In India, cholera, malaria, dysentery; at home bronchial pneumonia. Had they sent Sophie too early to Homelands; or, softened by the Indian sun, too late? There was no answer. Nothing to do but to order a white marble angel to stand over the place where she lay, with the words 'Gone to be with Jesus' on its plinth. They would miss the long letters, garrulous, cheerful, and the spelling so vastly improved. They would read again and again the truly beautiful letter from Mrs Armitage; how popular Sophie had been with everybody, how greatly she would be missed; how peacefully she had died after the briefest illness; and how Doctor Bowen had said what excellent nursing she had been given.

Doctor Bowen had said that; he had been struck by Mrs Osgood's demeanour; he had thought her imperturbable, but she was obviously extremely upset. 'You must not take it to heart, Mrs Osgood. If good nursing would have pulled her through you would have done it. To be honest, I had my doubts from the first. So little stamina, poor child.'

8

IN LONDON, SPRING HAD TAKEN A HESITANT STEP OR TWO. THE
weeping willow in Mr Fothergill's sheltered little garden had
changed colour and was dripping its green-gold hair over the
first crocuses; in a week there would be a pool of them, golden,
white, pale and dark purple. The window of the dining room
looked out upon the garden and Mr Fothergill studied it and
the morning with approval before settling down to his breakfast, the egg poached, the bacon grilled, fried food did not
agree with him. To the left of his place lay his post and the slim
silver paperknife. He had no hesitation about opening and
glancing at his letters while he ate; troublesome communica-
tions always went to the office. This morning he had two
invitations, four acceptances of invitations that he had sent out
and two impersonal notices, one informing him about a concert, the other concerned with a picture exhibition. All in
order. There remained the last letter and that gave him a
distinct jolt.

Dear Mr Fothergill,
  I am sorry to trouble you, but I can think of no one else to
whom to turn. I rather fear that unless I can talk to somebody, I may go mad. Something has happened here which
has made me think that I may have done what Inspector
Fowler said I did. I would come to you, but it is difficult for
me to get away. Could you possibly come to see me? If I did
it, I do not even know to whom to give myself up.

He had, almost deliberately, put her out of his mind. He'd liked her, admired her tremendously, had been anxious—and still was—to be of service to her. Aware that he was old enough to be her father. She was, he understood, still at school. Now and then when he thought about her, he had had a curious sensation, rather like a man who, suffering from some disquieting symptom is given a comforting diagnosis; nothing but a touch of indigestion. He had supplied his own diagnosis. It was his age. Men around forty were often attracted to young girls; some married, usually with disastrous results; others behaved scandalously in railway carriages. But he had once told her, and he had written that if ever she needed him ... As she now most obviously did.

He rang his bell and Mrs Hawkins came, glanced at what was left on his plate and said, 'Wasn't it to your liking, sir?' almost as much upset as Mrs Osgood had been over the breaking of *her* long record.

'Ask Hawkins to pack my bag, will you, Mrs Hawkins, and bring it round to the office. I may be away for a couple of days. Just what I need for the night. And a clean shirt. And if you would ask him, on his way, to send a telegram it would save me time. But of course I must look up the trains. Wait ...' In more of a fluster, as she termed it, he went into the next room and came back, having consulted the railway timetable and wrote on the back of one of the envelopes, 'Burns, Homelands, Gorston-on-Sea : be with you at six or soon after. Fothergill.'

He then set out for his office and although in private gardens and public places the crocuses had come up with their message of promise, he did not observe them.

Hugh Ampton heaved one of his vast, old-man's sighs.

'I thought that was over and done with. You're quite right to go, James. But for God's sake be careful. It was a damned narrow shave and any resuscitation ... It's a pretty incoherent letter, you know.'

'Is it? I thought that in the circumstances ...'

'About which you know nothing, me dear boy. Somebody, female, young, who writes that she may go mad, may well be so already.'

'I thought it a reasonable letter. Plainly something has upset her. I think she showed good sense in appealing to me.'

'That is true. And something to be thankful for. James, we

231

cannot, whatever the circumstances, have this thing dragged up again. God knows why she should now suspect herself. It's a form of dementia, as we well know. And by all accounts her mother died raving . . . Dear boy, if you can't talk her out of it, persuade her that she's ill. Bring her back with you and put her in that place at Barnet.'

'What place at Barnet?'

'A nursing home where people wrong in the head are kindly treated, well looked after and never heard of again.'

'If I may say so, Uncle Hugo, you are adopting a very unprofessional attitude. The magistrates' decision made provision for the possibility of further evidence being forthcoming. It may well be that whatever has happened to make her write such a letter is in the nature of further evidence.'

'James, if she stood in this room and gave me proof positive that she was guilty, ten times over, I'd shove her into Barnet rather than have the case reopened.'

'And you such a stickler for the law! Why?'

'That I cannot tell you. When I give my word, I give my word. I have told you, as clearly as I can what I wish you to do, and what I wish you not to do. Get along to Lowestoft and be eloquent. Be persuasive. Unless you want to bring my head in sorrow to the grave.'

'I have a few things to do before I can leave. I propose to catch the two-forty,' Mr Fothergill said, a trifle stiffly.

It was hot in Uttahpore, but outside the palace fountains played, cooling the air which, entering the vast tall room, was still further cooled by the punkahs, great overhead fans worked by little boys. The Rajah and John Vincent Cornwall, both clad in white linen, both extended at full length on couches woven from thin canes, flexible, yielding to every movement, every curve of the body, but not, like cushions, holding the heat, were very comfortable indeed. And the Rajah at least was happy. The British department to whom he had applied for an Educational Director had sent him, out of the thousands of people at their command, his old fag-master, J. V. Cornwall, once his god. J.V. had always been lenient. 'Oh, chuck it in the fire, Bunjo,' he would say of some burnt toast, 'and make some more.' He said, 'Look here, Bunjo, you're filthy; go and scrub up.' He had been kind where unkindness was the rule, and once when Bunjo had inadvertently offended another elder boy

232

and was due to be beaten, J.V. had intervened. 'Damn it all, Carrington, if he needs a hiding, I'll do it. He is my fag.' There had been no hiding; J.V. had said, 'Bunjo, you are a filthy dirty little tyke, but you're a heathen, you don't know any better. Don't get across Carrington again.' Bunjo had adored J.V. who all too soon had vanished into the English gentleman's world.

Their meeting after so many years had been ecstatic. What the Rajah of Uttahpore had been prepared to provide for some anonymous English educational officer was not nearly good enough for J.V. And the idea of J.V. making long journeys through the dust and the heat to the villages where schools had been planned, and were being built, was quite unthinkable. 'Sahni will do whatever you say, J.V. We will let him go. You stay here and come with me to watch the gathering of the wild elephants. By torchlight, it is quite a sight.'

Bunjo, not unaware that he was now in the ascendant, was extremely indulgent in a way that almost any man in John Vincent Cornwall's place would have found very flattering, very delightful. Old school friends, endlessly reminiscing. But ... And whenever John Vincent Cornwall came to examine that *but*, being no fool, he saw something from which he shied away.

'Twice,' Bunjo said on this particular evening, 'I remember that you were visited, and taken out by a very fine gentleman. I even remember his name. Lord Mersea. Is my memory not exceptional?'

'It was always good. Anything you forgot, Bunjo, was something you didn't want to remember. Yes, you're absolutely right, Lord Mersea did come twice. He was a friend of my father's.'

'And very handsome.'

'I suppose so. To tell you the truth I never took much notice. But he was witty ... At least, I could make him laugh and he could make me laugh. And I very well remember saying to him that I'd sooner spend the long vacation with him than with my uncle and aunt in Bristol. But he didn't take to the idea, and in fact that year I had a marvellous holiday, with a kind of tutor chap. We went up the Rhine. Actually I did have some splendid holidays. My uncle and aunt were pretty dull, but they did arrange decent holidays. And of course there was money in trust.'

'So fortunate, J.V.! But not enough, eh?'

'Not enough.'

'Permit me to say how glad I am. Otherwise you would not be here with me. And here you shall never lack money. I am the third richest man in the world and what is mine is yours.'

'You pay me more than adequately,' J.V. said, shying away from a gleam in the eye, a note in the voice.

'Between such old friends as we are, there must be no talk of pay, J.V.'

It would come, with the certainty of death. The moment to which everything was leading. And what then? Refuse and be out on your ear? The Board would not listen; an independent Indian prince, the third richest man in the world, could not be wrong in their sight. They would simply say that Cornwall had had the plummiest job in the trade and lost it, probably through drinking. A dismal prospect. But the alternative was hideous. Submit and go on being pampered, every day listen to the leper bell in one's mind, tolling 'Unclean! Unclean!' What a predicament to find himself in. At his age, too. Sometimes John Vincent Cornwall found himself asking what he had ever done to deserve such bad luck.

'That's all right, sir,' the cab driver said. 'We got our nose-bags. We don't mind a bit of a wait.'

He produced the one that belonged to the horse, and also two identical bits of old blanket. Back in his seat he wrapped himself in one of the pieces and ate his bread and cheese. After London the bracing east coast air was very bracing indeed, and Mr Fothergill shivered a little as he rang the bell and waited.

All telegrams were automatically delivered to Mrs Armitage, so that in case of bad news it could be broken gently. She explained this as she handed over the opened envelope and then asked, 'Who is Fothergill, Charlotte dear?' That was one of the least tolerable things about the last five days, the assumption that nothing had happened, that nothing had changed.

'My solicitor.'

'Good gracious! What on earth do you want with a solicitor?'

Even Mrs Armitage's calm was shattered.

'I wish to talk to him. About everything.'

'I should most strongly advise you not to. Your position is

234

and always has been very delicate. You may well find yourself back in gaol.'

Charlotte said nothing. 'And if you refer to the more recent tragedy'—Mrs Armitage was still choosing her words well—'I should warn you that anything you may say that is derogatory to Mrs Osgood's reputation will be slanderous. She would not hesitate to take action.'

That also was received in silence. 'Come now, Charlotte, you are not yourself. You have been quite ill, you know. Half of what you *think* happened has no reality outside your own mind. You are really in no condition to talk to an outsider. Send a telegram to Mr Fothergill, telling him not to bother; that you will write. You will find that when you come to put whatever you want to say into writing it will amount to almost nothing.'

'It is about myself that I wish to talk to Mr Fothergill. When my father went abroad Mr Fothergill took over the responsibility for me.'

Mrs Armitage did a bit more coaxing, issued some more warnings. Then, finding that Charlotte was not to be moved, took counsel with Mrs Osgood who said, 'I don't see what there is to worry about. She can't do me any harm. If she tells the truth, she'll come out of it badly. And a lawyer's just the person to tell her so.'

'Oh, Augusta, there is so much more to it than that. I am concerned for the good name of the school.'

'She can't hurt that either, when you come to think of it. Twenty years, only one death. Not bad when you think where they come from and how delicate most of them are when they arrive.'

Uninformed as she was, Mrs Osgood could take only the most narrow view.

Now, rising up, extending the white hand, offering a sweet, sad smile so tentative that it was hardly a smile at all, Mrs Armitage welcomed Mr Fothergill.

'I thought that if I saw you first, Mr Fothergill, I could prepare you. Do sit down. May I offer you a glass of sherry?'

'No, thank you.' The nameless instinct was at work again. James's hackles had bristled at the first sight of the once pretty, still attractive woman in the black and white that somehow said 'widow'.

'Perhaps a cup of tea?'

235

'I was able to obtain a cup of tea at Ipswich when I changed trains.'

'Oh yes, a very tedious journey. I know, of course, whisky! Gentlemen do prefer . . .'

Augusta thought that her whisky was a secret, secret because Mrs Armitage, before she knew her really well had once said that it was something no lady would drink. Augusta could provide the whisky. But that also Mr Fothergill refused. Mr Fothergill assumed his listening attitude, fingers linked, all but the first lying down, the first pressed close together and just touching his mouth.

'It is all so very difficult; almost impossible,' Mrs Armitage began in her gentlest, most plaintive voice. 'Perhaps I should begin by telling you that I know everything about Charlotte; her real name, the ghastly crime of which she was accused . . . everything. My late husband's cousin is the wife of the rector at Biddlesford. She asked me to take Charlotte in. Naturally she told me the circumstances, and I felt so sorry for her, a mere child. Mrs Greenfield—that is my husband's cousin— could not have known then; and indeed I did not suspect myself for quite some time, that Charlotte's dreadful experience had deranged her.'

Despite the warmth of the room Mr Fothergill felt another little shiver.

'In what way, Mrs Armitage?'

'It began with Miss Lamb . . .' Miss Lamb, an assistant mistress, properly dismissed had chosen to leave without saying goodbye to anyone. Charlotte chose to believe that she had drowned herself, and took the blame because she had left Miss Lamb alone for two minutes. 'She ran out, Mr Fothergill, up and down the beach, along the lane. It was raining at the time, she came in drenched and quite distraught. She had to be put to bed.' Charlotte had been demonstrably wrong about Miss Lamb having taken nothing with her; but she refused absolutely to believe the evidence of her own eyes. Mrs Armitage then moved on to Sophie's death. 'Quite tragic, but the child had had the best attention; the doctor came twice each day; Mrs Osgood is such a good nurse that this was our first loss in twenty years. But Charlotte is now convinced that she is responsible for that mishap. This is very difficult; it seems, Mr Fothergill, that when Charlotte's brother was ill he benefited by a steam kettle, and Charlotte claims that she placed a steam

236

kettle in the sickroom, a kettle which boiled dry and made fumes which she believes choked the child. The disturbing thing is that she claims to have done this *in her sleep*.'

Mr Fothergill's expression betrayed nothing.

'I need hardly tell you that no spirit-stove or boiled-dry kettle was found in the sickroom. I never saw the articles in question; Mrs Osgood did and says that they belonged to Miss Lamb and that when she left she took them with her. The point is, Mr Fothergill, though Charlotte has never said so in so many words to me, that I fear this tendency to self-blame, over Miss Lamb, over Sophie Wrenn, has now extended to self-blame over her little brother's death. I suspect that because when talking about the spirit-stove, she said, in a most agonised voice, "What else may I not have done in my sleep?" She was so upset, poor child, at the very thought, that once again we were obliged to put her to bed, and for her own sake keep her there until the funeral was over. She is not really well physically, and I am afraid that you will find her *most* confused in mind. There is, incidentally, no possibility of her having walked in her sleep without being detected. When the sickroom is occupied, Mrs Osgood whose room is next door, leaves *her* door open.'

Lucid, concise; extraordinarily so for a woman; and sympathetic, too. Mr Fothergill found himself wondering why he did not like, or trust Mrs Armitage. His mind came up with an explanation. That widowed look! Dealing as they did with wills and bequests, estates and money in trust, Fothergill, Ampton and Fothergill had many contacts with widows and his experience had taught him that the frailest-looking, the most bereaved-looking were often the most rapacious, all too ready to add two and two together, and if it were to their advantage, making five. Still he must not be prejudiced; he must be fair. She had offered sanctuary, and been, on the face of it, ill-rewarded.

He made one of his non-committal statements.

'You appear to have had a trying time.'

Mrs Armitage then performed the act for which, half-consciously, he had been waiting. She drew out a little lace-edged handkerchief and delicately touched her eyes.

'I have indeed. You see, if Charlotte manages to convince you that she was responsible for Miss Lamb's death, for Sophie's and for that poor little boy's ... Where do I stand? How would parents feel if they knew that *Charlotte Cornwall*

237

had been here for over a year, and that I, knowing her history, had taken her in. They would be appalled.'

'Yes. I see that.'

He gave nothing away. Mrs Armitage felt that she had covered every point, forestalled whatever Charlotte might have to say about Homelands. She said, 'I am very fond of Charlotte, and very sorry for her, and to see somebody young become a prey to such delusions, to become, one might say, mad, under one's very eyes, is so *sad*. But I have the school to consider, and one thing I must ask you, Mr Fothergill ... If she manages to convince you that somnambulism is concerned with what the magistrates' court called further evidence, please arrange for her removal, so that when she is charged again, it will not be from this address.'

A not unreasonable request.

'I will remember that.'

'In a just world,' Mrs Armitage said, just touching her eyes again, 'she would never be charged at all, whatever she may say. She is so deluded, so deranged. Far the kindest thing to do would be to put her in some place where she would be taken care of and her ravings would not be taken seriously. But of course such places are expensive and I simply cannot afford ... Oh, and I omitted to tell you one other thing which has rather complicated matters. Mrs Osgood *does* believe in the sleep-walking, and having an inordinate fear of fire, has insisted upon locking poor Charlotte in every night.'

'Perhaps I should see her now.'

Mrs Armitage rang her bell, a prearranged signal, and turning back to him said, 'I'm afraid you will find her much altered in appearance.'

Even thus forewarned, and even though the rose-shaded lamplight was kind, Mr Fothergill was shocked to realise that he might have passed Charlotte in the street and not recognised her. He had never thought her 'bonny', by which old-fashioned term he meant young, healthy, plumpish, but he had always thought her attractive and that in happier circumstances she could have been more so. Now he looked upon a wreck, bone thin, pale as tallow, with a furrow of bewilderment between eyes darkly shadowed. Even the hair which he had admired looked dull and brittle. And what in the world had happened to her hands?

'Mr Fothergill. It was so good of you to come at once.'

238

'I would have come by an earlier train, Miss Charlotte, but I had an appointment which I could not cancel without causing seven people great inconvenience.'

As it was he had forgone his lunch, and the cup of over-stewed railway tea had done nothing but growl in his stomach ever since he had swallowed it.

She sat down, folding those swollen, raw-looking hands in her lap and he resumed his seat, his listening posture. As she did not immediately begin to speak, he said, kindly, 'I am very sorry to hear that you have been ill.'

'I wasn't. It was the medicine. At least, something in the medicine. Or in the food. They didn't want me at the funeral, you see. They didn't want me to talk to Doctor Bowen.'

Delusions, Mr Fothergill knew, often centred about *They*; the deluded had enemies, the anonymous *They*, who dogged their footsteps, threatened their lives, tried to cheat them out of their rights. However, in this case *They* might be taken to mean Mrs Armitage and Mrs Osgood.

Again it was left to him to break the silence.

'You wanted to talk to me, Miss Charlotte.'

'Yes.' The scowl of bewilderment deepened and she put one hand to her throat. 'I simply don't know where to begin. They think I'm out of my mind already. What has Mrs Armitage been saying to you?'

'Nothing of the slightest importance. I am here to listen to *you*.' He waited, giving her a chance to speak, and then prompted her. 'You said in your letter that something had happened here ... Suppose you start by telling me about that.'

She told him about Sophie being ill; the argument about the oil-stove, of how she had accused Mrs Osgood of neglect and Mrs Osgood had accused her of placing the spirit-stove, with too little water, too much Friars' Balsam, in the sickroom.

'I did not remember anything about it, Mr Fothergill. But I was willing to accept the possibility that I had done it. For one thing I do walk in my sleep—when I am worried. This is very difficult to explain, you may not believe me. They don't. The fact is that you only *know* that you have walked in your sleep if something happens, or there is something to show. For example, once I was very worried about Thomas; he was to spend the night in the cellar and I suppose I meant to let him out. Cook heard me, she thought I was a burglar and nearly hit

239

me with a flat-iron. So then I knew. Another time . . .' She told him about fetching the mottled book from Miss Lamb's room. 'So you see it is possible. I was prepared to admit it and then Mrs Armitage said something about what else had I done in my sleep. And that made me begin to think. But then . . .' She wrestled with her throat again and her eyes flickered wildly. '*Then* they said I hadn't put the little stove there. That there was no such stove in the house; that this conversation had never taken place—except in my mind; that I had invented it all. And of course by that time I wasn't very clear in my mind. Whatever it was that Mrs Osgood gave me . . . I couldn't really think, do you see?'

'I do indeed.'

'There was another thing, too. Nothing to do with sleep-walking. May I tell you about that? There was Miss Lamb . . .' She told him how certain she had been that Miss Lamb had taken nothing with her and how Mrs Osgood had seemed to prove otherwise. 'Once you begin to doubt yourself, Mr Fothergill, it is so easy . . . especially when there is nobody to talk to. You were the only person I could think of. But of course none of this is really important. The dreadful, the really dreadful thing . . . whether Mrs Armitage really said it, or whether it was only my mind . . . I must face it. I could have killed Vincent. In my sleep. What do you think?'

'I should need to know a great deal more, my dear Miss Charlotte, before I could even begin to answer that question.' Except in his response to his hackles he was not a man of impulse, but he gave way to one now. Without stopping to ask himself: Where can she go? What shall I do with her? he said, 'That can wait. I think that the first thing is to get you out of this place.'

'If only you could! But . . .' she seemed to shrink. 'Mr Fothergill, I don't want to go to a place that Mrs Armitage once mentioned. For people, you know, wrong in the head. It was when she said that that I thought I would rather go to gaol. In a way I am, *now*. Locked in every night. And watched. It was with the utmost difficulty that I succeeded in posting my letter to you.'

'I assure you, the farthest we shall go tonight will be Lowestoft.' It was a bit disconcerting that his stomach at that moment growled: *And I hope I shall have something to eat there.* 'We must have much more talk,' Mr Fothergill said. 'And then

240

we shall see. How long would it take you to put into a bag what you would need for a night, a couple of nights?'

'Five minutes.'

'When you have done it, go out to the cab which is waiting. I will do all the explaining.'

Mrs Armitage, leaving them together, had suggested that when the interview was over the bell should be rung and she hoped that Mr Fothergill would stay to share their little dinner. When Charlotte opened the door a very pleasant odour —roast partridge?—drifted in.

Mr Fothergill knew something of women; he had not lived like a monk all these years, the reason why he was still a bachelor was that he had not, so far, encountered a woman with whom he wished to share his life, his interests, his placid, well-ordered household. But when women said five minutes, he knew that they meant ten, fifteen, so he waited ten minutes before he rang the bell. When Mrs Armitage drifted in prepared to offer sherry again, he said, 'I have decided to take Miss Burns away, Mrs Armitage. I think that may spare you any further embarrassment.'

'Where do you propose to take her, Mr Fothergill?'

He answered with that good, dependable phrase, 'That all depends.'

'Thank you. Now you must have dinner. After such a journey, and an interview which must have been, to say the least, trying.'

She was well-disposed towards him; he had listened without interrupting and she imagined that he had dismissed Charlotte to prepare for a move, later this evening, or tomorrow.

'I am afraid I must be off, Mrs Armitage. Miss Burns should be waiting in the cab.'

'I can never be sufficiently grateful, Mr Fothergill.'

This time he ignored the proffered hand.

'So now,' Mrs Osgood said, 'we have no teacher at all.' But she was not concerned; that side of the school was no concern of hers. Something else was and she intended to speak about it. 'And you knew who she was and what she'd done. Yet you took her in, and never a word to me.' Mrs Osgood was no fool; she had quickly put two and two together. Reaching back to the time when Mrs Armitage had suggested getting rid of Miss Lamb and she had said, 'What if Miss Burns decides to go?'

and Mrs Armitage said, 'She can never do that,' and running on to the effect that the word *inquest* had had. Mrs Osgood read very little except the papers, but those she read pretty thoroughly. Charlotte, half-drugged, self-accusing, had supplied quite enough for Mrs Osgood to go upon, and Mrs Armitage, openly accosted, had admitted the truth. Charlotte Burns was Charlotte Cornwall, who had been accused and not quite acquitted of murdering her little brother and who had, in Mrs Osgood's opinion, murdered Sophie Wrenn.

Mrs Osgood did not immediately take action. Let the funeral get over. Let Mrs Armitage, who had brought the dangerous girl into the house, devise some quiet way of getting her out. *Then* Mrs Osgood intended to say a few things which she knew she should have said a long time ago.

'No,' Mrs Armitage said, settling down to her partridge on its little square of toast. 'Not even Mamselle to help. But we shall manage.'

Mamselle had not, on the day of Sophie's death, been able to rush to help; nor had she been able to attend the funeral. Her father had been smitten down by an apoplectic stroke. The doctor, Mamselle had said in a hasty little letter, held out no hope.

'The great thing is, Augusta,' Mrs Armitage said, dealing neatly with her partridge, 'poor Charlotte has gone and I have reason to hope that, whatever becomes of her, Homelands will not be involved. I rather think that I managed to convince Mr Fothergill that he should think twice before crediting anything she said. And the fact that he removed her so promptly rather indicates . . .'

'She should never have come here. You knew what she was, what she'd done. But you took her in, a murderess, and never a word to me!'

'Augusta, I tried to explain that.'

'So you did.' Mrs Osgood spoke with her mouth full. 'Word of honour, something told you in confidence by your husband's cousin's wife.' Despite the mouthful her voice achieved a brutal mimicry of Mrs Armitage's. 'What about your word to me? Partners! Well, one thing it's made me see the light. Things are going to be very different here.'

'A little difficult, Augusta. Until Easter. At Easter assistant mistresses are ten a penny.'

'The next one I intend to have a good look at. Hitherto,'

Mrs Osgood said, removing, not very daintily, a little splinter of bone from her mouth, 'I left all that side to you. And you made a pretty mess of it, let me tell you. First Miss Lamb, I could have told you she was a crank. And interfering. And then this.'

'Augusta, need we hark? The whole thing is over.'

'Not with me. You saw to your side, I saw to mine. And to my mind you've made a proper mess-up.'

Not a nice term.

'And what do you mean by that, Augusta?'

'What I say. The same as you would have said if I'd mucked up some cooking. As I said, I saw the light. I've plodded on, like a donkey, pandering to you all these years because I thought you were so *clever*. Now I know, and as I said, things are going to be different. No more foolery,' Mrs Osgood said, including in one scornful glance the well-set table, the half-eaten birds on the plates, the sherry trifle on the sideboard. 'There'll be no more dinners,' she said, pouring into the one simple word a lifetime of scorn and twenty years' resentment. 'What you want after tea, you'll get for yourself. And the same with coffee in the morning. I never liked it. Give me a good cup of tea any time. Then there's Eva, dressed up like a monkey half her time; prancing about answering bells. We'll have no more of her and her like; a decent handy little skivvy in the kitchen. And the fees as I've said, time and again, *down*. Maybe then we could get up to forty again. With less than that there's no profit, scrimp as I may.'

Mrs Osgood had the advantage; her rage had been long smouldering and what she meant to say planned. Mrs Armitage was taken by surprise. And upset enough, both by the manner and the content of Mrs Osgood's speech that she was unable to continue with her excellent dinner. She placed her knife and fork in the correct position on her unemptied plate. She had a flashing vision of what life would be under Augusta's dominance. Herself in the kitchen, boiling an egg for supper; answering the doorbell; Augusta sitting in at every interview; Augusta dictating what the lower fees should be, and people all over the world saying that Homelands must be going down.

At the same time she realised that she had never *liked* Augusta, that vulgar woman, but had put up with her because she was so useful. Now she hated her. Trying to dominate;

trying to reduce everything to her own common level.

She said in a sweet, chilly voice, 'You appear to be dissatisfied with me; and to be frank, the rearrangements you visualise do not appeal to me. I think the time has come to wind up this enterprise.'

'And just what do you mean by that?'

'I intend to sell the school. I think that as a going concern it must be worth at least fifteen hundred pounds. From that we can deduct the thousand pounds which I gave for the house and some contents, and your two hundred and fifty which provided beds and cutlery. The remainder, after defraying the cost of advertising and the legal fees, we will divide between us as we have always divided the profits. What is it, Augusta, are you feeling unwell?'

Mrs Osgood had seen the staggering injustice between capital and labour. Mrs Armitage had provided most of the capital, she most of the labour and now, after twenty years, the capital was as good as new; it had not sweated over hot stoves, watched by sickbeds; its feet had not worn flat, nor its legs developed varicose veins. In short it had not aged. She had, and now, at the end of it all, she would have no home, just her two hundred and fifty pounds back, a tiny mite more, and what she had saved from her half of the profits—when there were profits. For years now they had been negligible. There was something very wrong somewhere, yet it was difficult to put a finger on it. Despite the difference in the amount invested, profits had been shared equally. Fair, even generous on the face of it.

She said, hoarsely, 'It'll leave us without a roof to our heads.'

Mrs Armitage knew to a penny how much she had saved in the days of the school's heyday. Fourteen hundred pounds, eleven shillings. Augusta, with her far less luxurious manner of life must have saved rather more.

'You will be able to buy a cottage somewhere.'

For herself, Viola Armitage knew exactly what she was going to do, if luck favoured her again. God let Mamselle's father hold out until the school was sold. Then she would be first in Provence. The house in the sun there would be her own. Mamselle could come along if she wished—as she indubitably would—and make from her wealth a contribution to the household expenses. But she would be, as she had been here, a guest, and Mrs Armitage, in her own house, would still be dominant.

'It's all wrong,' Mrs Osgood said, having now put her finger on the nub of the matter. 'As you say, we always shared the profits. But *after* upkeep. There was that new guttering, and all the painting, and the time when some tiles blew off. It was *your* property being mended up, every time. Not mine. I'd have much more in the bank if the profits had been divided *before* money was spent on your property.'

'And much less,' Mrs Armitage said, reasonably, 'had the profits been divided in accordance to the amount invested, as is, I believe, the usual custom.'

'But look at the work I've put in.'

'Augusta, we have both worked. We are no longer young. I think it is full time that we took a rest.'

She saw herself lying on a chaise-longue, on a sun-drenched, rose-wreathed terrace and Mamselle, still infatuated, but under control, bringing her grapes, warm from the vine.

9

In the cab, talk was, if not impossible, disjointed. The horse, headed for home, put on a turn of speed which anyone except his owner would have thought impossible. Mr Fothergill asked Charlotte if she would like to change places with him as the draught seemed to be coming from her side, and she replied that she was quite comfortable; that her cloak was very warm. She also said, 'It is such a comfort to feel that I can leave everything to you, Mr Fothergill. I was beginning to think that I was losing my mind. I feel better now.'

He sat and thought things over. Carrying one speculation to its furthest limits he wondered how far, in law, sleep-walking would be accepted as a defence against a murder charge. Rack his brain as he might he could not recall a case of any kind in which somnambulism was concerned. And the plea, in itself, would attract just the kind of publicity which Hugo Ampton so wished to avoid. Having carried that thought as far as it would go, he brooded over the things she had told him. He could see Mrs Armitage's reason for insisting that Miss Lamb had left in the ordinary way; suicide attracted attention too, and scandal was bad for a school. That Charlotte should first have been accused of putting the spirit-stove in the sickroom, and then assured that she had not done so, was more difficult to understand; unless the women were trying to unhinge her mind; but if they had succeeded in doing so, what then? Suppose the poor girl had not written to him, or that he had not been there to be written to, what would have happened? Would they have found a public lunatic asylum? Or kept her there, broken, convinced that she was crazy and grateful for shelter.

The whole thing smacked of melodrama, for which Mr Fothergill had little taste. But he was very glad that he had given her his address and that she had had the sense to send for him. Good sense there, and indeed none of her conversation so far had showed any lack either of sense or sanity.

The Three Ships Hotel, which the cabman recommended as the best of those that stayed open during the winter, which, as he explained, it could afford to do, since it was run by a family, had recently been embellished by gas-lighting, and in its glare Charlotte looked so ghastly that the landlady, who combined the role of cook with that of receptionist, took her to be far gone in consumption, brought—too late—to benefit from the famous bracing air.

'My name is Fothergill. This is Miss Burns. We need two rooms, in one of which a fire should be lighted immediately.' He also had noticed that Charlotte looked even worse now; perhaps he had been unwise to have moved her; he should have insisted that she went straight to bed, sent for the doctor, kept watch over her. Patently impossible! 'I think, Miss Charlotte, that you should go to bed at once and I think you should see a doctor.'

'Honestly, Mr Fothergill, there is no need. I am much better. And if you could bear it, I should like to continue our talk.'

Mr Fothergill's stomach reminded him angrily that it had had no lunch and that its dinner was overdue.

'Then we will have something to eat,' he said. The hotel was so quiet, had such an only-just-open atmosphere, that he had small hope of a good meal. Cold meat and some lumpy mashed potato.

'There's a good fire in the dining room,' said the woman, indicating the door.

The fire was splendid, great chunks of driftwood burning orange and blue. There were two other guests, but they had almost completed their meal; they were fish-buyers and had to be up early in the morning. The table to which the waiter—son of the house—led the way, was within the fire's ambience, and the tablecloth was clean, Mr Fothergill was pleased to see. There was oxtail soup and roast shoulder of mutton. At this season the Three Ships geared its menu to those in the fish trade whose tastes were simple, and who were too nearly connected with fish to wish to eat it.

Murder, possible murder, was not a dinner-table subject, but before Mr Fothergill could say that serious talk should be left until afterwards, Charlotte seemed to have forestalled his thought.

She said, 'The sight of that fire reminds me . . .' and gave a wry account of her experiment with driftwood. Mr Fothergill's stomach approved of the soup while his eye noticed that Charlotte ate slowly, without appetite.

Finishing with the story of the driftwood, Charlotte said, 'Mrs Osgood's soup was always so *thick*. A meal in itself, as they say. Miss Lamb once said that Mrs Osgood had such an affinity with barley that she should have been a brewer. That was the kind of thing we used to laugh about.'

He was glad that she had been happy enough to laugh, even in that horrible place. And since Charlotte herself had mentioned the woman, he felt it safe to say, 'She sounds quite a character.'

'Oh, she was. And so kind. Apart from you, Mr Fothergill, quite the kindest person I ever met.' A few examples of Miss Lamb's kindness, ingenuity and wit, took them through the soup.

Charlotte refused the roast lamb.

'I honestly could not, Mr Fothergill. I am no longer hungry.'

'Could you drink a glass of wine?'

'Oh yes.'

The light white wines which Mr Fothergill knew were the favourites with ladies were not available. So with his tender, succulent mutton, his beautifully roasted potatoes, onion sauce and red currant jelly, Mr Fothergill drank a surprisingly good claret and Charlotte sipped. The subject of Miss Lamb came to an abrupt halt as Charlotte, abandoning the lighter side said, 'I know that it had always been her ambition to have a school of her own. And she had almost attained that, in a way . . . And then to be dismissed, for absolutely no reason. I never felt the same towards Mrs Armitage again.' Her expression changed. Darkened.

'Prior to that you got on well with her?' Mr Fothergill ventured.

'Oh yes. Everybody did. I see now that she was an arch humbug. And, under that soft manner, intensely cruel . . . perhaps the word I need is ruthless. She was totally concerned with her own comfort and well-being, and I think she only took me in because I was a kind of slave labour.'

The son of the house apologised; there was no pudding. There had been a Bakewell tart, but both the earlier diners had taken two helpings and all he had to offer now was Stilton cheese.

Mr Fothergill's stomach was pacified; Charlotte said she could eat no more. The son of the house threw a ship's timber on to the fire and quickly cleared the table. The time had come.

Charlotte said, 'Mr Fothergill, you said you need to know much more before you could answer my question. What more can I tell you?'

The chairs were hard and upright, Mr Fothergill could not lean back and adopt his listening attitude, so he leaned forward, his elbows on the table, his hands supporting his head.

He said, 'So far as I can see, in every case when you have walked in your sleep—or been said to have walked in your sleep—there has been some purpose, some emotional involvement. The common denominator is a concern for something, or somebody. Were you concerned, in any way, about Vincent?'

'That question I asked myself, Mr Fothergill. And the answer, hateful as it is, is *Yes*. Mrs Cornwall was very angry and Vincent turned to me for protection, he hid his face in my skirt. And I stood there . . . I thought—what will he do when I am gone and he has no one to turn to? I remember thinking that; because I was about to ask Papa for permission to go to London. Mrs Cornwall was very fond of Vincent, he was her first-born, her son . . . But he was becoming wilful, and she only liked him when he was amenable. And she was a very jealous woman.' The scowl which had eased slightly, clamped down again, and she lifted her hand and made that wrestling movement at her throat. 'It is difficult to explain. I can only tell you that I stood there and foresaw trouble, if Vincent should ever say, instead of "I'll tell Mamma", "I'll tell Papa". He was capable of it. And I thought that her next baby might be a boy—Amelia she hardly noticed. I remember thinking that I wished I could take him with me. That was, of course, quite impossible. But did this thing in my mind . . . the thing that makes me do in my sleep what I know, while awake, to be

249

impossible, make me get up in the night and try to take him away? And did he make a noise? Did I smother him?'

To this there was no certain answer. Mr Fothergill said, very gently, 'Miss Charlotte, the child was also stabbed.'

Her brow furrowed, her eyes flickered. Speaking more slowly, she said, 'Yes, I know. But there is a connection, in a way. I don't know whether even *you*, Mr Fothergill, will understand.'

'I shall endeavour to.'

'I loved Papa's razors. I learned to tell the days of the week on them. When I was very small, when Mamma was alive and well, I'd go into his dressing room and he'd say, "Charlie, this is Tuesday," or whatever the day was, "which razor must I use?" He'd put them in different positions, so that I could not cheat. And when I could read the names and say "This one", and be right, he would be so pleased . . .' Her voice trailed off for a moment, like that of a very old person, recalling happy, youthful days. Then she went on, 'But I hated them, too, when they were open; so sharp, so cruel.'

Mr Fothergill waited; now completely puzzled. Where was the connection?

She said, 'Obviously in my sleep I do things that I would not otherwise do; things I am afraid to do. I should never have dared defy Mrs Cornwall by letting Thomas out of the cellar. I should never have dared go into Miss Lamb's room, in fact from the time that she died, to the time when I fetched the book that was so helpful, I had never entered her room. As for defying Mrs Osgood by taking in the little stove . . . You see? And there is another connection—that afternoon I had been teaching Vincent some of the alphabet. In this sleeping mind of mine, the razors . . . the letters I had learned, the thing I was so much afraid of . . . with Vincent already smothered . . . and dead. Can you see, Mr Fothergill? Can you see?'

He was accustomed to listening to long rambling discourses, reducing them into short dry statements that made sense, and now, in a moment of severe strain and distress, the habit held.

'You wish me to understand that you *stabbed* Vincent with a razor. My dear girl, that is impossible.'

'So it would seem,' she said with a dogged kind of patience, 'that I could enter the sickroom, move about, go into the dispensary, with Mrs Osgood asleep behind an open door . . .

Impossible. But they said I did. I know that afterwards they said otherwise, to confuse me, because they did not want an inquest. But why, if, as they said later, I made it all up in my mind, was it ever said? And with such anger?'

Logical? Up to a point. But there was a flaw in her self-accusation . . . and if she were not to tip over the narrow ledge, the balance between sanity and madness, he must . . . he must . . . he must . . .

Behind a face that showed nothing except deep thought, he reviewed her argument. Except for the razor, it was plausible, but with a mad kind of plausibility; the result of her determination to accuse herself. He believed, as he had always believed, that she was innocent. His instinct had so informed him from the very first, and that instinct had been confirmed by the verdict of the magistrates' court which had been to say in effect that a good deal more evidence would be needed before they were convinced of her guilt.

What was needed now, he realised, was evidence to convince her that she was innocent. He looked across the table and saw her eyes fixed upon him with an expression far more tragic and disturbed than she had ever worn while in gaol. She had not doubted her innocence then.

He tried the old tactic of a shock question.

'What did you do with the nightdress?'

'I never touched it,' she replied promptly. 'If you remember, Mr Sawyer proved that Inspector Fowler was wrong in saying that I did.'

'Ah, yes. I am not interested in that one. I am asking about the nightdress—or perhaps some other garment—which you were wearing on this occasion when you walked, *if* you walked, in your sleep.'

She stared, completely bewildered.

'It could hardly have emerged unsullied,' he reminded her.

'I can't see it at all, Mr Fothergill. Isn't that strange? I can just visualise all the rest, but not that. Let me think.'

She put her disfigured hands to her head and was silent.

'No,' she said at last. 'I cannot imagine . . . I think we must accept that as another of the impossible things that sleep-walkers do. I mean I must have disposed of it somehow. But that doesn't matter very much, does it?'

'Only as a matter of interest.' What matters, he thought, is that you should be rid of this obsession.

251

He tried again, this time saying with a seeming casualness, 'The doctor's evidence was to the effect that the wound was inflicted by a *knife*.'

'No. When I see it, in my mind, I see a razor. For the reasons I have told you . . .'

Suddenly he saw what he must do. He reached out and rang the bell. The son of the house, disturbed from his own supper, came and said, not too graciously, 'You rang, sir?'

'Would you please bring me a loaf of bread?'

'A loaf of bread, sir?'

'A loaf of bread. Miss Charlotte, I shall not be a minute.'

He knew that he was taking a risk; in her present state anything might happen; but he dared not risk avoiding the risk.

'Now, Miss Charlotte,' he said, coming back to the table, 'we are going to make a little experiment. Will you put these on.' He handed her his own gloves, kid, fur-lined. The child had been wearing a woollen vest and a flannel nightshirt, so Mr Fothergill enveloped the loaf in two layers of his own flannel nightshirt; near enough, he thought. He then opened his own razor and held it out to her.

She shrank away. 'I told you, Mr Fothergill, I cannot bear . . . while I am awake.'

'I would do it myself,' he said gallantly, 'but then you might think I was fumble-fingered, or something. Just make this one effort. For my sake. Good. I have always thought you were brave. Now, will you stab the loaf . . .'

He was actually trembling with trepidation. Even through the gloves, she might cut her fingers; but better cut fingers than a wounded mind.

The razor behaved as expected; the flannel withstood its rounded end and as she pressed harder, still failing to penetrate, the blade closed back towards the handle, trapping her fingers. He opened it instantly. 'Are you hurt?' But he could see that the kid of the gloves, though marked, had not been sliced.

'I'll try again.'

'Indeed you will not. Next time you might cut yourself. Miss Charlotte, you could try a thousand times, I might try. A circus strong man might try. It is impossible to *stab* with a razor.'

For a moment the wretchedness vanished from her face,

leaving it, though thinner and paler, much as he remembered it. Then it collapsed into misery again.

'But I told you, sleepwalkers do seemingly impossible things.'

'Only within limits,' he said, rather sternly. 'The nature of inanimate objects remains constant. A razor does not know whether it is being handled by a waking or a sleeping person. Let us suppose that the story of the spirit-stove was true. It may seem *unlikely*, that is as far as I would go, that you could move about without waking Mrs Osgood; but she probably was very sound asleep. So there you did not perform the impossible. And the stove behaved in an ordinary way; it did not go off like a firework; or begin to play a tune.' He paused to allow that piece of reasoning to find its mark.

'Then why did I seem to see . . .?'

'Because you have a very lively imagination. And because, since Miss Lamb's disappearance, you have been under an almost intolerable strain. And because on the occasion of her disappearance, a trick was played upon you which made you doubt yourself. Then, when you were in great distress over the little girl's death, you were accused of being responsible for it; and at the same time there was a suggestion made that you had been responsible for the crime. Mrs Armitage's version was that you at once accused yourself, I prefer yours, that it was she who put the idea into your head. Your mind was already troubled, and your health much undermined. Such states of mind and body make people more susceptible than they ordinarily are . . .' He could say that with certainty; it accounted for half the last-minute alterations in wills. 'Nor,' he continued in his dispassionate lawyer's voice, 'may we completely ignore the effects of Mrs Osgood's medicine. It was probably opium, a drug under whose influence some people have pleasant imaginary experiences, and others have dreams, hallucinations, of a most disturbing kind. I think that when all these factors are taken into consideration, Miss Charlotte . . .'

He could see that she was about to cry.

She said, lips and chin trembling, eyes filling, 'Mr Fothergill . . . the relief!' And then she burst into a healing flood of tears which he welcomed. He had always thought that nature had given women the ability to cry and feel better as some faint compensation for their obvious disadvantages in a man-made world. He had seen grief, disappointment, even sheer rage washed away by tears. He also knew that any woman, weeping, either had no handkerchief or a perfectly inadequate one.

He knew all the rules. You let them cry for a bit; then you made comforting gestures, said soothing words, proffered the handkerchief and withdrew, or seemed to withdraw your attention. He tried to adhere to the rules, letting her cry while he folded his nightshirt and put it, and the razor, out of sight on the floor beside his chair. He was, however, a little early with the comforting gesture, and the sharpness of her shoulder bones under his hand, gave him a distinct pang. He thought—She needs feeding up. And he remembered Mrs Hawkins's splendid cooking.

'There, there,' he said. 'It's over now.' He said, 'Have a good cry and forget about it.' He said, 'Have this handkerchief.'

But when she had recovered, the sobbing dying away into little gulps and the handkerchief plied, and her face, still pallid, hollowed, but cleansed of fear and doubt, lifted towards him, and she said, 'Mr Fothergill, how to thank you . . .' he had a disquieting thought about the resilience of youth. It was something as definite as the nature of inanimate things which he had earlier mentioned. It was something that he had lost. He was indeed spent. It had been a long tiring day; her letter, the tedious journey; the shock her appearance had given him; the need to take that instant decision to remove her; and then the experiment, which might at worst have sent her over the narrow borderline, at least have injured her fingers. Such things took toll when a man was forty.

Also, he was aware that he had turned a pretty dangerous corner. When he had proved that she could not have stabbed with a razor, she might, the sense of guilt sufficiently implanted, have said, 'Then I must have used a knife.' And then he would have been at a loss. But thank God that had not happened.

Charlotte mopped her face and said, 'Mr Fothergill, I am sorry to have behaved so badly.'

'You have behaved impeccably. I think we could both do with a drink. What would you like?'

'Oh, please, a cup of tea. I have not had a cup of proper tea . . . Miss Lamb made hers with condensed milk, which is very different. And I always suspected that at breakfast and teatime what we were given was made from used tea-leaves.'

Mr Fothergill again rang the bell. The son of the house

254

answered it, even less graciously, and Mr Fothergill said that they wanted a tray of tea and a large brandy. He added that the loaf might be taken away.

'So what did they want it for?' the young man asked his mother who made the tea while he fetched the brandy. 'They didn't touch it.'

She said, 'All the better. It'll do for toast in the morning.'

'School food,' Mr Fothergill was saying to Charlotte, 'is notoriously bad. I can so well remember. I had not been exactly pampered, but my Uncle Hugo, with whom I had lived since the death of my parents, kept a very good table. Nothing that I was offered at school seemed to me even remotely edible. So I refrained from eating it. I must admit that I also cherished a hope that Uncle Hugo, informed that his nephew was starving to death might rush to the rescue and remove me. In fact nobody noticed, or cared whether James Fothergill ate or fasted. On the third day I ate some very peculiar grey stew. After which, of course, I never looked back. But it had an effect, I made up my mind that once I was grown up and earning I would have proper food. That is, quite possibly, the only resolution that I have kept.'

He sipped his brandy and looked at her with approval and possessiveness. She was of his making, this now-calm, almost smiling girl, enjoying her tea and with every minute, every breath, seeming to move further from the poor, broken, half-demented thing who had entered that rose-coloured room.

'To have kept one is something. Mine usually came to nothing. Except one. Not, I am afraid a very worthy one . . .'

'The least worthy are the easiest to keep. There is nothing very admirable about deciding to eat well.' He thought of Mrs Hawkins's cooking; that would soon put some flesh on her bones. As he, given the chance, would put happiness and gaiety into her spirit. How best to go about it; invite her in so many words; tacitly assume that she would go home with him? Home. Poor child, she had not known a proper home since her mother died. What she had said about learning to read from the razors and thus pleasing her father, had hinted at a happy family life at one time. Soon disrupted. Somewhere along the road she had lost that Papa; and her Mamma; she had lost Vincent, Miss Lamb and a little girl of whom she had obviously been fond. So far nothing but loss.

The mention of the one resolution to which she had adhered

had reminded Charlotte of the person with whom it was concerned.

She said, gravely, 'Mr Fothergill, earlier this evening I made a statement which I wish to withdraw. I said that I could not return to my stepmother. That was stupid. St Lawrence Square is my home, the proper place for me to be until I can find some occupation. I am saying this now because . . . Well, I have been so much trouble to you already; I should not like you to worry about what to do with me tomorrow.'

'I have been giving the matter some thought.' Shyness made him sound rather more pompous than usual. 'Frankly, I do not consider that St Lawrence Square is the proper place for you in your present condition.'

Young James who sometimes took a puckish delight in poking fun at Mr Fothergill, commented: What an expression! It sounds as though she were pregnant!

Mr Fothergill coloured slightly, but pressed on.

'I have an alternative to suggest. I have plenty of room. I have a married couple who would, I know, do their best to make you comfortable. I think you would find my friends congenial. And I should be only too delighted if you would accept my hospitality.'

'You mean that I should go home with you?' Something that he had always sensed to be there always, so far obscured, a lively brightness flooded into her face.

He said humbly, 'Yes. I would do my very best to make you happy.'

'Mr Fothergill, I should be happy just to be with you!'

Too much significance must not be attached to that simple statement; made in the aftermath of emotional stress, probably influenced by gratitude. But it was something to be going on with. And one good thing about being forty was that one had learned patience.

'Then that is settled. You have given me great pleasure. Now . . .' He consulted his watch. 'The only good train in the morning leaves at seven-twenty. That means an early start. So I think we should begin to think about getting to bed.'

Young James had something to say about that expression, too.